A Terrified Teacher at Ghoul School! vol.8

Mai Tanaka

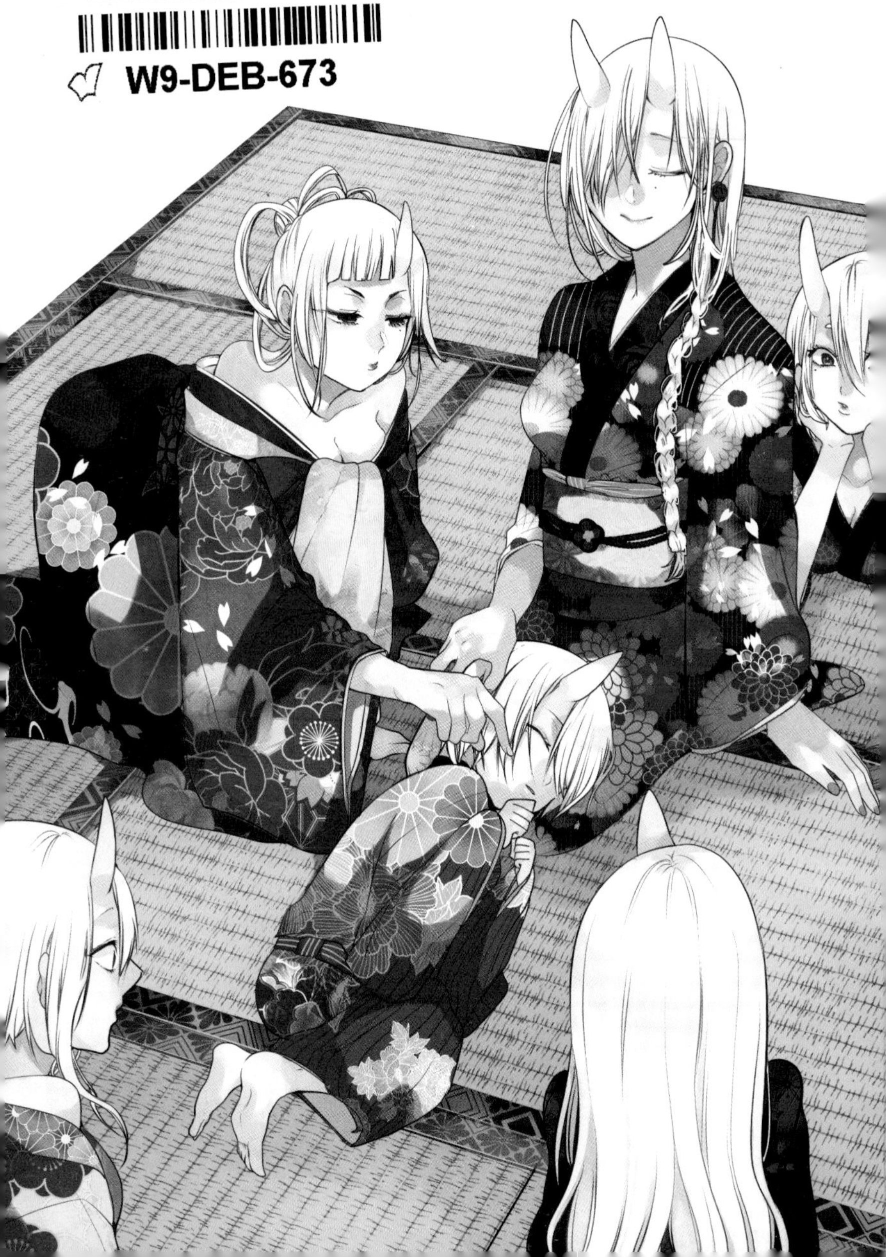

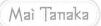

CONTENTS

Forty-Sixth Period
🔹 Summer! The Beach! Fishing!! --- 003

Forty-Seventh Period
🔹 Abe no Seimei, Haruaki Abe, and
Shutendouji (Part 1) ------------ 023

Forty-Eighth Period
🔹 Abe no Seimei, Haruaki Abe, and
Shutendouji (Part 2) ------------ 045

Forty-Ninth Period
🔹 Abe no Seimei, Haruaki Abe, and
Shutendouji (Part 3) ------------ 073

Fiftieth Period
🔹 Hiji-tan's August 31 ------------ 105

Fifty-First Period
🔹 The Great Hyakki Academy Island
Chase!! -------------------------- 127

🔹 Side Story: Haru & Ame _____ 149

Fifty-Second Period
🔹 Haruaki vs. Sano-kun!! The Strength
Test Showdown!! ---------------- 157

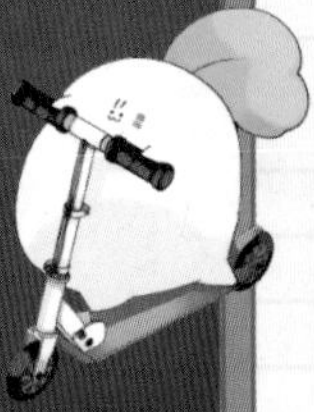

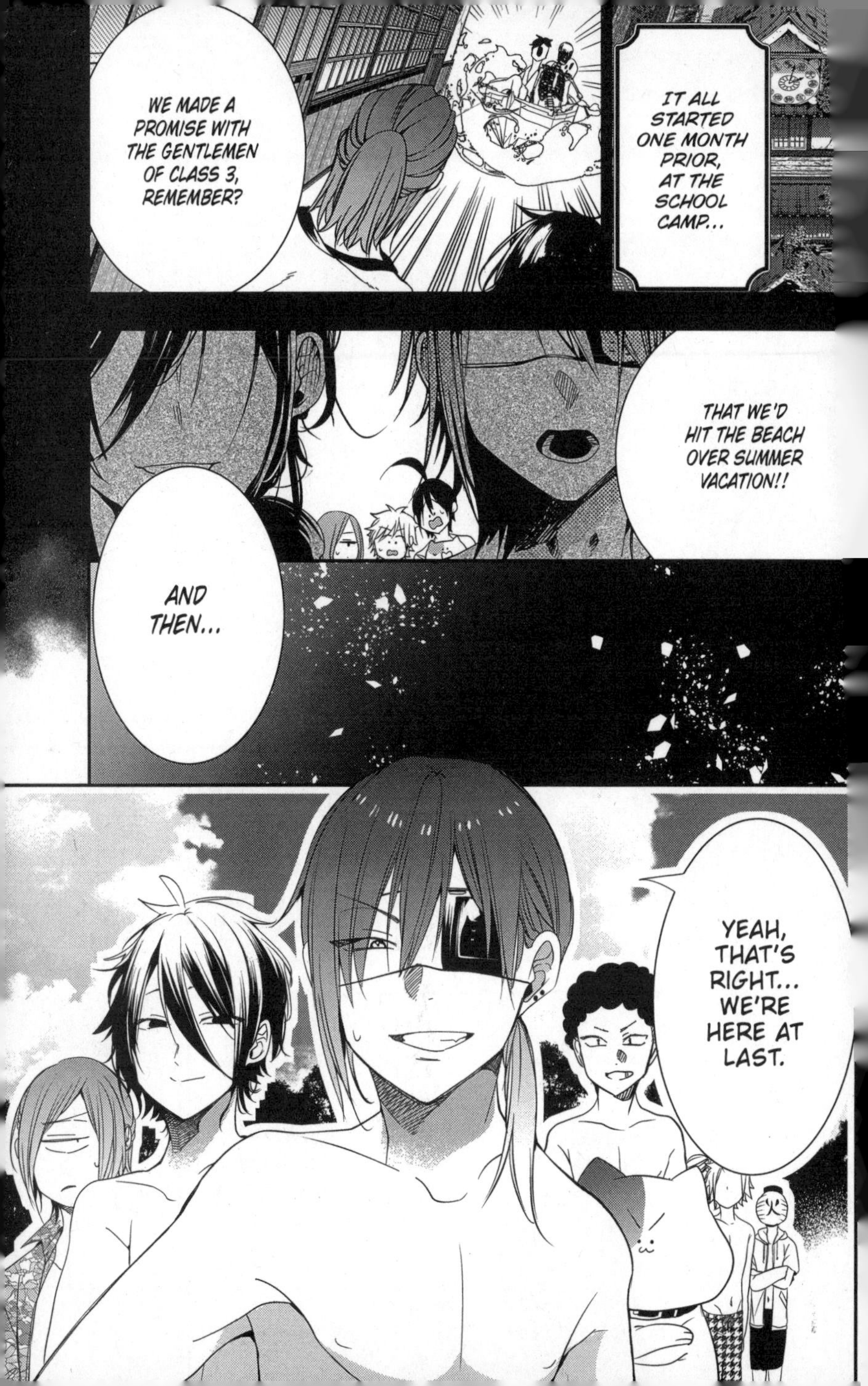
IT ALL STARTED ONE MONTH PRIOR, AT THE SCHOOL CAMP...
WE MADE A PROMISE WITH THE GENTLEMEN OF CLASS 3, REMEMBER?
THAT WE'D HIT THE BEACH OVER SUMMER VACATION!!
AND THEN...
YEAH, THAT'S RIGHT... WE'RE HERE AT LAST.

Forty-Sixth Period: Summer! The Beach! Fishing!!

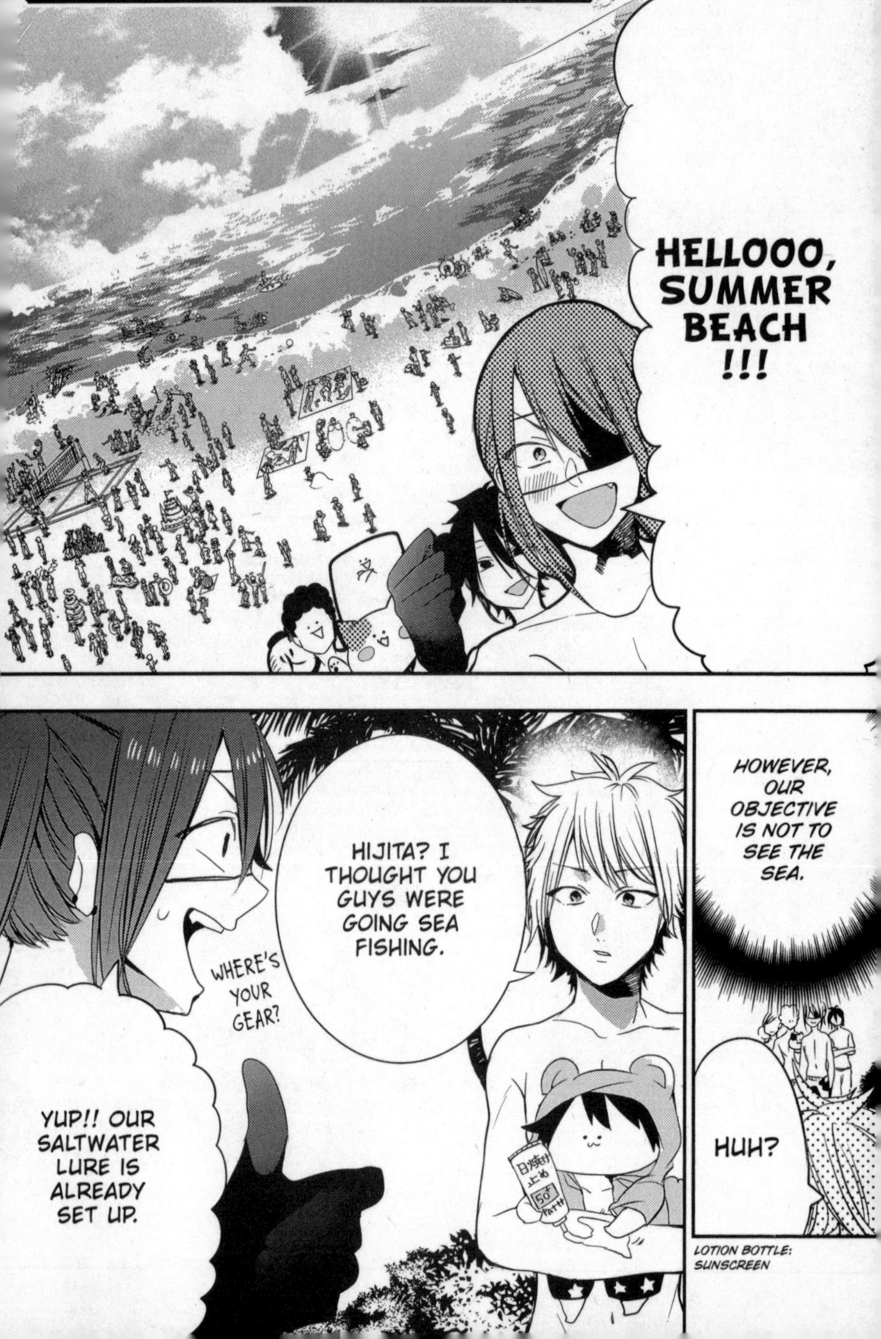
HELLOOO, SUMMER BEACH !!!
HOWEVER, OUR OBJECTIVE IS NOT TO SEE THE SEA.
HUH?
HIJITA? I THOUGHT YOU GUYS WERE GOING SEA FISHING.
WHERE'S YOUR GEAR?
YUP!! OUR SALTWATER LURE IS ALREADY SET UP.

LOTION BOTTLE: SUNSCREEN

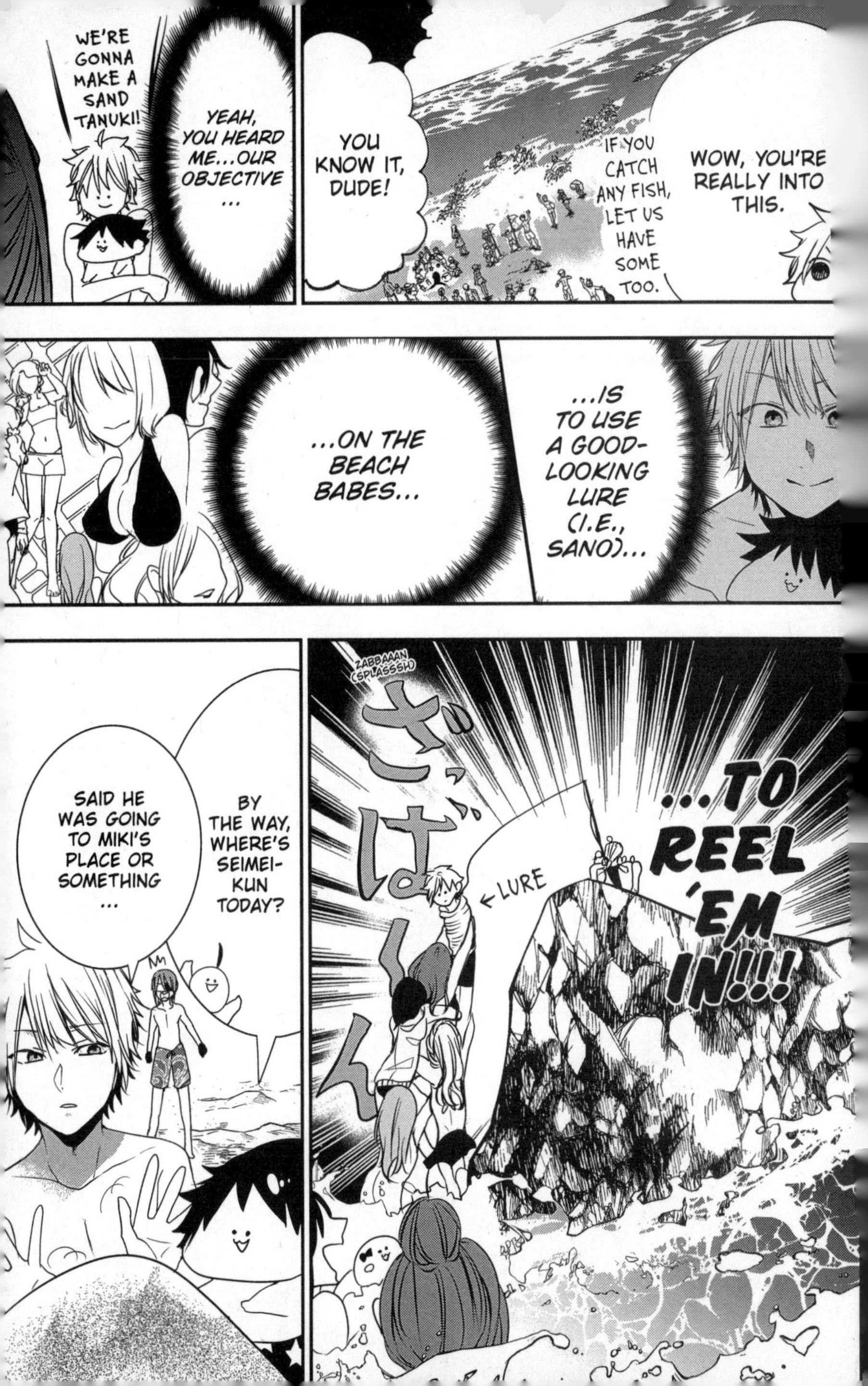
WOW, YOU'RE REALLY INTO THIS.
IF YOU CATCH ANY FISH, LET US HAVE SOME TOO.
YOU KNOW IT, DUDE!
YEAH, YOU HEARD ME...OUR OBJECTIVE ...
WE'RE GONNA MAKE A SAND TANUKI!!
...IS TO USE A GOOD-LOOKING LURE (I.E., SANO)...
...ON THE BEACH BABES...
ZABBAAAN (SPLASSSH)
...TO REEL 'EM IN!!!
← LURE
BY THE WAY, WHERE'S SEIMEI-KUN TODAY?
SAID HE WAS GOING TO MIKI'S PLACE OR SOMETHING ...

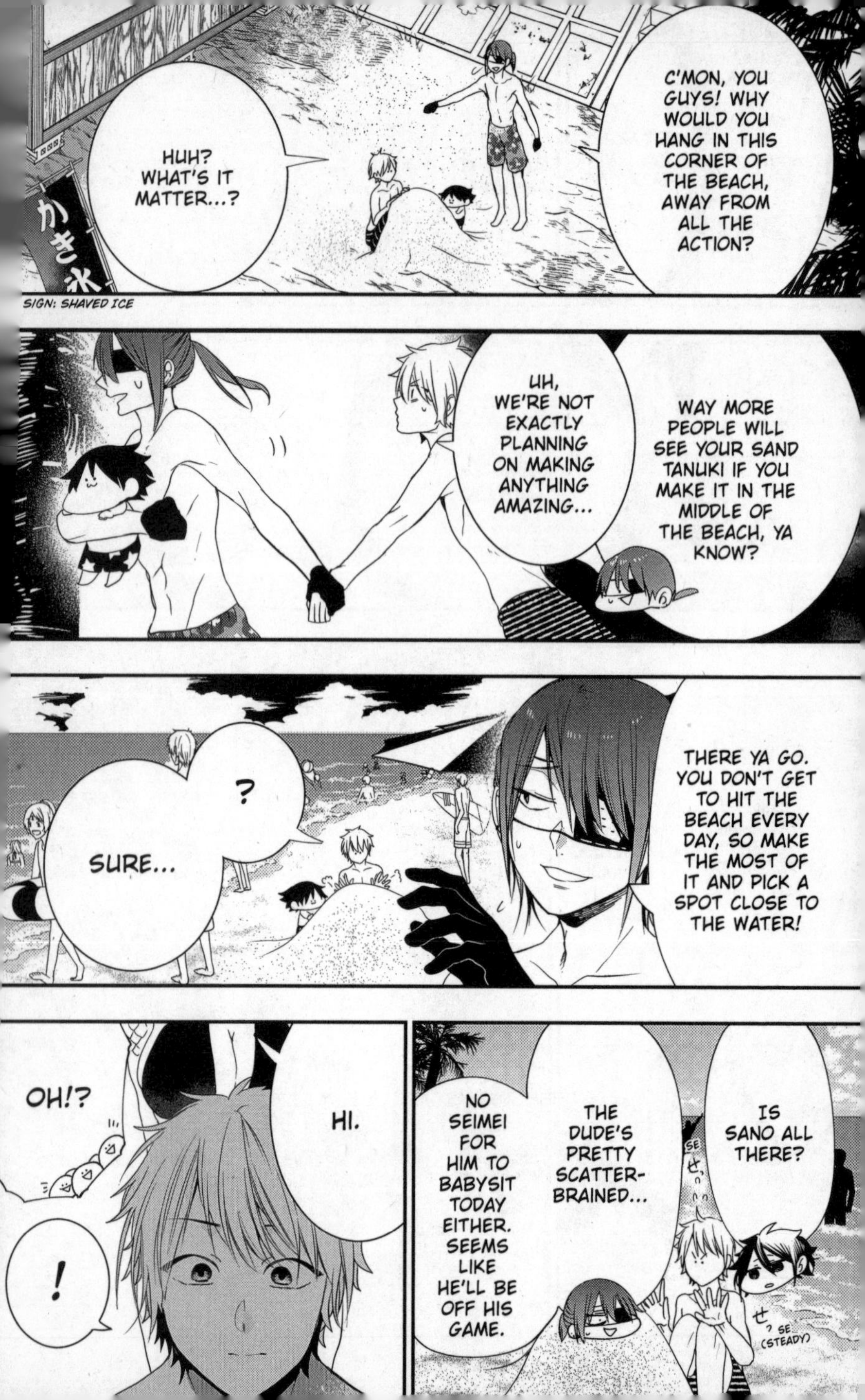
C'MON, YOU GUYS! WHY WOULD YOU HANG IN THIS CORNER OF THE BEACH, AWAY FROM ALL THE ACTION?
HUH? WHAT'S IT MATTER...?
かき氷
SIGN: SHAVED ICE
WAY MORE PEOPLE WILL SEE YOUR SAND TANUKI IF YOU MAKE IT IN THE MIDDLE OF THE BEACH, YA KNOW?
UH, WE'RE NOT EXACTLY PLANNING ON MAKING ANYTHING AMAZING...
THERE YA GO. YOU DON'T GET TO HIT THE BEACH EVERY DAY, SO MAKE THE MOST OF IT AND PICK A SPOT CLOSE TO THE WATER!
?
SURE...
IS SANO ALL THERE?
SE せ
THE DUDE'S PRETTY SCATTER-BRAINED...
NO SEIMEI FOR HIM TO BABYSIT TODAY EITHER. SEEMS LIKE HE'LL BE OFF HIS GAME.
せ SE (STEADY)
HI.
OH!?
!

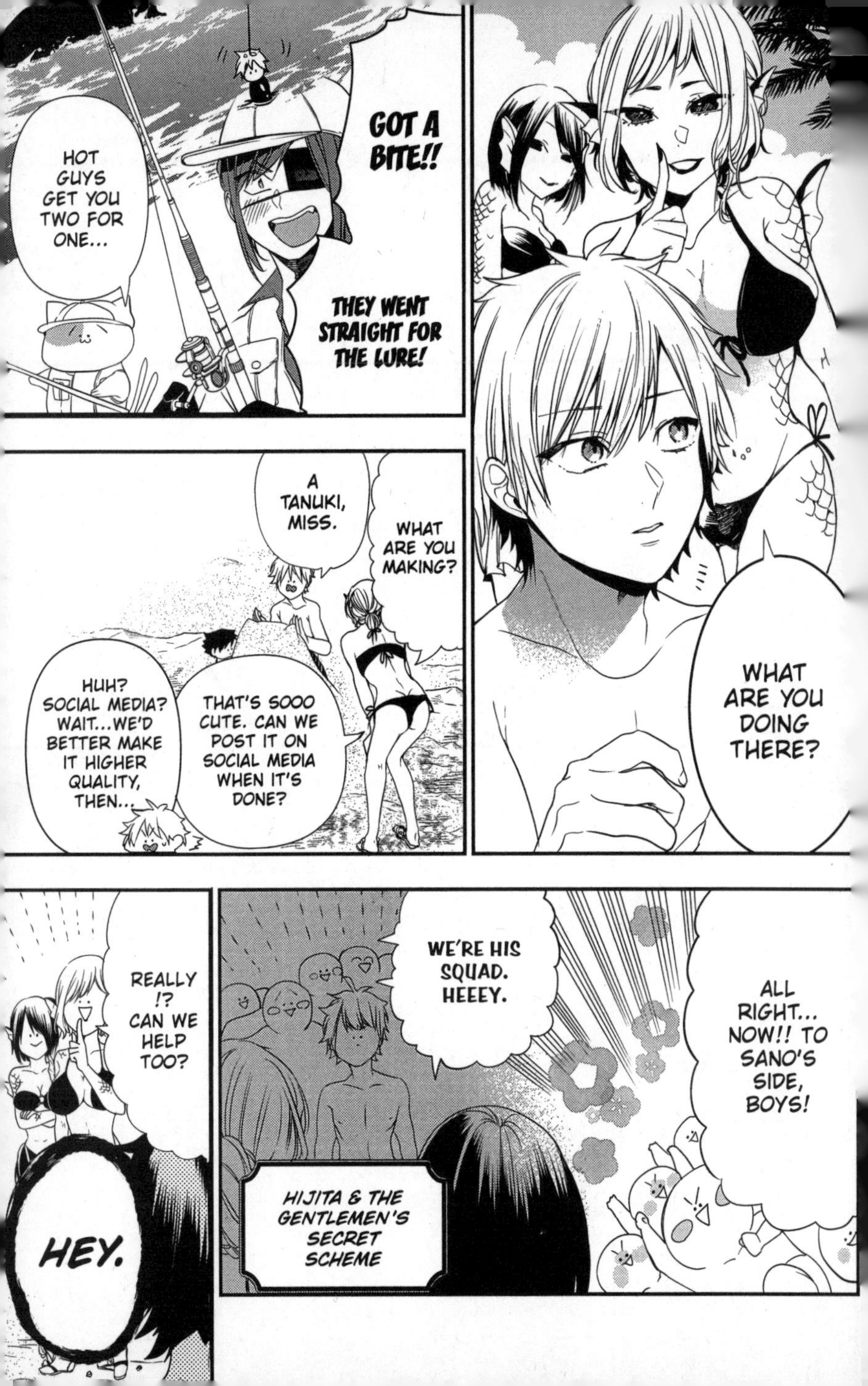
WHAT ARE YOU DOING THERE?
GOT A BITE!!
THEY WENT STRAIGHT FOR THE LURE!
HOT GUYS GET YOU TWO FOR ONE...
WHAT ARE YOU MAKING?
A TANUKI, MISS.
THAT'S SOOO CUTE. CAN WE POST IT ON SOCIAL MEDIA WHEN IT'S DONE?
HUH? SOCIAL MEDIA? WAIT...WE'D BETTER MAKE IT HIGHER QUALITY, THEN...
ALL RIGHT... NOW!! TO SANO'S SIDE, BOYS!
WE'RE HIS SQUAD. HEEEY.
HIJITA & THE GENTLEMEN'S SECRET SCHEME
REALLY!? CAN WE HELP TOO?
HEY.

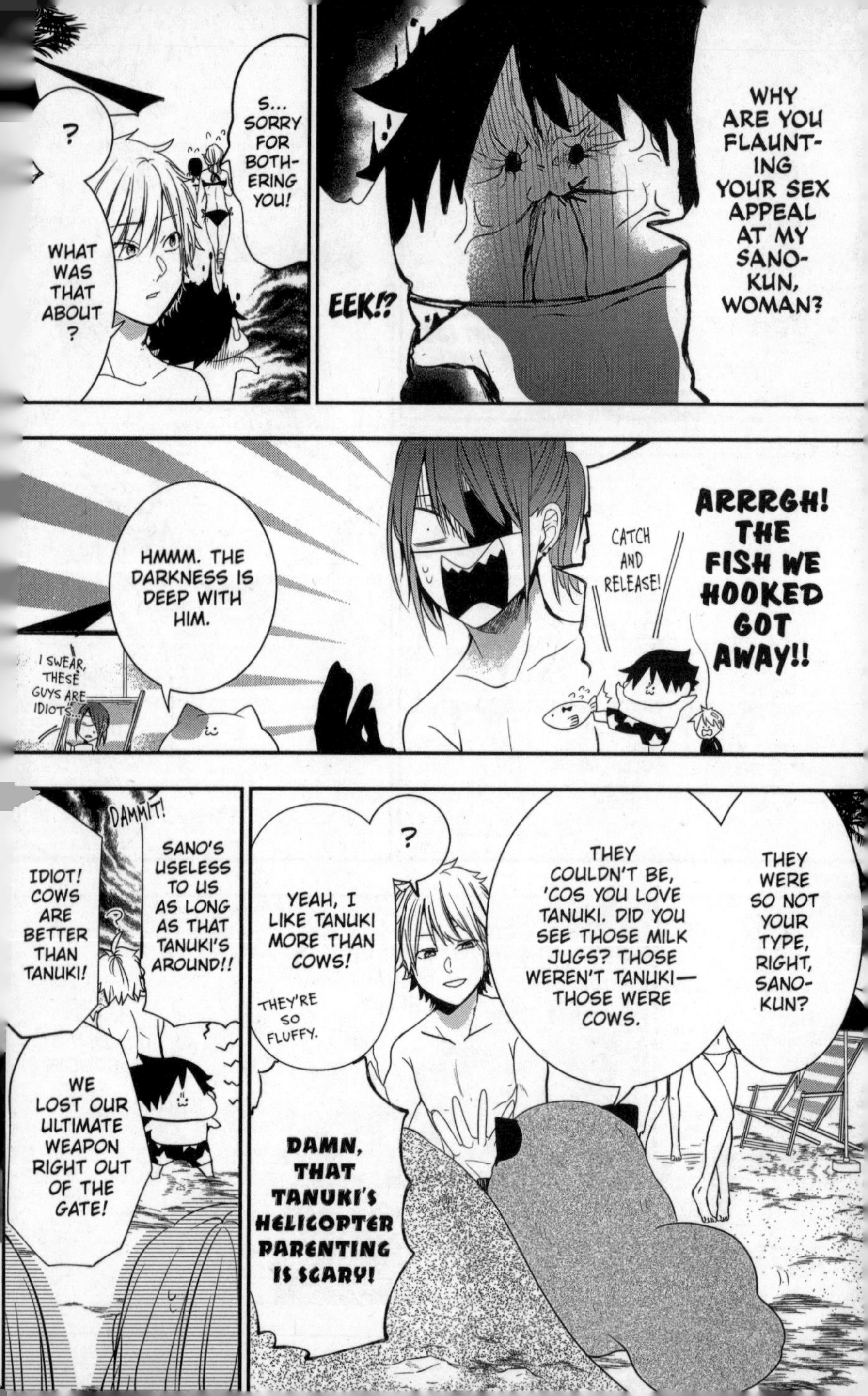
WHY ARE YOU FLAUNTING YOUR SEX APPEAL AT MY SANO-KUN, WOMAN?
EEK!?
S... SORRY FOR BOTHERING YOU!
?
WHAT WAS THAT ABOUT?
ARRRGH! THE FISH WE HOOKED GOT AWAY!!
CATCH AND RELEASE!
HMMM. THE DARKNESS IS DEEP WITH HIM.
I SWEAR, THESE GUYS ARE IDIOTS...
THEY WERE SO NOT YOUR TYPE, RIGHT, SANO-KUN?
THEY COULDN'T BE, 'COS YOU LOVE TANUKI. DID YOU SEE THOSE MILK JUGS? THOSE WEREN'T TANUKI—THOSE WERE COWS.
?
YEAH, I LIKE TANUKI MORE THAN COWS!
THEY'RE SO FLUFFY.
DAMN, THAT TANUKI'S HELICOPTER PARENTING IS SCARY!
DAMMIT!
SANO'S USELESS TO US AS LONG AS THAT TANUKI'S AROUND!!
IDIOT! COWS ARE BETTER THAN TANUKI!
WE LOST OUR ULTIMATE WEAPON RIGHT OUT OF THE GATE!

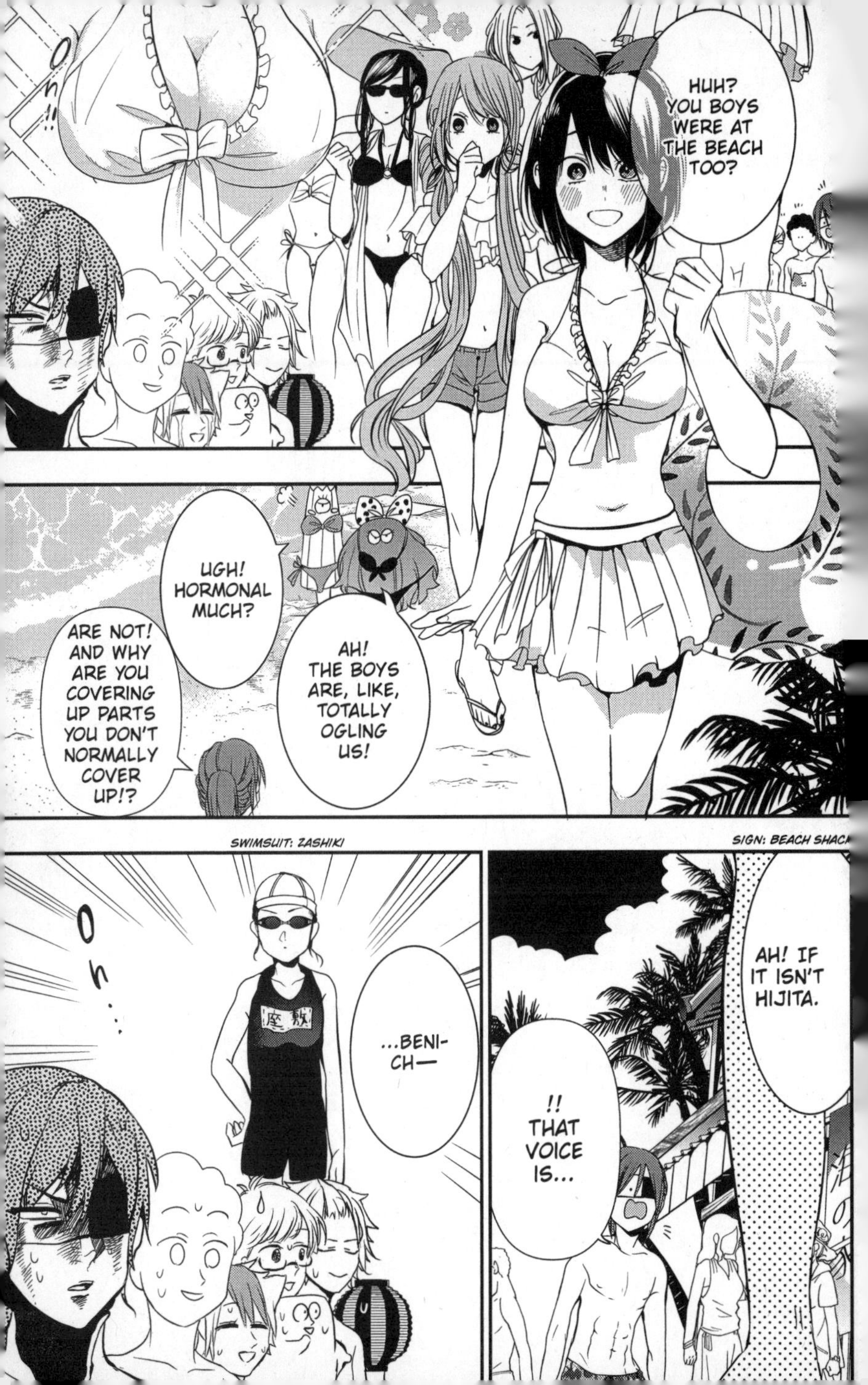
HUH? YOU BOYS WERE AT THE BEACH TOO?
On!!
AH! THE BOYS ARE, LIKE, TOTALLY OGLING US!
UGH! HORMONAL MUCH?
ARE NOT! AND WHY ARE YOU COVERING UP PARTS YOU DON'T NORMALLY COVER UP!?
SIGN: BEACH SHACK
SWIMSUIT: ZASHIKI
AH! IF IT ISN'T HIJITA.
!! THAT VOICE IS...
...BENI-CH—
On...
座敷

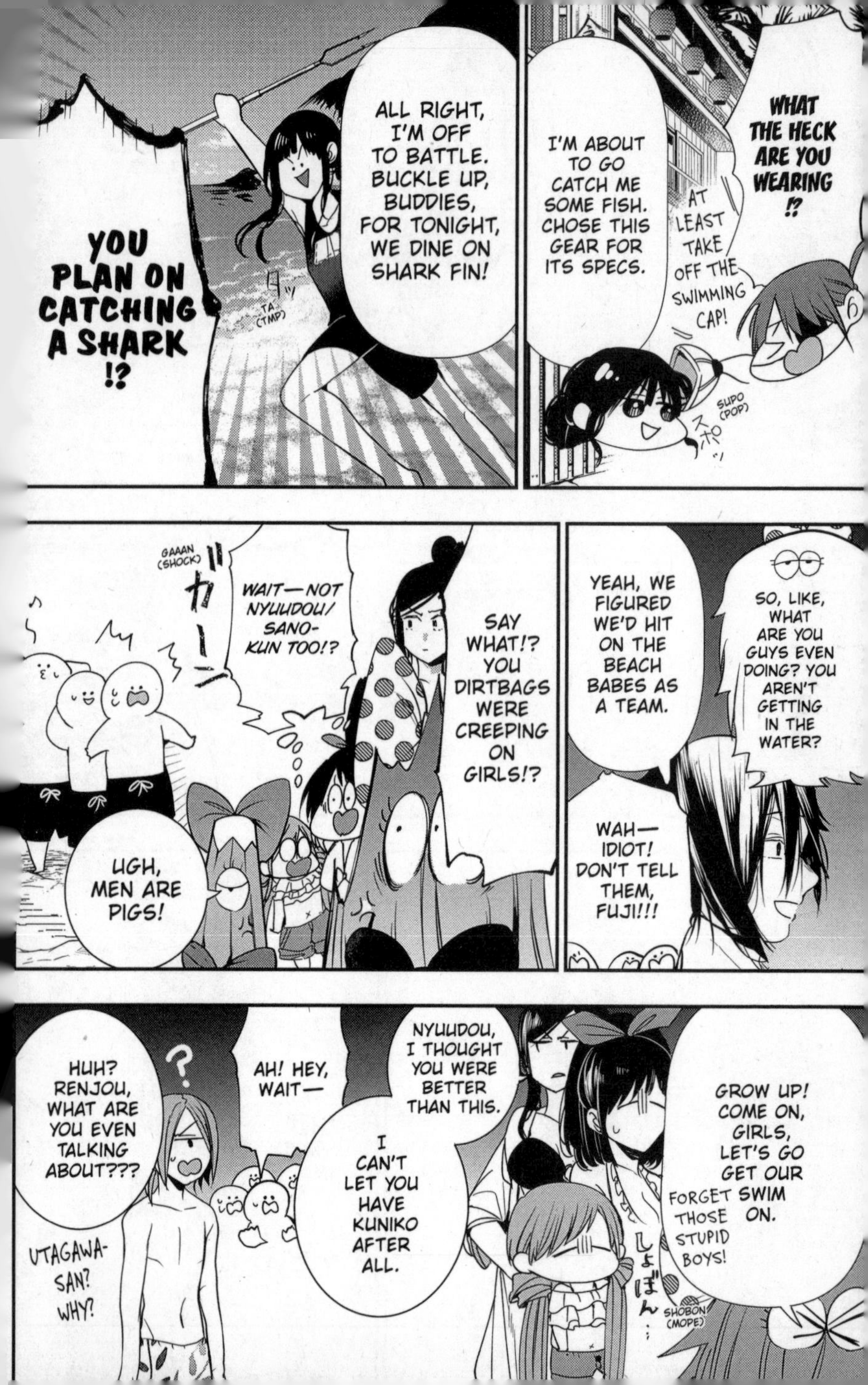
WHAT THE HECK ARE YOU WEARING!?
I'M ABOUT TO GO CATCH ME SOME FISH. CHOSE THIS GEAR FOR ITS SPECS.
AT LEAST TAKE OFF THE SWIMMING CAP!
SUPO (POP)
ALL RIGHT, I'M OFF TO BATTLE. BUCKLE UP, BUDDIES, FOR TONIGHT, WE DINE ON SHARK FIN!
TA (TMP)
YOU PLAN ON CATCHING A SHARK!?
SO, LIKE, WHAT ARE YOU GUYS EVEN DOING? YOU AREN'T GETTING IN THE WATER?
YEAH, WE FIGURED WE'D HIT ON THE BEACH BABES AS A TEAM.
WAH— IDIOT! DON'T TELL THEM, FUJI!!!
SAY WHAT!? YOU DIRTBAGS WERE CREEPING ON GIRLS!?
WAIT—NOT NYUUDOU/SANO-KUN TOO!?
GAAAN (SHOCK)
UGH, MEN ARE PIGS!
GROW UP! COME ON, GIRLS, LET'S GO GET OUR SWIM ON.
FORGET THOSE STUPID BOYS!
SHOBON (MOPE)
NYUUDOU, I THOUGHT YOU WERE BETTER THAN THIS.
I CAN'T LET YOU HAVE KUNIKO AFTER ALL.
AH! HEY, WAIT—
HUH? RENJOU, WHAT ARE YOU EVEN TALKING ABOUT???
UTAGAWA-SAN? WHY?

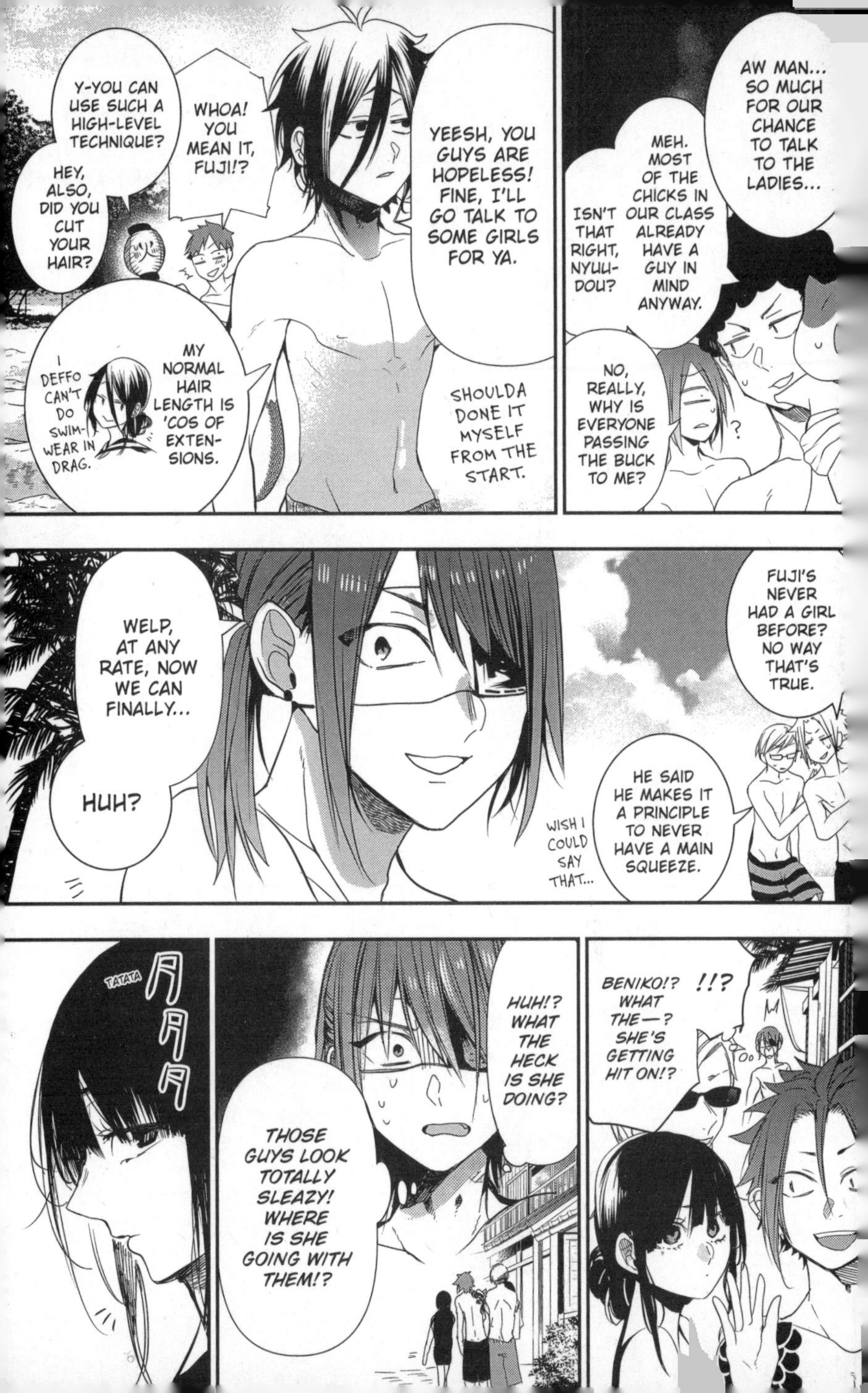
AW MAN... SO MUCH FOR OUR CHANCE TO TALK TO THE LADIES...
MEH. MOST OF THE CHICKS IN OUR CLASS ALREADY HAVE A GUY IN MIND ANYWAY.
ISN'T THAT RIGHT, NYUU-DOU?
NO, REALLY, WHY IS EVERYONE PASSING THE BUCK TO ME?
?
YEESH, YOU GUYS ARE HOPELESS! FINE, I'LL GO TALK TO SOME GIRLS FOR YA.
WHOA! YOU MEAN IT, FUJI!?
Y-YOU CAN USE SUCH A HIGH-LEVEL TECHNIQUE?
HEY, ALSO, DID YOU CUT YOUR HAIR?
SHOULDA DONE IT MYSELF FROM THE START.
MY NORMAL HAIR LENGTH IS 'COS OF EXTENSIONS.
I DEFFO CAN'T DO SWIMWEAR IN DRAG.
FUJI'S NEVER HAD A GIRL BEFORE? NO WAY THAT'S TRUE.
HE SAID HE MAKES IT A PRINCIPLE TO NEVER HAVE A MAIN SQUEEZE.
WISH I COULD SAY THAT...
WELP, AT ANY RATE, NOW WE CAN FINALLY...
HUH?
!!?
BENIKO!? WHAT THE—? SHE'S GETTING HIT ON!?
HUH!? WHAT THE HECK IS SHE DOING?
THOSE GUYS LOOK TOTALLY SLEAZY! WHERE IS SHE GOING WITH THEM!?
TATATA

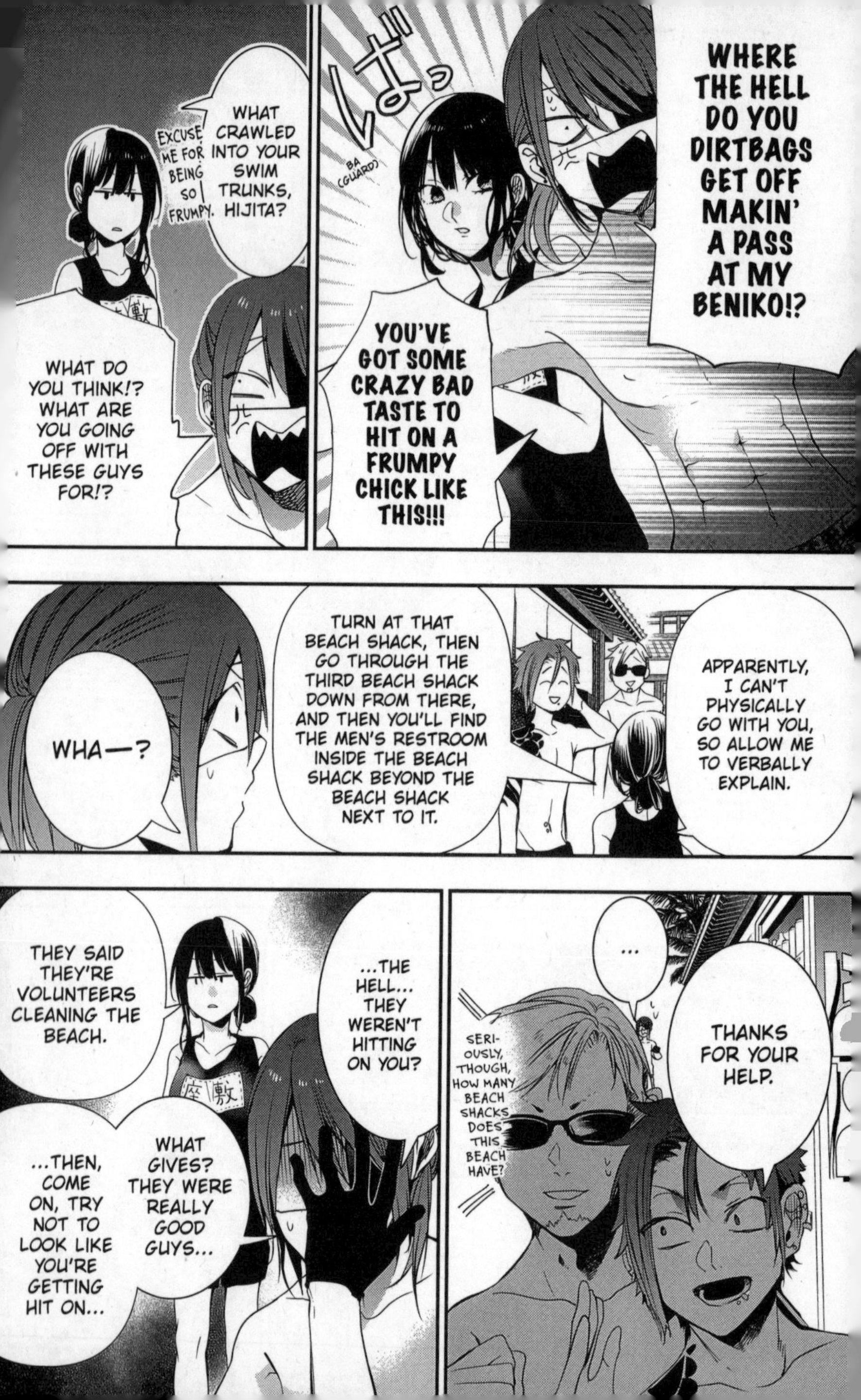
WHERE THE HELL DO YOU DIRTBAGS GET OFF MAKIN' A PASS AT MY BENIKO!?
ばっ
BA (GUARD)
YOU'VE GOT SOME CRAZY BAD TASTE TO HIT ON A FRUMPY CHICK LIKE THIS!!!
WHAT CRAWLED INTO YOUR SWIM TRUNKS, HIJITA?
EXCUSE ME FOR BEING SO FRUMPY.
WHAT DO YOU THINK!? WHAT ARE YOU GOING OFF WITH THESE GUYS FOR!?
APPARENTLY, I CAN'T PHYSICALLY GO WITH YOU, SO ALLOW ME TO VERBALLY EXPLAIN.
TURN AT THAT BEACH SHACK, THEN GO THROUGH THE THIRD BEACH SHACK DOWN FROM THERE, AND THEN YOU'LL FIND THE MEN'S RESTROOM INSIDE THE BEACH SHACK BEYOND THE BEACH SHACK NEXT TO IT.
WHA—?
THANKS FOR YOUR HELP.
...
SERIOUSLY, THOUGH, HOW MANY BEACH SHACKS DOES THIS BEACH HAVE?
...THE HELL... THEY WEREN'T HITTING ON YOU?
THEY SAID THEY'RE VOLUNTEERS CLEANING THE BEACH.
WHAT GIVES? THEY WERE REALLY GOOD GUYS...
...THEN, COME ON, TRY NOT TO LOOK LIKE YOU'RE GETTING HIT ON...

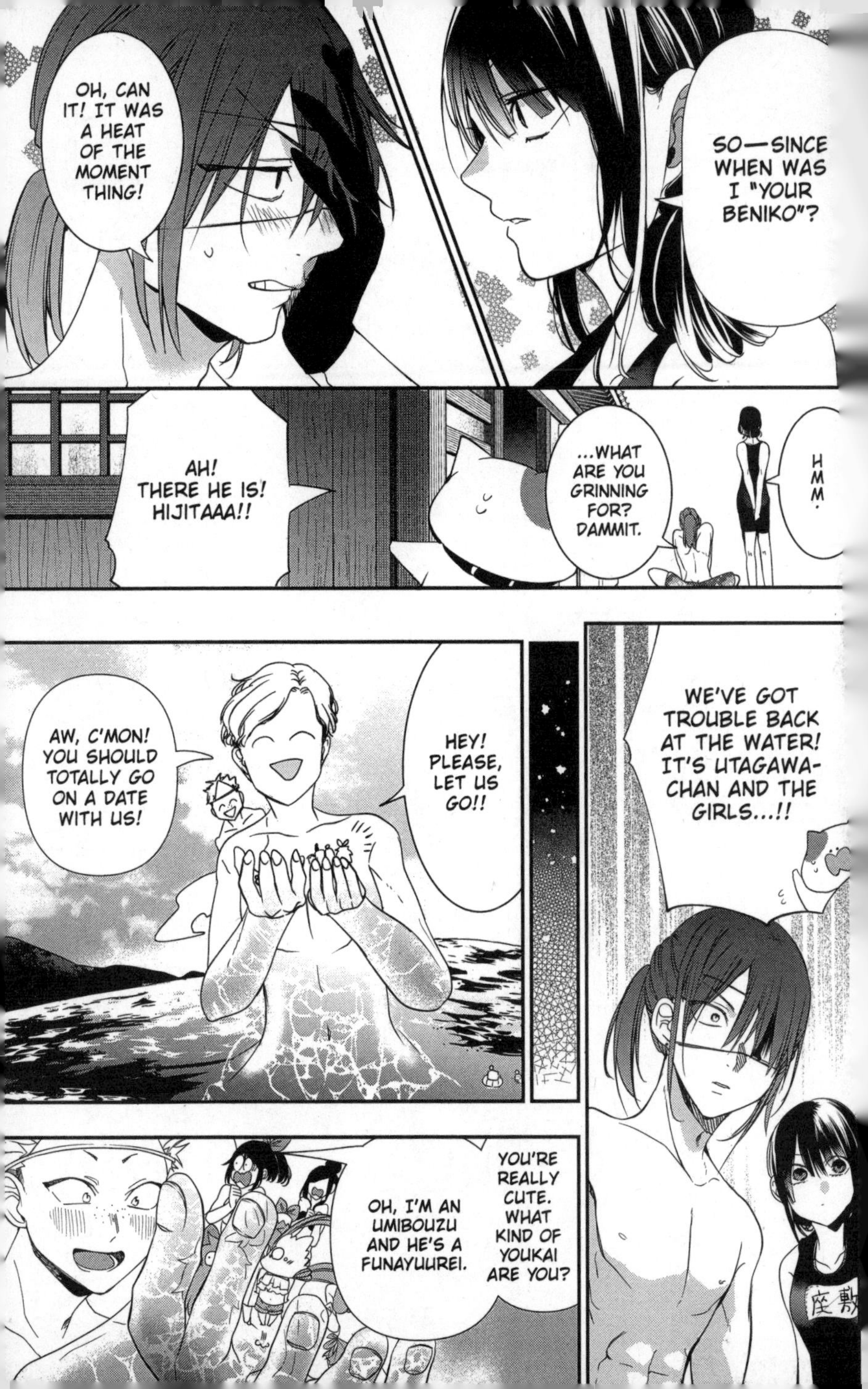
SO—SINCE WHEN WAS I "YOUR BENIKO"?
OH, CAN IT! IT WAS A HEAT OF THE MOMENT THING!
HMM.
...WHAT ARE YOU GRINNING FOR? DAMMIT.
AH! THERE HE IS! HIJITAAA!!
WE'VE GOT TROUBLE BACK AT THE WATER! IT'S UTAGAWA-CHAN AND THE GIRLS...!!
座敷
HEY! PLEASE, LET US GO!!
AW, C'MON! YOU SHOULD TOTALLY GO ON A DATE WITH US!
YOU'RE REALLY CUTE. WHAT KIND OF YOUKAI ARE YOU?
OH, I'M AN UMIBOUZU AND HE'S A FUNAYUUREI.

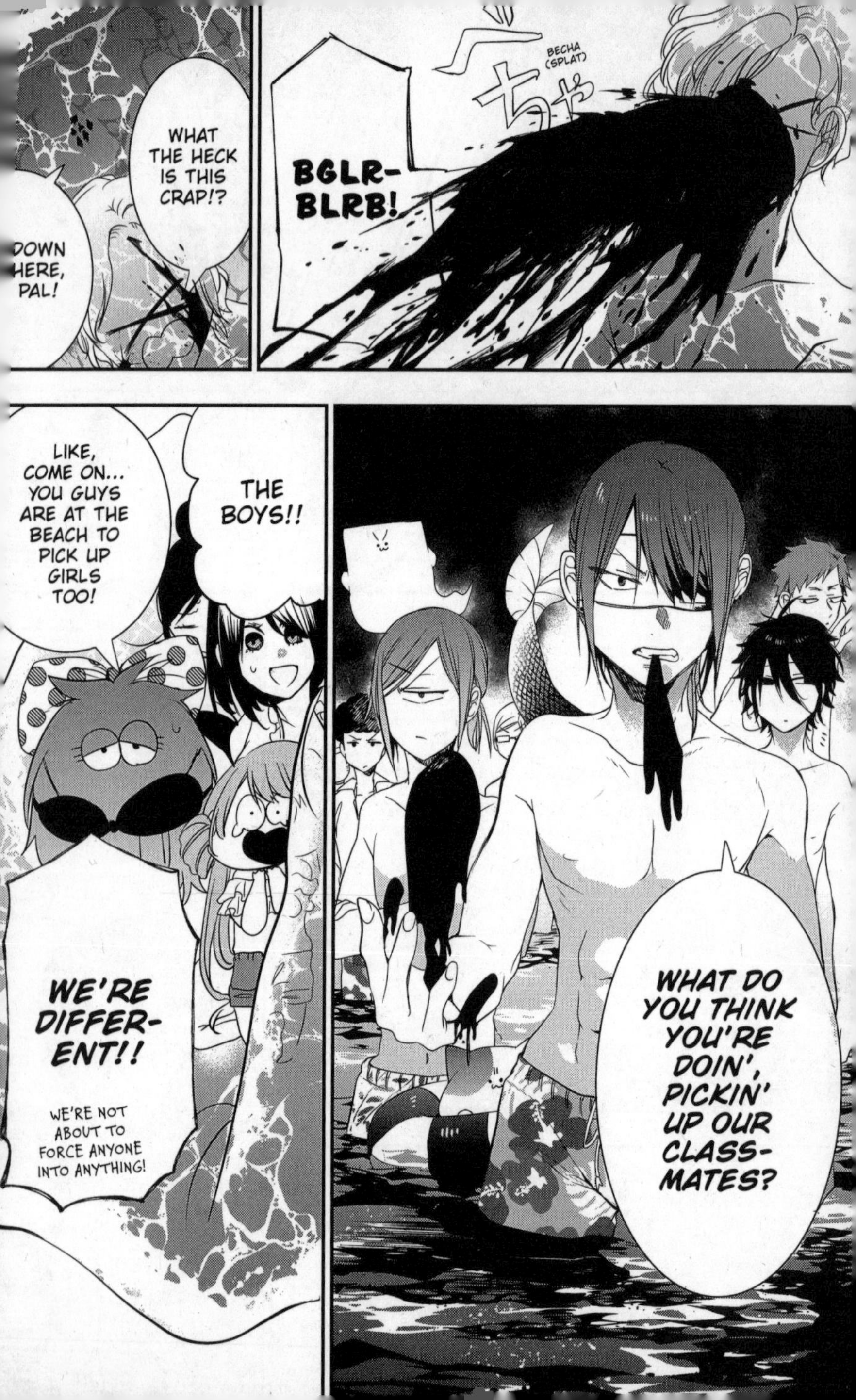
BECHA (SPLAT)
ちゃ
BGLR-BLRB!
WHAT THE HECK IS THIS CRAP!?
DOWN HERE, PAL!
WHAT DO YOU THINK YOU'RE DOIN', PICKIN' UP OUR CLASSMATES?
THE BOYS!!
LIKE, COME ON... YOU GUYS ARE AT THE BEACH TO PICK UP GIRLS TOO!
WE'RE DIFFERENT!!
WE'RE NOT ABOUT TO FORCE ANYONE INTO ANYTHING!

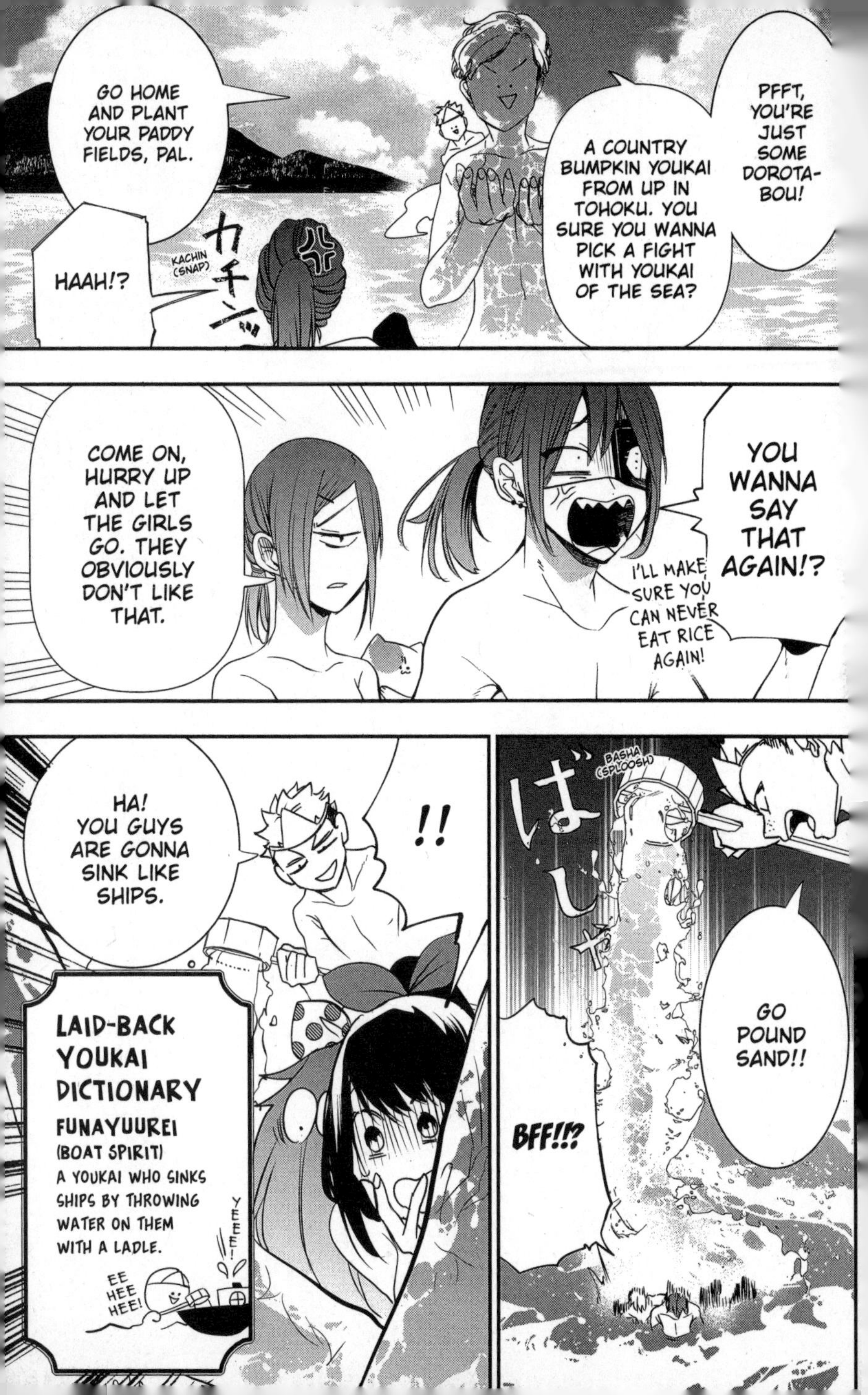
PFFT, YOU'RE JUST SOME DOROTA-BOU!
A COUNTRY BUMPKIN YOUKAI FROM UP IN TOHOKU. YOU SURE YOU WANNA PICK A FIGHT WITH YOUKAI OF THE SEA?
GO HOME AND PLANT YOUR PADDY FIELDS, PAL.
KACHIN (SNAP)
HAAH!?
YOU WANNA SAY THAT AGAIN!?
I'LL MAKE SURE YOU CAN NEVER EAT RICE AGAIN!
COME ON, HURRY UP AND LET THE GIRLS GO. THEY OBVIOUSLY DON'T LIKE THAT.
BASHA (SPLOOSH)
GO POUND SAND!!
BFF!!?
!!
HA! YOU GUYS ARE GONNA SINK LIKE SHIPS.
YEEE!
LAID-BACK YOUKAI DICTIONARY
FUNAYUUREI (BOAT SPIRIT)
A YOUKAI WHO SINKS SHIPS BY THROWING WATER ON THEM WITH A LADLE.
EE HEE HEE!

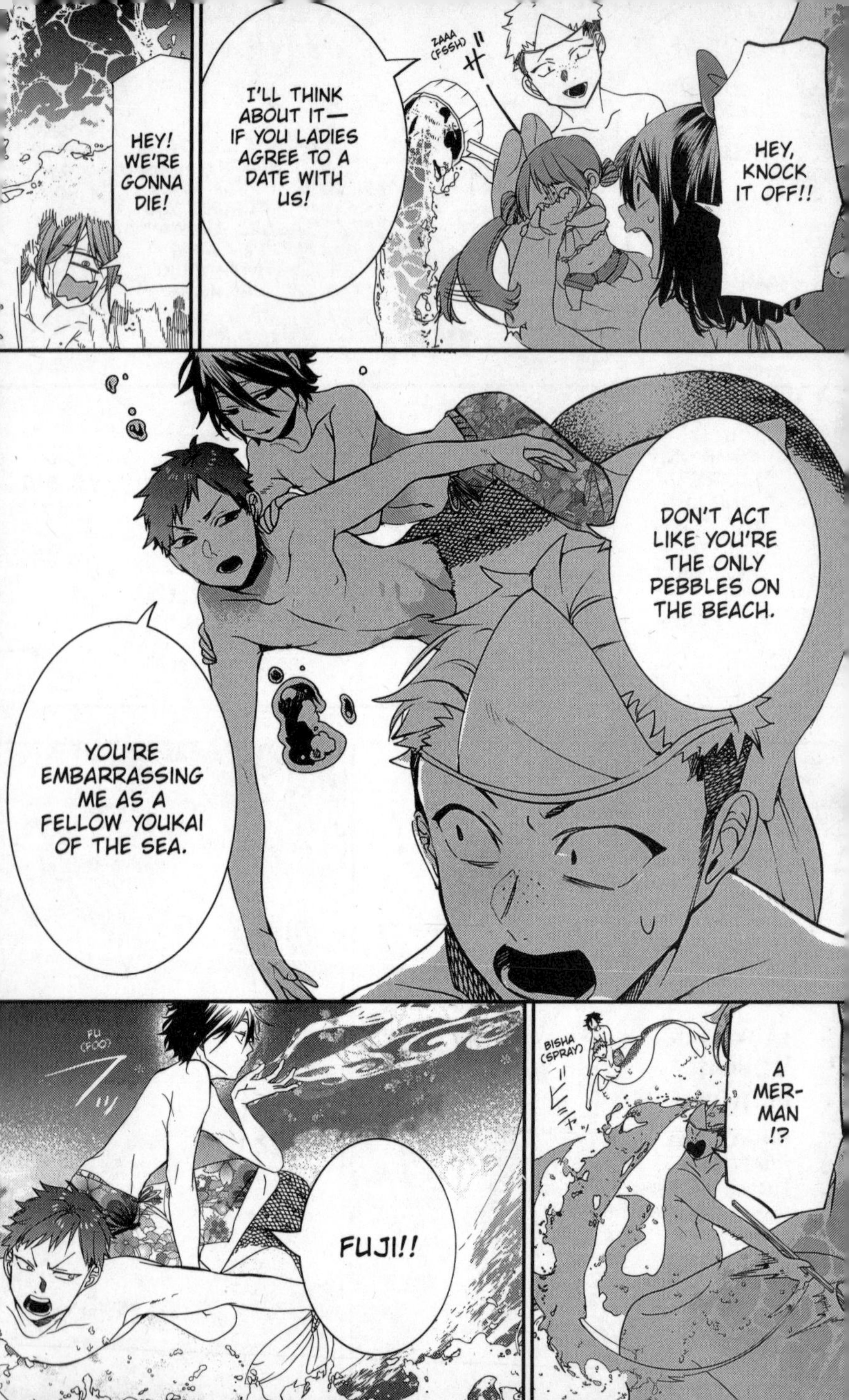
HEY, KNOCK IT OFF!!
ZAAA (FSSH)
I'LL THINK ABOUT IT— IF YOU LADIES AGREE TO A DATE WITH US!
HEY! WE'RE GONNA DIE!
DON'T ACT LIKE YOU'RE THE ONLY PEBBLES ON THE BEACH.
YOU'RE EMBARRASSING ME AS A FELLOW YOUKAI OF THE SEA.
BISHA (SPRAY)
A MER-MAN!?
FU (FOO)
FUJI!!

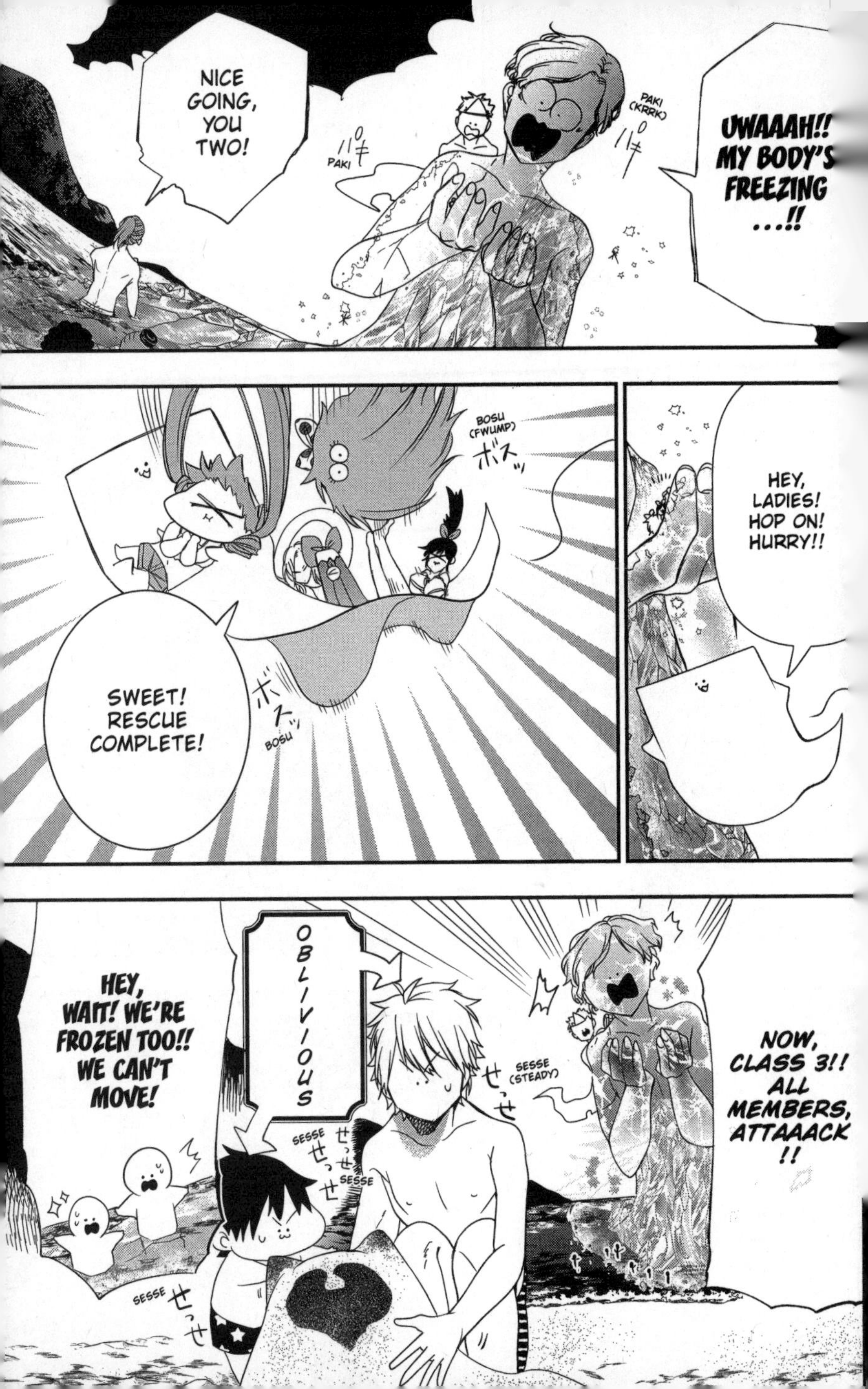
UWAAAH!! MY BODY'S FREEZING ...!!
PAKI (KRRK)
パキ
PAKI
パキ
NICE GOING, YOU TWO!
HEY, LADIES! HOP ON! HURRY!!
BOSU (FWUMP)
ボスッ
SWEET! RESCUE COMPLETE!
ボスッ
BOSU
NOW, CLASS 3!! ALL MEMBERS, ATTAAACK!!
SESSE (STEADY)
せっせ
OBLIVIOUS
SESSE
せっせ
SESSE
せっせ
HEY, WAIT! WE'RE FROZEN TOO!! WE CAN'T MOVE!
SESSE
せっせ

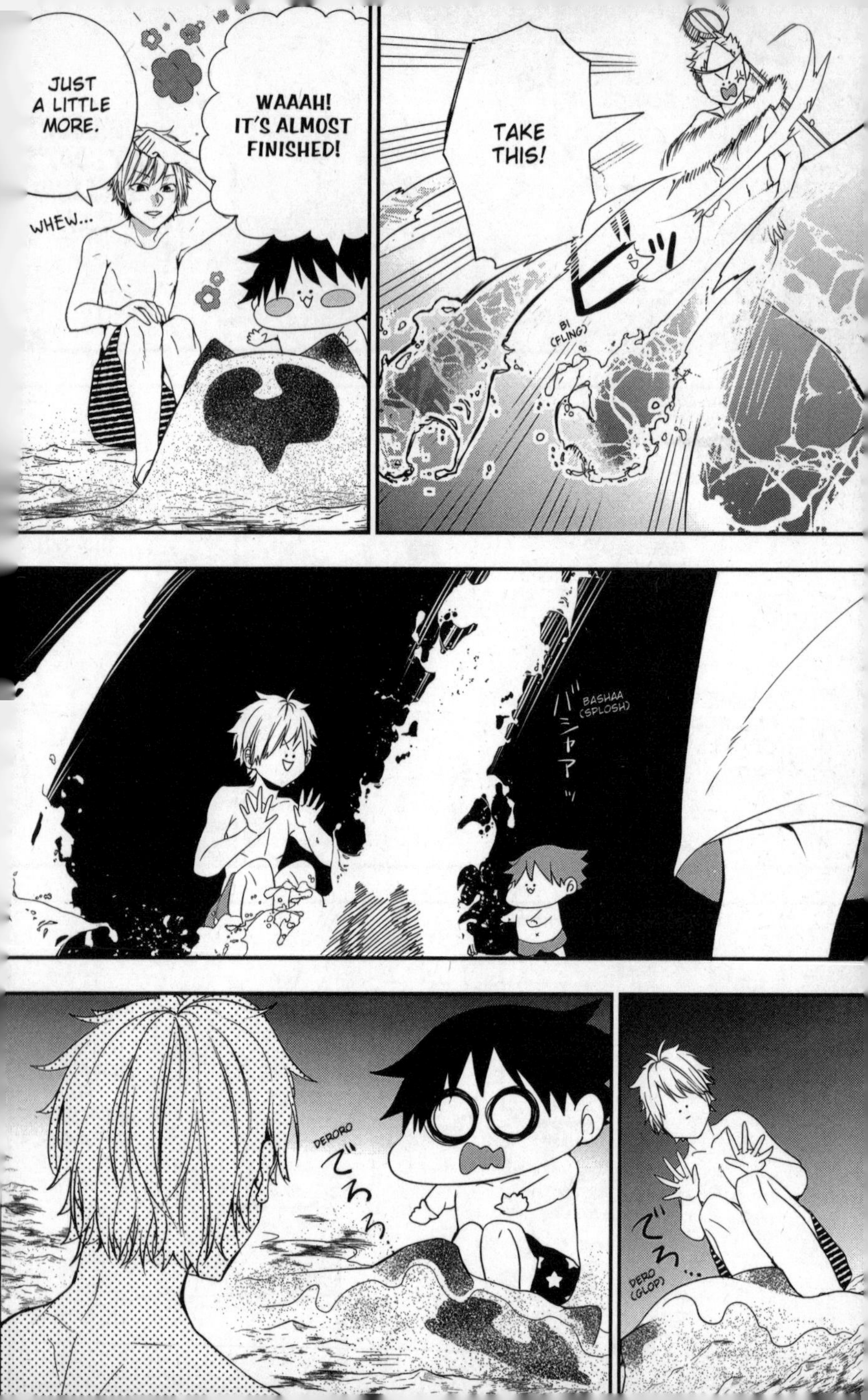

TAKE THIS!
ビッ
BI (FLING)
WAAAH! IT'S ALMOST FINISHED!
JUST A LITTLE MORE.
WHEW...
バシャアッ
BASHAA (SPLOSH)
でろ…
DERO (GLOP)
でろろ
DERORO

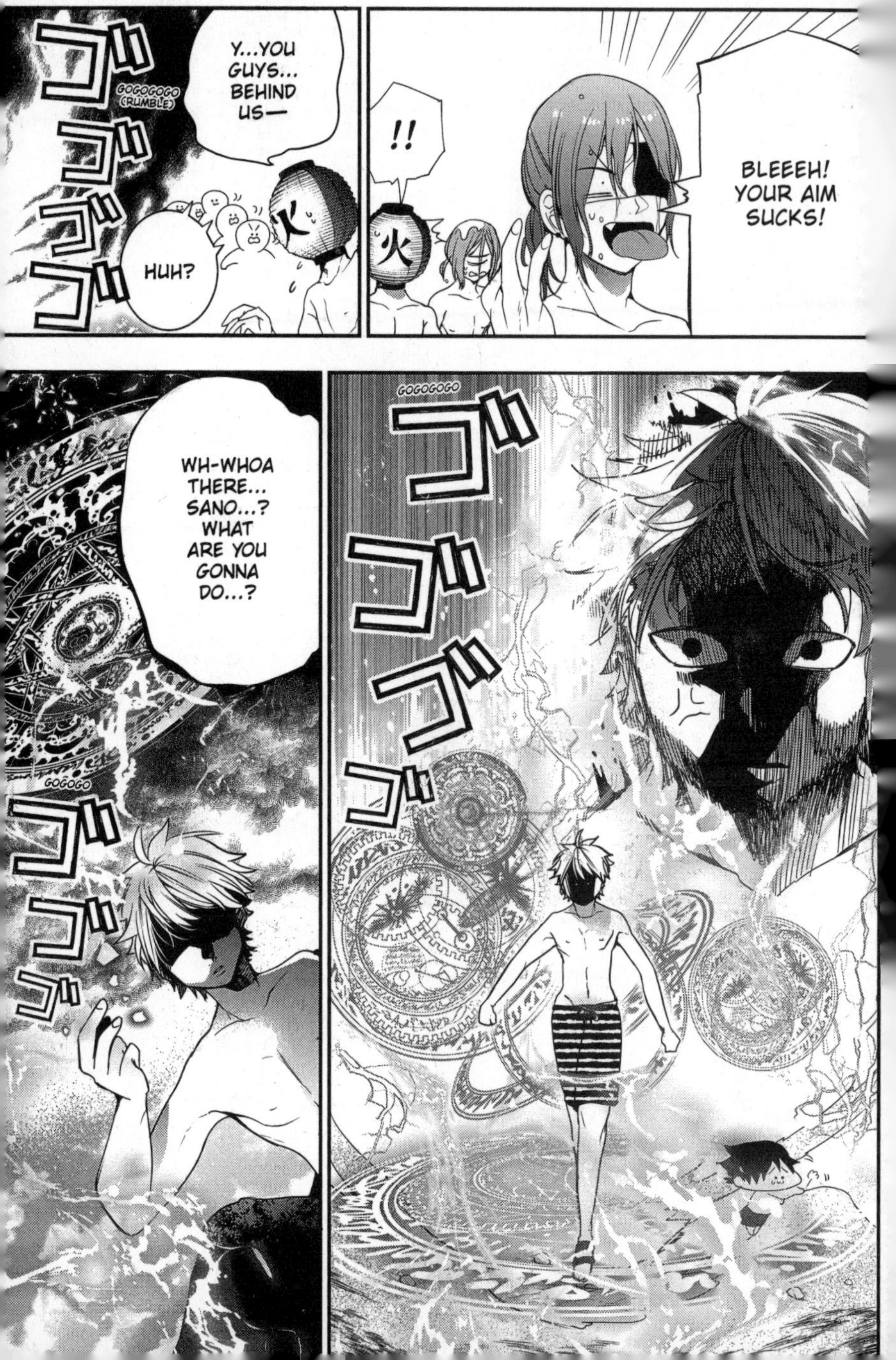
BLEEEH! YOUR AIM SUCKS!
!!
火
火
Y...YOU GUYS... BEHIND US—
HUH?
GOGOGOGO (RUMBLE)
ゴゴゴゴ
GOGOGOGO
ゴゴゴゴ
WH-WHOA THERE... SANO...? WHAT ARE YOU GONNA DO...?
GOGOGO
ゴゴゴ

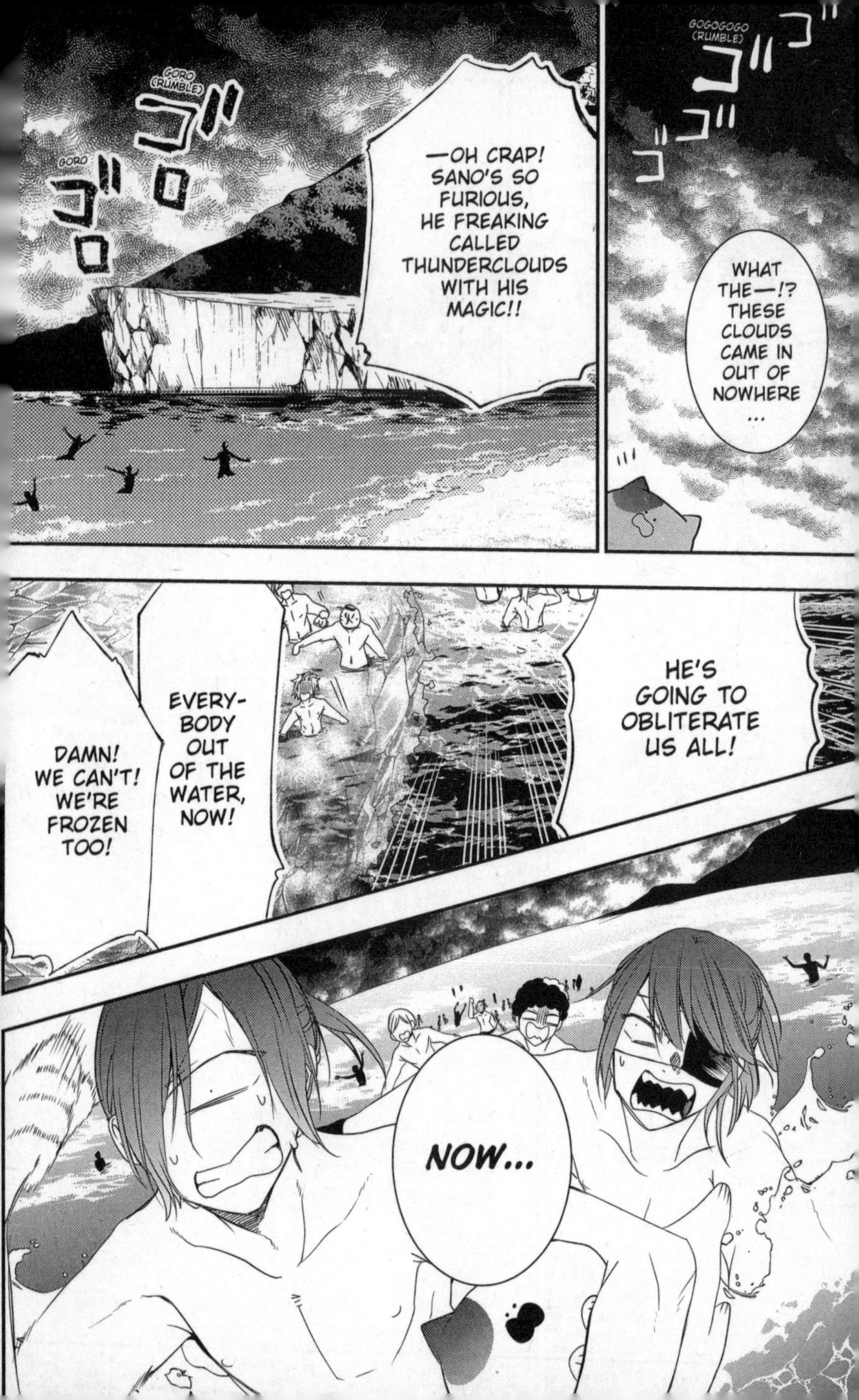
GOGOGOGO (RUMBLE)
WHAT THE—!? THESE CLOUDS CAME IN OUT OF NOWHERE...
GORO (RUMBLE)
GORO
—OH CRAP! SANO'S SO FURIOUS, HE FREAKING CALLED THUNDERCLOUDS WITH HIS MAGIC!!
HE'S GOING TO OBLITERATE US ALL!
EVERY-BODY OUT OF THE WATER, NOW!
DAMN! WE CAN'T! WE'RE FROZEN TOO!
NOW...

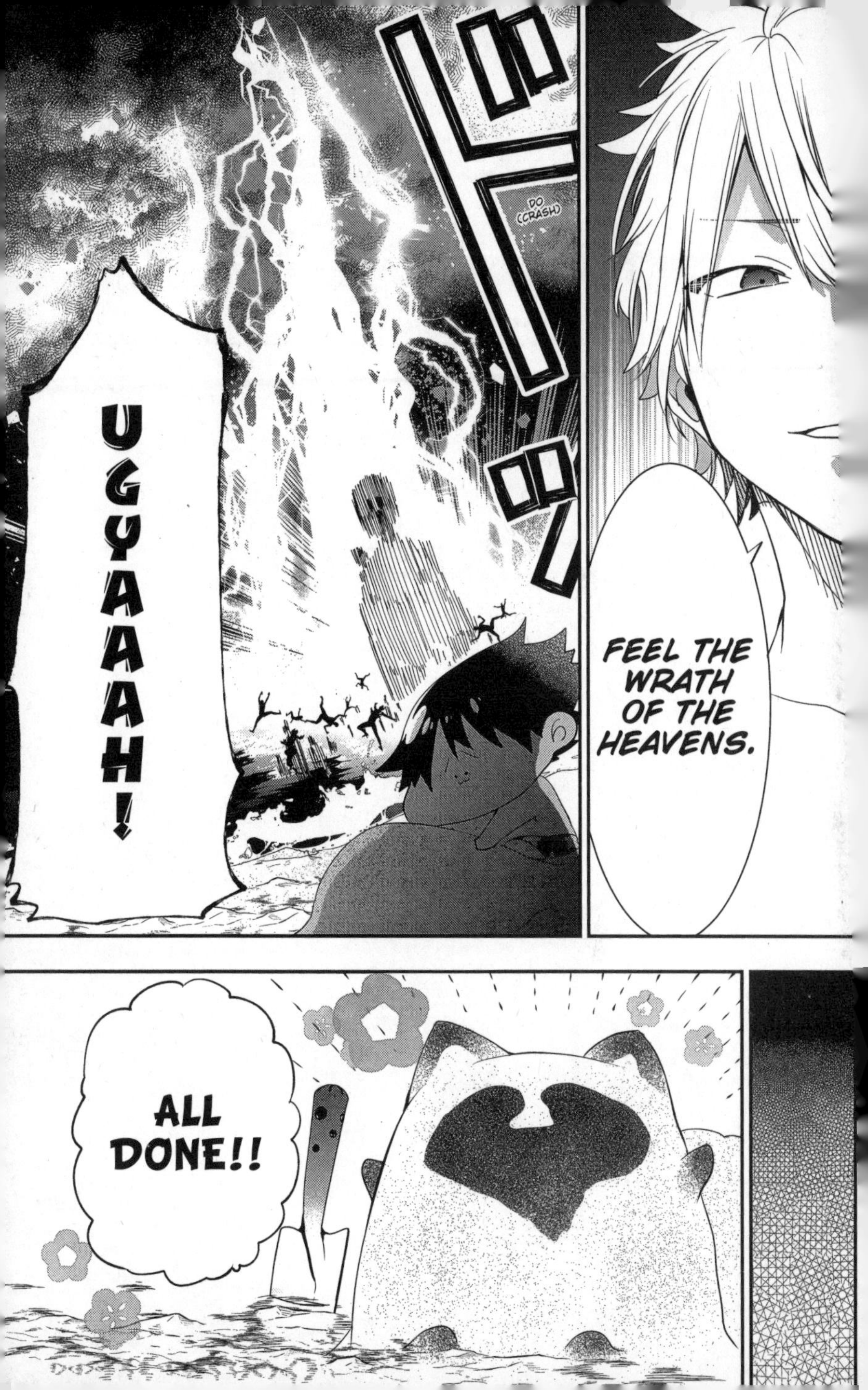
FEEL THE WRATH OF THE HEAVENS.
DO (CRASH)
UGYAAAAH!
ALL DONE!!

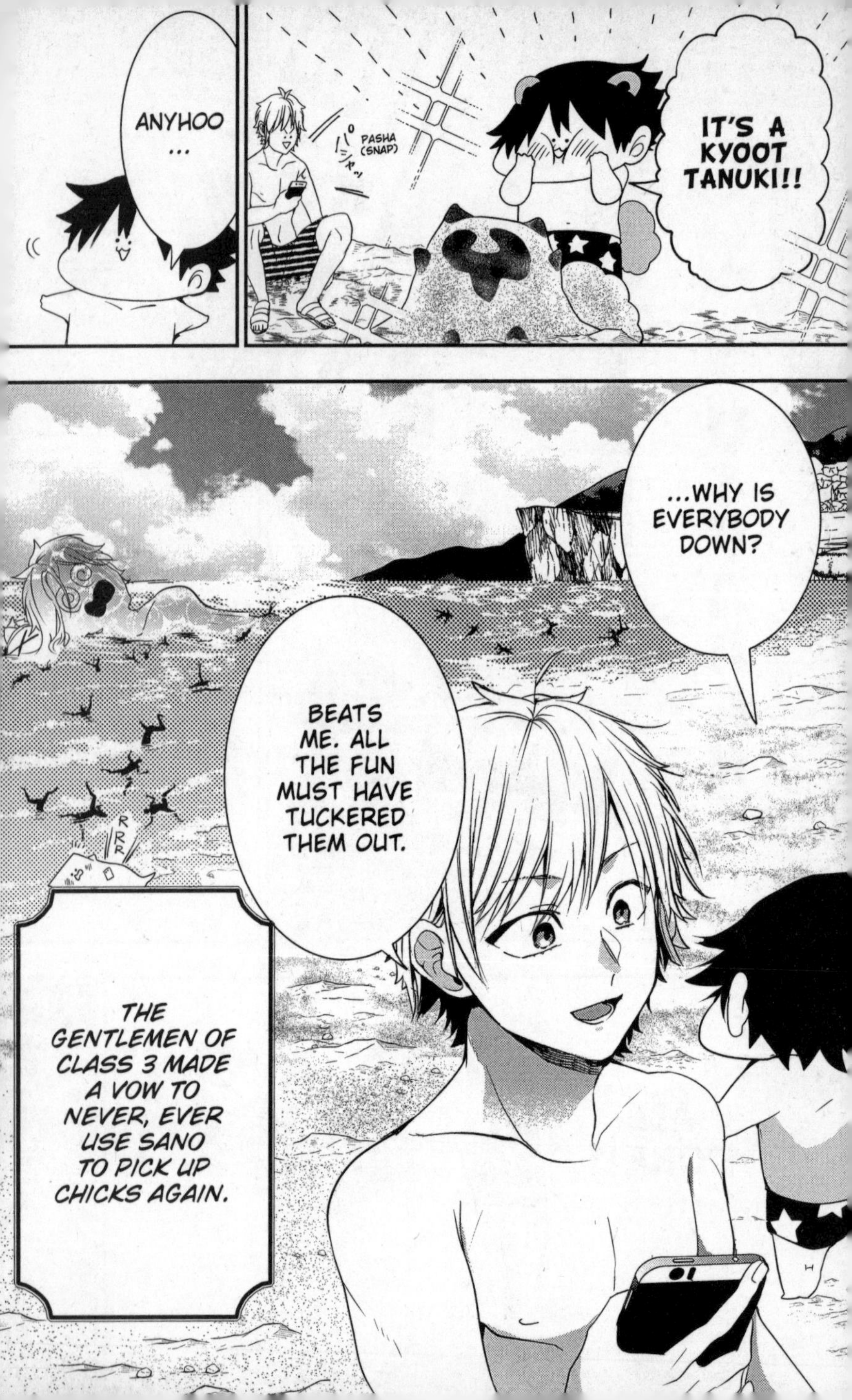
IT'S A KYOOT TANUKI!!
PASHA (SNAP)
ANYHOO ...
...WHY IS EVERYBODY DOWN?
BEATS ME. ALL THE FUN MUST HAVE TUCKERED THEM OUT.
RRR
THE GENTLEMEN OF CLASS 3 MADE A VOW TO NEVER, EVER USE SANO TO PICK UP CHICKS AGAIN.

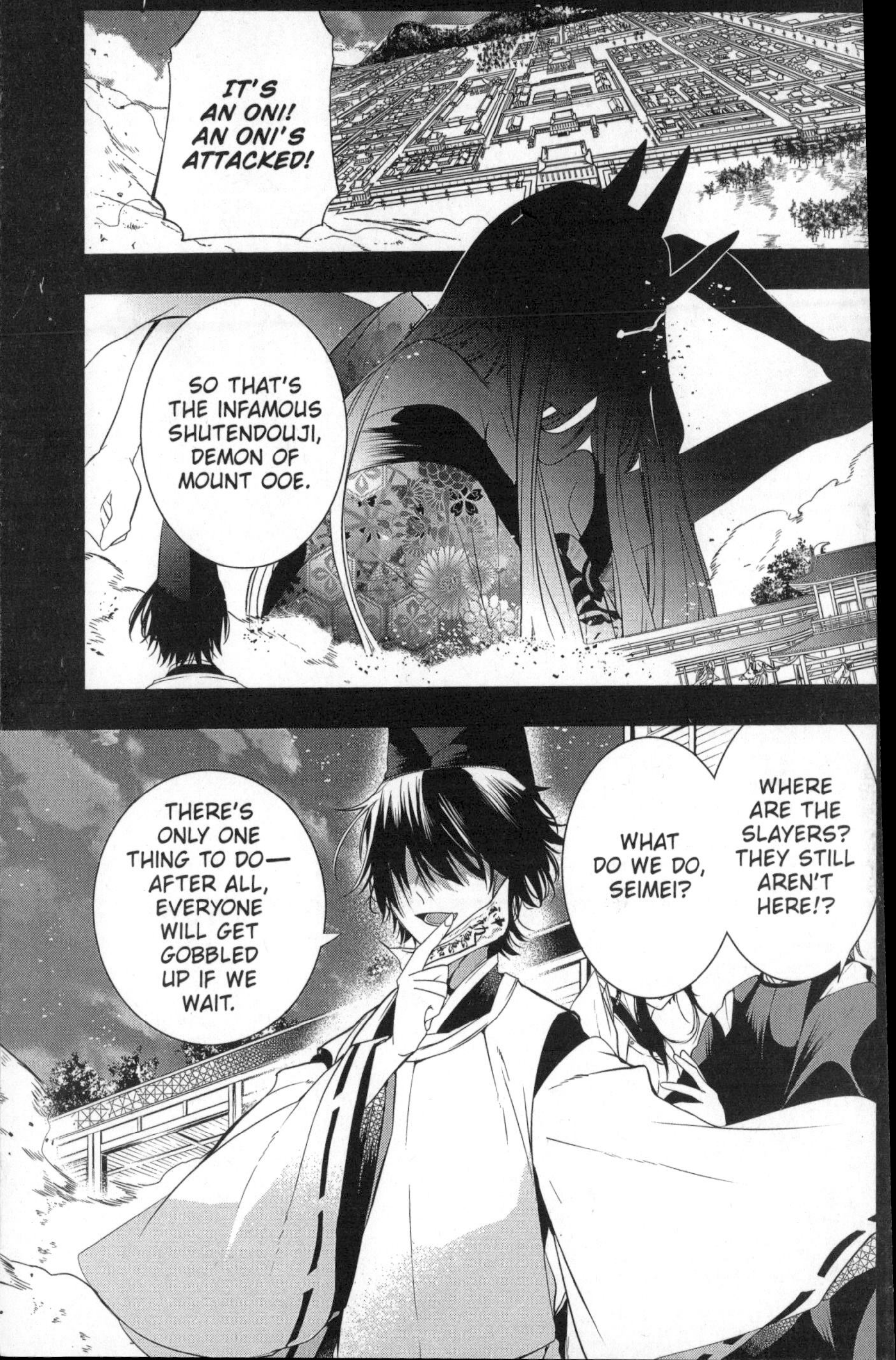
IT'S AN ONI! AN ONI'S ATTACKED!
SO THAT'S THE INFAMOUS SHUTENDOUJI, DEMON OF MOUNT OOE.
WHERE ARE THE SLAYERS? THEY STILL AREN'T HERE!?
WHAT DO WE DO, SEIMEI?
THERE'S ONLY ONE THING TO DO—AFTER ALL, EVERYONE WILL GET GOBBLED UP IF WE WAIT.

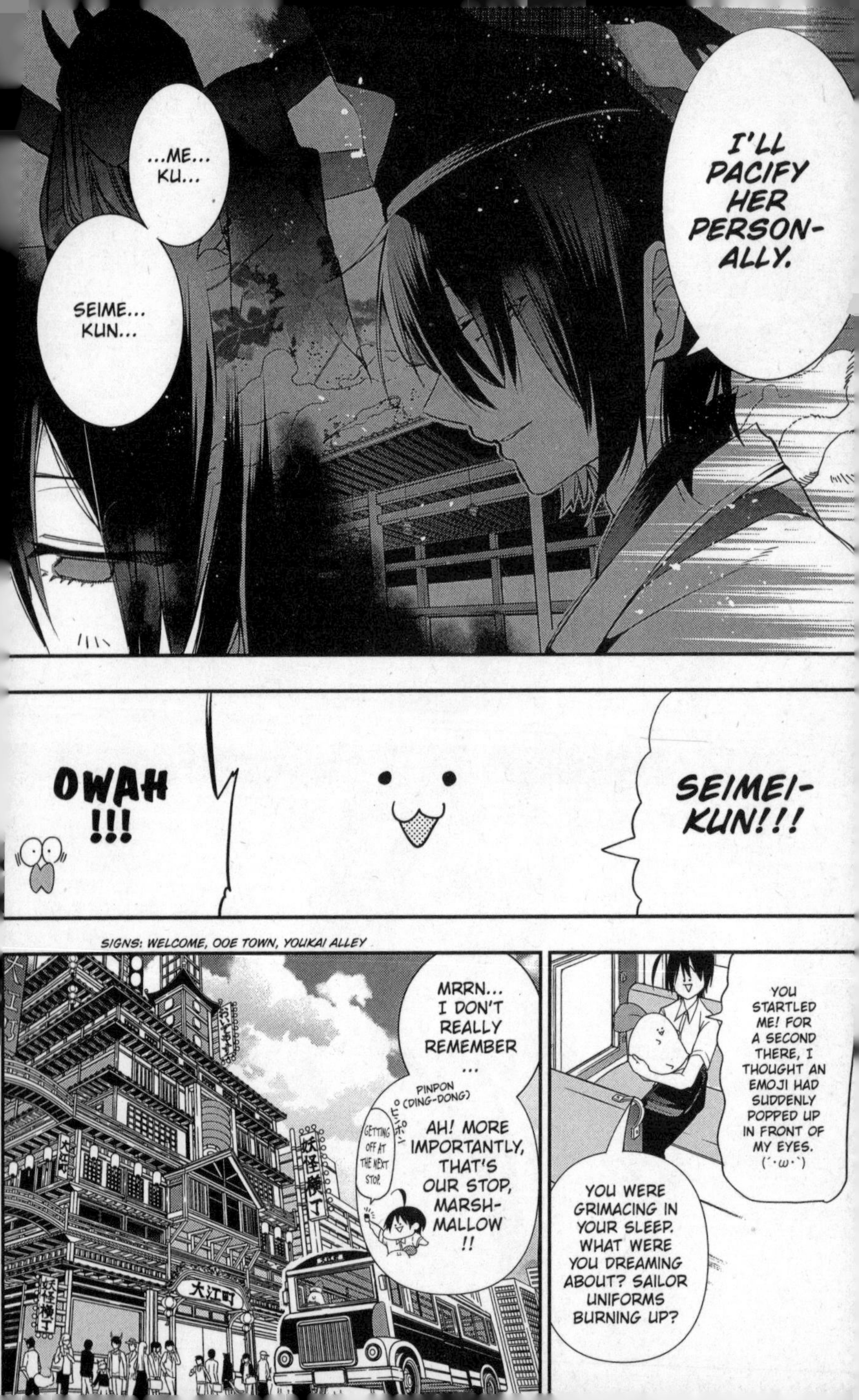

I'LL PACIFY HER PERSON-ALLY.
...ME... KU...
SEIME... KUN...
SEIMEI-KUN!!!
OWAH !!!
SIGNS: WELCOME, OOE TOWN, YOUKAI ALLEY
YOU STARTLED ME! FOR A SECOND THERE, I THOUGHT AN EMOJI HAD SUDDENLY POPPED UP IN FRONT OF MY EYES. (´･ω･`)
YOU WERE GRIMACING IN YOUR SLEEP. WHAT WERE YOU DREAMING ABOUT? SAILOR UNIFORMS BURNING UP?
MRRN... I DON'T REALLY REMEMBER ...
PINPON (DING-DONG)
GETTING OFF AT THE NEXT STOP.
AH! MORE IMPORTANTLY, THAT'S OUR STOP, MARSH-MALLOW !!
妖怪横丁
大江町

Forty-Seventh Period — Abe no Seimei, Haruaki Abe, and Shutendouji (Part 1)

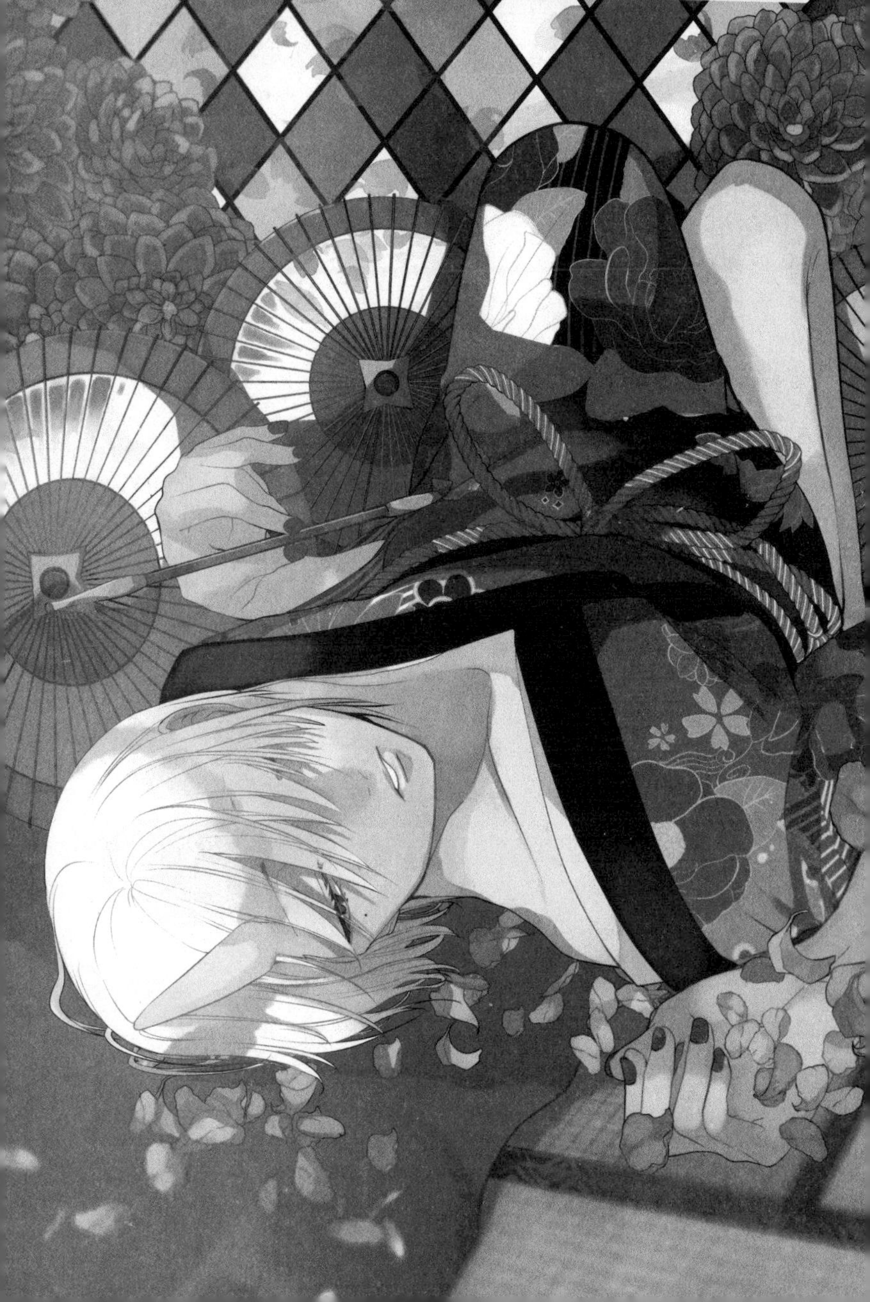

A TeRRified Teacher
at GHOUL School!

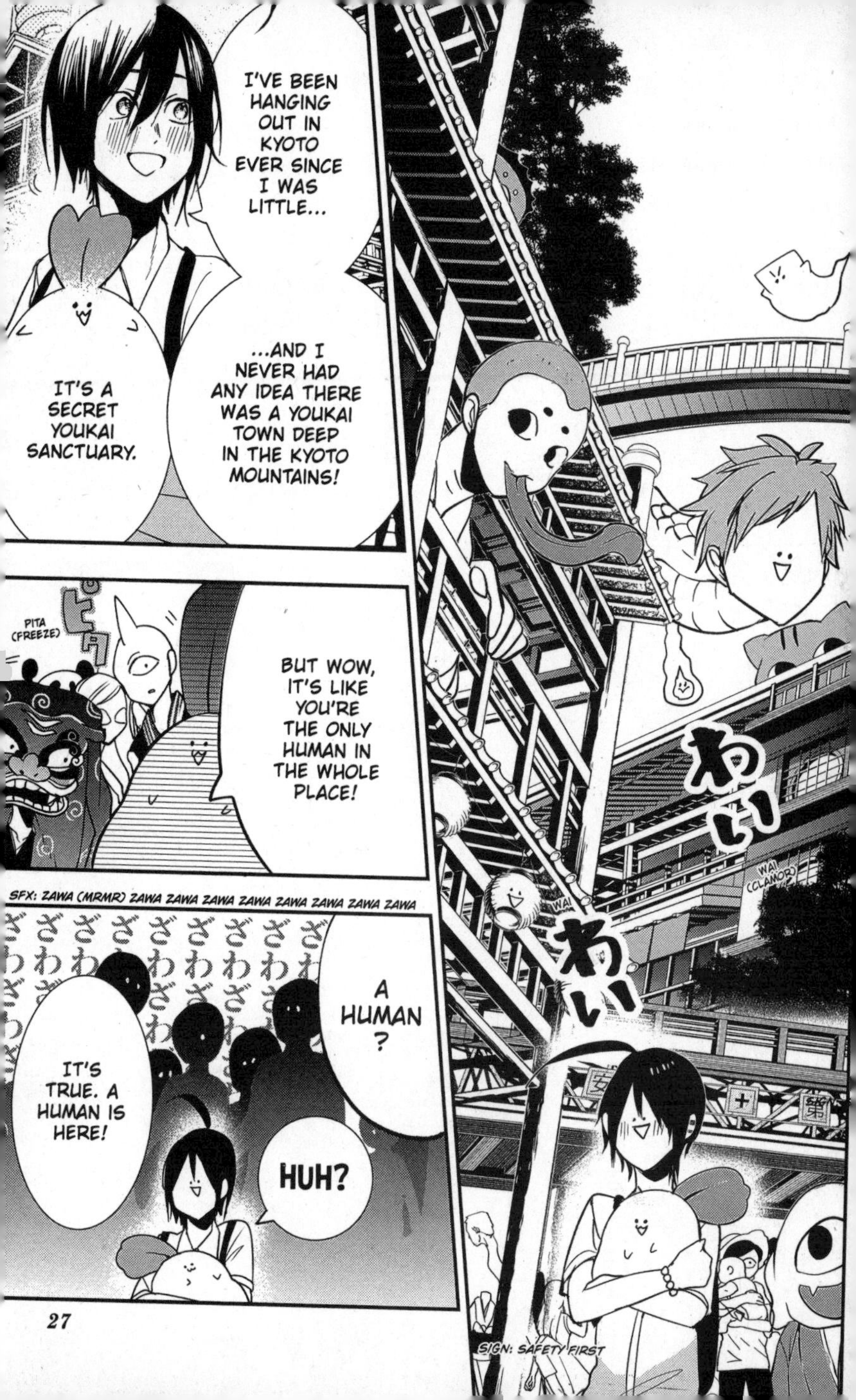
わい
WAI (CLAMOR)
WAI
わい
SIGN: SAFETY FIRST
I'VE BEEN HANGING OUT IN KYOTO EVER SINCE I WAS LITTLE...
...AND I NEVER HAD ANY IDEA THERE WAS A YOUKAI TOWN DEEP IN THE KYOTO MOUNTAINS!
IT'S A SECRET YOUKAI SANCTUARY.
BUT WOW, IT'S LIKE YOU'RE THE ONLY HUMAN IN THE WHOLE PLACE!
PITA (FREEZE)
SFX: ZAWA (MRMR) ZAWA ZAWA ZAWA ZAWA ZAWA ZAWA ZAWA ZAWA
A HUMAN?
IT'S TRUE. A HUMAN IS HERE!
HUH?

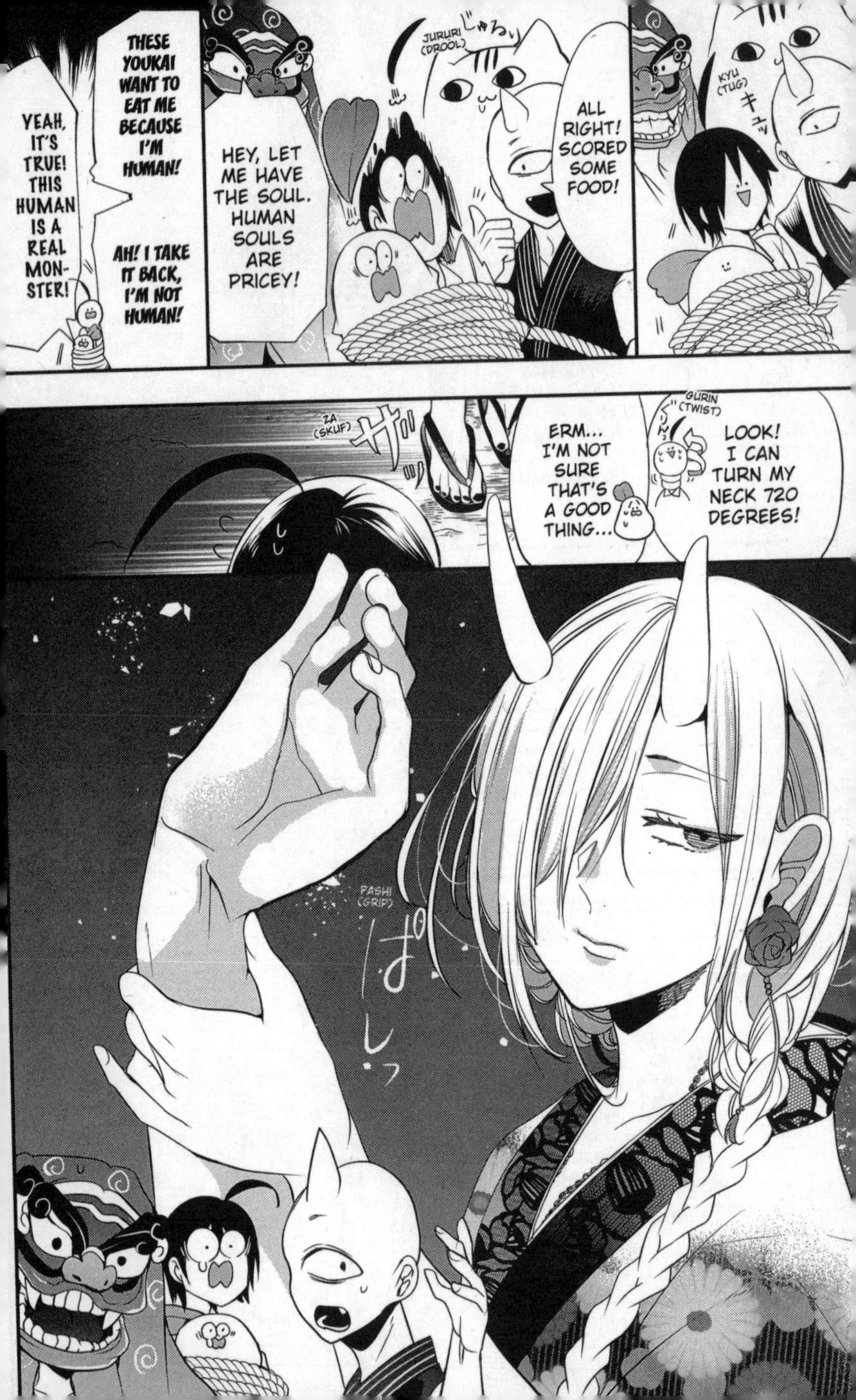
KYU (TUG)
キュッ
JURURI (DROOL)
ALL RIGHT! SCORED SOME FOOD!
HEY, LET ME HAVE THE SOUL. HUMAN SOULS ARE PRICEY!
THESE YOUKAI WANT TO EAT ME BECAUSE I'M HUMAN!
AH! I TAKE IT BACK, I'M NOT HUMAN!
YEAH, IT'S TRUE! THIS HUMAN IS A REAL MONSTER!
LOOK! I CAN TURN MY NECK 720 DEGREES!
GURIN (TWIST)
ERM... I'M NOT SURE THAT'S A GOOD THING...
ZA (SKUF)
FASHI (GRIP)

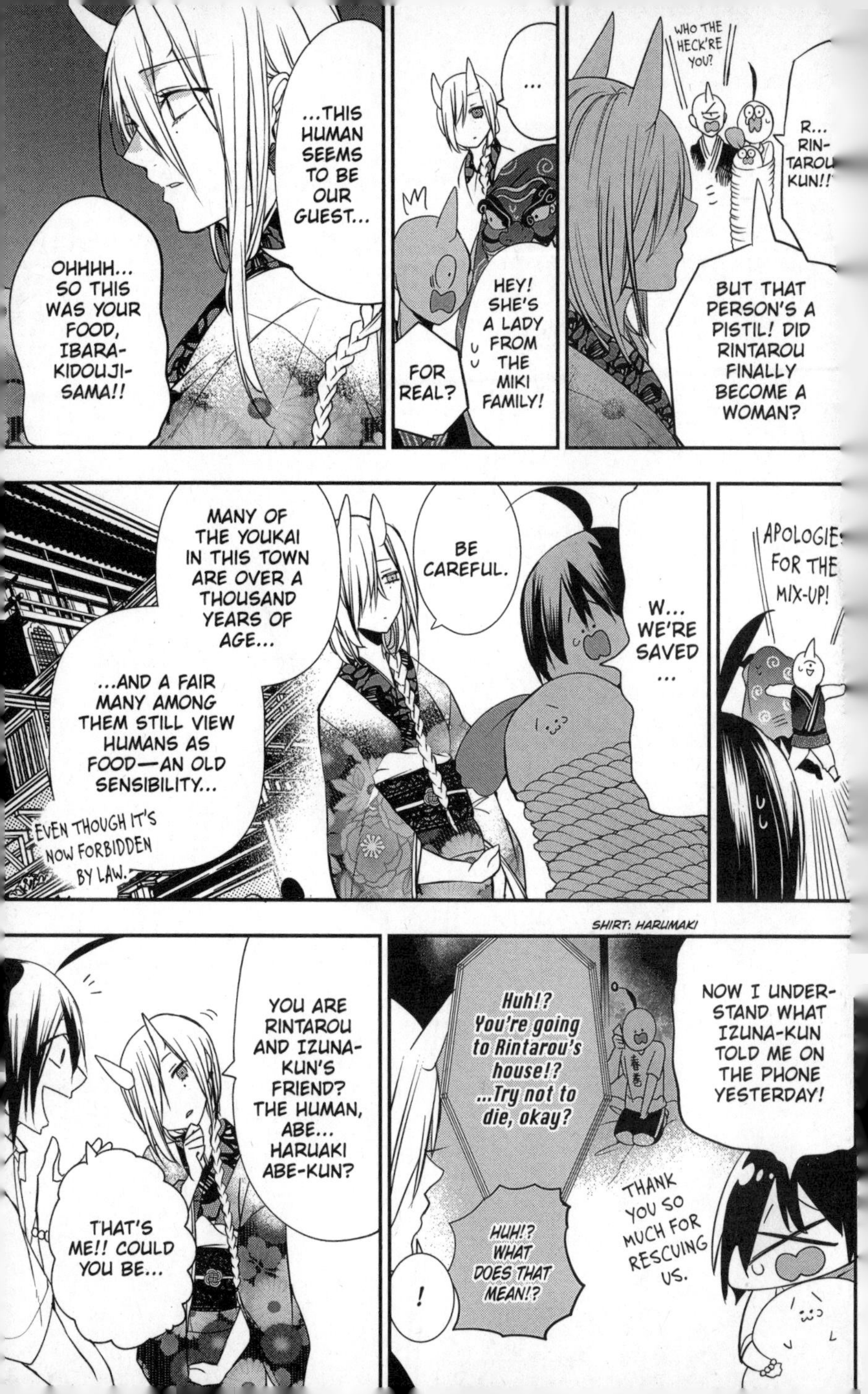
R... RINTAROU-KUN!!
WHO THE HECK'RE YOU?
BUT THAT PERSON'S A PISTIL! DID RINTAROU FINALLY BECOME A WOMAN?
...
HEY! SHE'S A LADY FROM THE MIKI FAMILY!
FOR REAL?
...THIS HUMAN SEEMS TO BE OUR GUEST...
OHHHH... SO THIS WAS YOUR FOOD, IBARA-KIDOUJI-SAMA!!
APOLOGIES FOR THE MIX-UP!
W... WE'RE SAVED...
BE CAREFUL.
MANY OF THE YOUKAI IN THIS TOWN ARE OVER A THOUSAND YEARS OF AGE...
...AND A FAIR MANY AMONG THEM STILL VIEW HUMANS AS FOOD—AN OLD SENSIBILITY...
EVEN THOUGH IT'S NOW FORBIDDEN BY LAW.
SHIRT: HARUMAKI
NOW I UNDERSTAND WHAT IZUNA-KUN TOLD ME ON THE PHONE YESTERDAY!
Huh!? You're going to Rintarou's house!? ...Try not to die, okay?
THANK YOU SO MUCH FOR RESCUING US.
HUH!? WHAT DOES THAT MEAN!?
!
YOU ARE RINTAROU AND IZUNA-KUN'S FRIEND? THE HUMAN, ABE... HARUAKI ABE-KUN?
THAT'S ME!! COULD YOU BE...

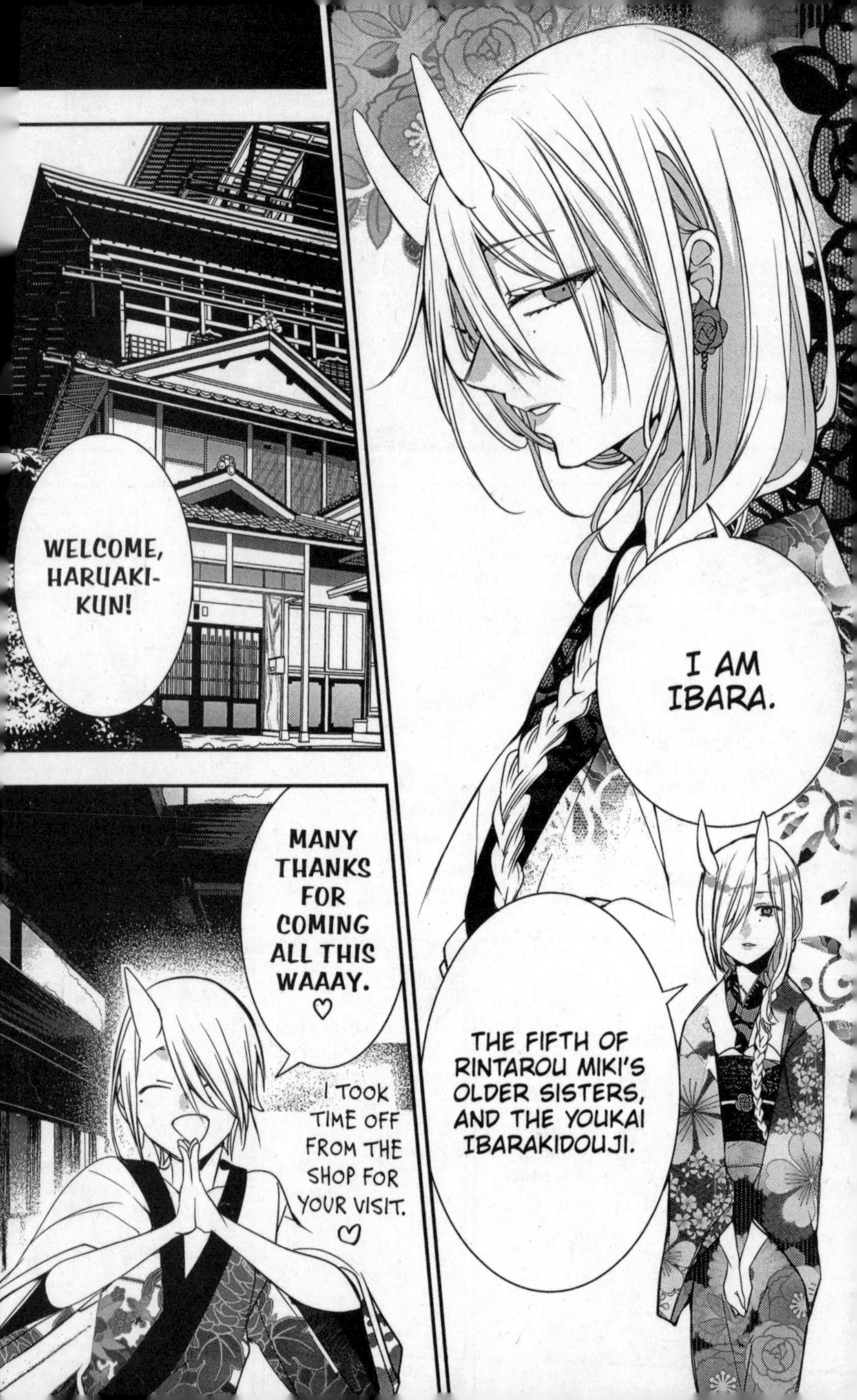
I AM IBARA.
THE FIFTH OF RINTAROU MIKI'S OLDER SISTERS, AND THE YOUKAI IBARAKIDOUJI.
WELCOME, HARUAKI-KUN!
MANY THANKS FOR COMING ALL THIS WAAAY. ♡
I TOOK TIME OFF FROM THE SHOP FOR YOUR VISIT. ♡

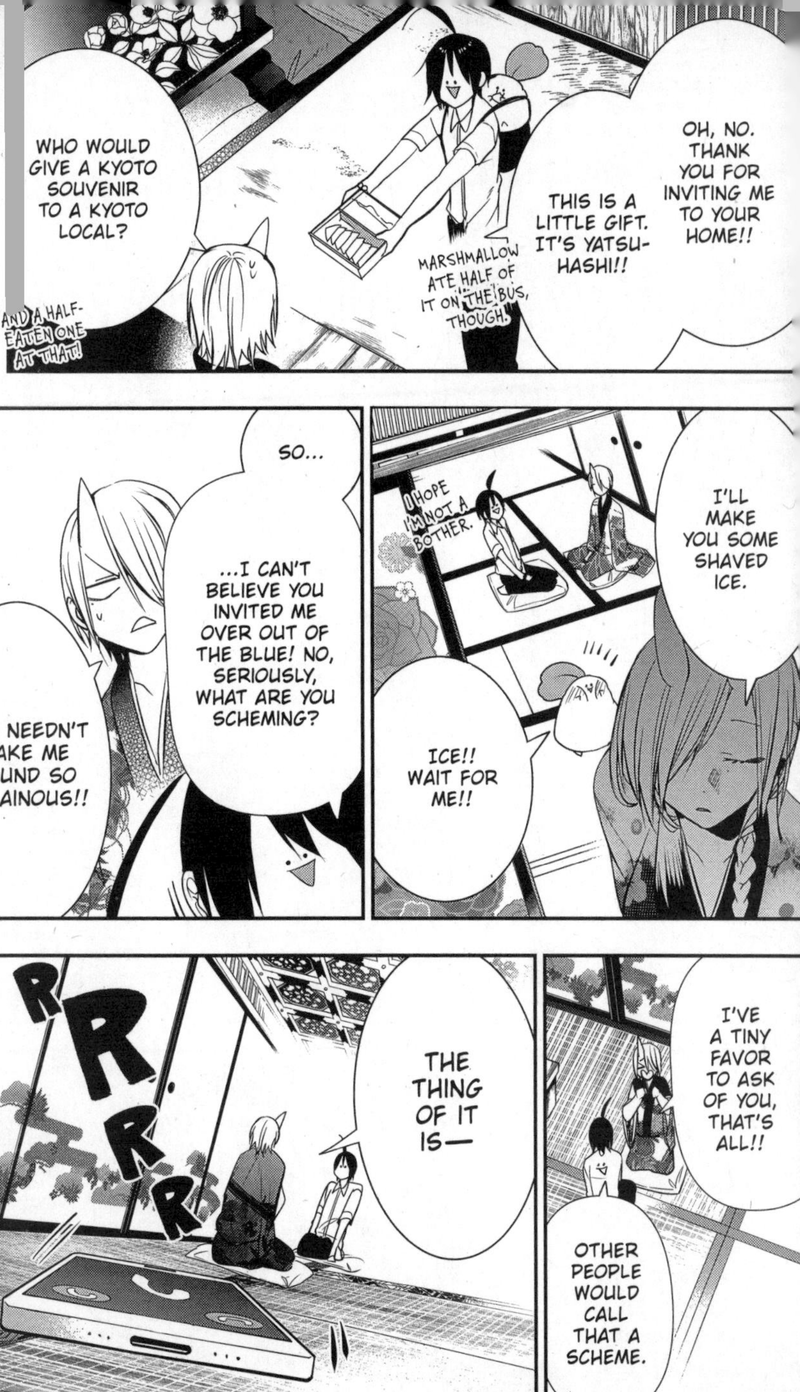
OH, NO. THANK YOU FOR INVITING ME TO YOUR HOME!!
THIS IS A LITTLE GIFT. IT'S YATSU-HASHI!!
MARSHMALLOW ATE HALF OF IT ON THE BUS, THOUGH.
WHO WOULD GIVE A KYOTO SOUVENIR TO A KYOTO LOCAL?
AND A HALF-EATEN ONE AT THAT!
I'LL MAKE YOU SOME SHAVED ICE.
I HOPE I'M NOT A BOTHER.
ICE!! WAIT FOR ME!!
SO...
...I CAN'T BELIEVE YOU INVITED ME OVER OUT OF THE BLUE! NO, SERIOUSLY, WHAT ARE YOU SCHEMING?
YOU NEEDN'T MAKE ME SOUND SO VILLAINOUS!!
I'VE A TINY FAVOR TO ASK OF YOU, THAT'S ALL!!
OTHER PEOPLE WOULD CALL THAT A SCHEME.
THE THING OF IT IS—
RRRR

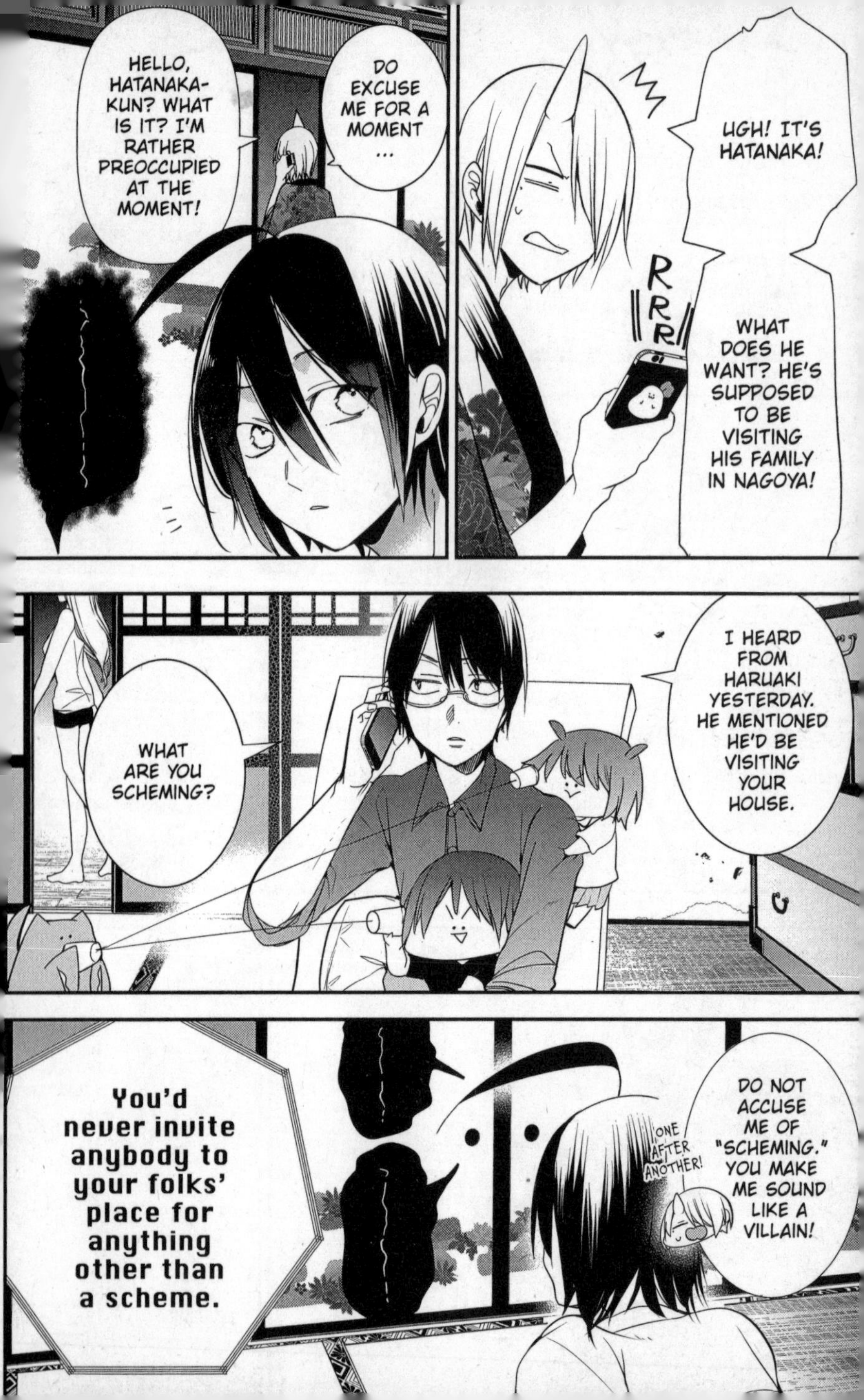
UGH! IT'S HATANAKA!
RRR
WHAT DOES HE WANT? HE'S SUPPOSED TO BE VISITING HIS FAMILY IN NAGOYA!
DO EXCUSE ME FOR A MOMENT ...
HELLO, HATANAKA-KUN? WHAT IS IT? I'M RATHER PREOCCUPIED AT THE MOMENT!
I HEARD FROM HARUAKI YESTERDAY. HE MENTIONED HE'D BE VISITING YOUR HOUSE.
WHAT ARE YOU SCHEMING?
DO NOT ACCUSE ME OF "SCHEMING." YOU MAKE ME SOUND LIKE A VILLAIN!
ONE AFTER ANOTHER!
You'd never invite anybody to your folks' place for anything other than a scheme.

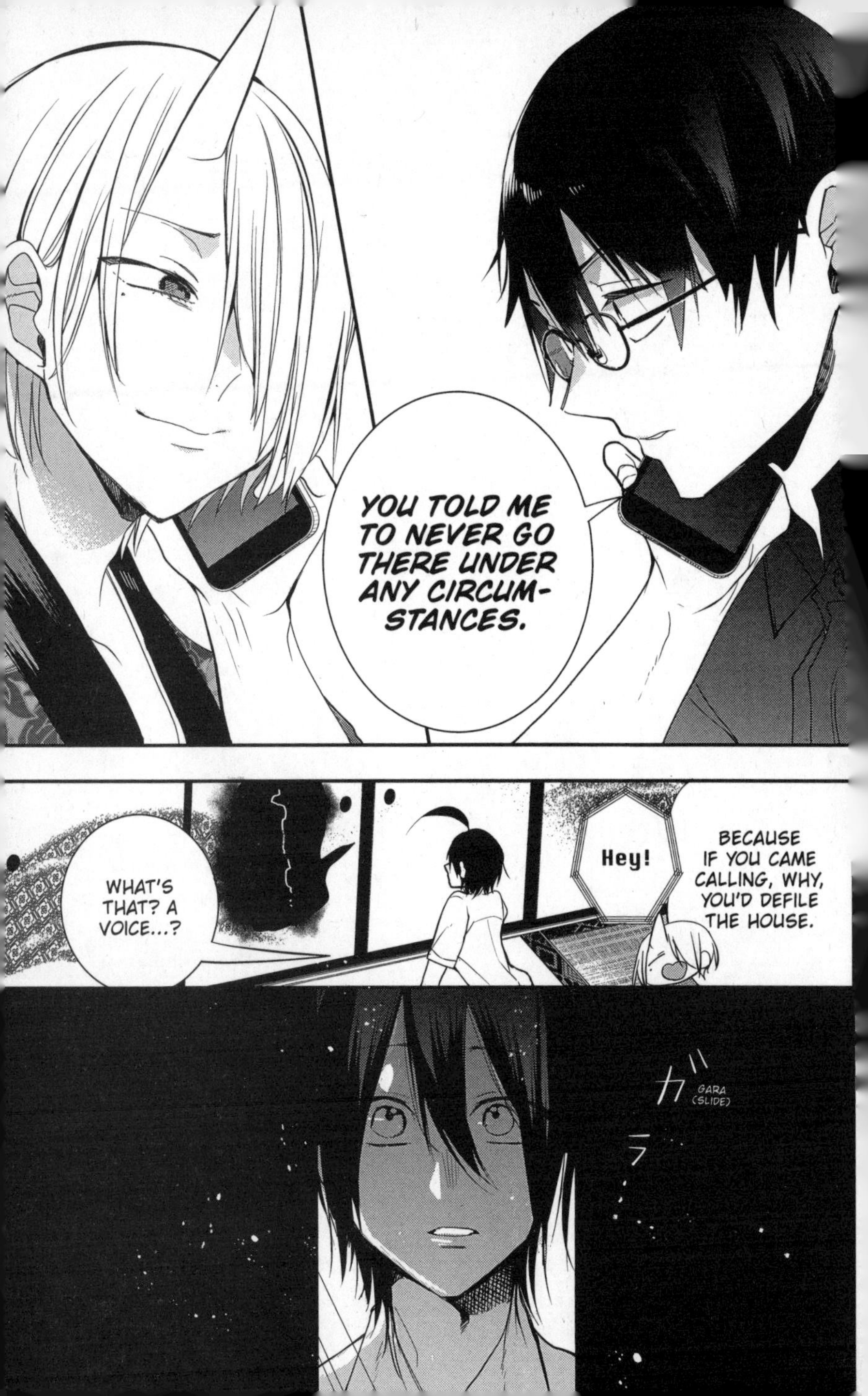
YOU TOLD ME TO NEVER GO THERE UNDER ANY CIRCUM-STANCES.
BECAUSE IF YOU CAME CALLING, WHY, YOU'D DEFILE THE HOUSE.
Hey!
WHAT'S THAT? A VOICE...?
ガラ
GARA (SLIDE)

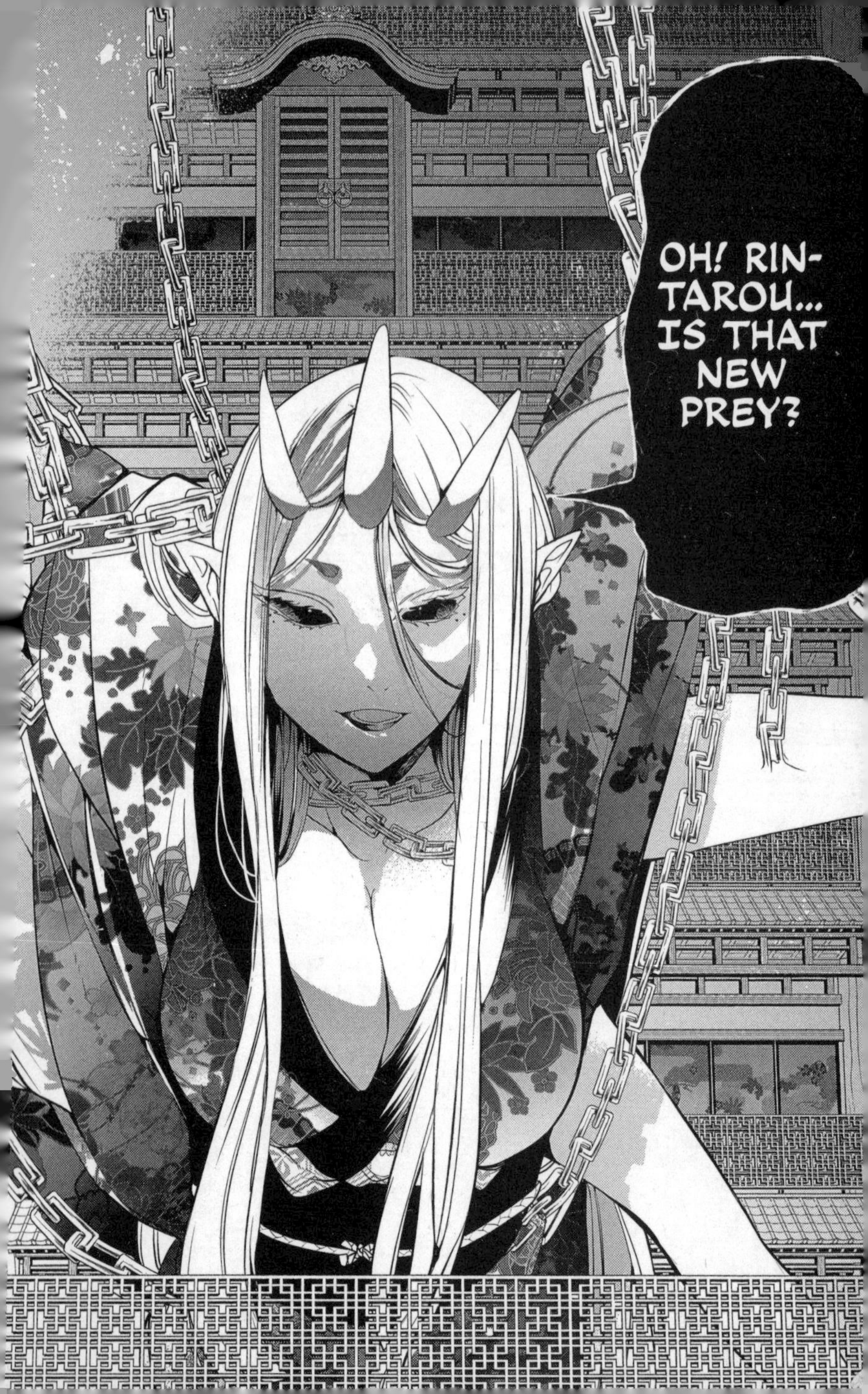
OH! RIN-TAROU... IS THAT NEW PREY?

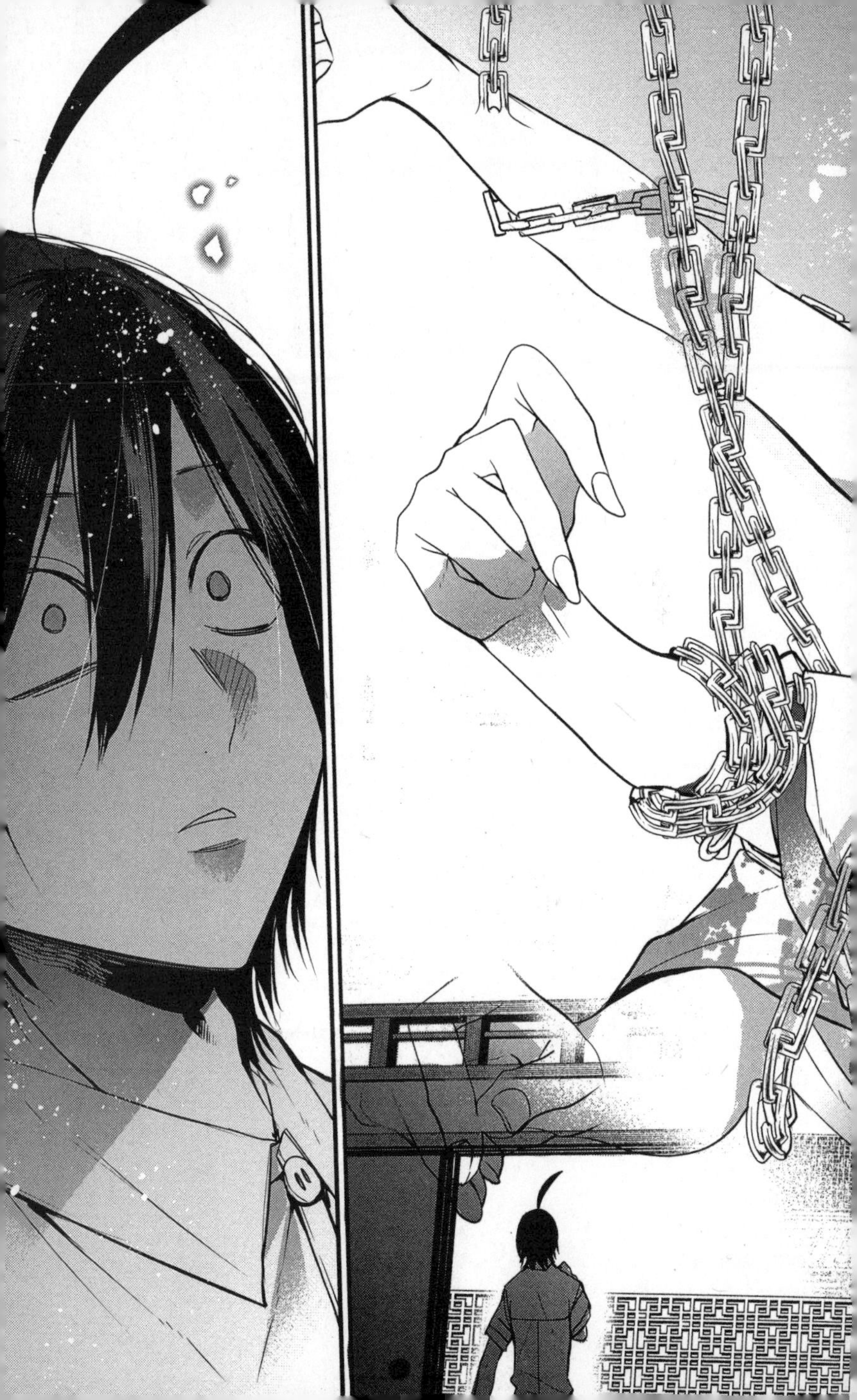

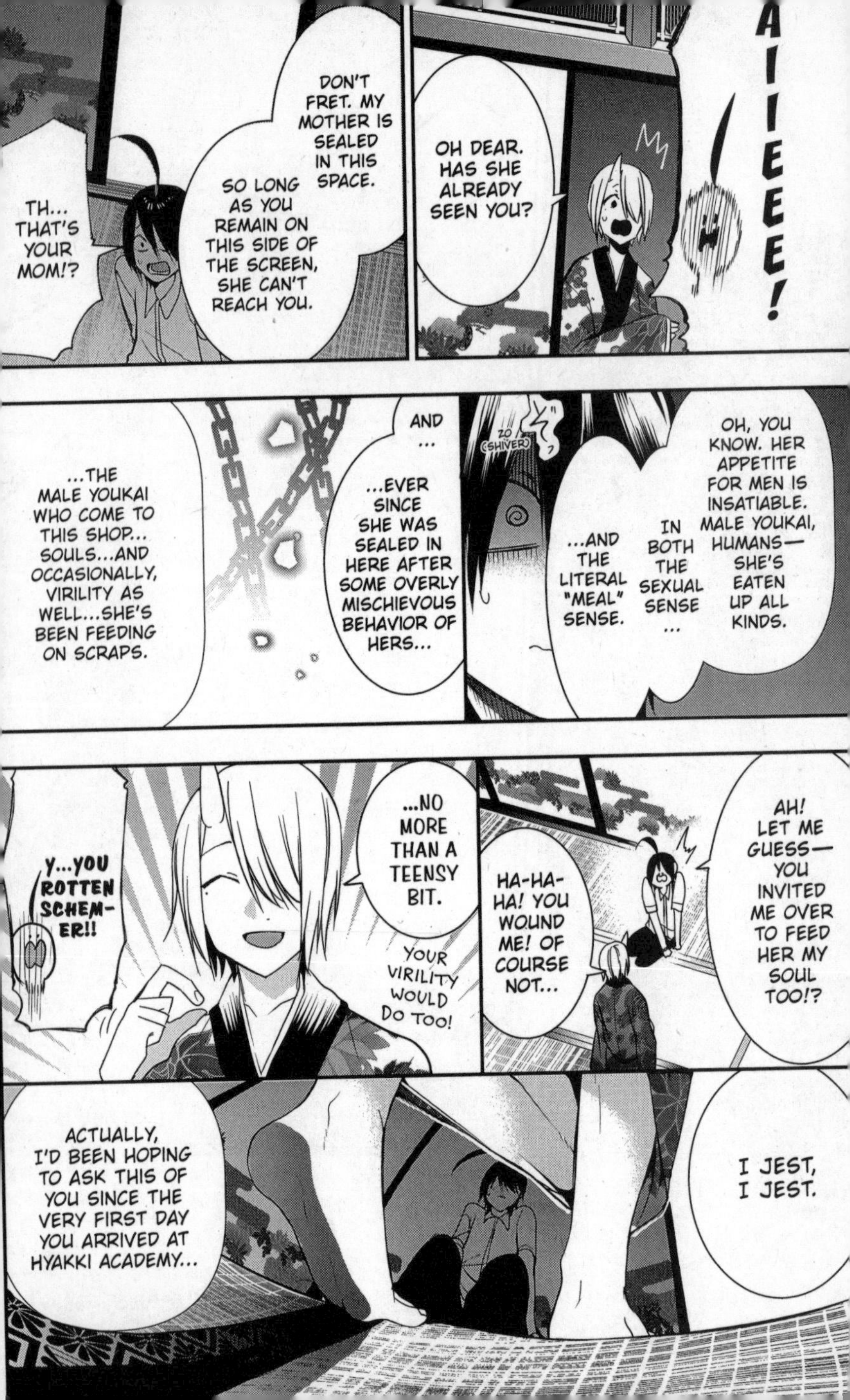
AIIEEE!
OH DEAR. HAS SHE ALREADY SEEN YOU?
DON'T FRET. MY MOTHER IS SEALED IN THIS SPACE.
SO LONG AS YOU REMAIN ON THIS SIDE OF THE SCREEN, SHE CAN'T REACH YOU.
TH... THAT'S YOUR MOM!?
OH, YOU KNOW. HER APPETITE FOR MEN IS INSATIABLE. MALE YOUKAI, HUMANS— SHE'S EATEN UP ALL KINDS.
IN BOTH THE SEXUAL SENSE...
...AND THE LITERAL "MEAL" SENSE.
ZO (SHIVER)
AND...
...EVER SINCE SHE WAS SEALED IN HERE AFTER SOME OVERLY MISCHIEVOUS BEHAVIOR OF HERS...
...THE MALE YOUKAI WHO COME TO THIS SHOP... SOULS...AND OCCASIONALLY, VIRILITY AS WELL...SHE'S BEEN FEEDING ON SCRAPS.
AH! LET ME GUESS— YOU INVITED ME OVER TO FEED HER MY SOUL TOO!?
HA-HA-HA! YOU WOUND ME! OF COURSE NOT...
...NO MORE THAN A TEENSY BIT.
YOUR VIRILITY WOULD DO TOO!
Y...YOU ROTTEN SCHEM-ER!!
I JEST, I JEST.
ACTUALLY, I'D BEEN HOPING TO ASK THIS OF YOU SINCE THE VERY FIRST DAY YOU ARRIVED AT HYAKKI ACADEMY...

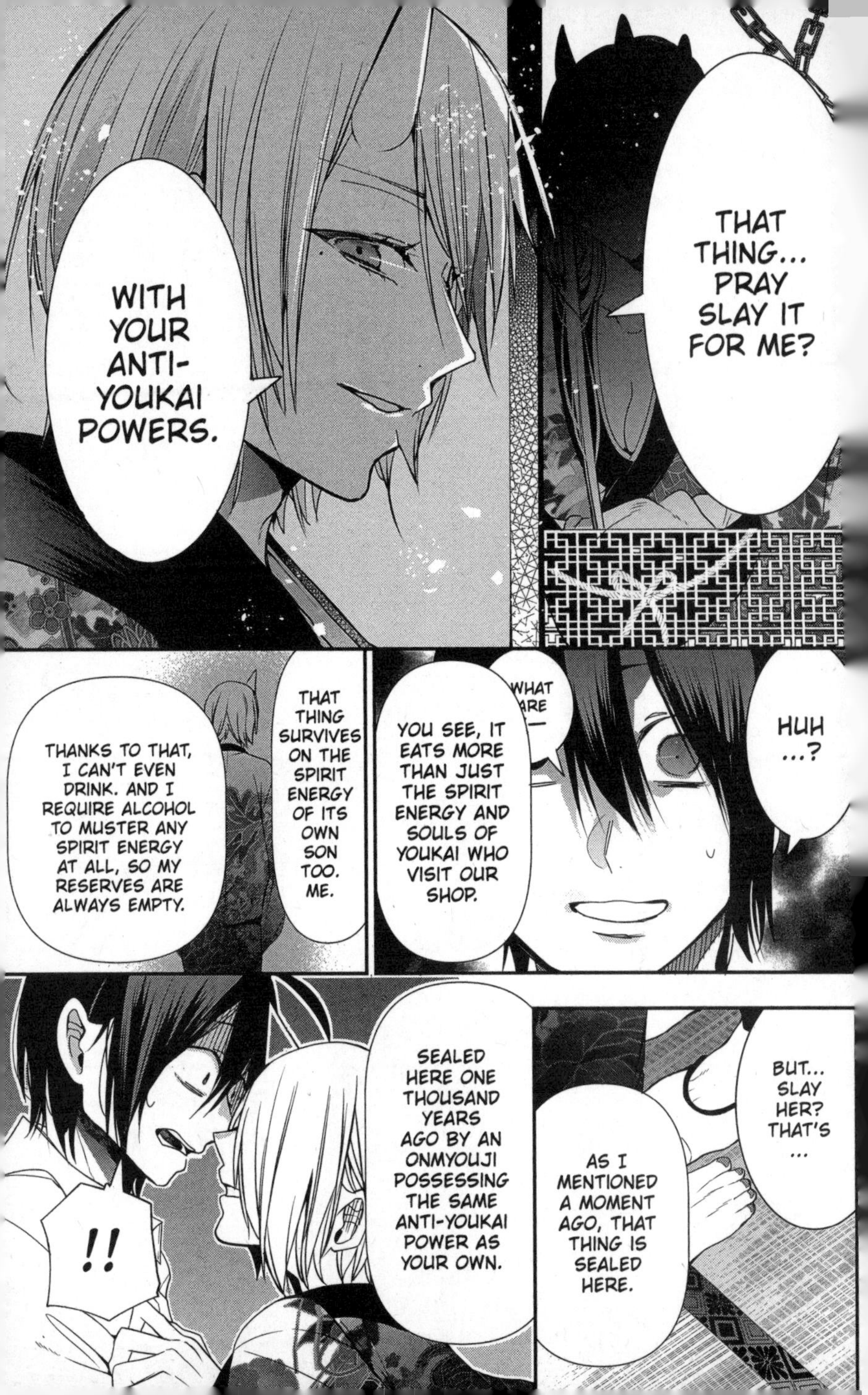
THAT THING... PRAY SLAY IT FOR ME?
WITH YOUR ANTI-YOUKAI POWERS.
HUH ...?
WHAT ARE—
YOU SEE, IT EATS MORE THAN JUST THE SPIRIT ENERGY AND SOULS OF YOUKAI WHO VISIT OUR SHOP.
THAT THING SURVIVES ON THE SPIRIT ENERGY OF ITS OWN SON TOO. ME.
THANKS TO THAT, I CAN'T EVEN DRINK. AND I REQUIRE ALCOHOL TO MUSTER ANY SPIRIT ENERGY AT ALL, SO MY RESERVES ARE ALWAYS EMPTY.
BUT... SLAY HER? THAT'S ...
AS I MENTIONED A MOMENT AGO, THAT THING IS SEALED HERE.
SEALED HERE ONE THOUSAND YEARS AGO BY AN ONMYOUJI POSSESSING THE SAME ANTI-YOUKAI POWER AS YOUR OWN.
!!

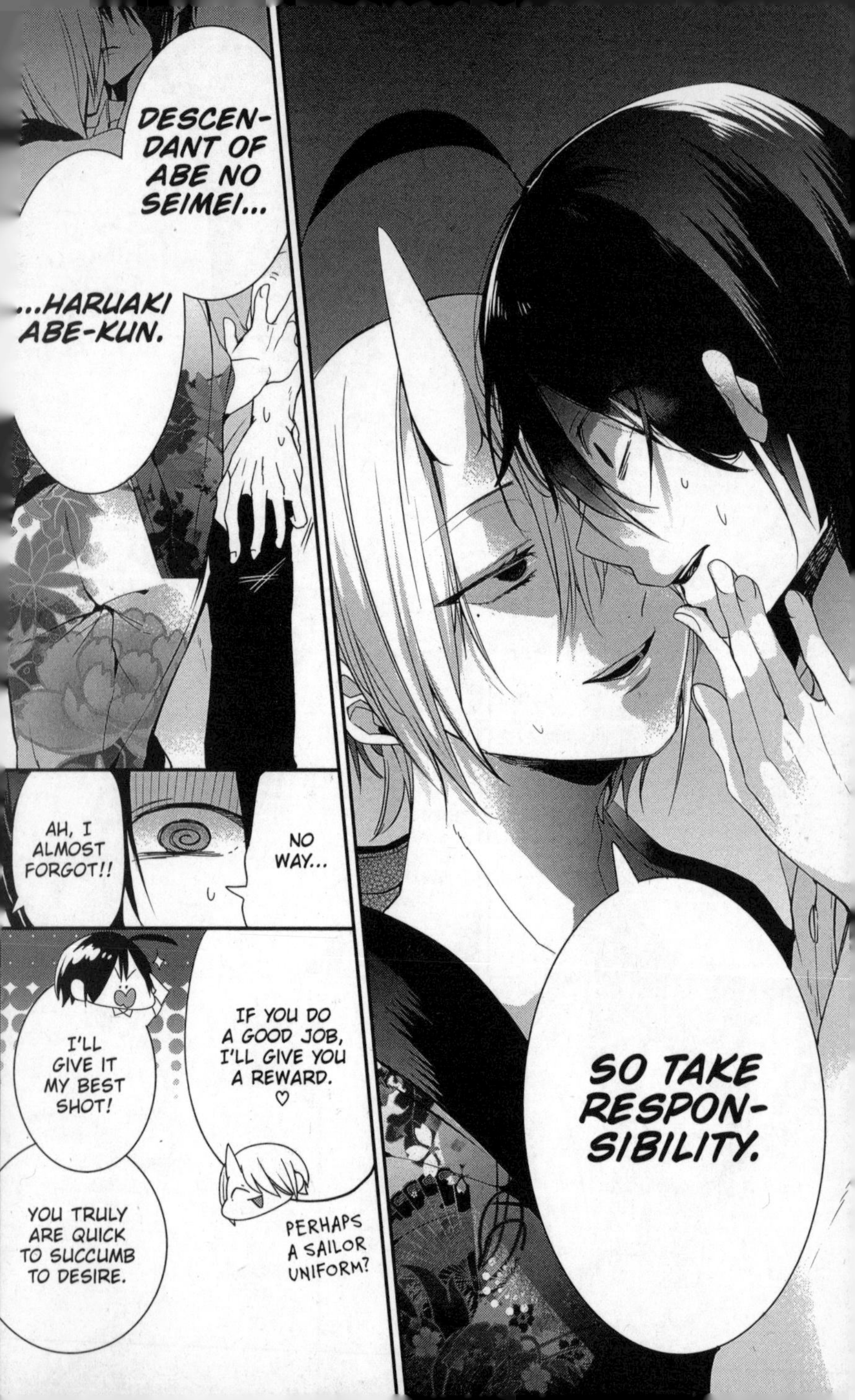
SO TAKE RESPON-SIBILITY.
DESCEN-DANT OF ABE NO SEIMEI...
...HARUAKI ABE-KUN.
NO WAY...
AH, I ALMOST FORGOT!!
IF YOU DO A GOOD JOB, I'LL GIVE YOU A REWARD. ♡
I'LL GIVE IT MY BEST SHOT!
PERHAPS A SAILOR UNIFORM?
YOU TRULY ARE QUICK TO SUCCUMB TO DESIRE.

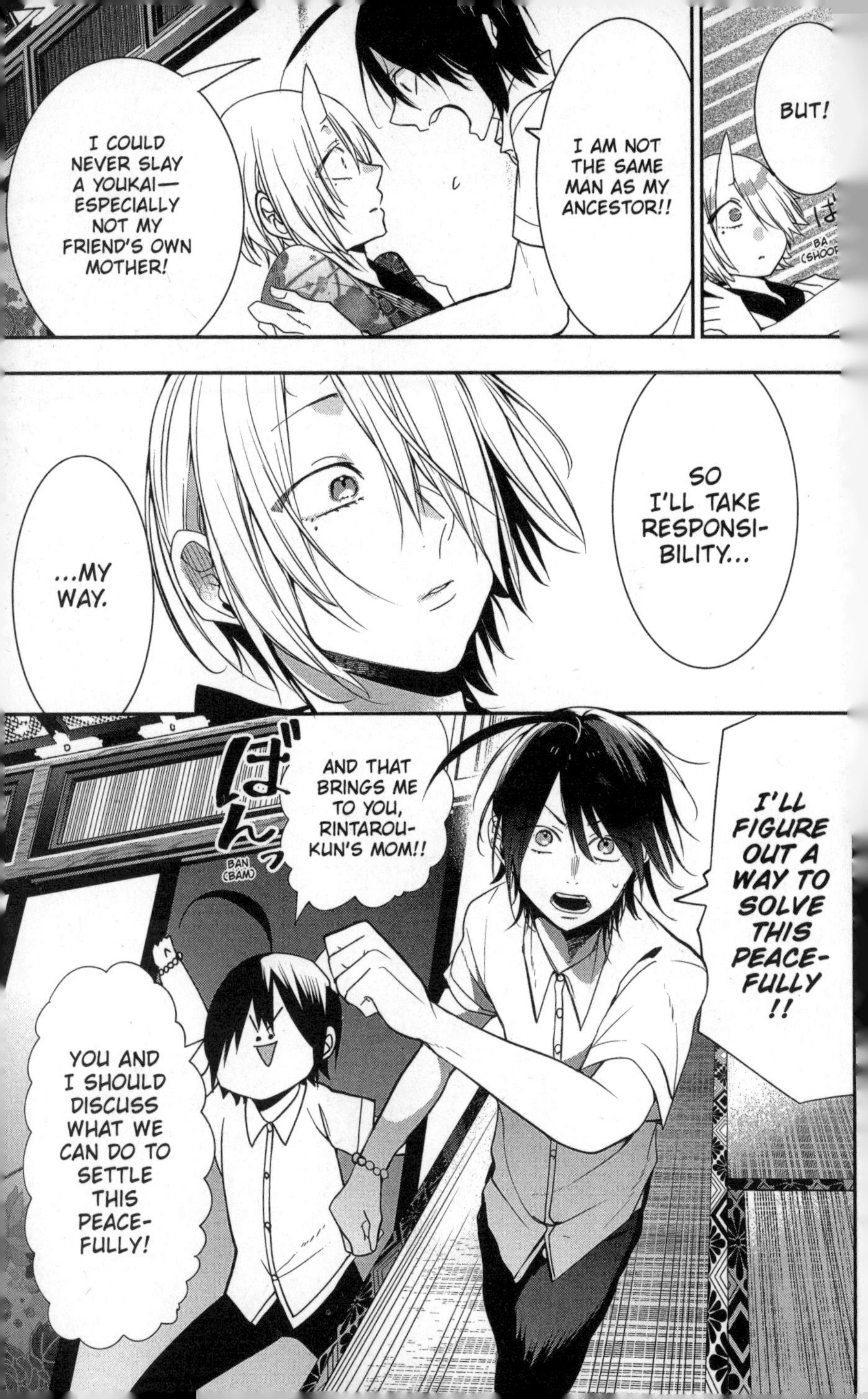
BUT!
ぱ
BA
I AM NOT THE SAME MAN AS MY ANCESTOR!!
I COULD NEVER SLAY A YOUKAI—ESPECIALLY NOT MY FRIEND'S OWN MOTHER!
SO I'LL TAKE RESPONSI-BILITY...
...MY WAY.
I'LL FIGURE OUT A WAY TO SOLVE THIS PEACE-FULLY!!
AND THAT BRINGS ME TO YOU, RINTAROU-KUN'S MOM!!
ばんっ
BAN (BAM)
YOU AND I SHOULD DISCUSS WHAT WE CAN DO TO SETTLE THIS PEACE-FULLY!

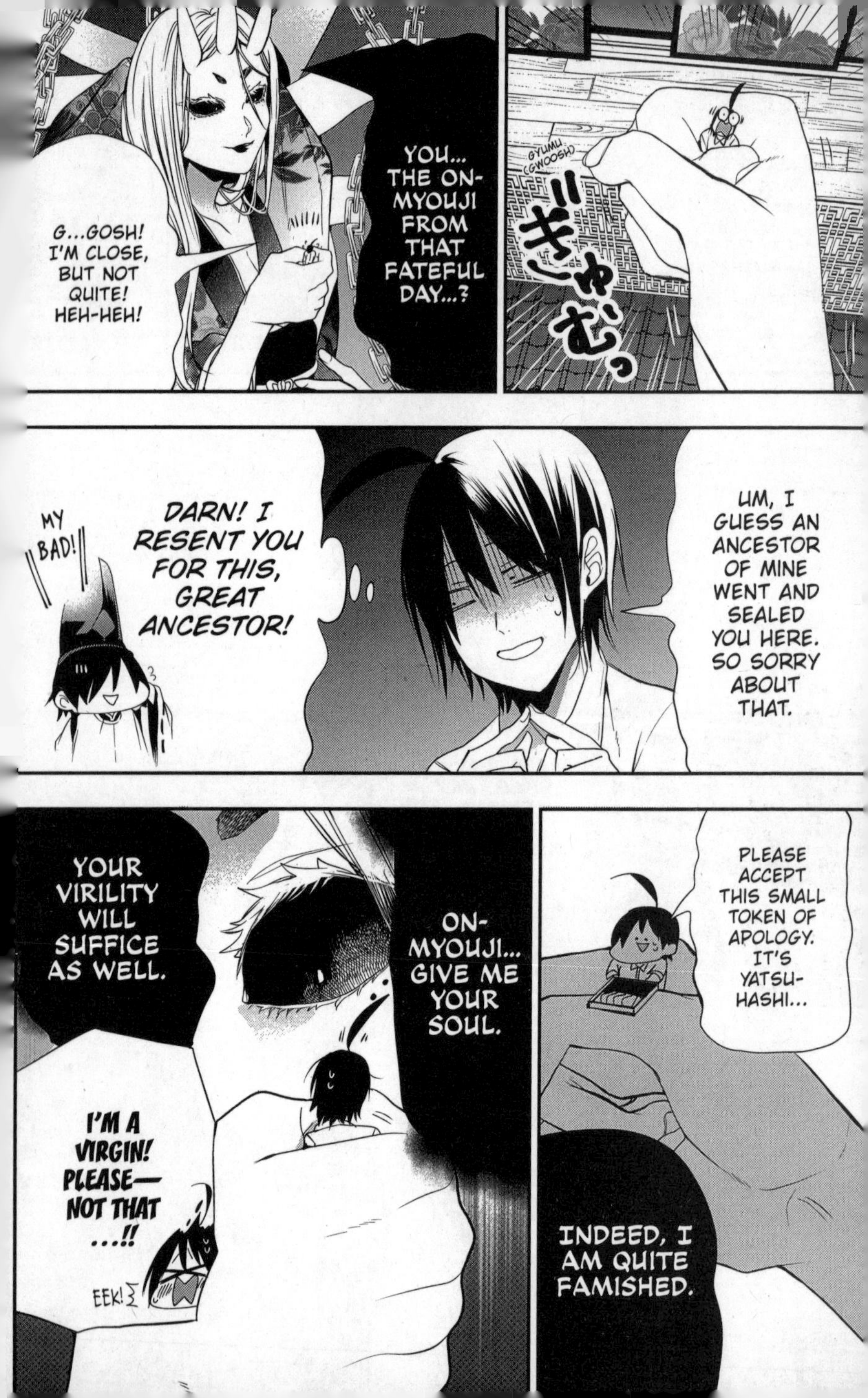
GYUMU (GWOOSH)
ぎゅむっ
YOU... THE ON-MYOUJI FROM THAT FATEFUL DAY...?
G...GOSH! I'M CLOSE, BUT NOT QUITE! HEH-HEH!
UM, I GUESS AN ANCESTOR OF MINE WENT AND SEALED YOU HERE. SO SORRY ABOUT THAT.
DARN! I RESENT YOU FOR THIS, GREAT ANCESTOR!
MY BAD!
PLEASE ACCEPT THIS SMALL TOKEN OF APOLOGY. IT'S YATSU-HASHI...
INDEED, I AM QUITE FAMISHED.
ON-MYOUJI... GIVE ME YOUR SOUL.
YOUR VIRILITY WILL SUFFICE AS WELL.
I'M A VIRGIN! PLEASE— NOT THAT ...!!
EEK!

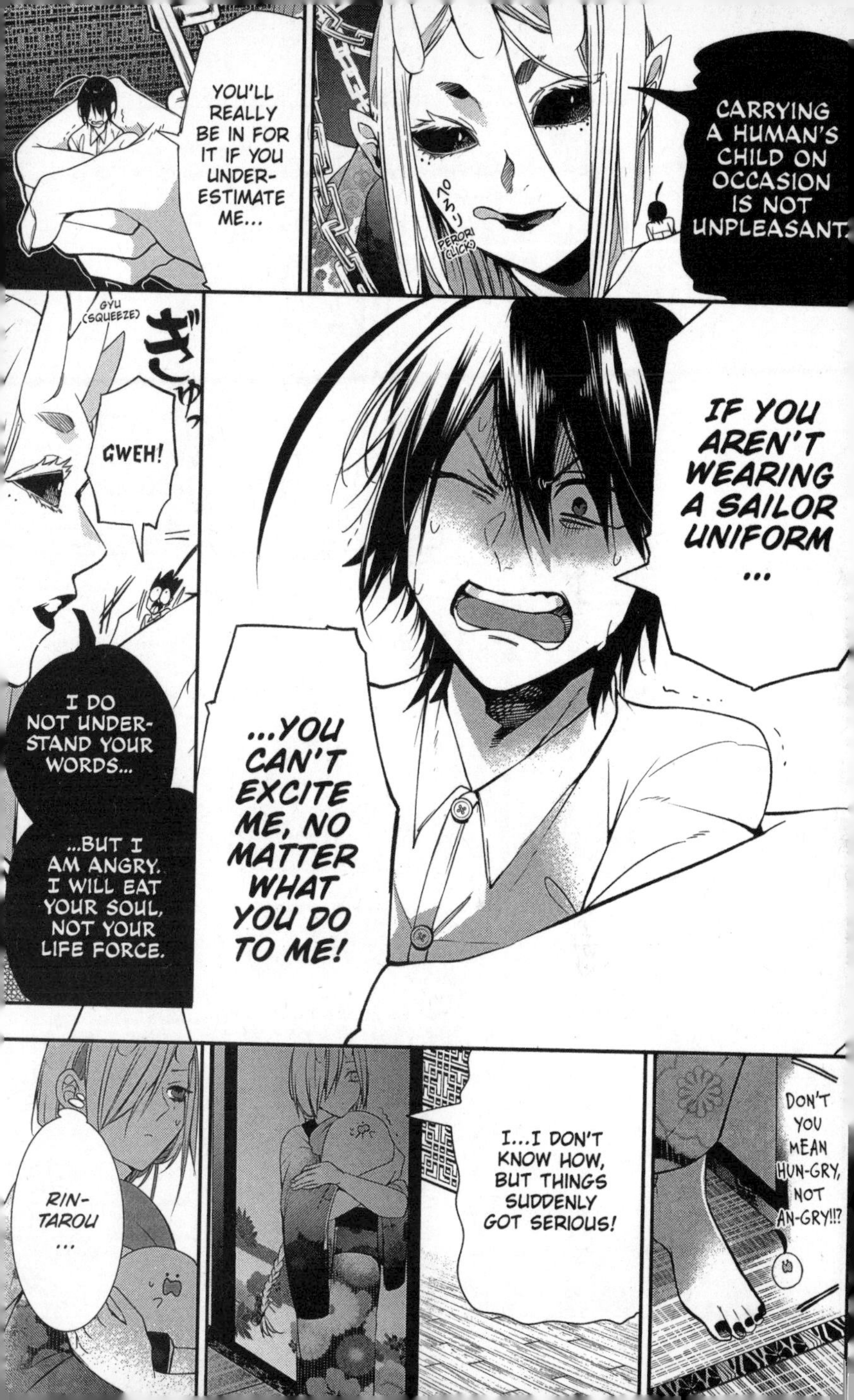
CARRYING A HUMAN'S CHILD ON OCCASION IS NOT UNPLEASANT.
PERORI (LICK)
YOU'LL REALLY BE IN FOR IT IF YOU UNDER-ESTIMATE ME...
IF YOU AREN'T WEARING A SAILOR UNIFORM...
...YOU CAN'T EXCITE ME, NO MATTER WHAT YOU DO TO ME!
GYU (SQUEEZE)
GWEH!
I DO NOT UNDER-STAND YOUR WORDS...
...BUT I AM ANGRY. I WILL EAT YOUR SOUL, NOT YOUR LIFE FORCE.
DON'T YOU MEAN HUN-GRY, NOT AN-GRY!!?
I...I DON'T KNOW HOW, BUT THINGS SUDDENLY GOT SERIOUS!
RIN-TAROU...

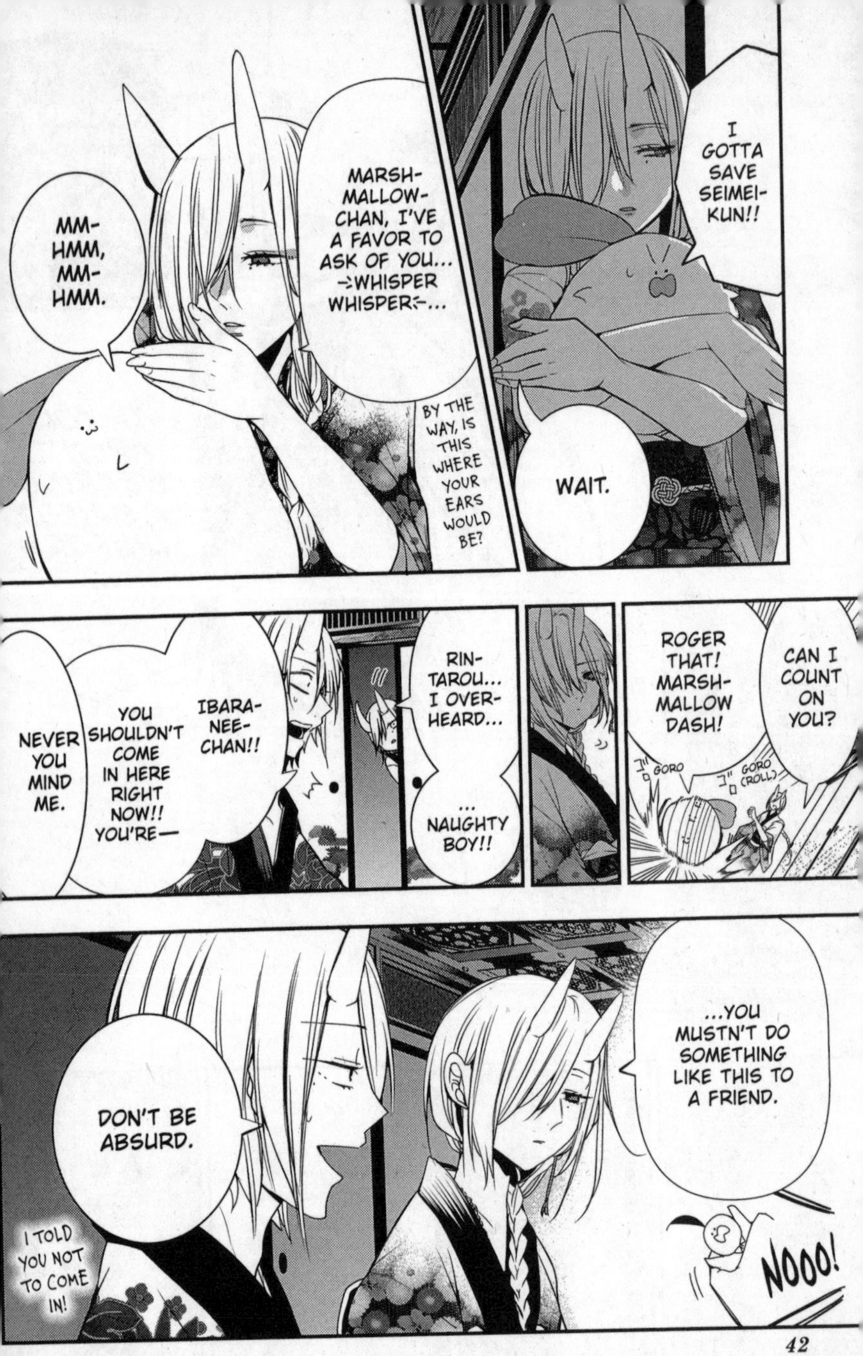
I GOTTA SAVE SEIMEI-KUN!!
WAIT.
MARSH-MALLOW-CHAN, I'VE A FAVOR TO ASK OF YOU... ⇒WHISPER WHISPER⇐...
MM-HMM, MM-HMM.
BY THE WAY, IS THIS WHERE YOUR EARS WOULD BE?
CAN I COUNT ON YOU?
ROGER THAT! MARSH-MALLOW DASH!
GORO
GORO (ROLL)
RIN-TAROU... I OVER-HEARD...
...NAUGHTY BOY!!
IBARA-NEE-CHAN!!
YOU SHOULDN'T COME IN HERE RIGHT NOW!! YOU'RE—
NEVER YOU MIND ME.
...YOU MUSTN'T DO SOMETHING LIKE THIS TO A FRIEND.
NOOO!
DON'T BE ABSURD.
I TOLD YOU NOT TO COME IN!

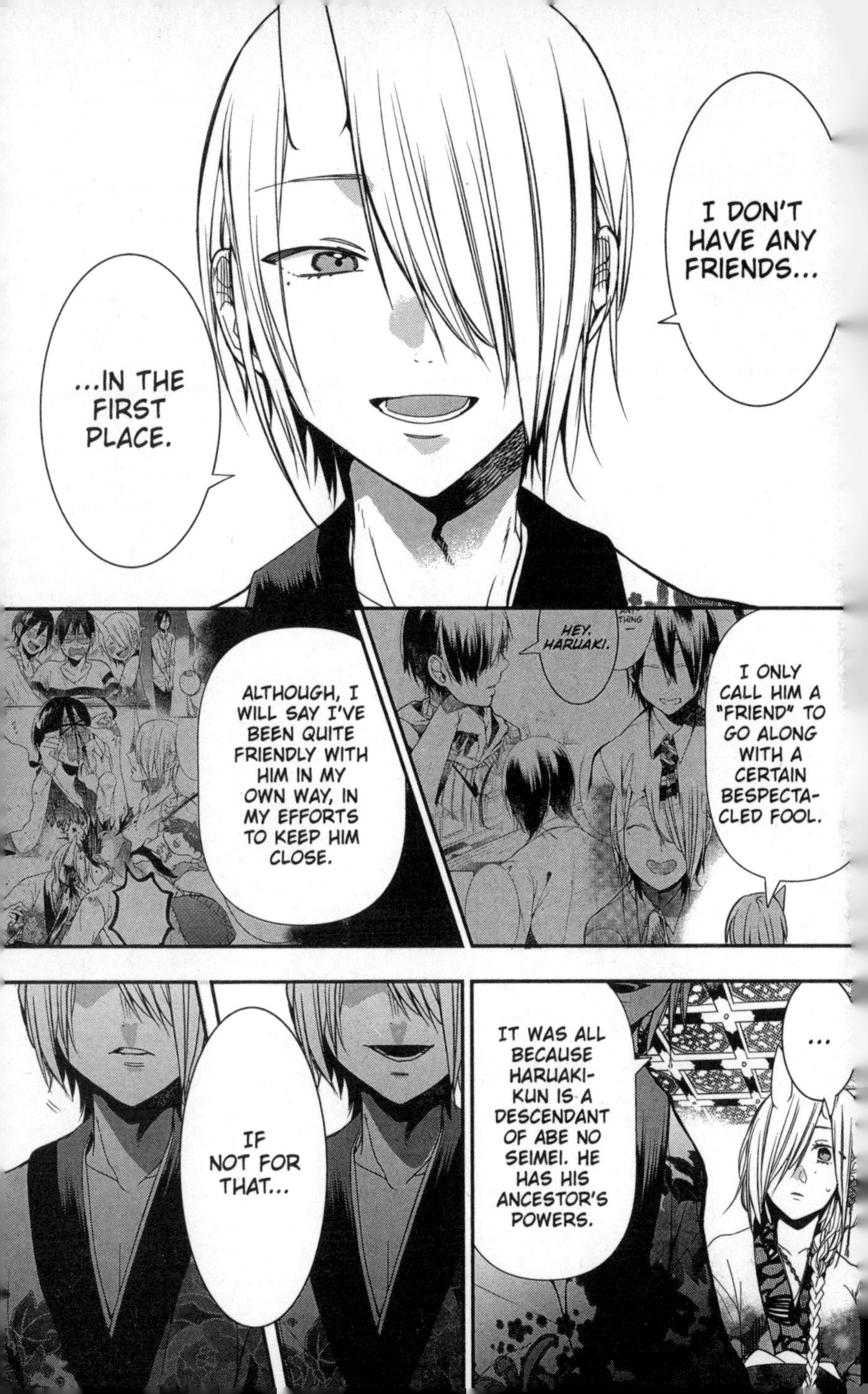

I DON'T HAVE ANY FRIENDS...
...IN THE FIRST PLACE.
I ONLY CALL HIM A "FRIEND" TO GO ALONG WITH A CERTAIN BESPECTACLED FOOL.
ANYTHING —
HEY. HARUAKI.
ALTHOUGH, I WILL SAY I'VE BEEN QUITE FRIENDLY WITH HIM IN MY OWN WAY, IN MY EFFORTS TO KEEP HIM CLOSE.
...
IT WAS ALL BECAUSE HARUAKI-KUN IS A DESCENDANT OF ABE NO SEIMEI. HE HAS HIS ANCESTOR'S POWERS.
IF NOT FOR THAT...

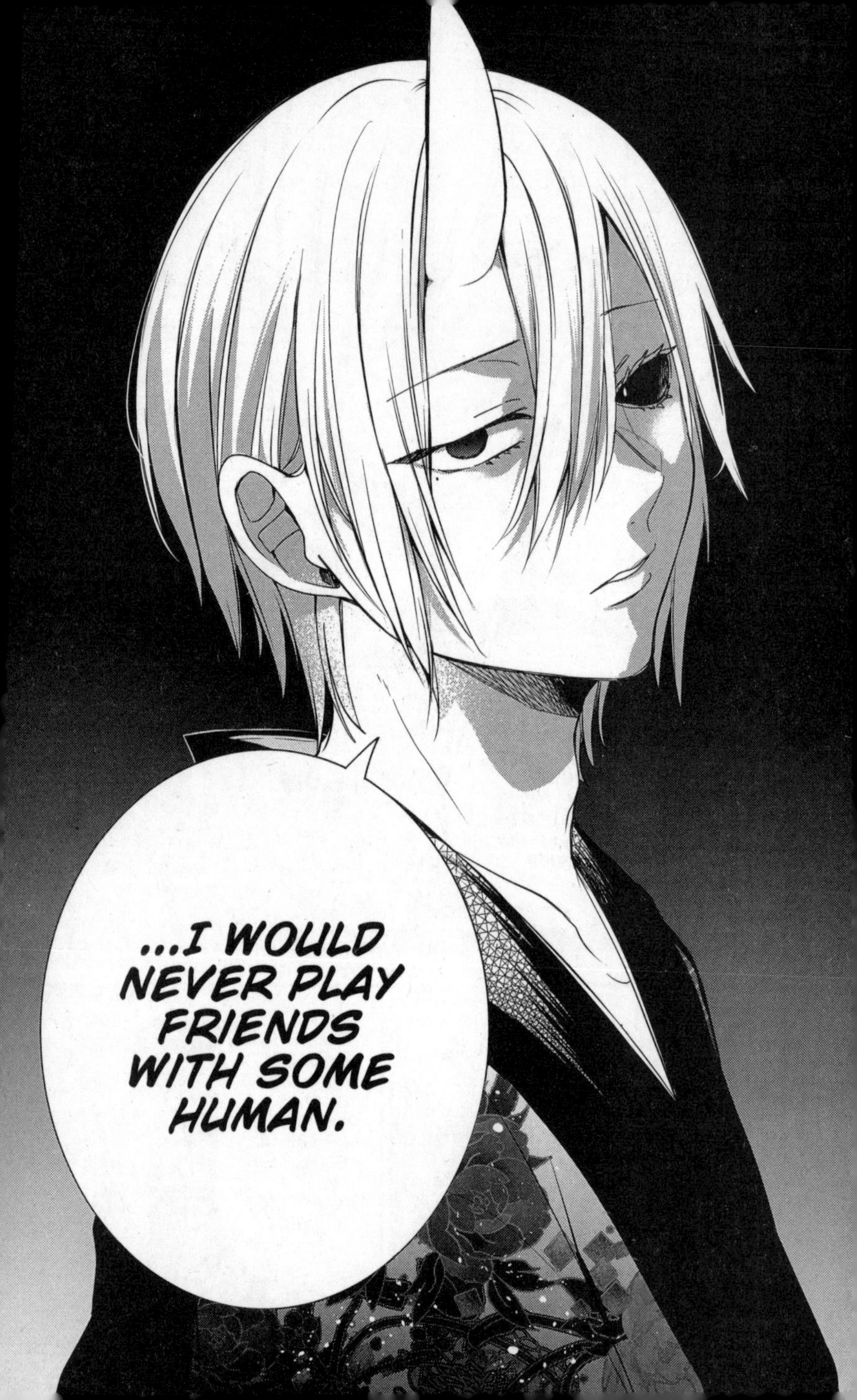
...I WOULD NEVER PLAY FRIENDS WITH SOME HUMAN.

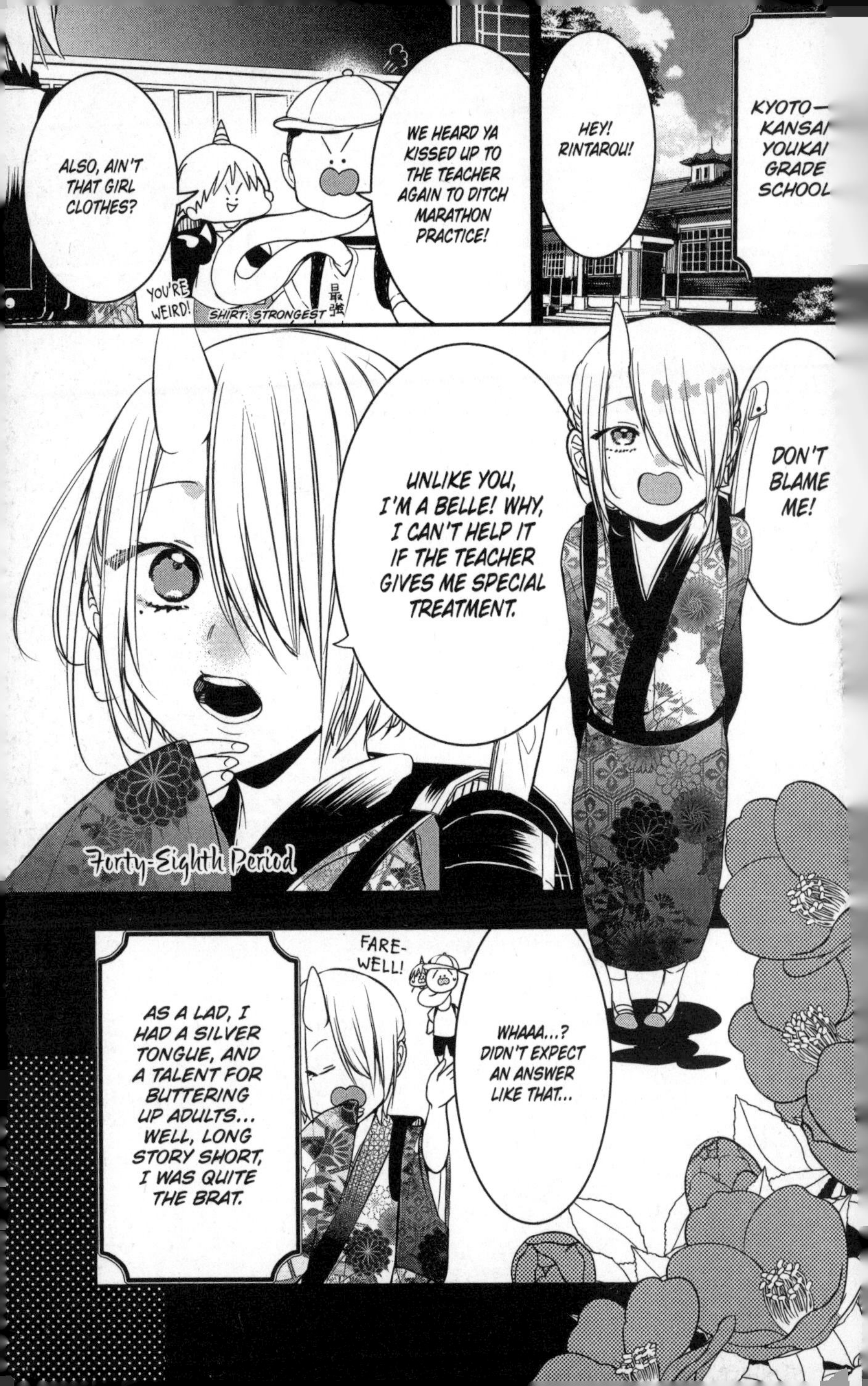
KYOTO—KANSAI YOUKAI GRADE SCHOOL
HEY! RINTAROU!
WE HEARD YA KISSED UP TO THE TEACHER AGAIN TO DITCH MARATHON PRACTICE!
SHIRT: STRONGEST 最強
ALSO, AIN'T THAT GIRL CLOTHES?
YOU'RE WEIRD!
DON'T BLAME ME!
UNLIKE YOU, I'M A BELLE! WHY, I CAN'T HELP IT IF THE TEACHER GIVES ME SPECIAL TREATMENT.
Forty-Eighth Period
WHAAA...? DIDN'T EXPECT AN ANSWER LIKE THAT...
FARE-WELL!
AS A LAD, I HAD A SILVER TONGUE, AND A TALENT FOR BUTTERING UP ADULTS... WELL, LONG STORY SHORT, I WAS QUITE THE BRAT.

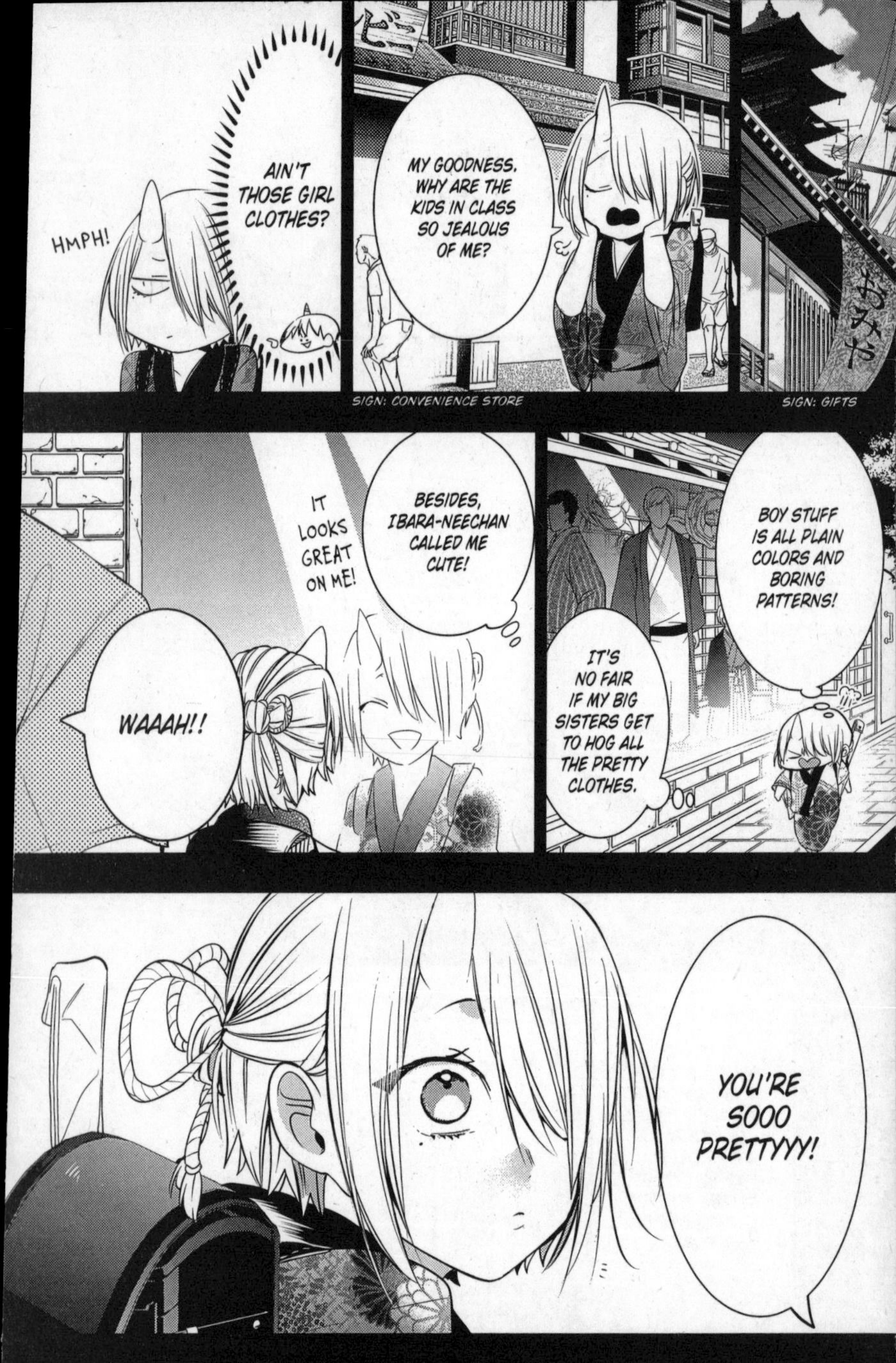
SIGN: GIFTS
MY GOODNESS. WHY ARE THE KIDS IN CLASS SO JEALOUS OF ME?
SIGN: CONVENIENCE STORE
AIN'T THOSE GIRL CLOTHES?
HMPH!
BOY STUFF IS ALL PLAIN COLORS AND BORING PATTERNS!
IT'S NO FAIR IF MY BIG SISTERS GET TO HOG ALL THE PRETTY CLOTHES.
BESIDES, IBARA-NEECHAN CALLED ME CUTE!
IT LOOKS GREAT ON ME!
WAAAH!!
YOU'RE SOOO PRETTYYY!

Forty-Eighth Period Abe no Seimei, Haruaki Abe, and Shutendouji (Part 2)

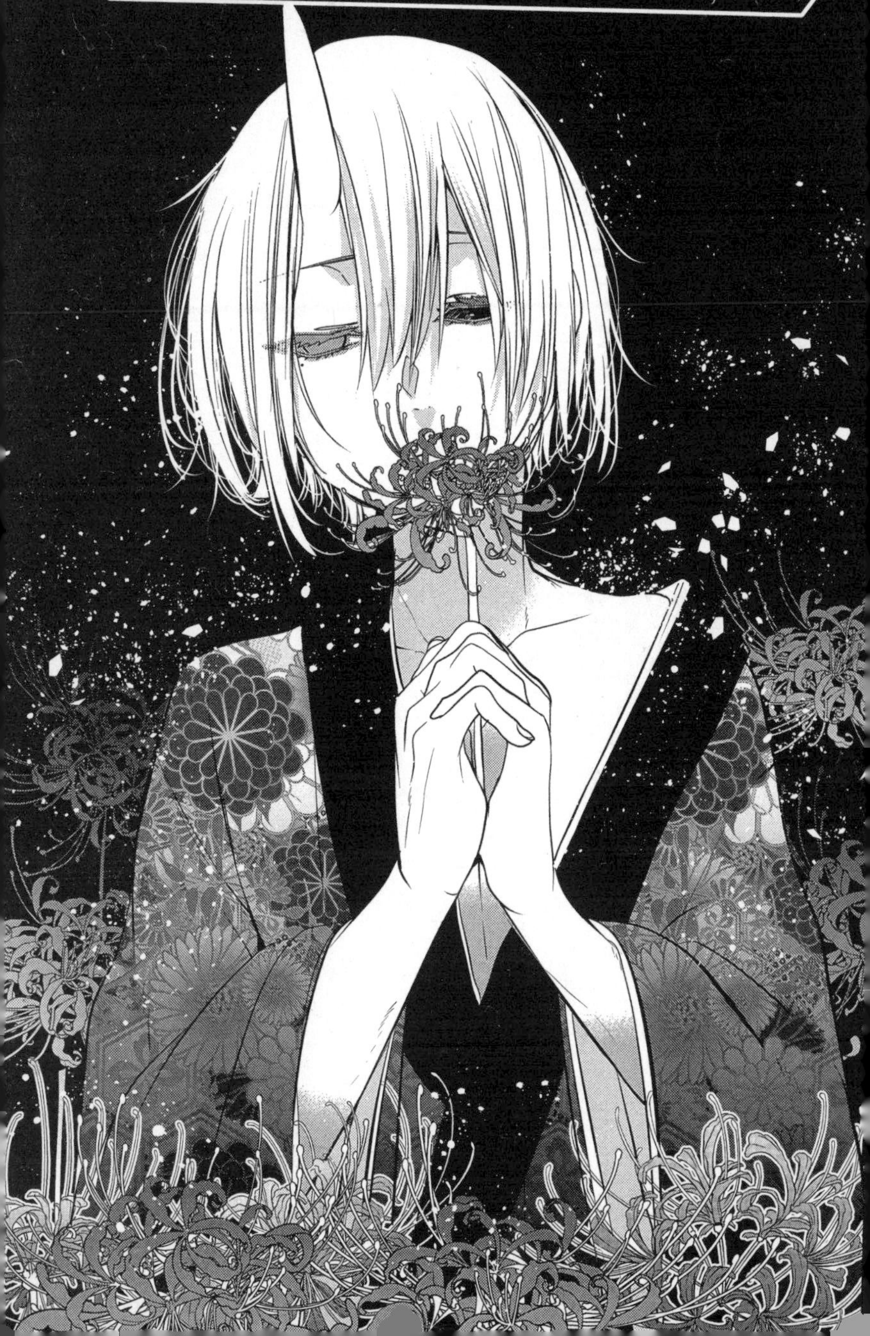

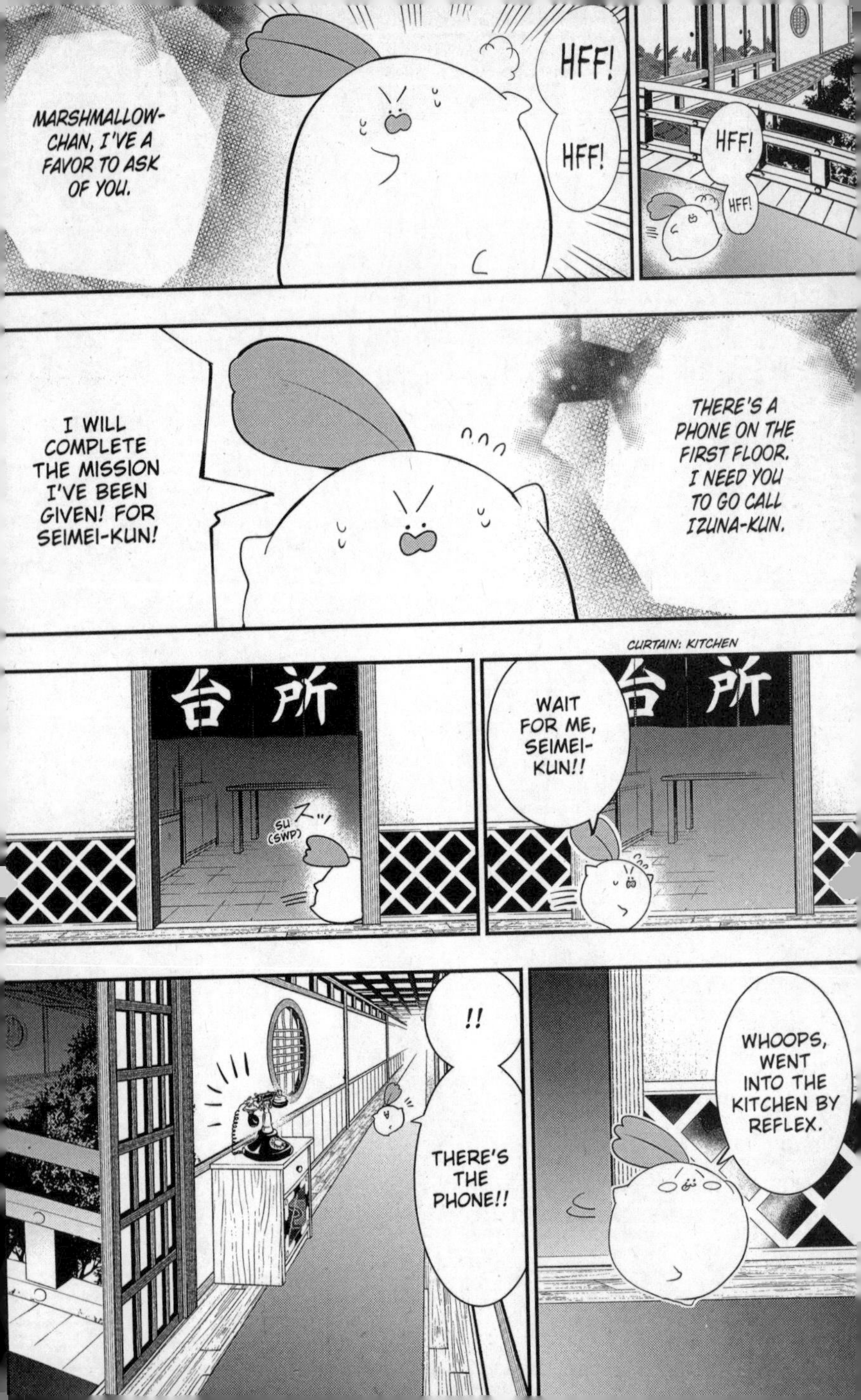

HFF!
HFF!
HFF!
HFF!
MARSHMALLOW-CHAN, I'VE A FAVOR TO ASK OF YOU.
THERE'S A PHONE ON THE FIRST FLOOR. I NEED YOU TO GO CALL IZUNA-KUN.
I WILL COMPLETE THE MISSION I'VE BEEN GIVEN! FOR SEIMEI-KUN!
CURTAIN: KITCHEN
台所
WAIT FOR ME, SEIMEI-KUN!!
台所
SU (SWP)
WHOOPS, WENT INTO THE KITCHEN BY REFLEX.
!!
THERE'S THE PHONE!!

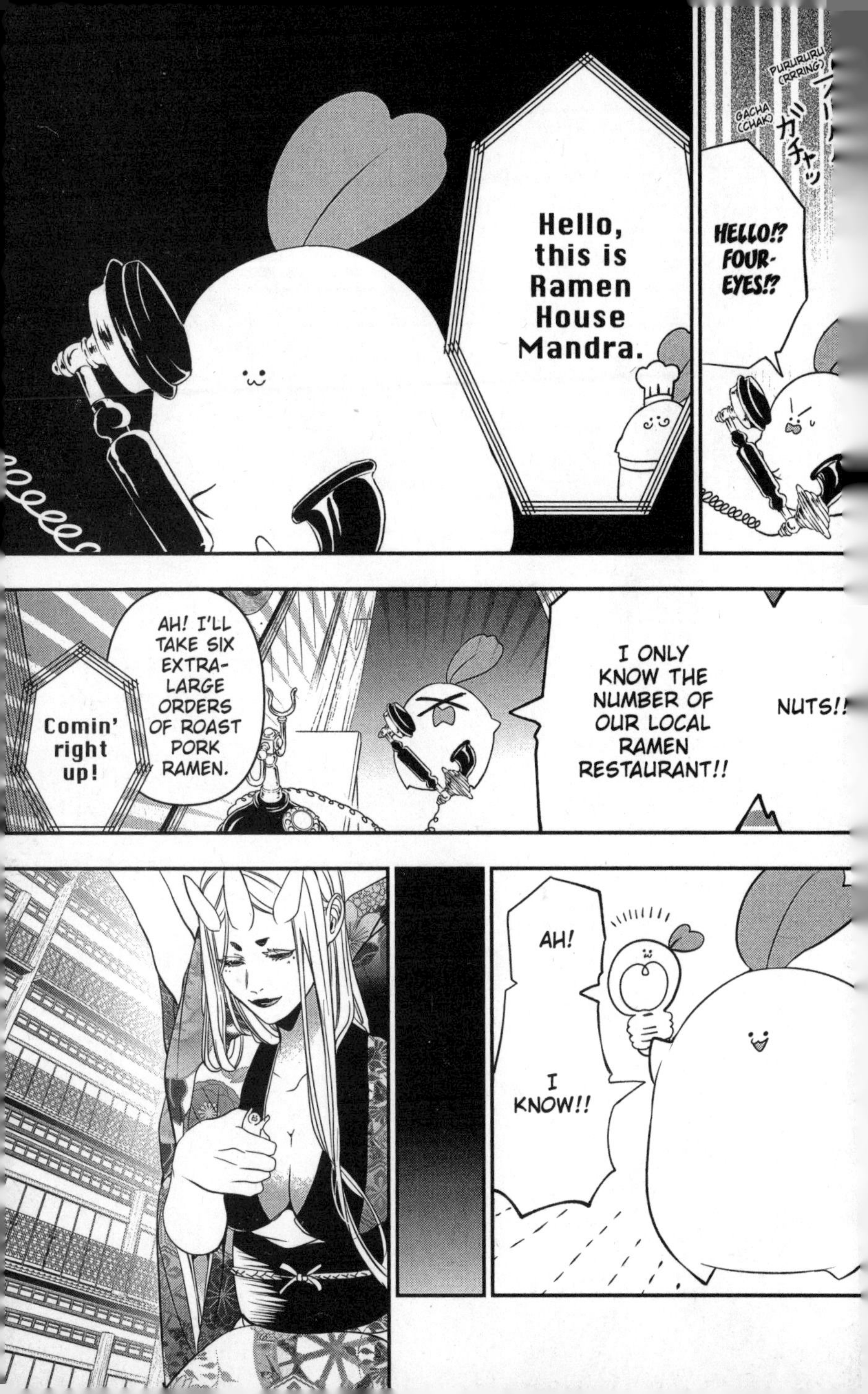
PURURURU (RRRING)
GACHA (CHAK)
ガチャッ
HELLO!? FOUR-EYES!?
Hello, this is Ramen House Mandra.
NUTS!!
I ONLY KNOW THE NUMBER OF OUR LOCAL RAMEN RESTAURANT!!
AH! I'LL TAKE SIX EXTRA-LARGE ORDERS OF ROAST PORK RAMEN.
Comin' right up!
AH!
I KNOW!!

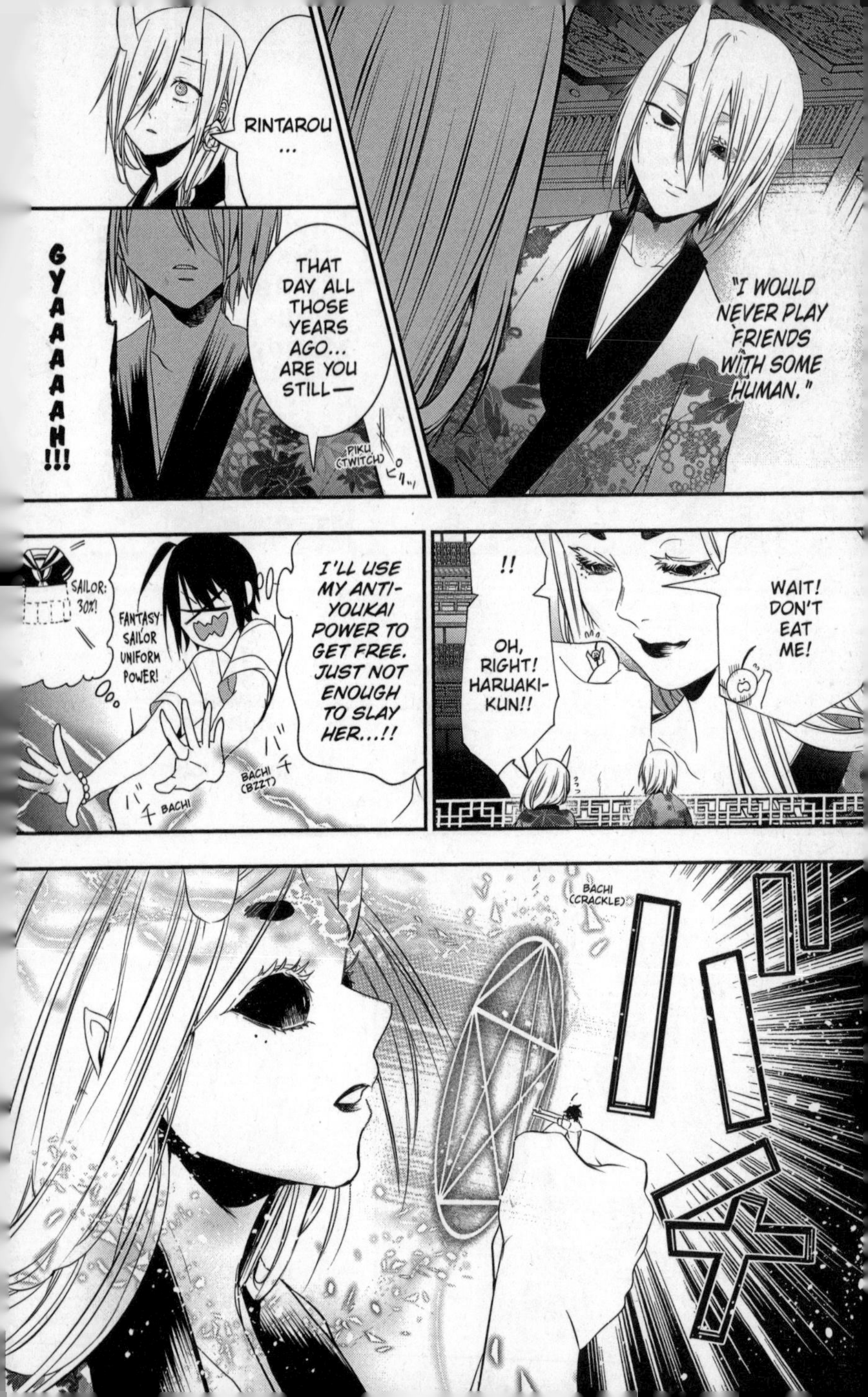
"I WOULD NEVER PLAY FRIENDS WITH SOME HUMAN."
RINTAROU ...
THAT DAY ALL THOSE YEARS AGO... ARE YOU STILL—
PIKU (TWITCH)
GYAAAAAAH!!!
WAIT! DON'T EAT ME!
!!
OH, RIGHT! HARUAKI-KUN!!
I'LL USE MY ANTI-YOUKAI POWER TO GET FREE. JUST NOT ENOUGH TO SLAY HER...!!
BACHI (BZZT)
SAILOR: 30%!
FANTASY SAILOR UNIFORM POWER!
BACHI
BACHI (CRACKLE)

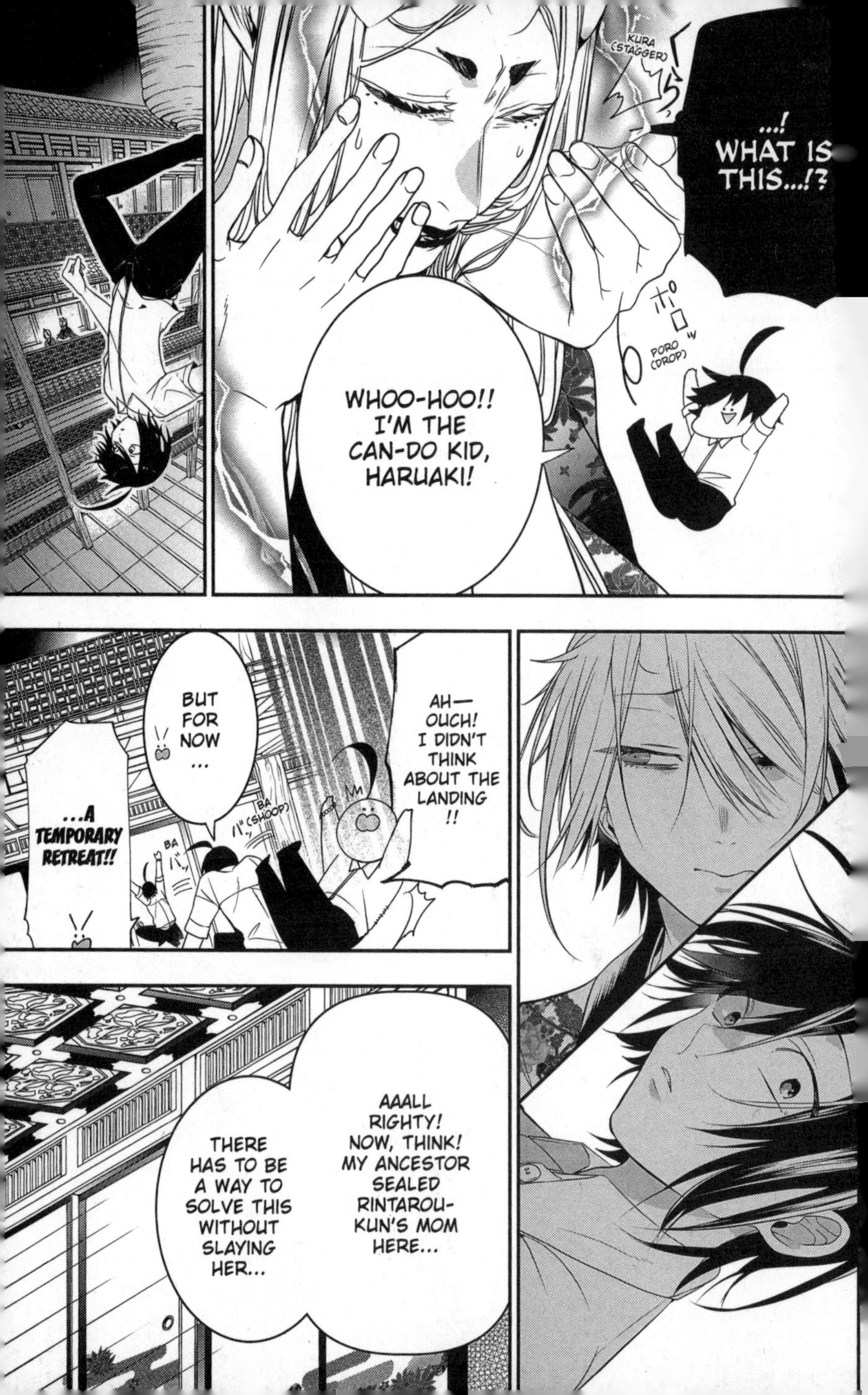
KURA (STAGGER)
...! WHAT IS THIS...!?
PORO (DROP)
WHOO-HOO!! I'M THE CAN-DO KID, HARUAKI!
AH— OUCH! I DIDN'T THINK ABOUT THE LANDING!!
BA (SHOOP)
BUT FOR NOW ...
BA
...A TEMPORARY RETREAT!!
AAALL RIGHTY! NOW, THINK! MY ANCESTOR SEALED RINTAROU-KUN'S MOM HERE...
THERE HAS TO BE A WAY TO SOLVE THIS WITHOUT SLAYING HER...

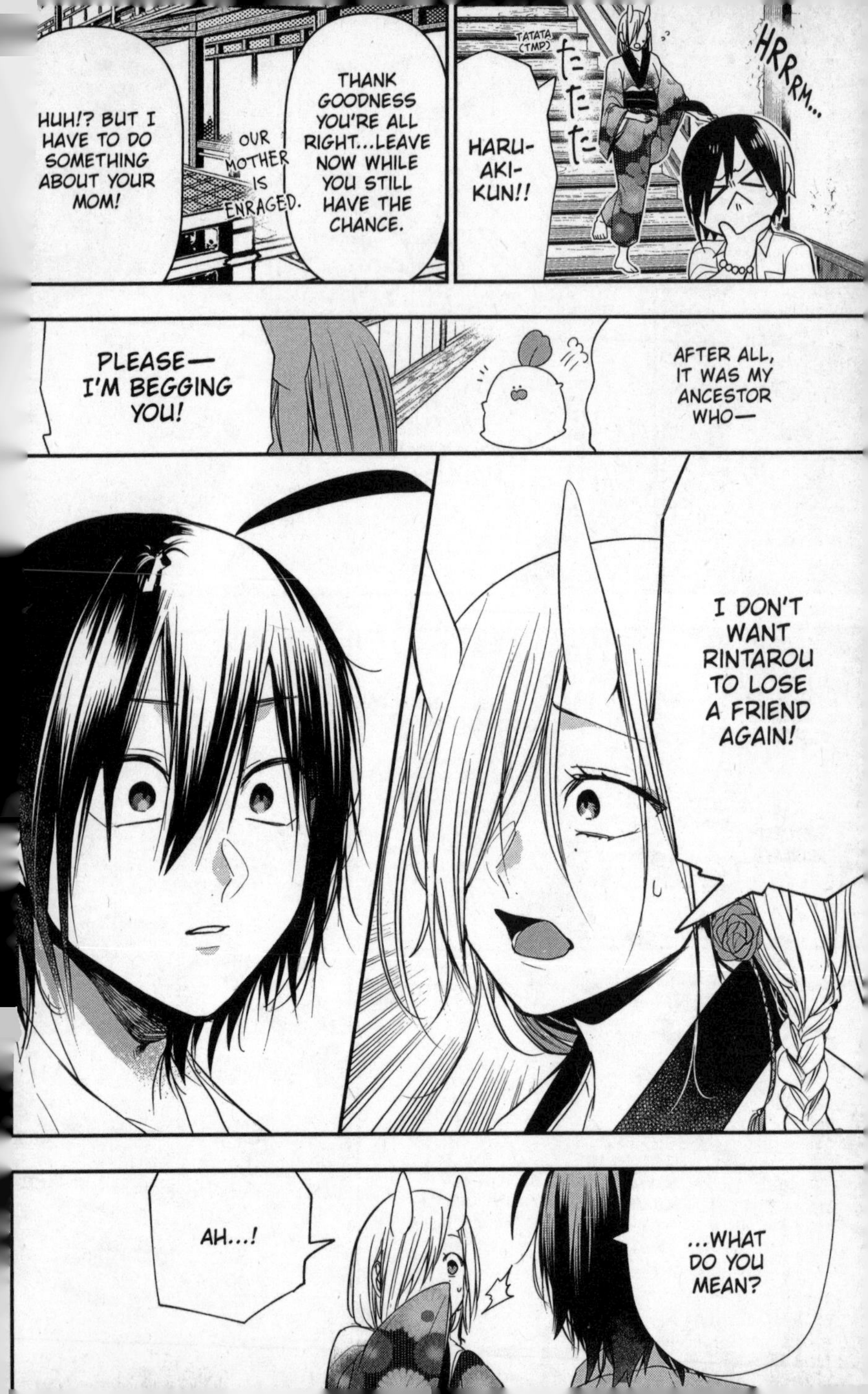
HRRRM...
TATATA (TMP)
たたた
HARU-AKI-KUN!!
THANK GOODNESS YOU'RE ALL RIGHT...LEAVE NOW WHILE YOU STILL HAVE THE CHANCE.
OUR MOTHER IS ENRAGED.
HUH!? BUT I HAVE TO DO SOMETHING ABOUT YOUR MOM!
AFTER ALL, IT WAS MY ANCESTOR WHO—
PLEASE— I'M BEGGING YOU!
I DON'T WANT RINTAROU TO LOSE A FRIEND AGAIN!
...WHAT DO YOU MEAN?
AH...!

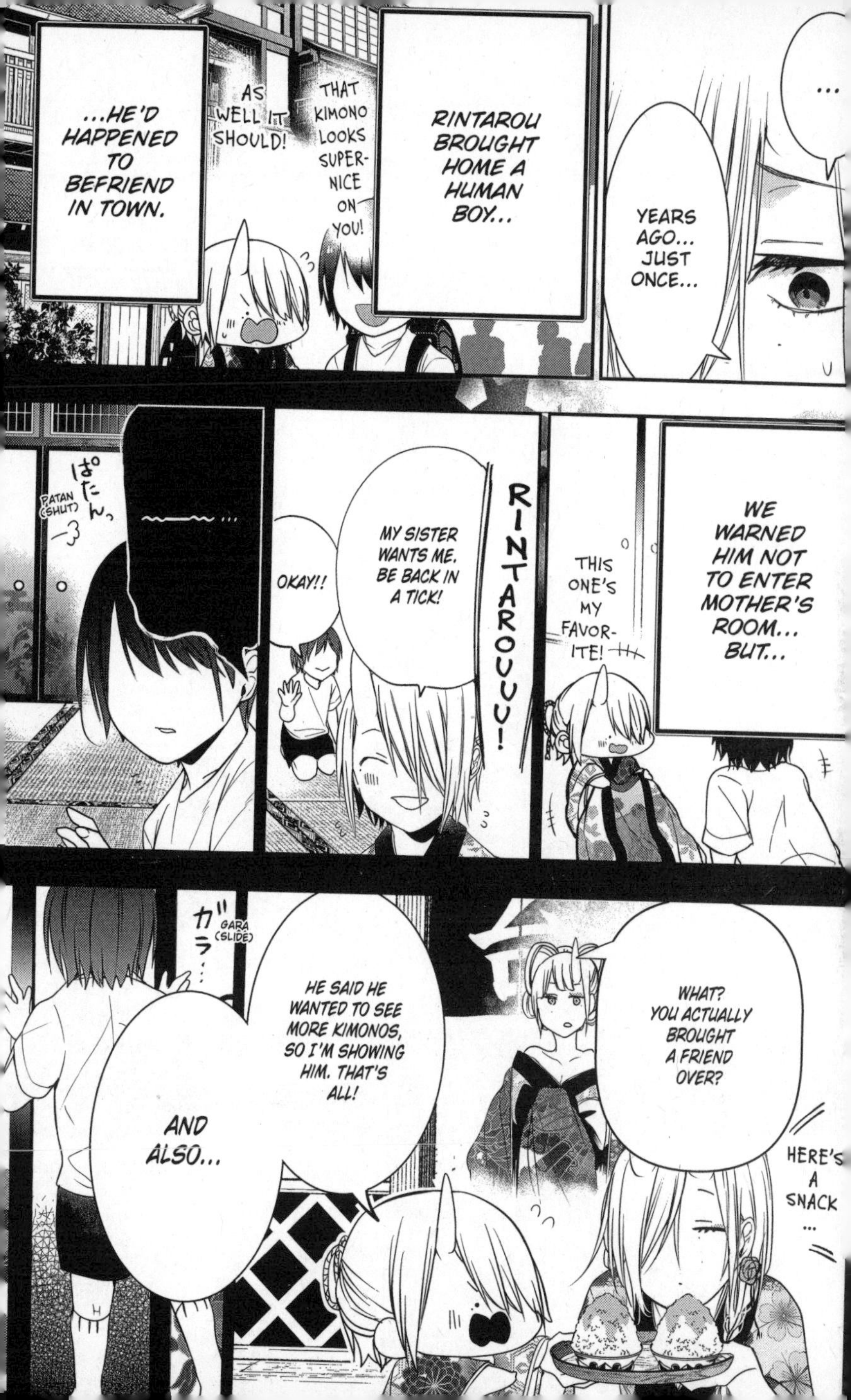
...
YEARS AGO... JUST ONCE...
RINTAROU BROUGHT HOME A HUMAN BOY...
THAT KIMONO LOOKS SUPER-NICE ON YOU!
AS WELL IT SHOULD!
...HE'D HAPPENED TO BEFRIEND IN TOWN.
WE WARNED HIM NOT TO ENTER MOTHER'S ROOM... BUT...
THIS ONE'S MY FAVORITE!
RINTAROUUU!
MY SISTER WANTS ME. BE BACK IN A TICK!
OKAY!!
ぱたん
PATAN (SHUT)
WHAT? YOU ACTUALLY BROUGHT A FRIEND OVER?
HERE'S A SNACK...
HE SAID HE WANTED TO SEE MORE KIMONOS, SO I'M SHOWING HIM. THAT'S ALL!
AND ALSO...
ガラ
GARA (SLIDE)

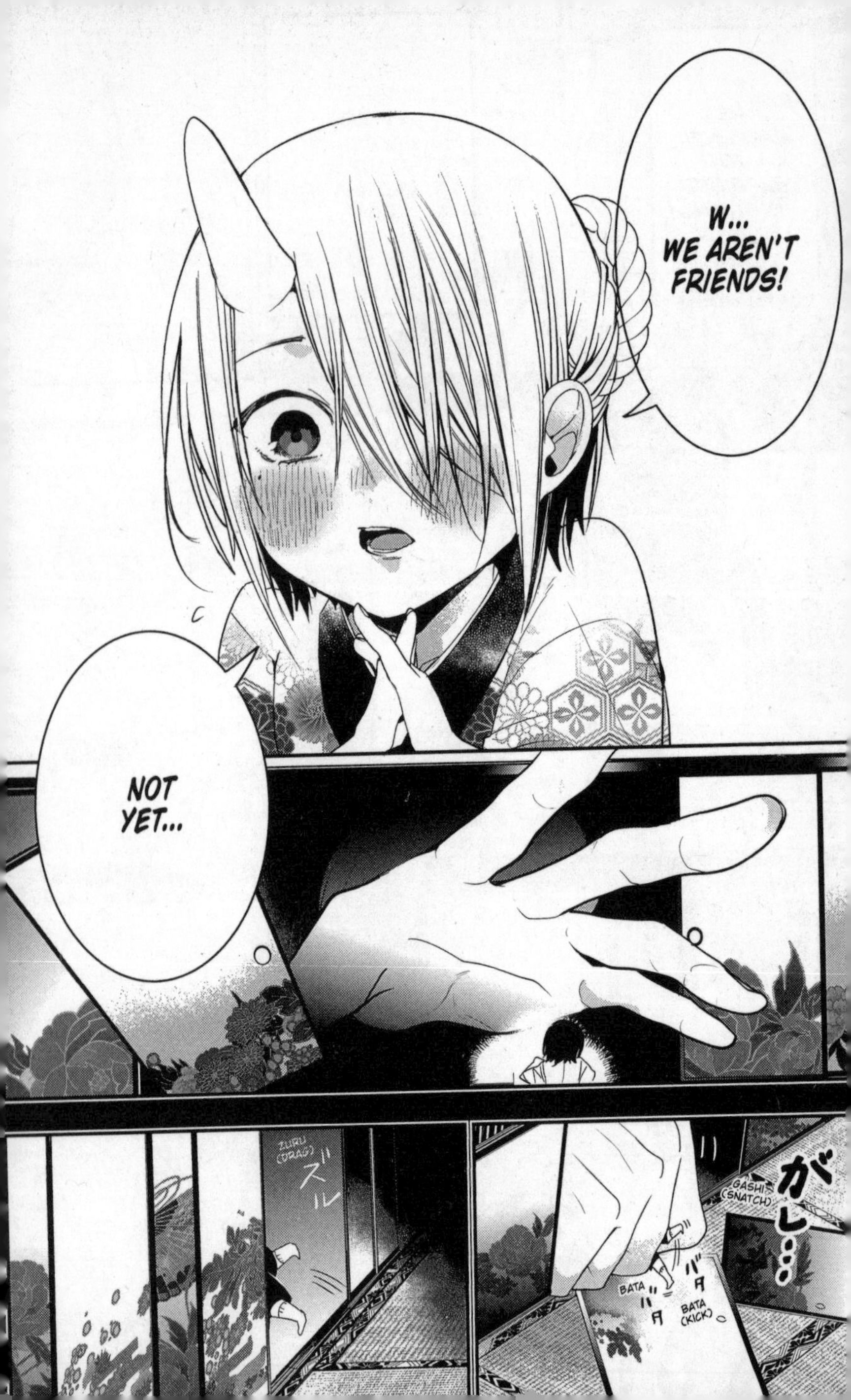
W... WE AREN'T FRIENDS!
NOT YET...
がし…
GASHI (SNATCH)
バタバタ
BATA BATA (KICK)
ズル
ZURU (DRAG)

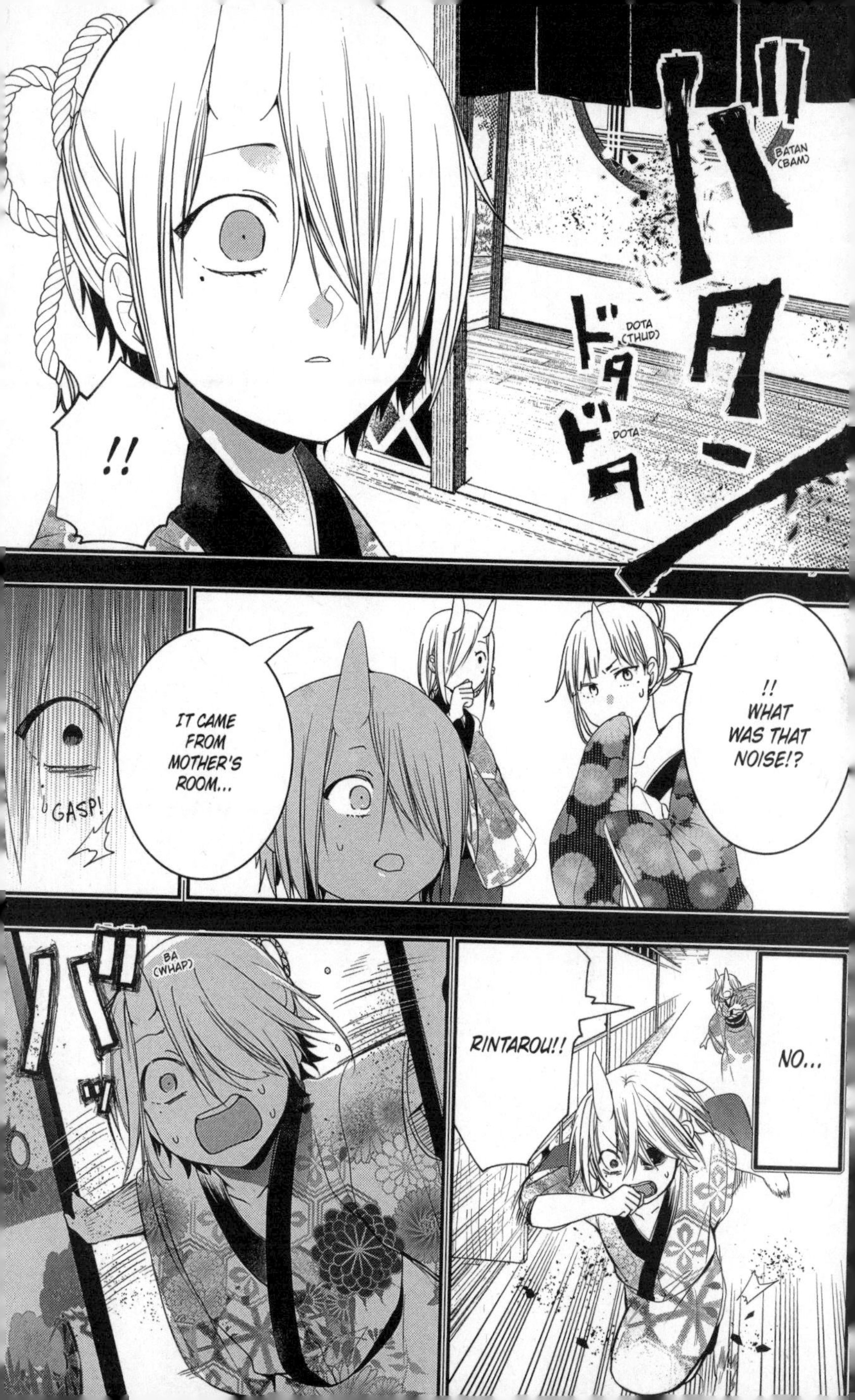
BATAN (BAM)
DOTA (THUD)
DOTA
!!
!! WHAT WAS THAT NOISE!?
IT CAME FROM MOTHER'S ROOM...
GASP!
NO...
RINTAROU!!
BA (WHAP)

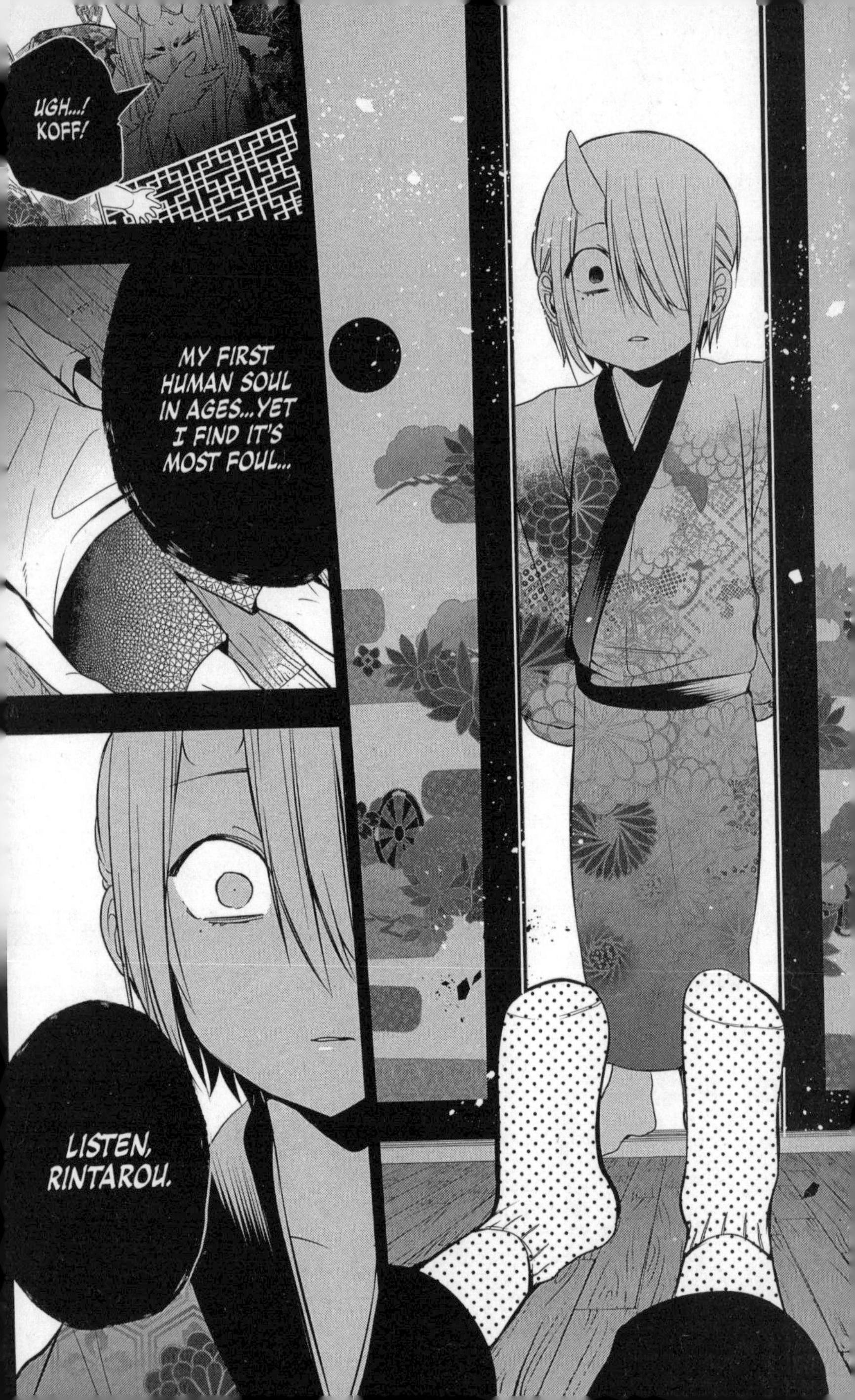
UGH...! KOFF!
MY FIRST HUMAN SOUL IN AGES...YET I FIND IT'S MOST FOUL...
LISTEN, RINTAROU.

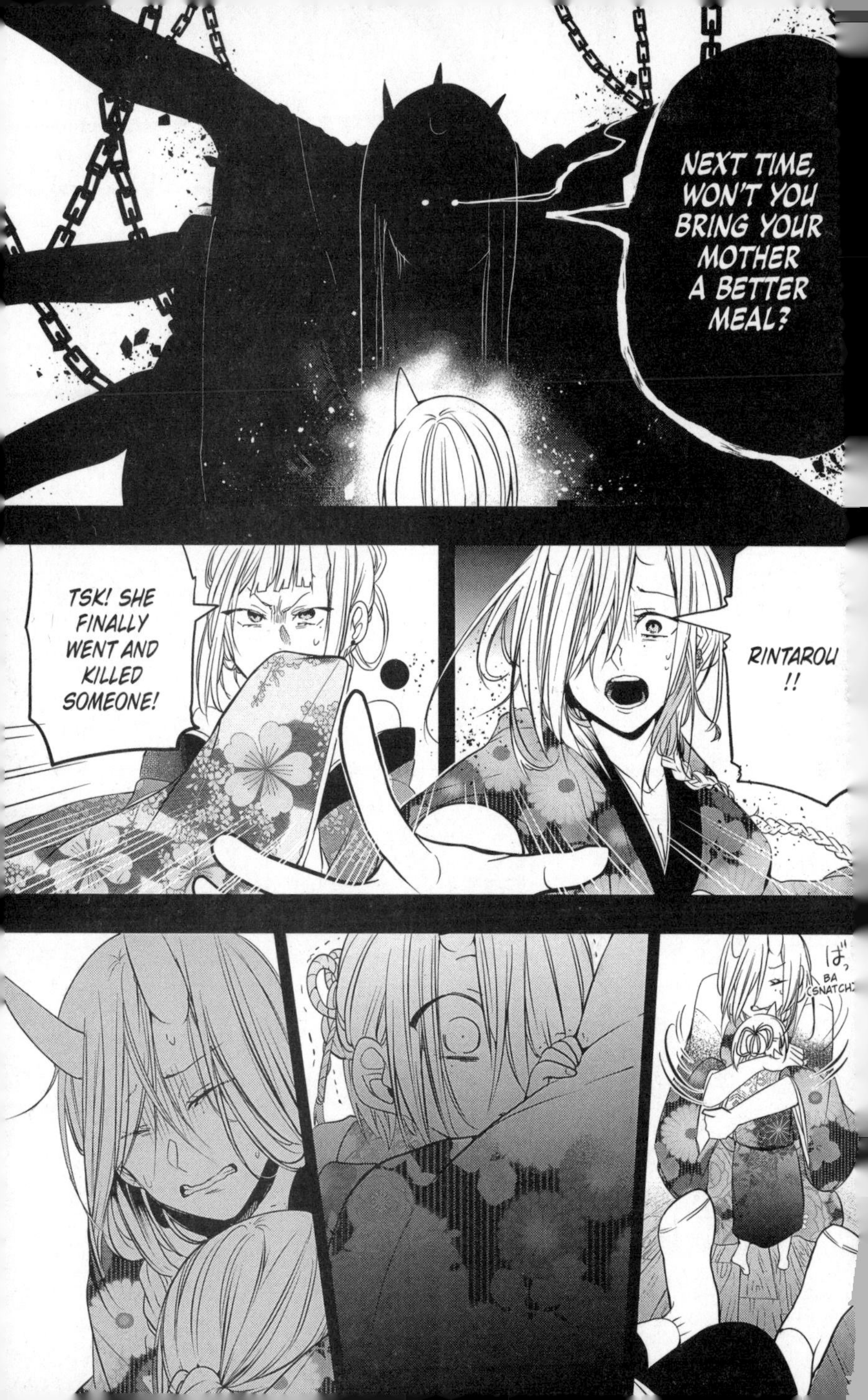
NEXT TIME, WON'T YOU BRING YOUR MOTHER A BETTER MEAL?
RINTAROU !!
TSK! SHE FINALLY WENT AND KILLED SOMEONE!
ばっ
BA (SNATCH)

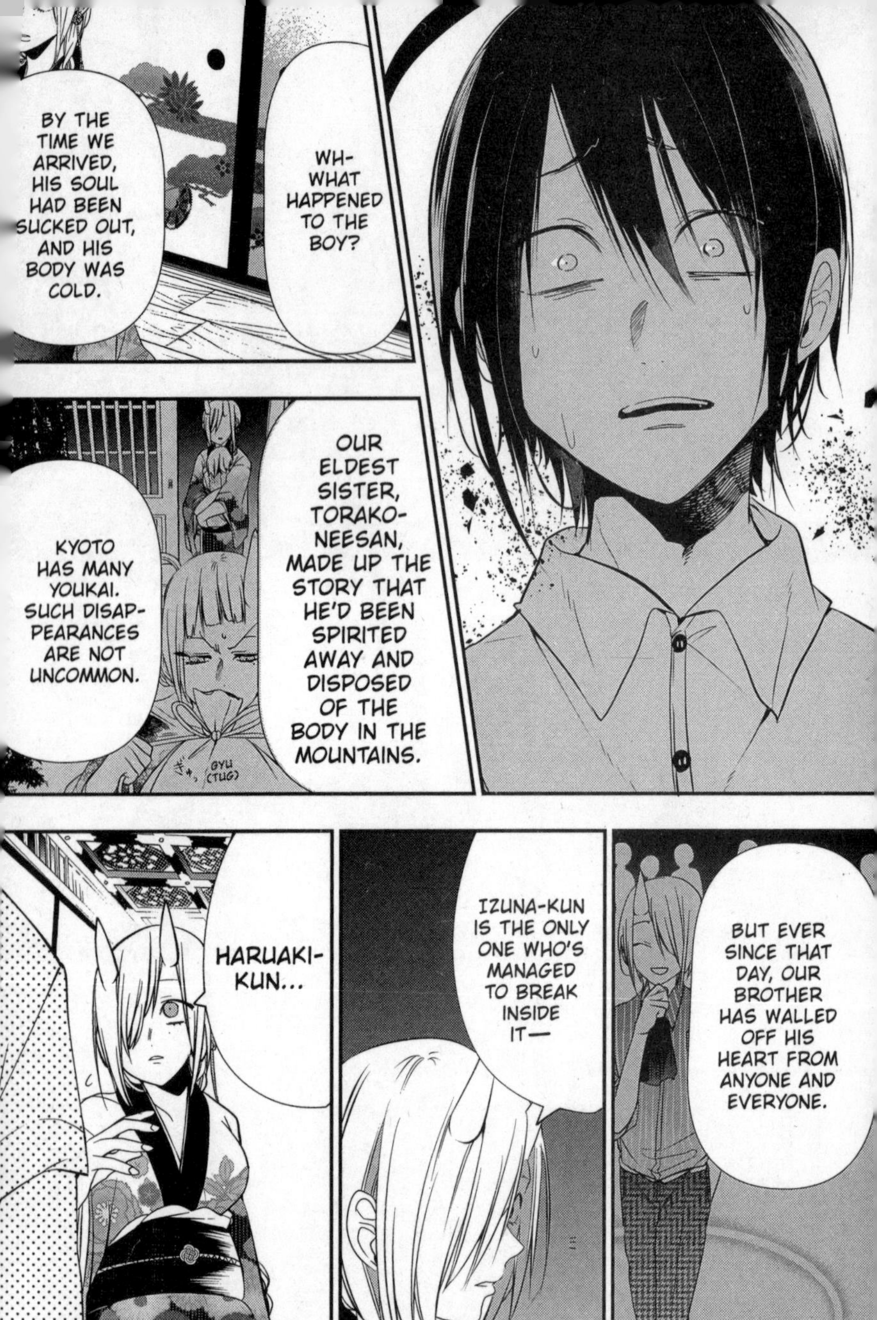
WH- WHAT HAPPENED TO THE BOY?
BY THE TIME WE ARRIVED, HIS SOUL HAD BEEN SUCKED OUT, AND HIS BODY WAS COLD.
OUR ELDEST SISTER, TORAKO-NEESAN, MADE UP THE STORY THAT HE'D BEEN SPIRITED AWAY AND DISPOSED OF THE BODY IN THE MOUNTAINS.
KYOTO HAS MANY YOUKAI. SUCH DISAPPEARANCES ARE NOT UNCOMMON.
GYU (TUG)
BUT EVER SINCE THAT DAY, OUR BROTHER HAS WALLED OFF HIS HEART FROM ANYONE AND EVERYONE.
IZUNA-KUN IS THE ONLY ONE WHO'S MANAGED TO BREAK INSIDE IT—
HARUAKI-KUN...

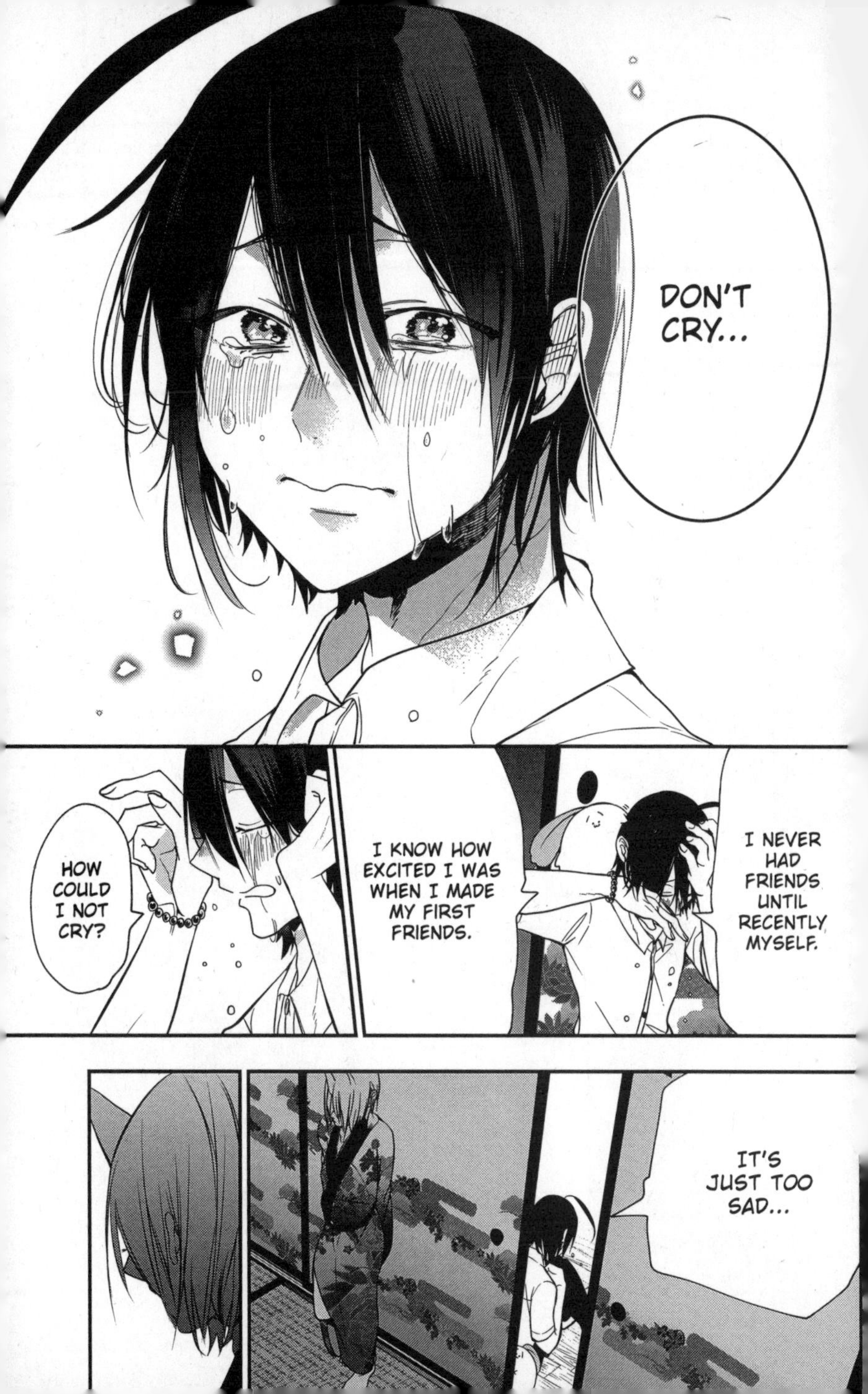
DON'T CRY...
I NEVER HAD FRIENDS UNTIL RECENTLY MYSELF.
I KNOW HOW EXCITED I WAS WHEN I MADE MY FIRST FRIENDS.
HOW COULD I NOT CRY?
IT'S JUST TOO SAD...

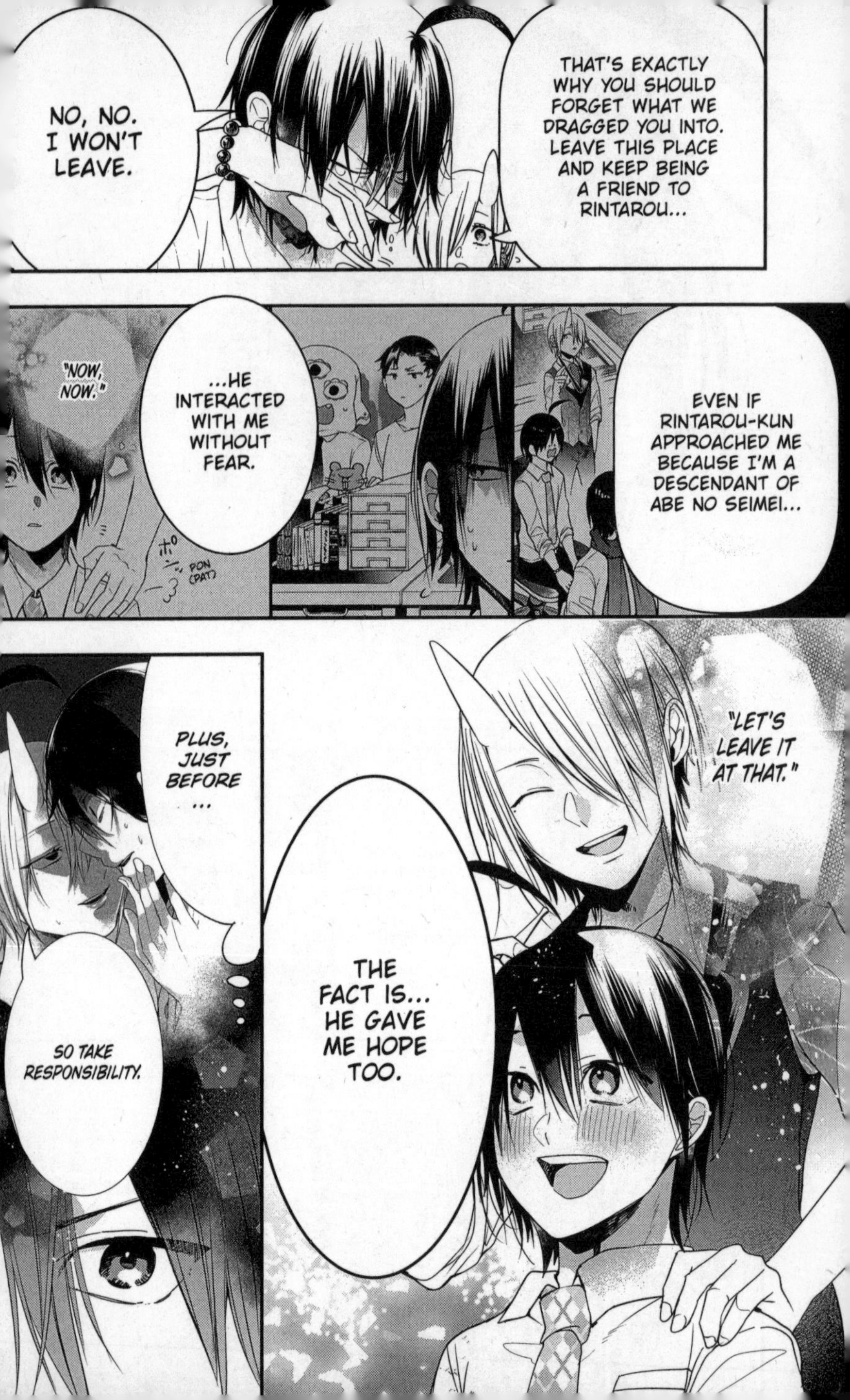
THAT'S EXACTLY WHY YOU SHOULD FORGET WHAT WE DRAGGED YOU INTO. LEAVE THIS PLACE AND KEEP BEING A FRIEND TO RINTAROU...
NO, NO. I WON'T LEAVE.
EVEN IF RINTAROU-KUN APPROACHED ME BECAUSE I'M A DESCENDANT OF ABE NO SEIMEI...
...HE INTERACTED WITH ME WITHOUT FEAR.
"NOW, NOW."
PON (PAT)
"LET'S LEAVE IT AT THAT."
THE FACT IS... HE GAVE ME HOPE TOO.
PLUS, JUST BEFORE ...
SO TAKE RESPONSIBILITY.

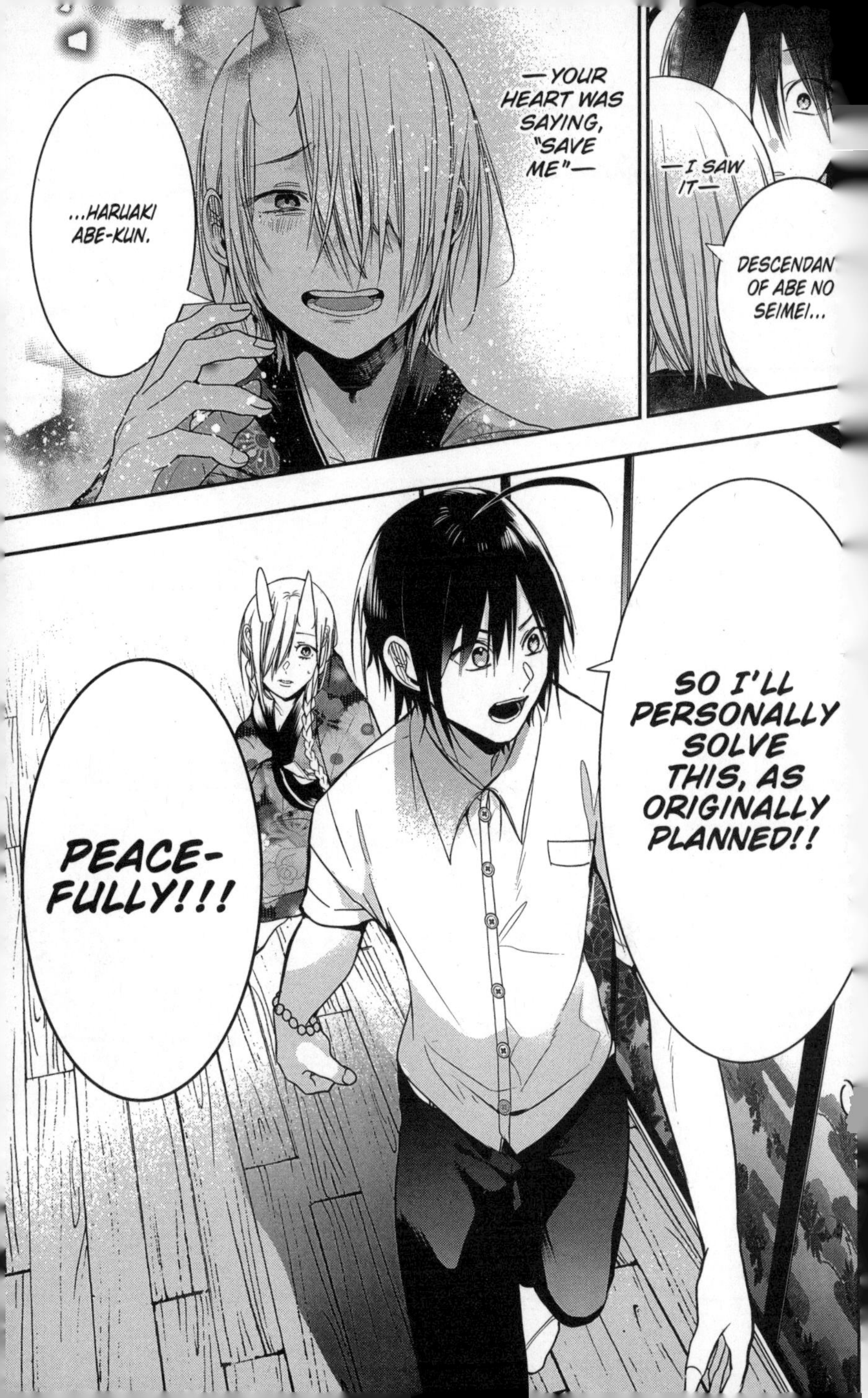
—I SAW IT—
DESCENDAN OF ABE NO SEIMEI...
—YOUR HEART WAS SAYING, "SAVE ME"—
...HARUAKI ABE-KUN.
SO I'LL PERSONALLY SOLVE THIS, AS ORIGINALLY PLANNED!!
PEACE-FULLY!!!

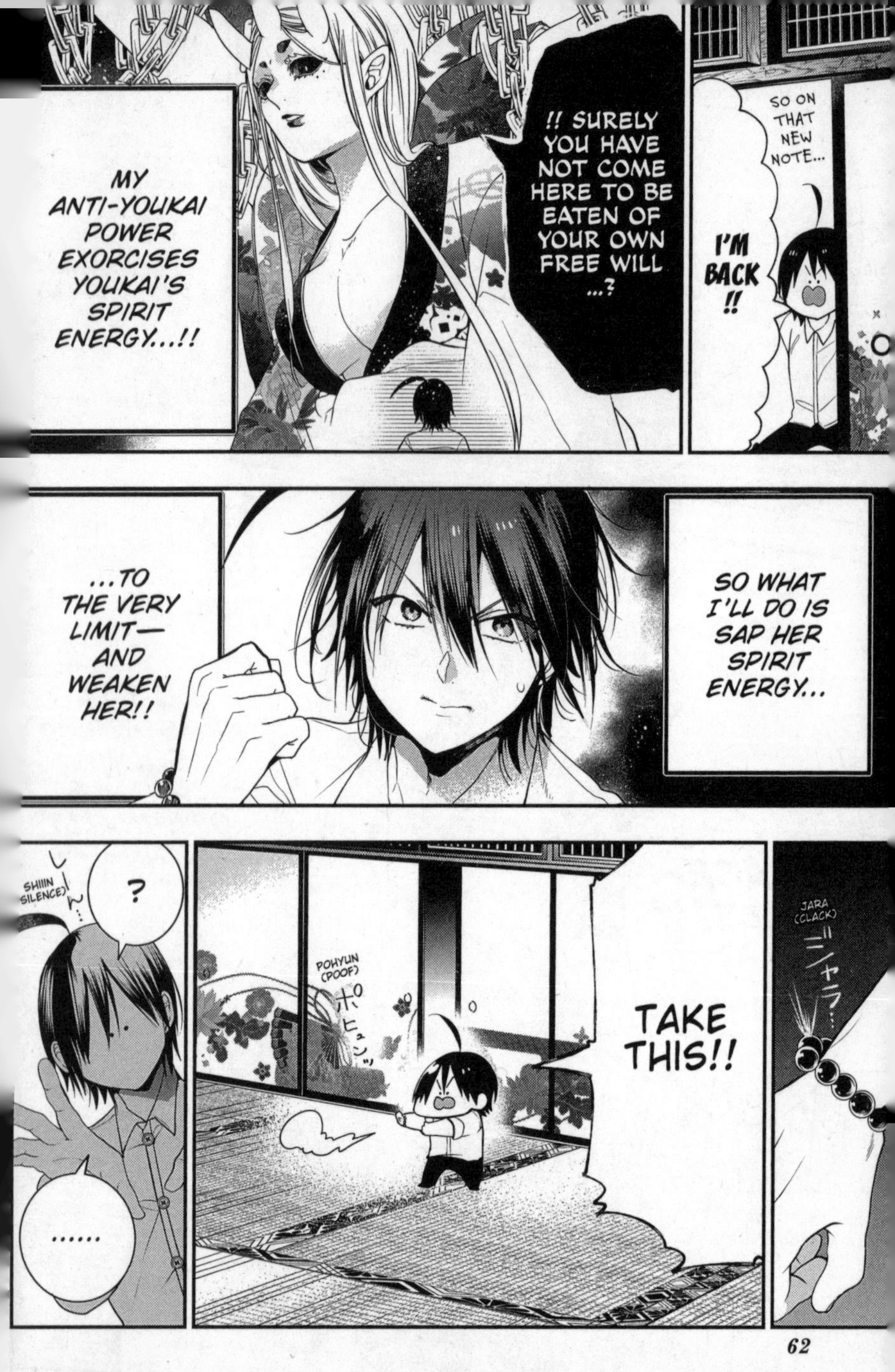
SO ON THAT NEW NOTE...
I'M BACK!!
!! SURELY YOU HAVE NOT COME HERE TO BE EATEN OF YOUR OWN FREE WILL ...?
MY ANTI-YOUKAI POWER EXORCISES YOUKAI'S SPIRIT ENERGY...!!
SO WHAT I'LL DO IS SAP HER SPIRIT ENERGY...
...TO THE VERY LIMIT—AND WEAKEN HER!!
JARA (CLACK)
ジャラ…
TAKE THIS!!
POHYUN (POOF)
ポヒュンッ
?
SHIIIN (SILENCE)
しーん…
......

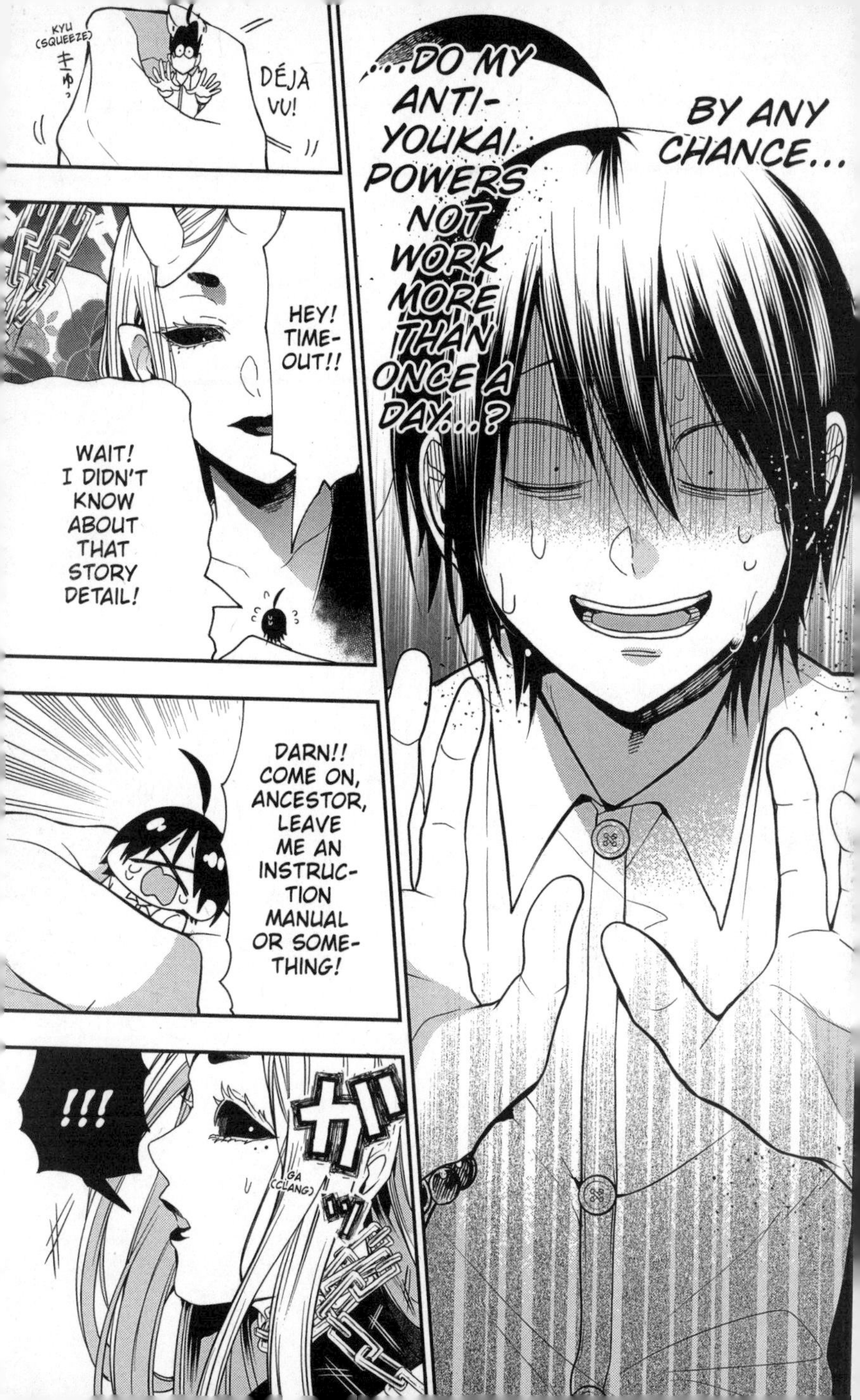
BY ANY CHANCE...
...DO MY ANTI-YOUKAI POWERS NOT WORK MORE THAN ONCE A DAY...?
DÉJÀ VU!
KYU (SQUEEZE)
きゅっ
HEY! TIME-OUT!!
WAIT! I DIDN'T KNOW ABOUT THAT STORY DETAIL!
DARN!! COME ON, ANCESTOR, LEAVE ME AN INSTRUC-TION MANUAL OR SOME-THING!
ガッ
GA (CLANG)
!!!

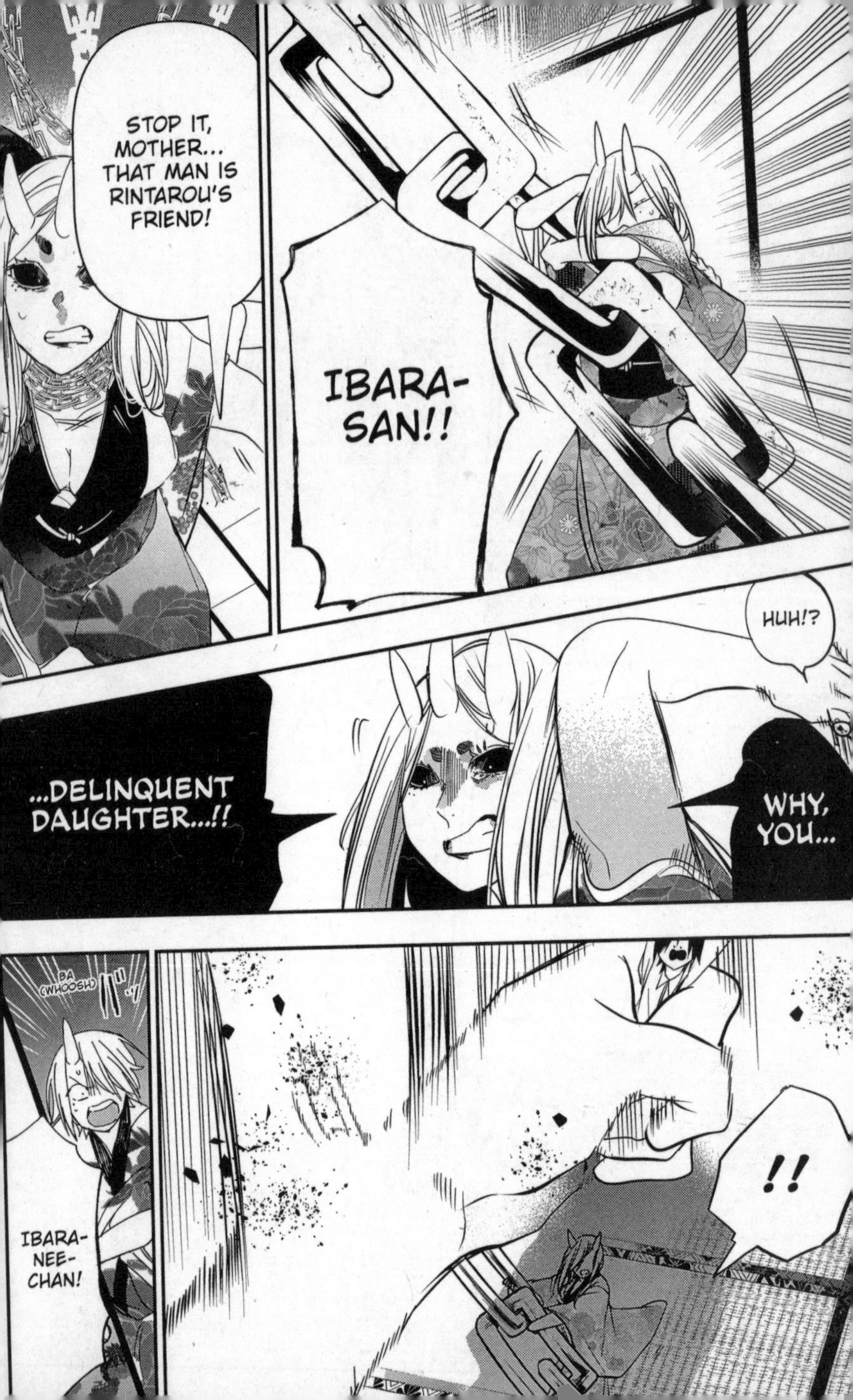
IBARA-SAN!!
STOP IT, MOTHER... THAT MAN IS RINTAROU'S FRIEND!
HUH!?
WHY, YOU...
...DELINQUENT DAUGHTER...!!
!!
BA (WHOOSH)
IBARA-NEE-CHAN!

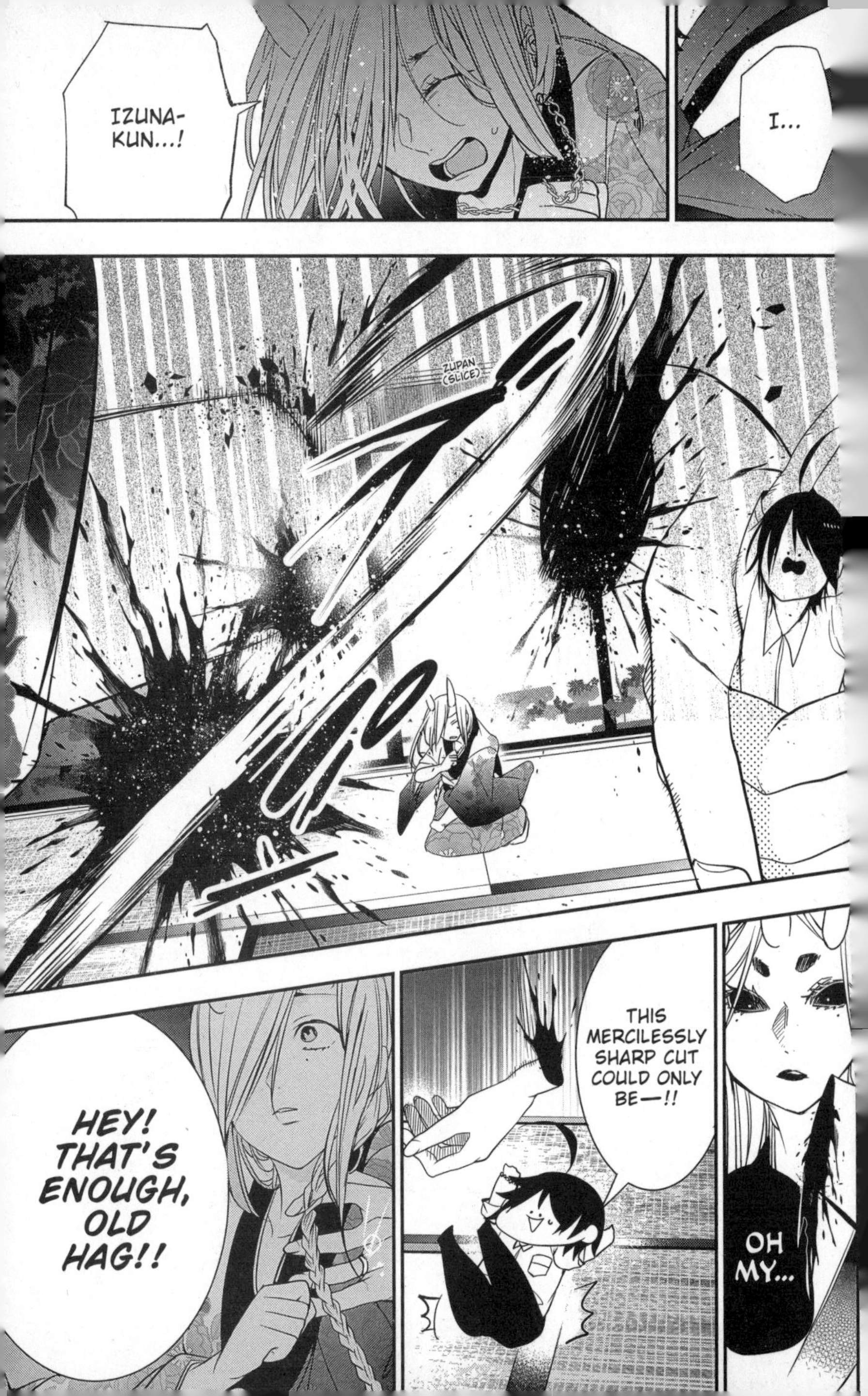
I...
IZUNA-KUN...!
ZUPAN (SLICE)
OH MY...
THIS MERCILESSLY SHARP CUT COULD ONLY BE—!!
HEY! THAT'S ENOUGH, OLD HAG!!

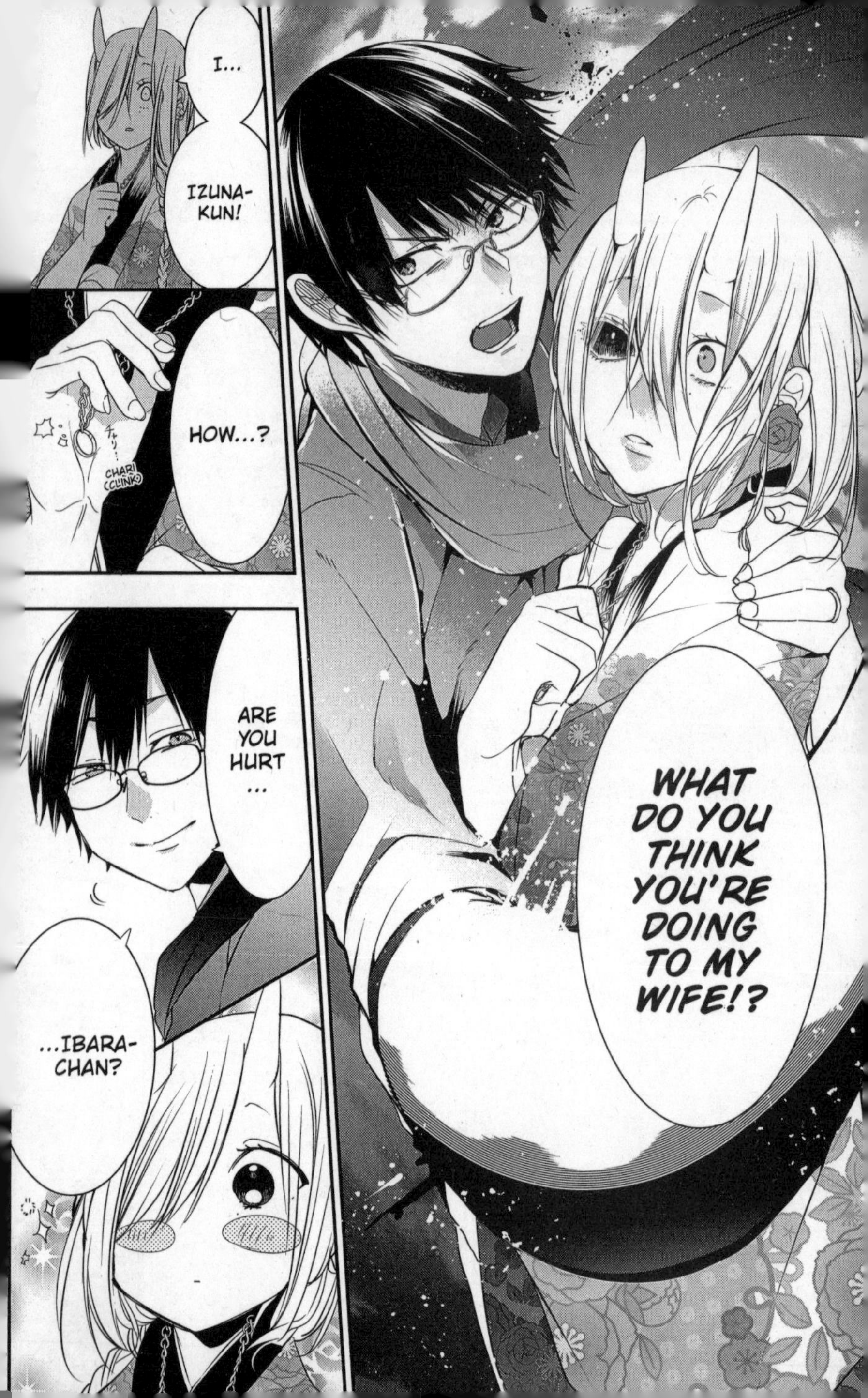
WHAT DO YOU THINK YOU'RE DOING TO MY WIFE!?
I...
IZUNA-KUN!
HOW...?
チャリ…
CHARI (CLINK)
ARE YOU HURT...
...IBARA-CHAN?

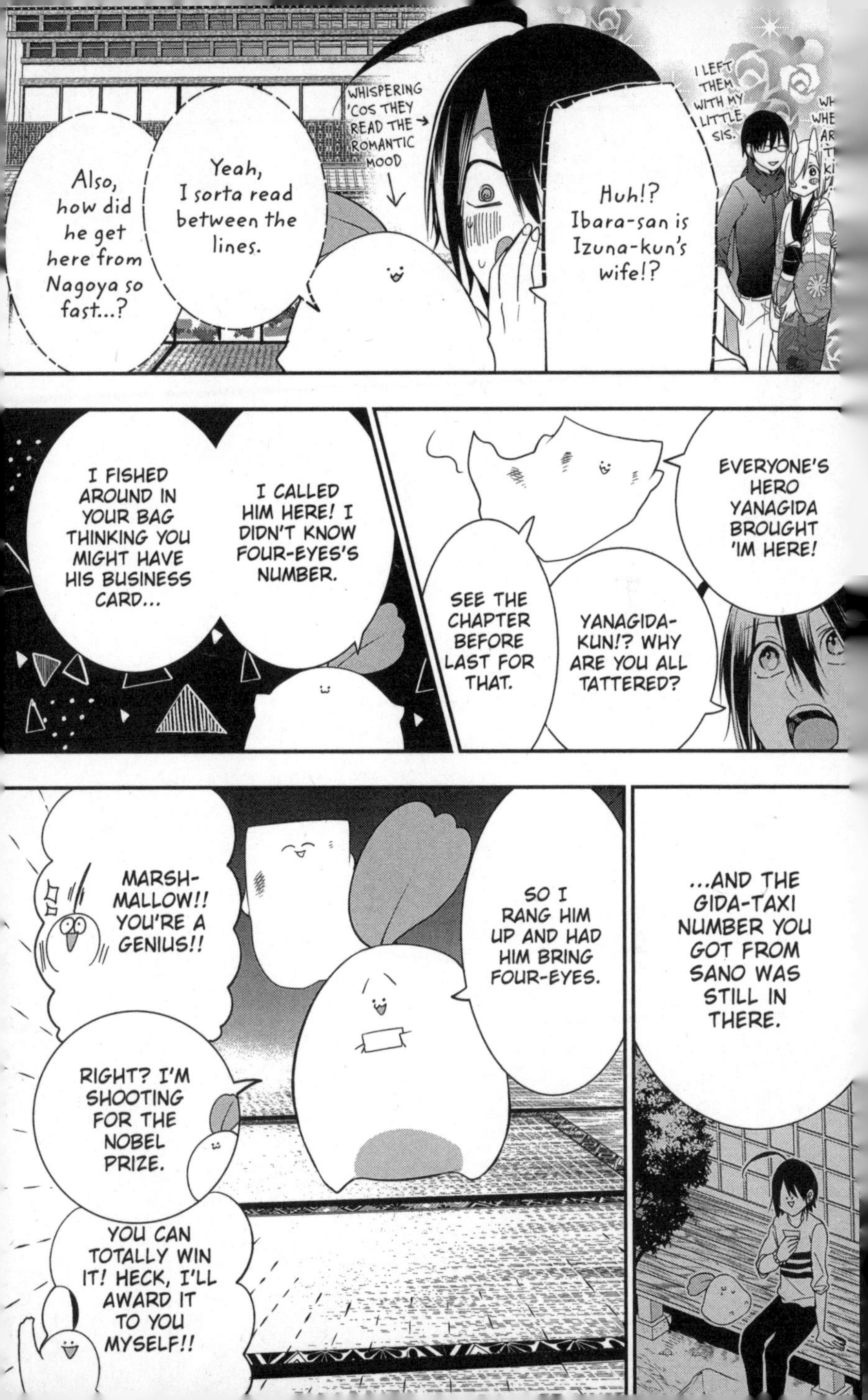
I LEFT THEM WITH MY LITTLE SIS.
Huh!? Ibara-san is Izuna-kun's wife!?
WHISPERING 'COS THEY READ THE ROMANTIC MOOD
Yeah, I sorta read between the lines.
Also, how did he get here from Nagoya so fast...?
EVERYONE'S HERO YANAGIDA BROUGHT 'IM HERE!
YANAGIDA-KUN!? WHY ARE YOU ALL TATTERED?
SEE THE CHAPTER BEFORE LAST FOR THAT.
I CALLED HIM HERE! I DIDN'T KNOW FOUR-EYES'S NUMBER.
I FISHED AROUND IN YOUR BAG THINKING YOU MIGHT HAVE HIS BUSINESS CARD...
...AND THE GIDA-TAXI NUMBER YOU GOT FROM SANO WAS STILL IN THERE.
SO I RANG HIM UP AND HAD HIM BRING FOUR-EYES.
MARSH-MALLOW!! YOU'RE A GENIUS!!
RIGHT? I'M SHOOTING FOR THE NOBEL PRIZE.
YOU CAN TOTALLY WIN IT! HECK, I'LL AWARD IT TO YOU MYSELF!!

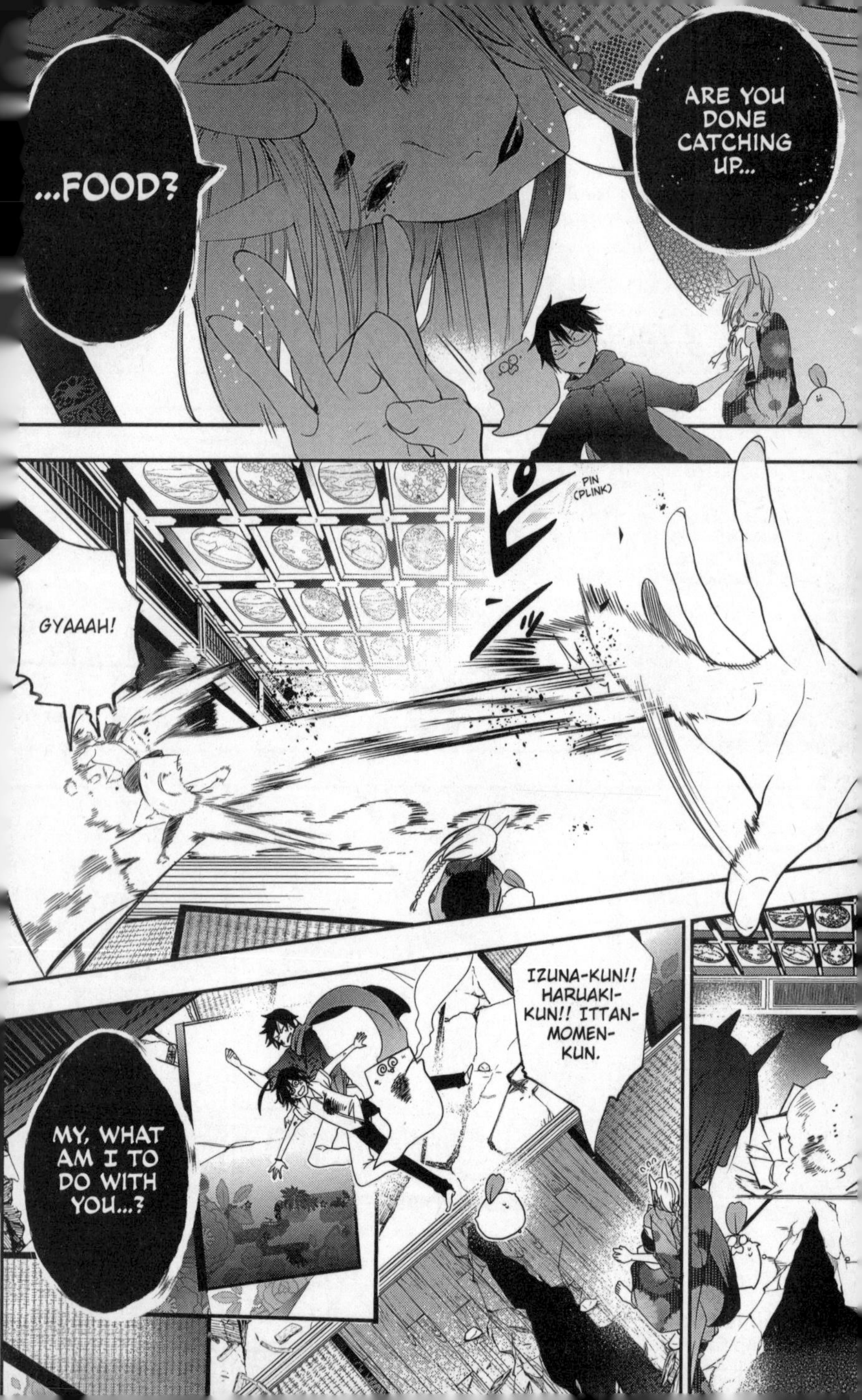
ARE YOU DONE CATCHING UP...
...FOOD?
PIN (PLINK)
GYAAAH!
IZUNA-KUN!! HARUAKI-KUN!! ITTAN-MOMEN-KUN.
MY, WHAT AM I TO DO WITH YOU...?

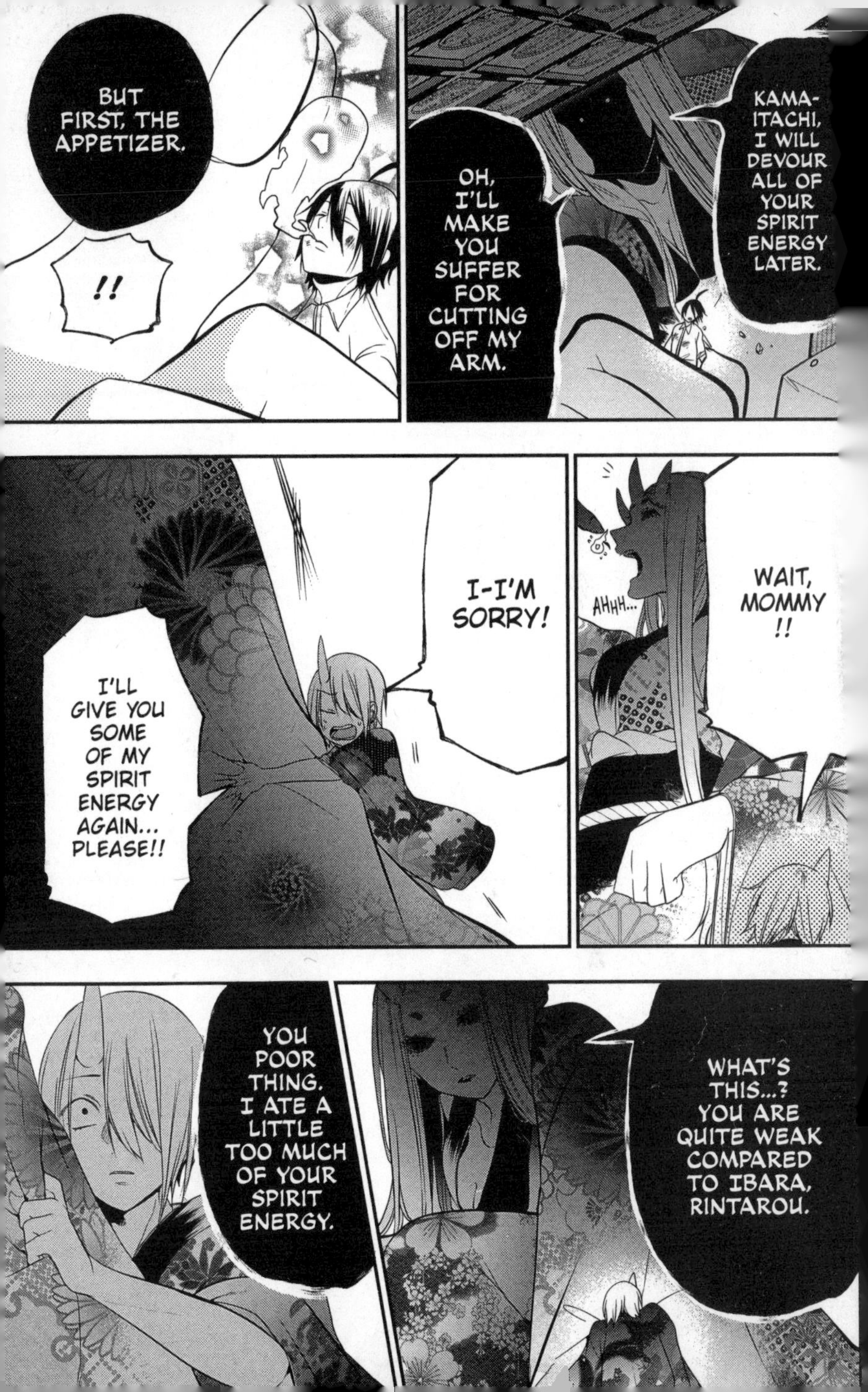
KAMA-ITACHI, I WILL DEVOUR ALL OF YOUR SPIRIT ENERGY LATER.
OH, I'LL MAKE YOU SUFFER FOR CUTTING OFF MY ARM.
BUT FIRST, THE APPETIZER.
!!
WAIT, MOMMY!!
AHHH...
I-I'M SORRY!
I'LL GIVE YOU SOME OF MY SPIRIT ENERGY AGAIN... PLEASE!!
WHAT'S THIS...? YOU ARE QUITE WEAK COMPARED TO IBARA, RINTAROU.
YOU POOR THING. I ATE A LITTLE TOO MUCH OF YOUR SPIRIT ENERGY.

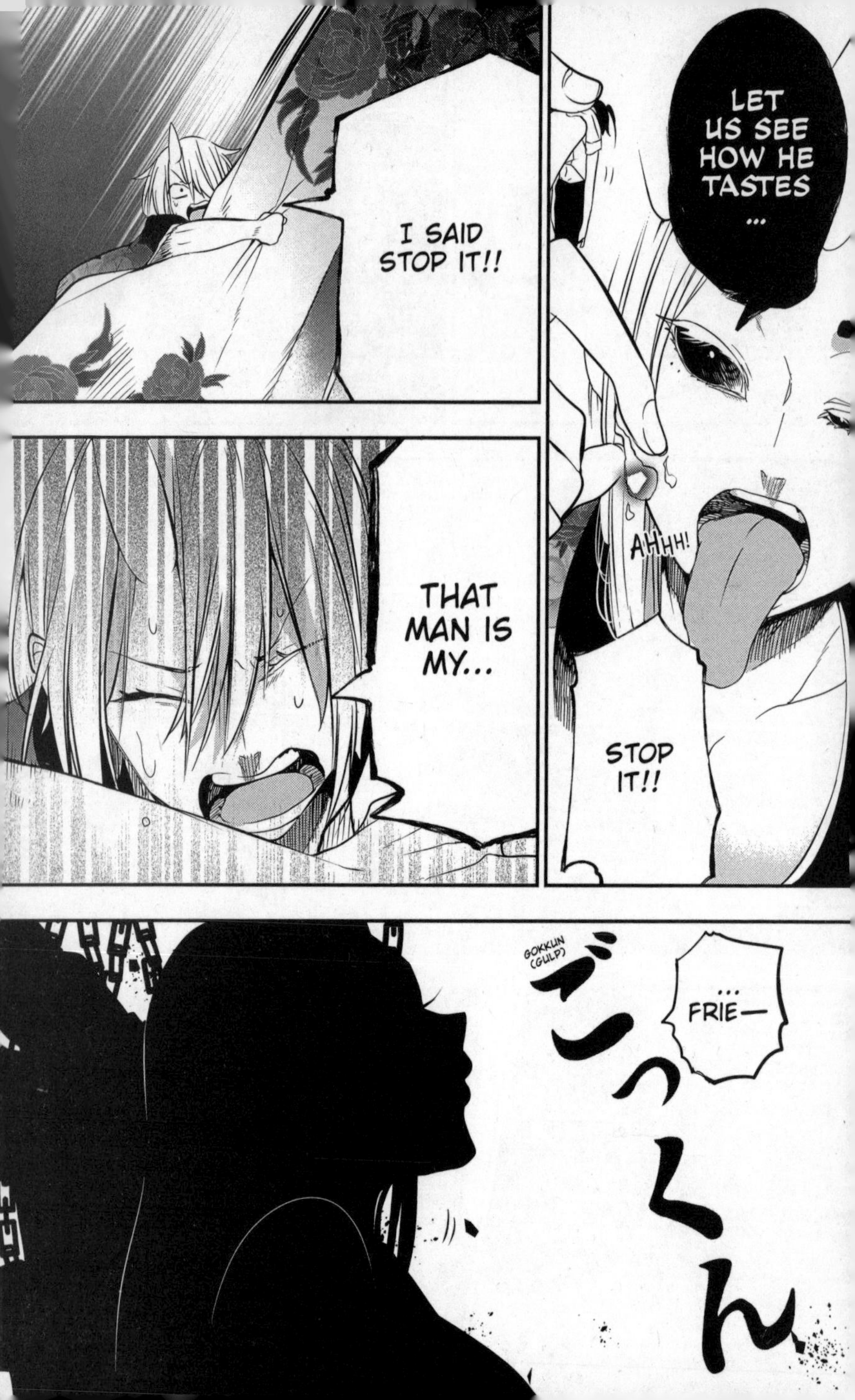
LET US SEE HOW HE TASTES ...
AHHH!
STOP IT!!
I SAID STOP IT!!
THAT MAN IS MY...
GOKKUN (GULP)
ごっくん
... FRIE—

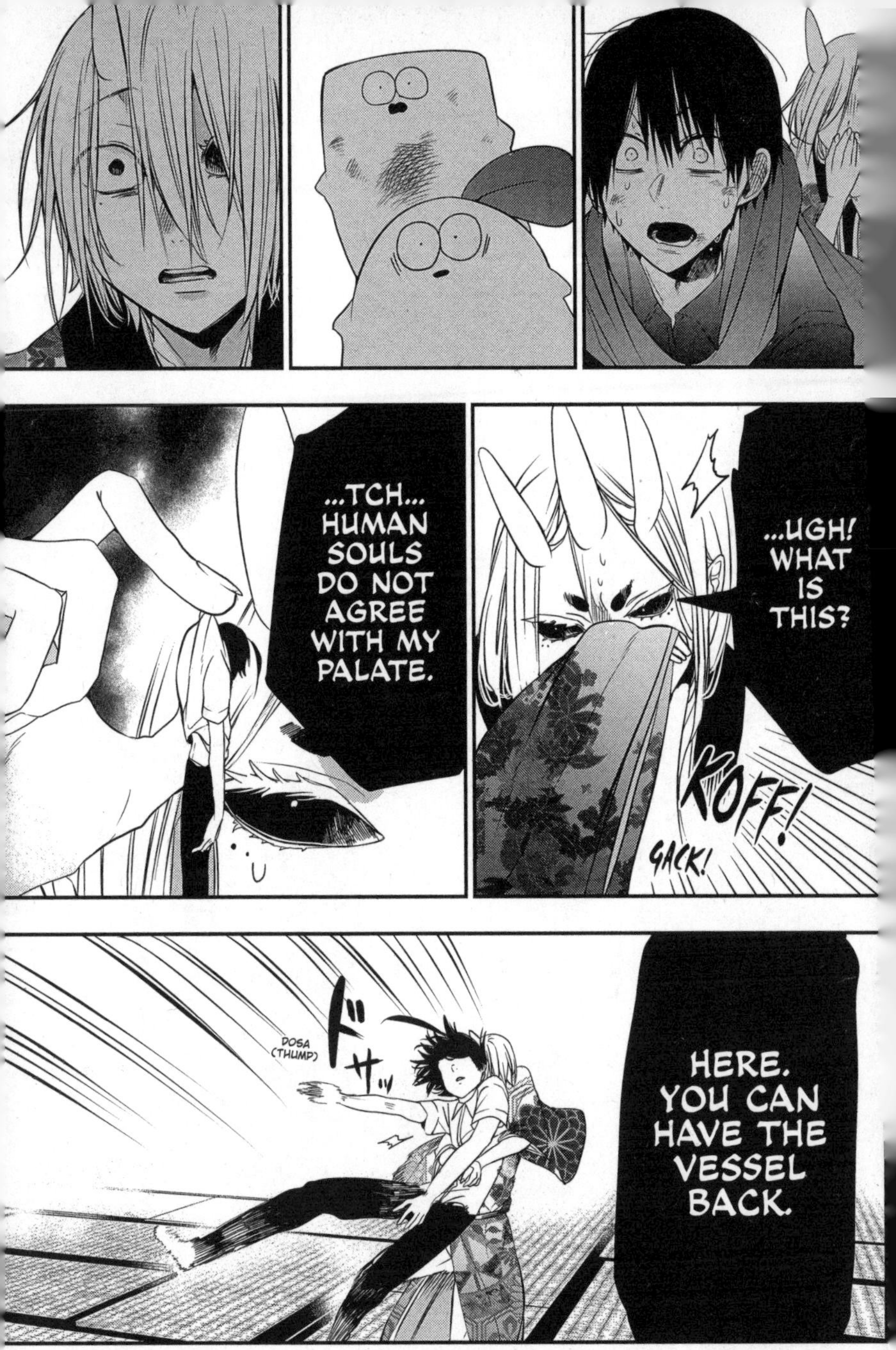
...UGH! WHAT IS THIS?
KOFF!
GACK!
...TCH... HUMAN SOULS DO NOT AGREE WITH MY PALATE.
HERE. YOU CAN HAVE THE VESSEL BACK.
DOSA (THUMP)

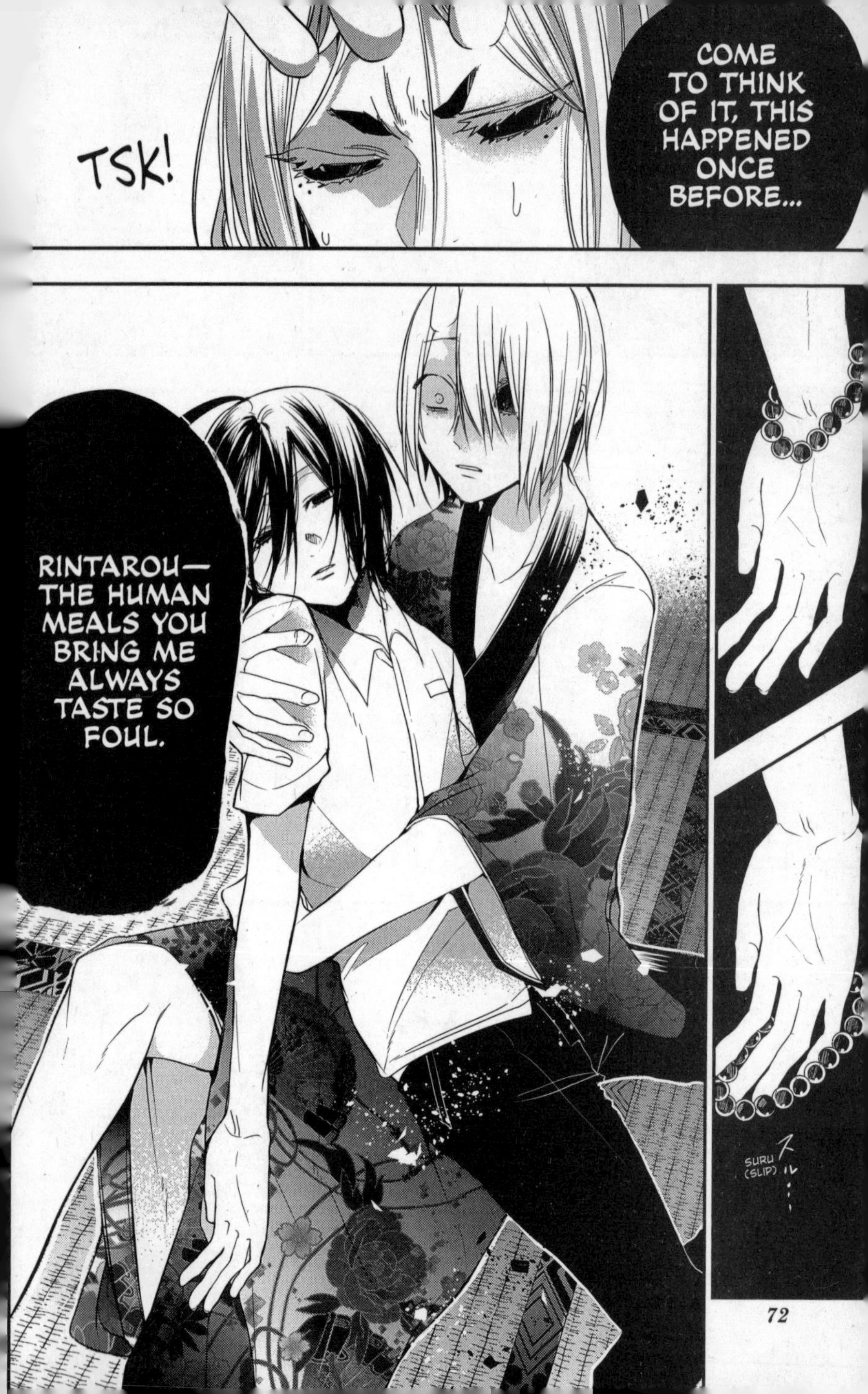
COME TO THINK OF IT, THIS HAPPENED ONCE BEFORE...
TSK!
SURU (SLIP)
RINTAROU— THE HUMAN MEALS YOU BRING ME ALWAYS TASTE SO FOUL.

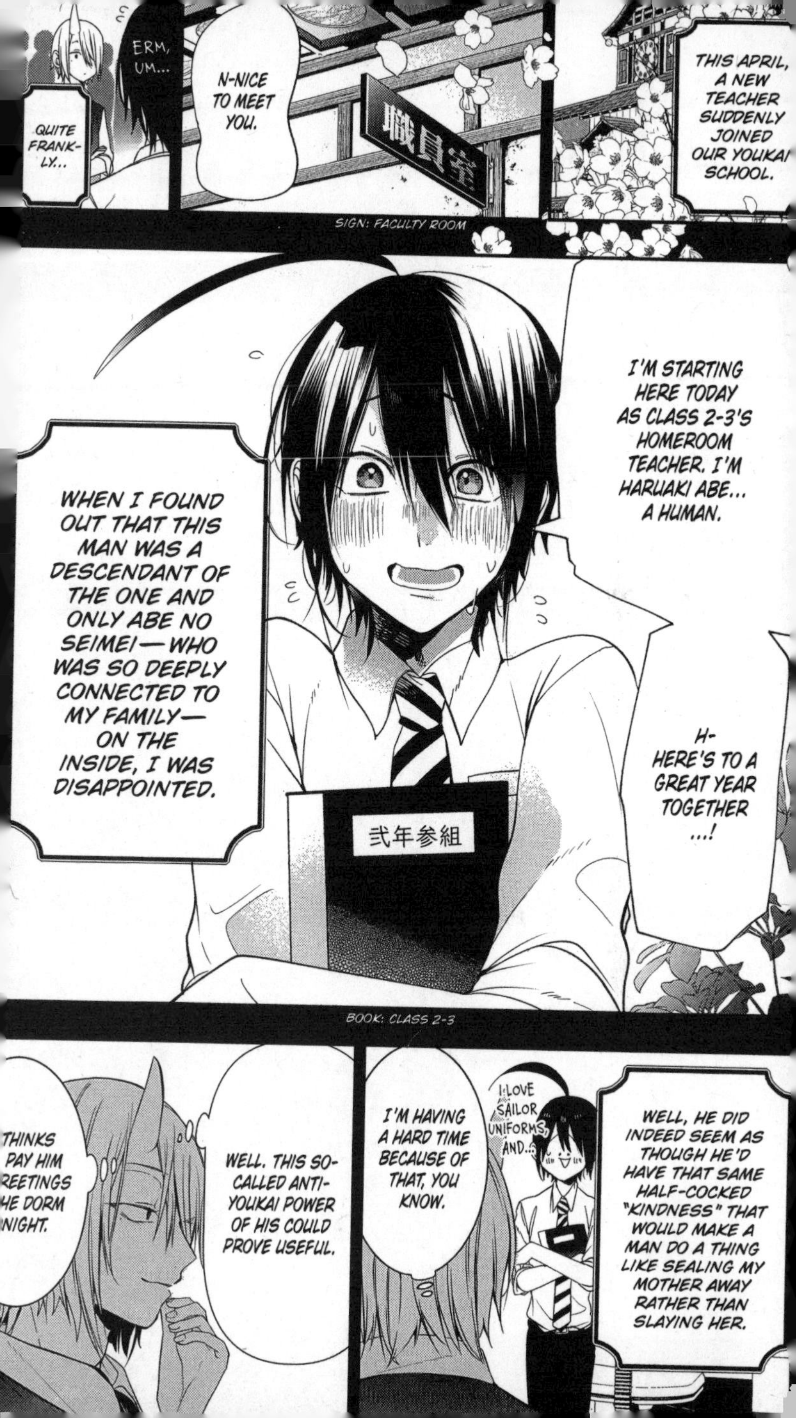

THIS APRIL, A NEW TEACHER SUDDENLY JOINED OUR YOUKAI SCHOOL.
職員室
N-NICE TO MEET YOU.
SIGN: FACULTY ROOM
ERM, UM...
QUITE FRANKLY...
I'M STARTING HERE TODAY AS CLASS 2-3'S HOMEROOM TEACHER. I'M HARUAKI ABE... A HUMAN.
H-HERE'S TO A GREAT YEAR TOGETHER...!
WHEN I FOUND OUT THAT THIS MAN WAS A DESCENDANT OF THE ONE AND ONLY ABE NO SEIMEI—WHO WAS SO DEEPLY CONNECTED TO MY FAMILY—ON THE INSIDE, I WAS DISAPPOINTED.
弐年参組
BOOK: CLASS 2-3
WELL, HE DID INDEED SEEM AS THOUGH HE'D HAVE THAT SAME HALF-COCKED "KINDNESS" THAT WOULD MAKE A MAN DO A THING LIKE SEALING MY MOTHER AWAY RATHER THAN SLAYING HER.
I LOVE SAILOR UNIFORMS, AND...
I'M HAVING A HARD TIME BECAUSE OF THAT, YOU KNOW.
WELL. THIS SO-CALLED ANTI-YOUKAI POWER OF HIS COULD PROVE USEFUL.
THINKS
PAY HIM
REETINGS
HE DORM
NIGHT.

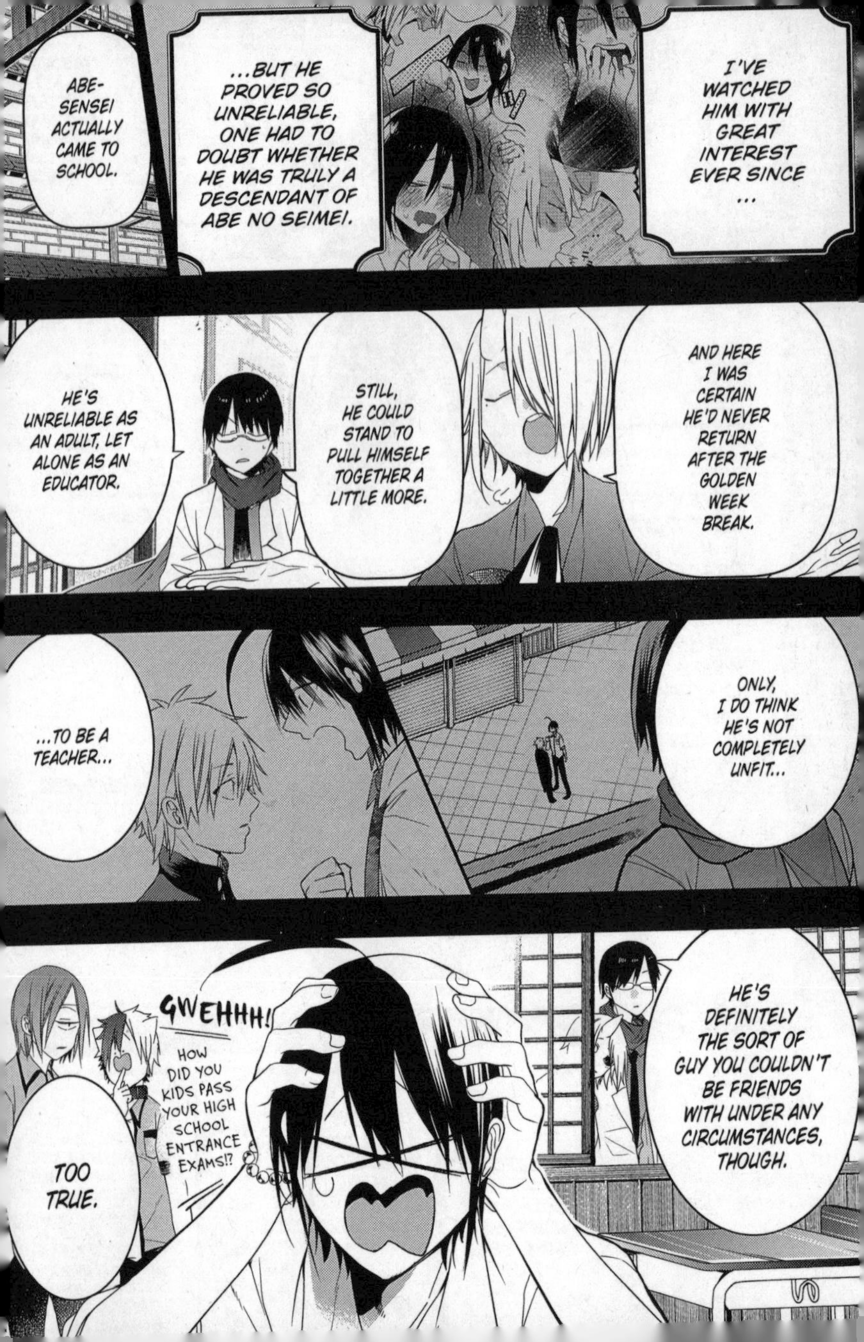
I'VE WATCHED HIM WITH GREAT INTEREST EVER SINCE ...
...BUT HE PROVED SO UNRELIABLE, ONE HAD TO DOUBT WHETHER HE WAS TRULY A DESCENDANT OF ABE NO SEIMEI.
ABE-SENSEI ACTUALLY CAME TO SCHOOL.
AND HERE I WAS CERTAIN HE'D NEVER RETURN AFTER THE GOLDEN WEEK BREAK.
STILL, HE COULD STAND TO PULL HIMSELF TOGETHER A LITTLE MORE.
HE'S UNRELIABLE AS AN ADULT, LET ALONE AS AN EDUCATOR.
ONLY, I DO THINK HE'S NOT COMPLETELY UNFIT...
...TO BE A TEACHER...
HE'S DEFINITELY THE SORT OF GUY YOU COULDN'T BE FRIENDS WITH UNDER ANY CIRCUMSTANCES, THOUGH.
GWEHHH!
HOW DID YOU KIDS PASS YOUR HIGH SCHOOL ENTRANCE EXAMS!?
TOO TRUE.

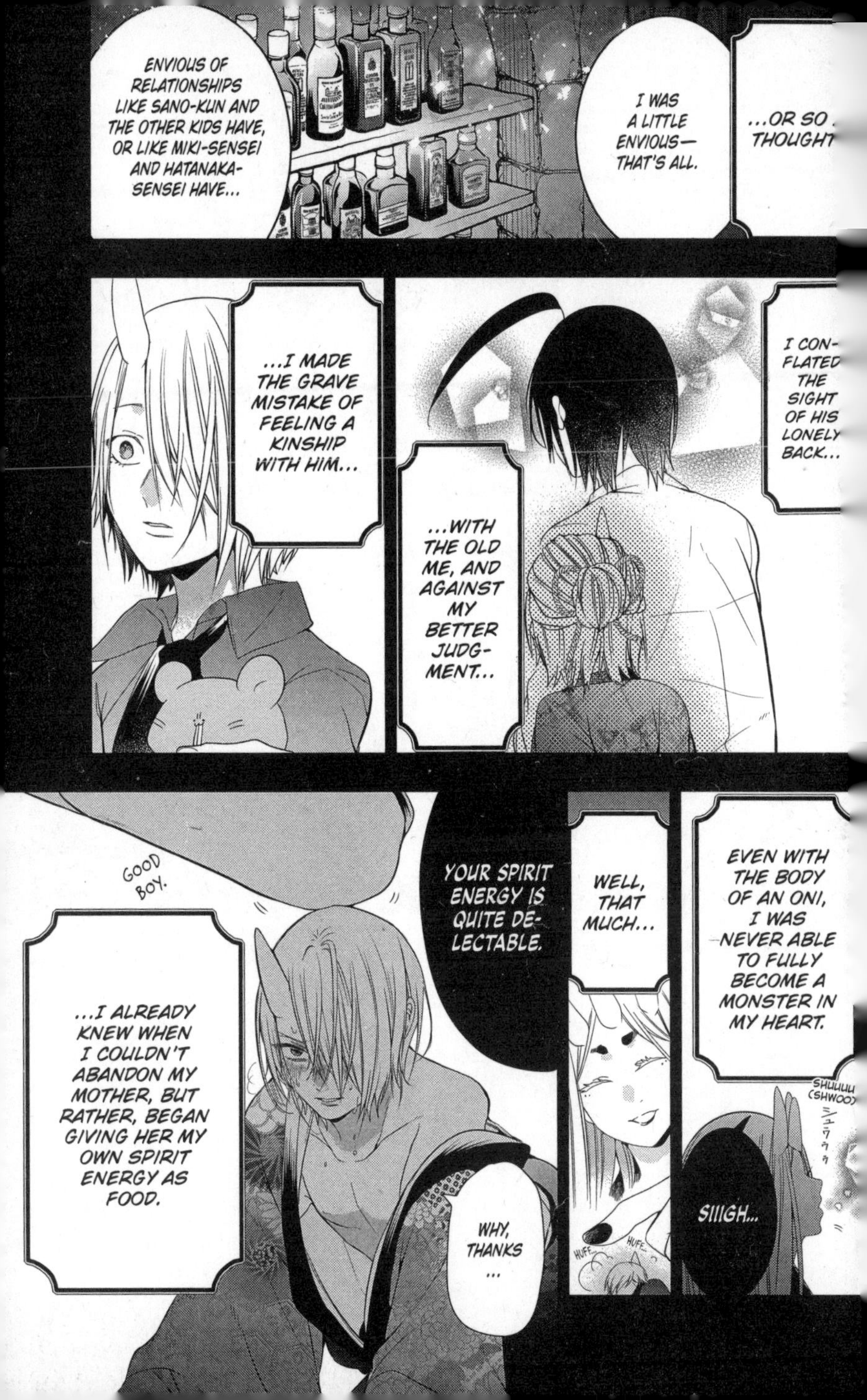
...OR SO
THOUGHT
I WAS A LITTLE ENVIOUS—THAT'S ALL.
ENVIOUS OF RELATIONSHIPS LIKE SANO-KUN AND THE OTHER KIDS HAVE, OR LIKE MIKI-SENSEI AND HATANAKA-SENSEI HAVE...
I CON-FLATED THE SIGHT OF HIS LONELY BACK...
...WITH THE OLD ME, AND AGAINST MY BETTER JUDG-MENT...
...I MADE THE GRAVE MISTAKE OF FEELING A KINSHIP WITH HIM...
EVEN WITH THE BODY OF AN ONI, I WAS NEVER ABLE TO FULLY BECOME A MONSTER IN MY HEART.
SHUUUU (SHWOO)
SIIIGH...
WELL, THAT MUCH...
HUFF... HUFF...
YOUR SPIRIT ENERGY IS QUITE DE-LECTABLE.
GOOD BOY.
...I ALREADY KNEW WHEN I COULDN'T ABANDON MY MOTHER, BUT RATHER, BEGAN GIVING HER MY OWN SPIRIT ENERGY AS FOOD.
WHY, THANKS ...

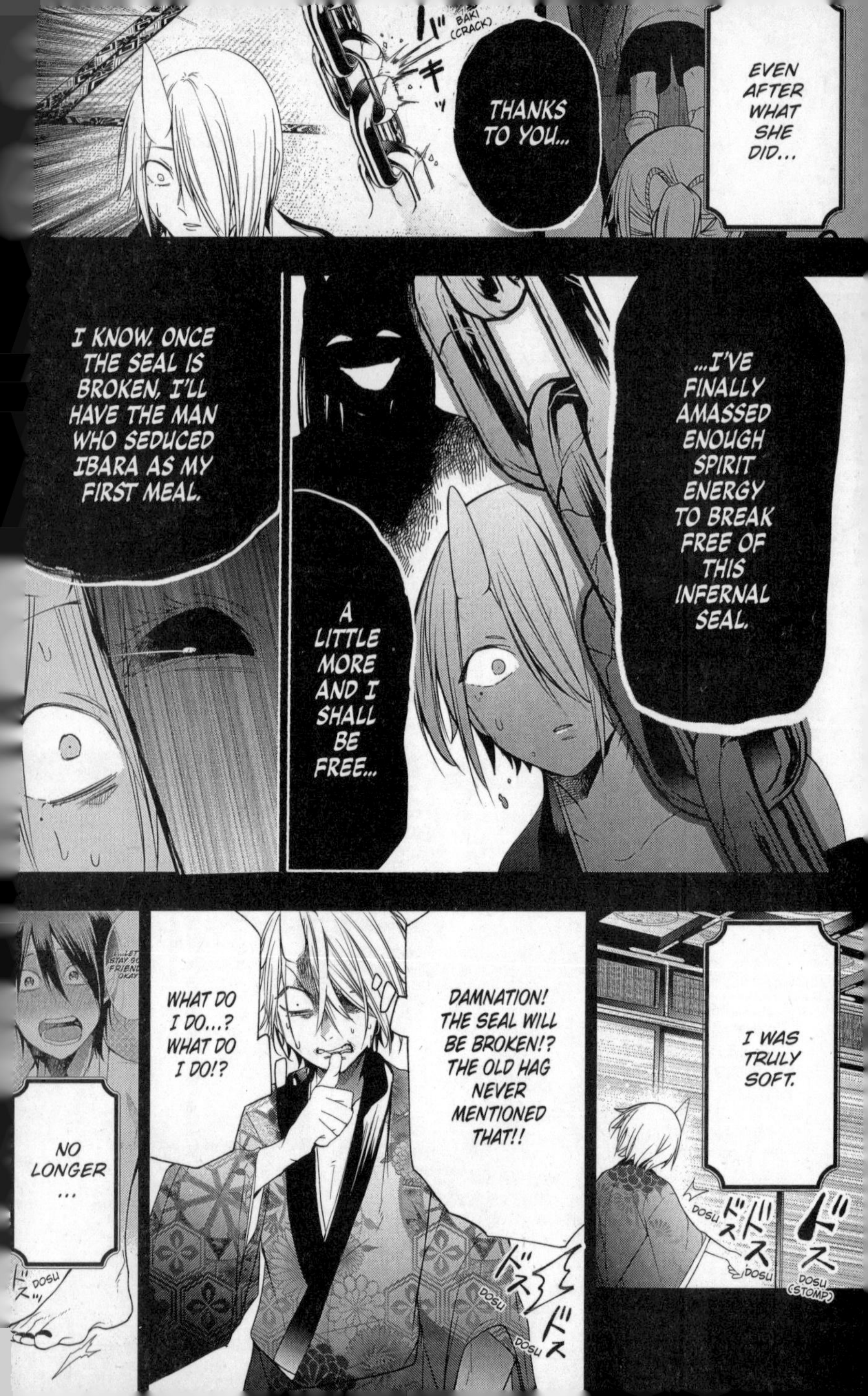
EVEN AFTER WHAT SHE DID...
THANKS TO YOU...
BAKI (CRACK)
...I'VE FINALLY AMASSED ENOUGH SPIRIT ENERGY TO BREAK FREE OF THIS INFERNAL SEAL.
A LITTLE MORE AND I SHALL BE FREE...
I KNOW. ONCE THE SEAL IS BROKEN, I'LL HAVE THE MAN WHO SEDUCED IBARA AS MY FIRST MEAL.
I WAS TRULY SOFT.
DOSU (STOMP)
DOSU
DOSU
DAMNATION! THE SEAL WILL BE BROKEN!? THE OLD HAG NEVER MENTIONED THAT!!
WHAT DO I DO...? WHAT DO I DO!?
DOSU
DOSU
NO LONGER...
DOSU

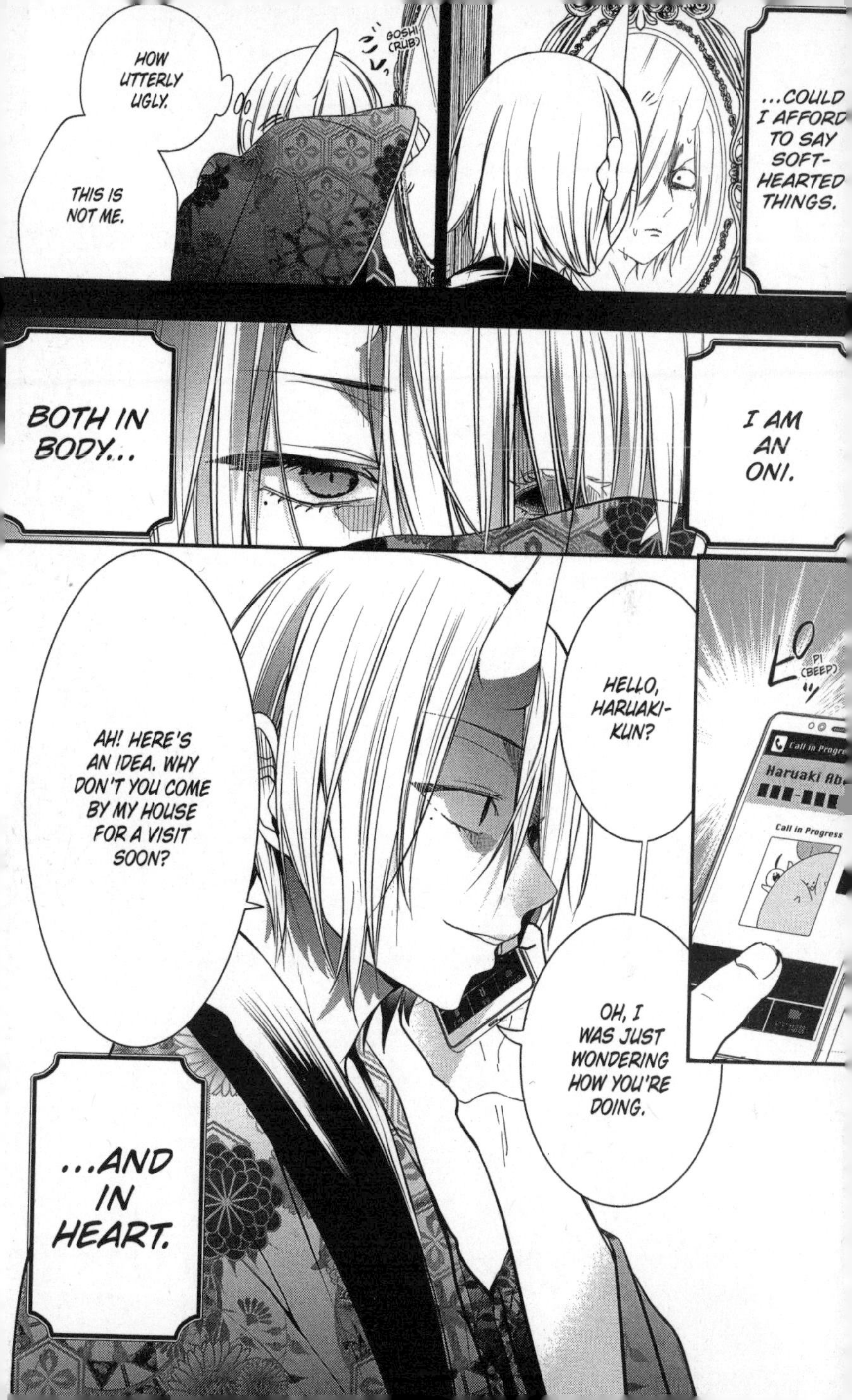
...COULD I AFFORD TO SAY SOFT-HEARTED THINGS.
GOSHI (RUB)
HOW UTTERLY UGLY.
THIS IS NOT ME.
I AM AN ONI.
BOTH IN BODY...
PI (BEEP)
Call in Progress
HELLO, HARUAKI-KUN?
OH, I WAS JUST WONDERING HOW YOU'RE DOING.
AH! HERE'S AN IDEA. WHY DON'T YOU COME BY MY HOUSE FOR A VISIT SOON?
...AND IN HEART.

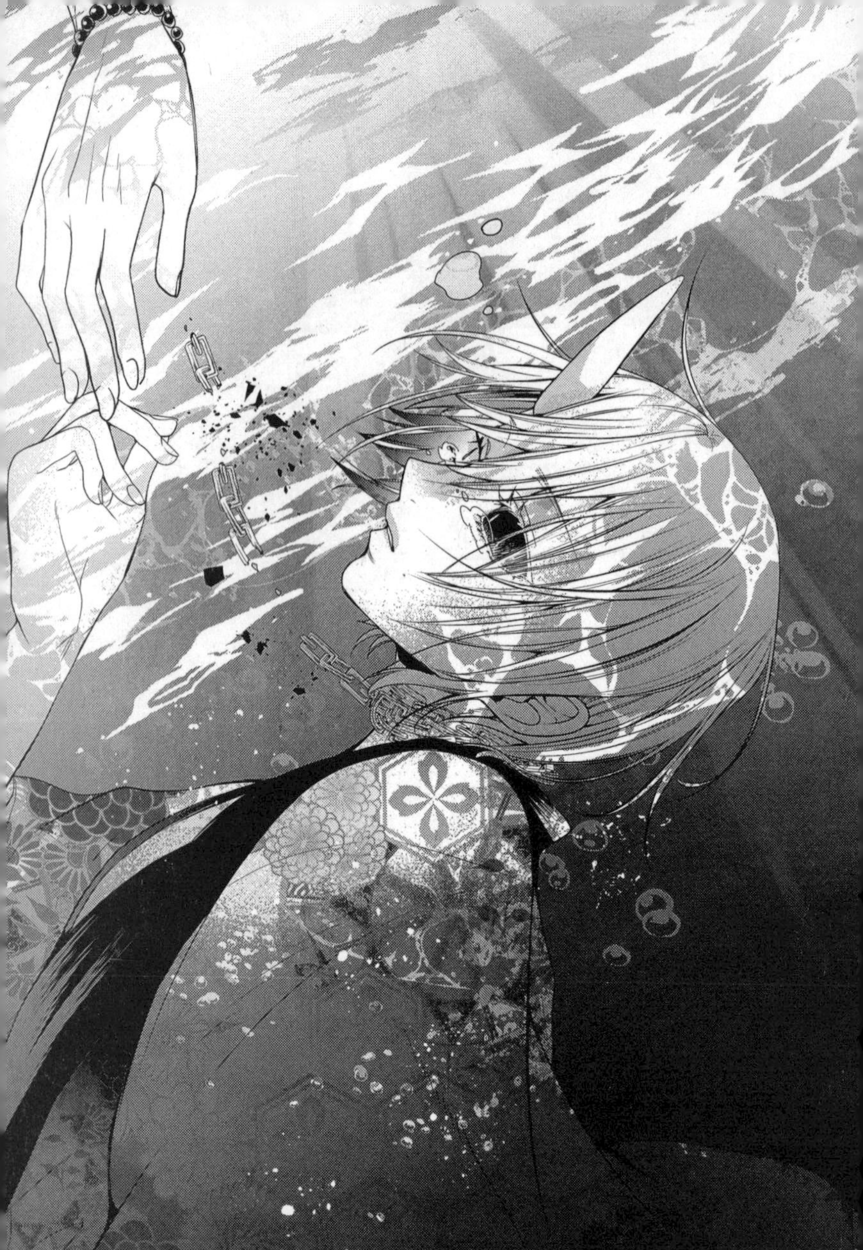

Forty-Ninth Period Abe no Seimei, Haruaki Abe, and Shutendouji (Part 3)

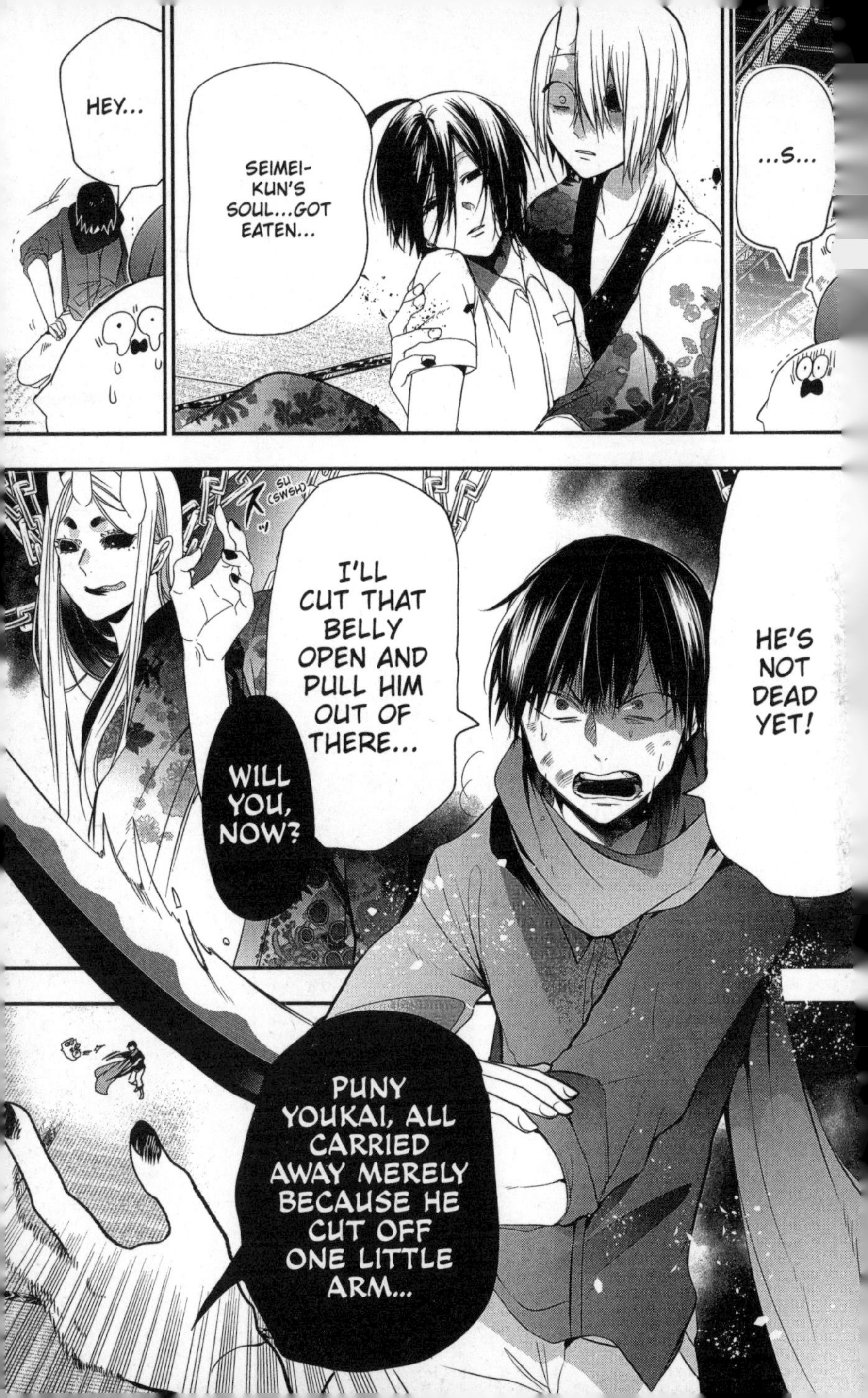
...S...
SEIMEI-KUN'S SOUL...GOT EATEN...
HEY...
HE'S NOT DEAD YET!
I'LL CUT THAT BELLY OPEN AND PULL HIM OUT OF THERE...
SU (SWSH)
WILL YOU, NOW?
PUNY YOUKAI, ALL CARRIED AWAY MERELY BECAUSE HE CUT OFF ONE LITTLE ARM...

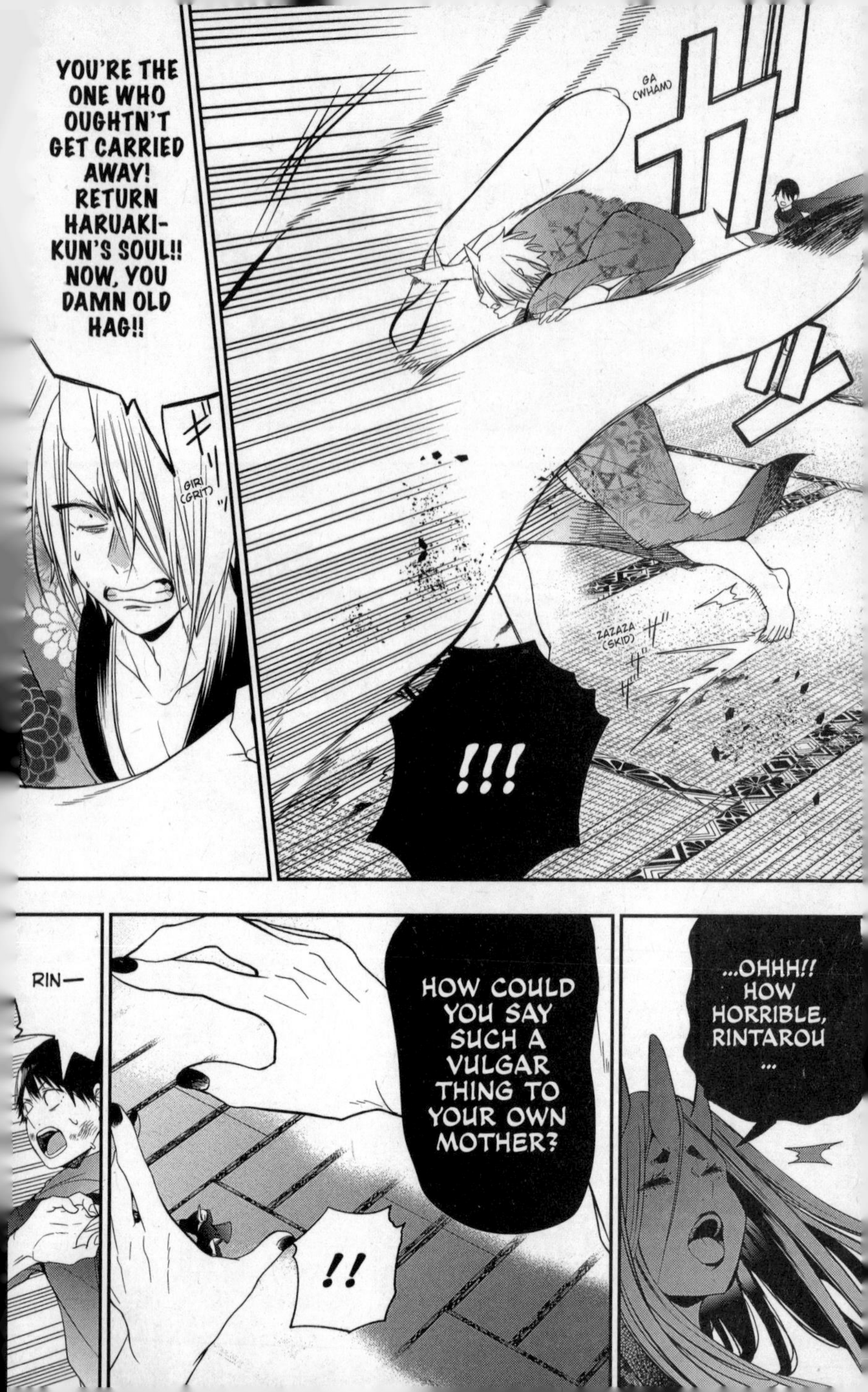
GA (WHAM)
ZAZAZA (SKID)
!!!
YOU'RE THE ONE WHO OUGHTN'T GET CARRIED AWAY! RETURN HARUAKI-KUN'S SOUL!! NOW, YOU DAMN OLD HAG!!
GIRI (GRIT)
...OHHH!! HOW HORRIBLE, RINTAROU ...
HOW COULD YOU SAY SUCH A VULGAR THING TO YOUR OWN MOTHER?
!!
RIN—

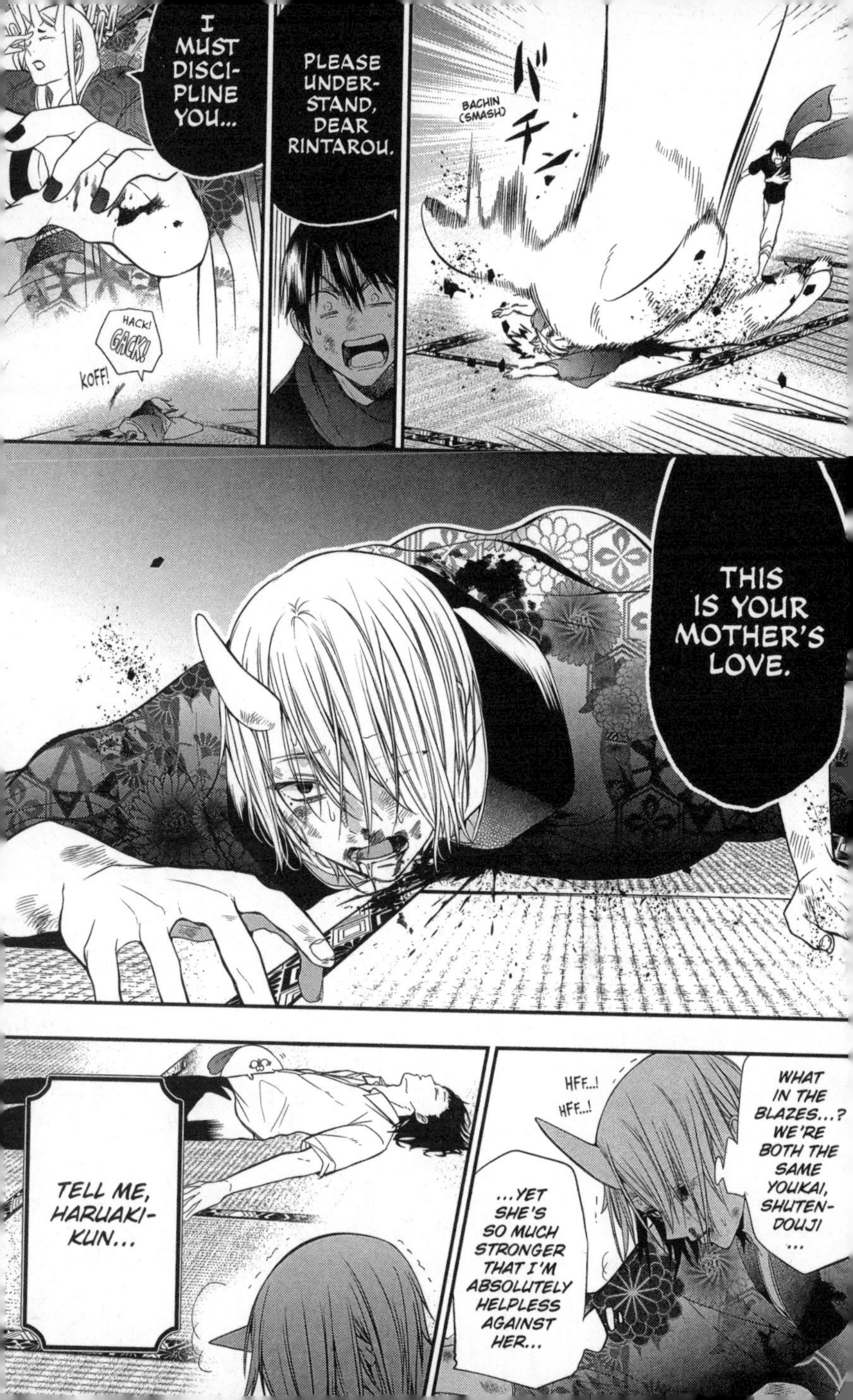
バチン
BACHIN (SMASH)
PLEASE UNDERSTAND, DEAR RINTAROU.
I MUST DISCIPLINE YOU...
HACK! GACK!
KOFF!
THIS IS YOUR MOTHER'S LOVE.
WHAT IN THE BLAZES...? WE'RE BOTH THE SAME YOUKAI, SHUTEN-DOUJI...
HFF...! HFF...!
...YET SHE'S SO MUCH STRONGER THAT I'M ABSOLUTELY HELPLESS AGAINST HER...
TELL ME, HARUAKI-KUN...

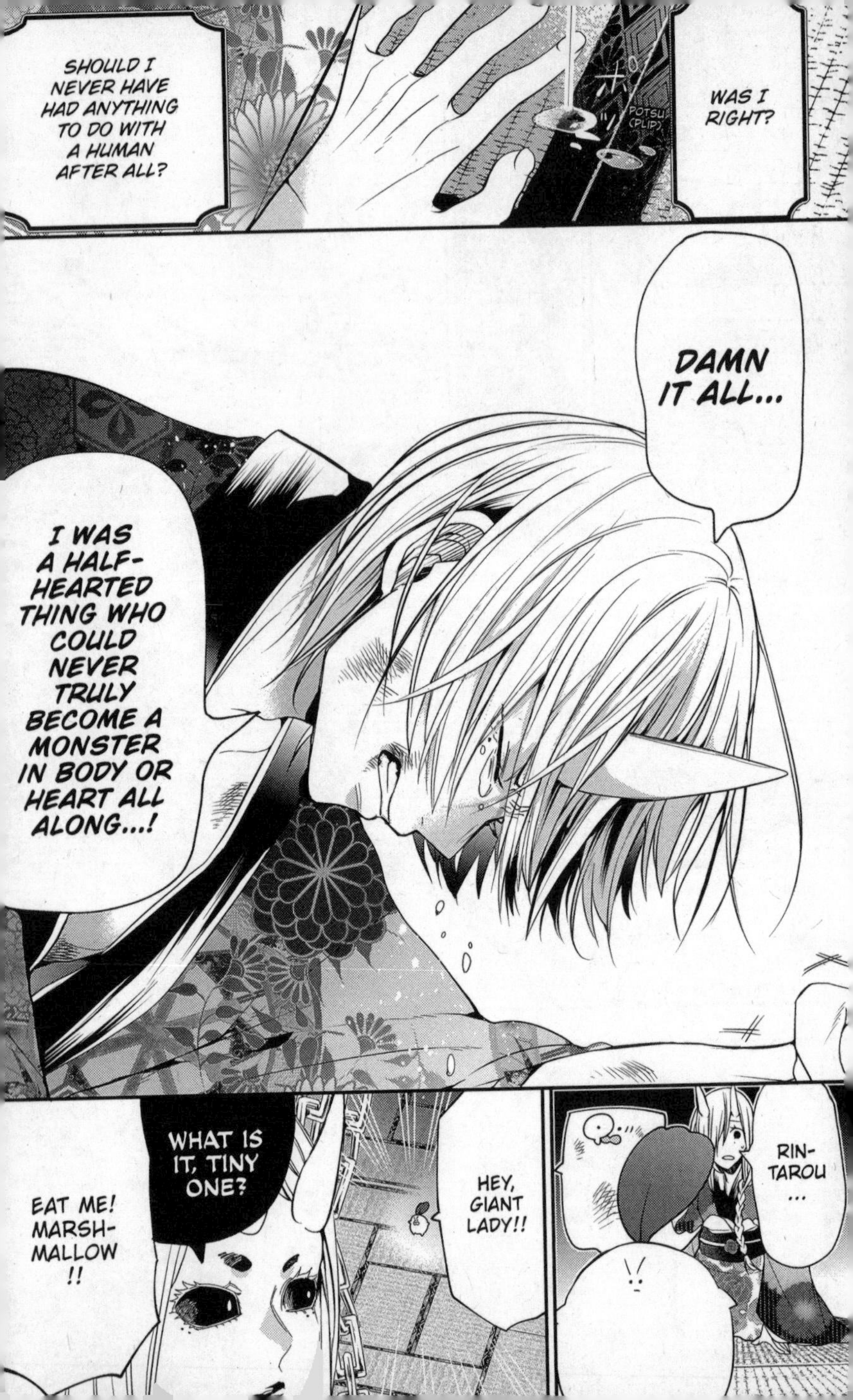
WAS I RIGHT?
POTSU (PLIP)
SHOULD I NEVER HAVE HAD ANYTHING TO DO WITH A HUMAN AFTER ALL?
DAMN IT ALL...
I WAS A HALF-HEARTED THING WHO COULD NEVER TRULY BECOME A MONSTER IN BODY OR HEART ALL ALONG...!
RIN-TAROU ...
HEY, GIANT LADY!!
WHAT IS IT, TINY ONE?
EAT ME! MARSHMALLOW !!

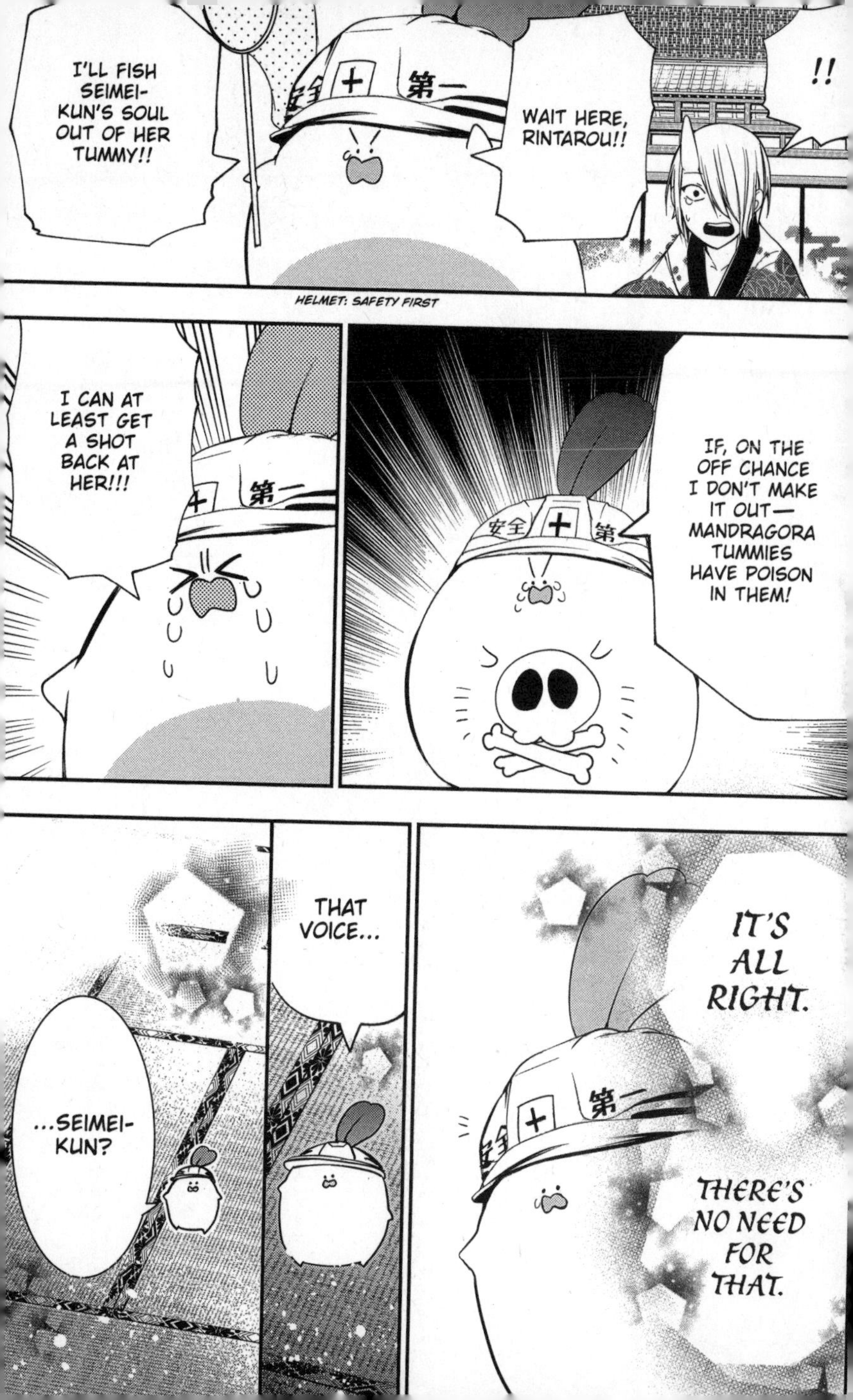
!!
WAIT HERE, RINTAROU!!
I'LL FISH SEIMEI-KUN'S SOUL OUT OF HER TUMMY!!
HELMET: SAFETY FIRST
IF, ON THE OFF CHANCE I DON'T MAKE IT OUT— MANDRAGORA TUMMIES HAVE POISON IN THEM!
I CAN AT LEAST GET A SHOT BACK AT HER!!!
IT'S ALL RIGHT.
THERE'S NO NEED FOR THAT.
THAT VOICE...
...SEIMEI-KUN?

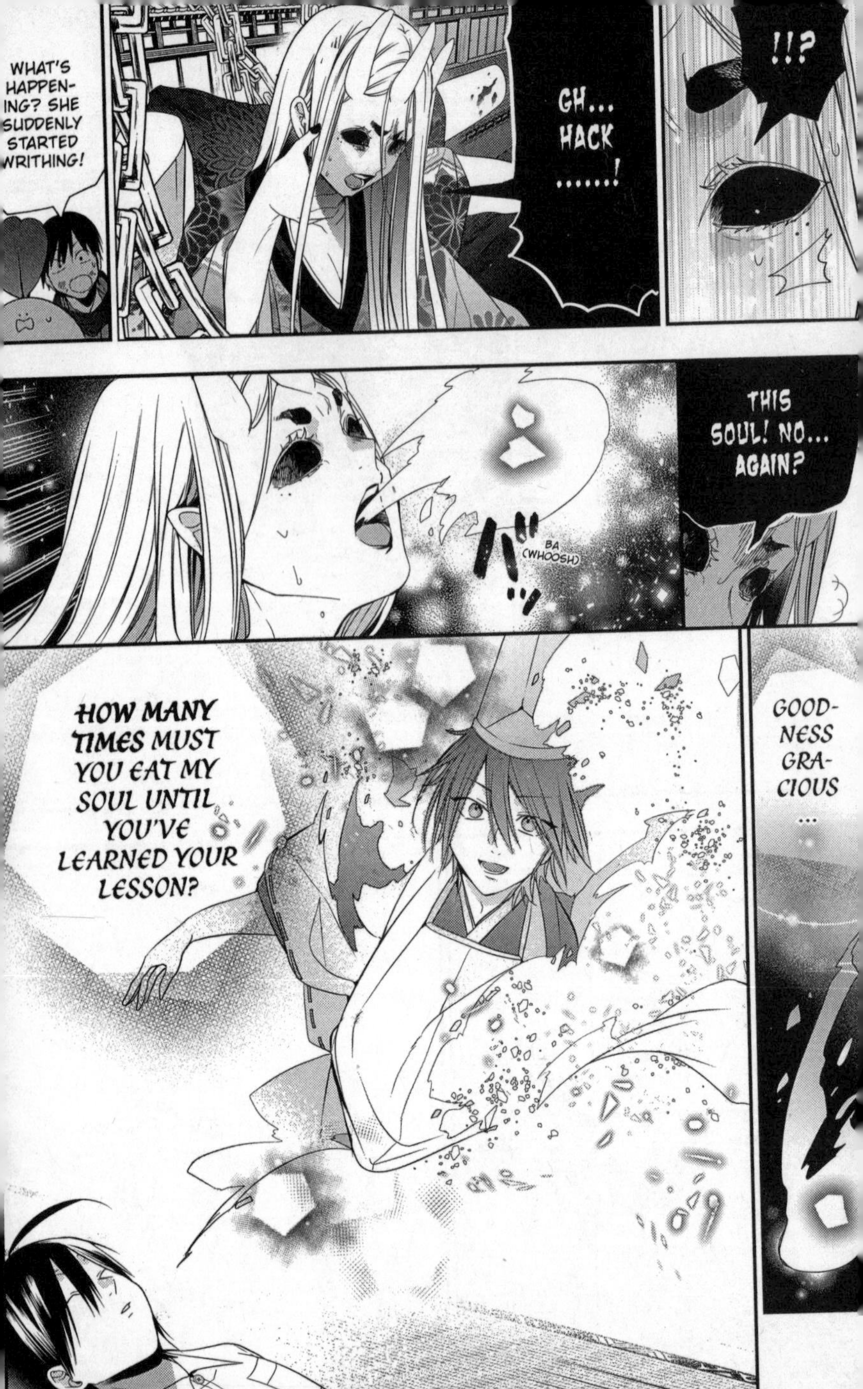
!!?
GH... HACK ......!
WHAT'S HAPPEN-ING? SHE SUDDENLY STARTED WRITHING!
THIS SOUL! NO... AGAIN?
BA (WHOOSH)
GOOD-NESS GRA-CIOUS ...
HOW MANY TIMES MUST YOU EAT MY SOUL UNTIL YOU'VE LEARNED YOUR LESSON?

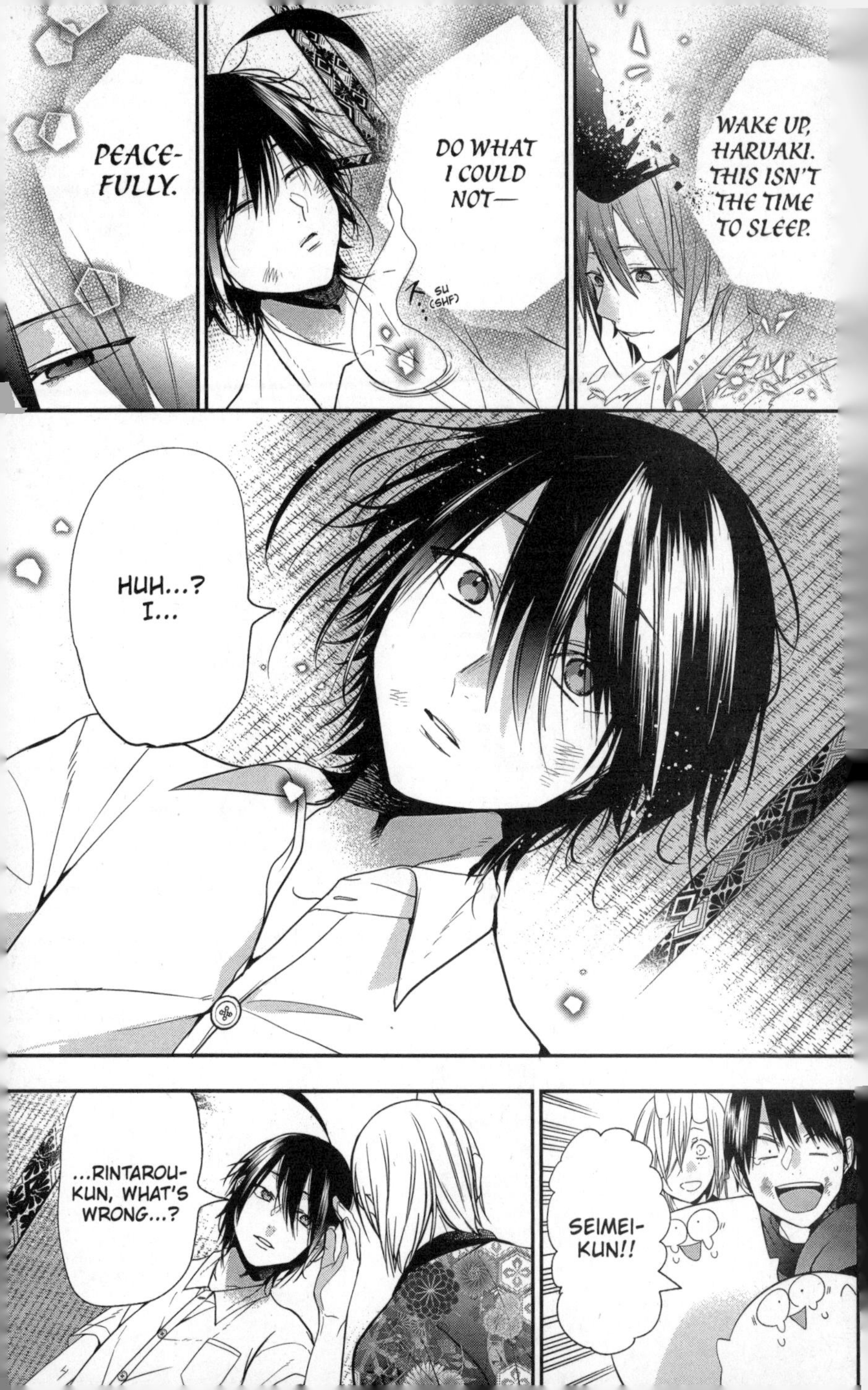
WAKE UP, HARUAKI. THIS ISN'T THE TIME TO SLEEP.
DO WHAT I COULD NOT—
SU (SHF)
PEACE-FULLY.
HUH...? I...
SEIMEI-KUN!!
...RINTAROU-KUN, WHAT'S WRONG...?

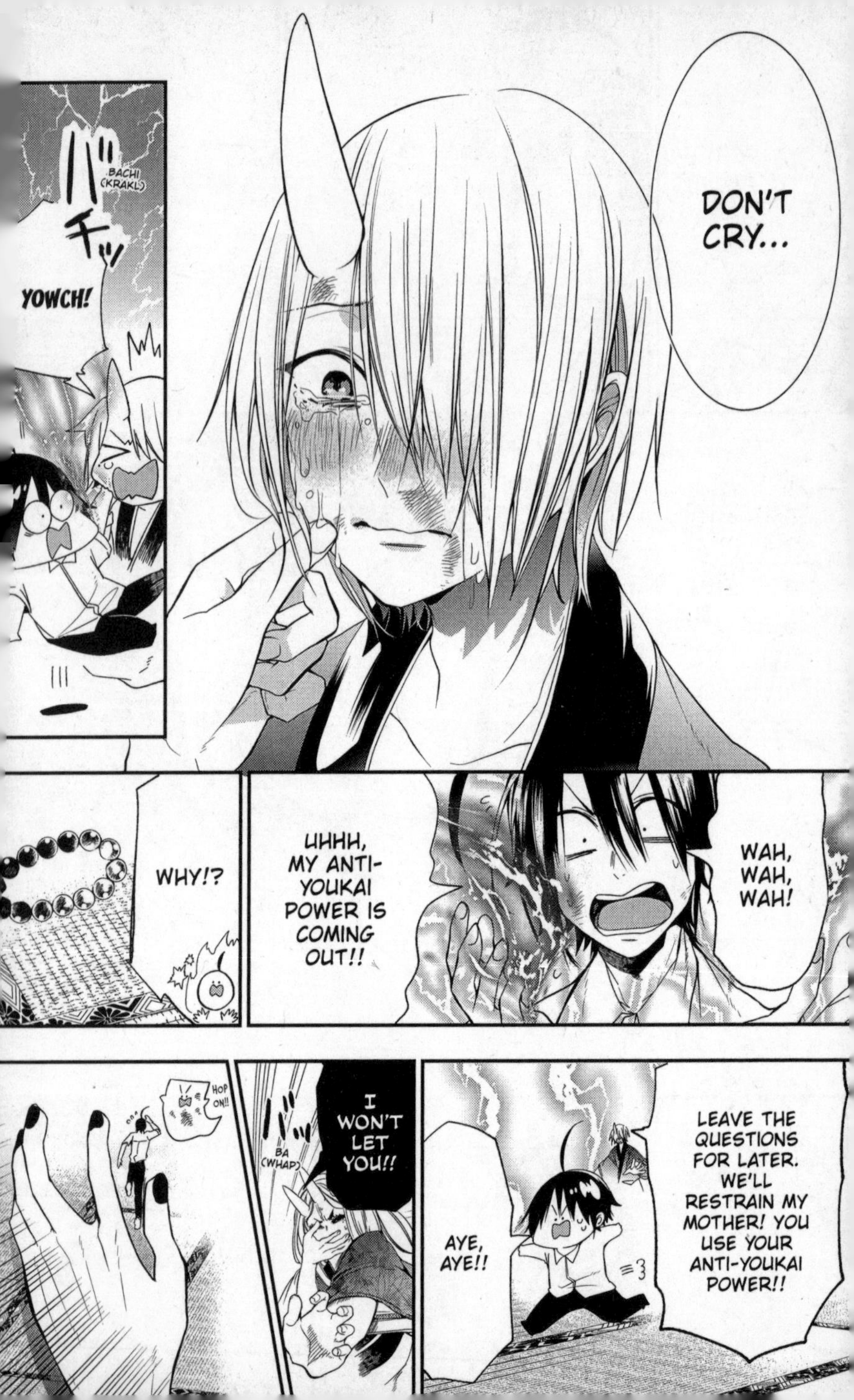
DON'T CRY...
バチッ
BACHI (KRAKL)
YOWCH!
WAH, WAH, WAH!
UHHH, MY ANTI-YOUKAI POWER IS COMING OUT!!
WHY!?
LEAVE THE QUESTIONS FOR LATER. WE'LL RESTRAIN MY MOTHER! YOU USE YOUR ANTI-YOUKAI POWER!!
AYE, AYE!!
I WON'T LET YOU!!
BA (WHAP)
HOP ON!!

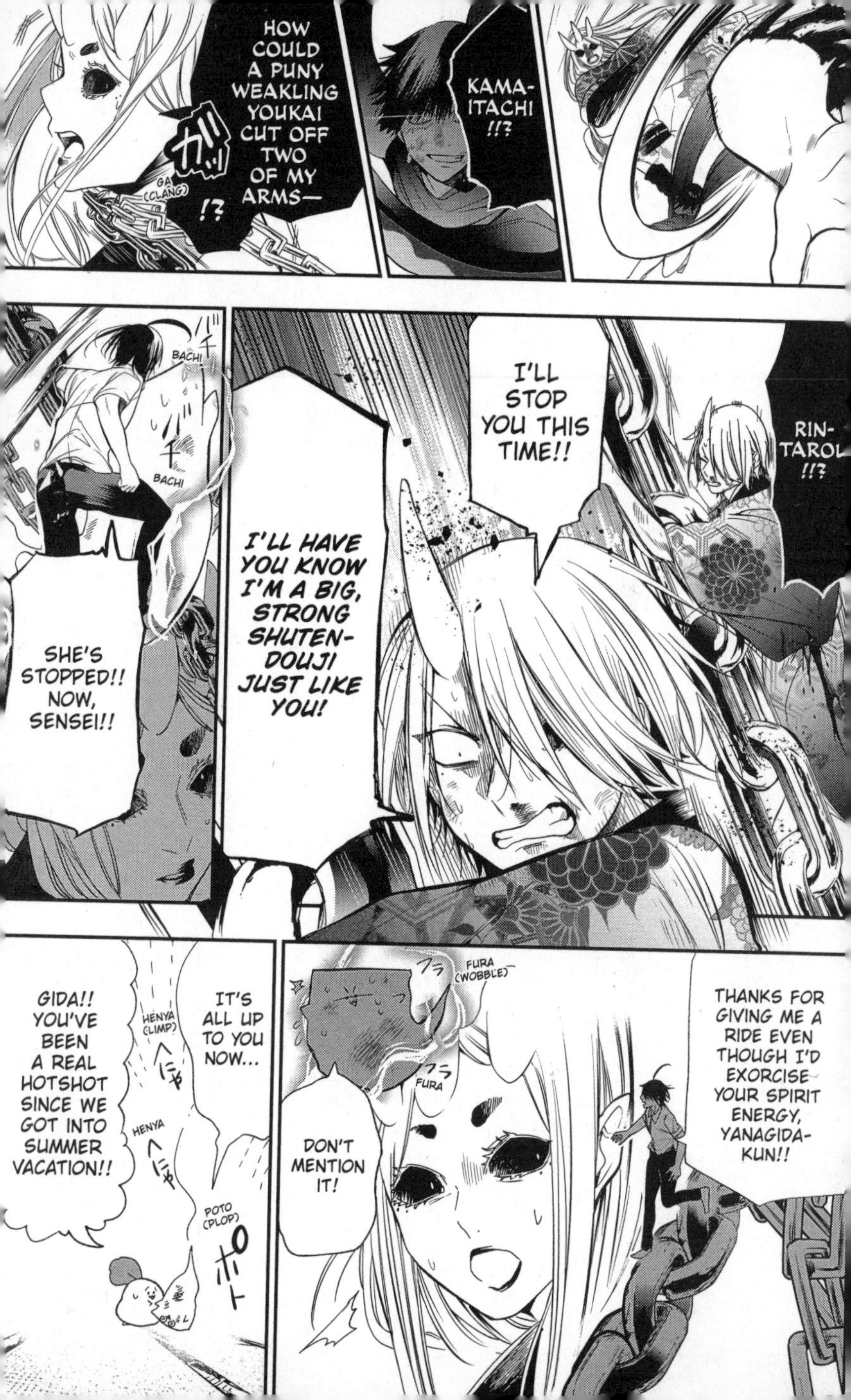
KAMA-ITACHI!!?
HOW COULD A PUNY WEAKLING YOUKAI CUT OFF TWO OF MY ARMS—
GA (CLANG)
!?
RIN-TAROU!!?
I'LL STOP YOU THIS TIME!!
I'LL HAVE YOU KNOW I'M A BIG, STRONG SHUTEN-DOUJI JUST LIKE YOU!
BACHI!
BACHI
SHE'S STOPPED!! NOW, SENSEI!!
THANKS FOR GIVING ME A RIDE EVEN THOUGH I'D EXORCISE YOUR SPIRIT ENERGY, YANAGIDA-KUN!!
FURA (WOBBLE)
FURA
DON'T MENTION IT!
IT'S ALL UP TO YOU NOW...
HENYA (LIMP)
HENYA
GIDA!! YOU'VE BEEN A REAL HOTSHOT SINCE WE GOT INTO SUMMER VACATION!!
POTO (PLOP)

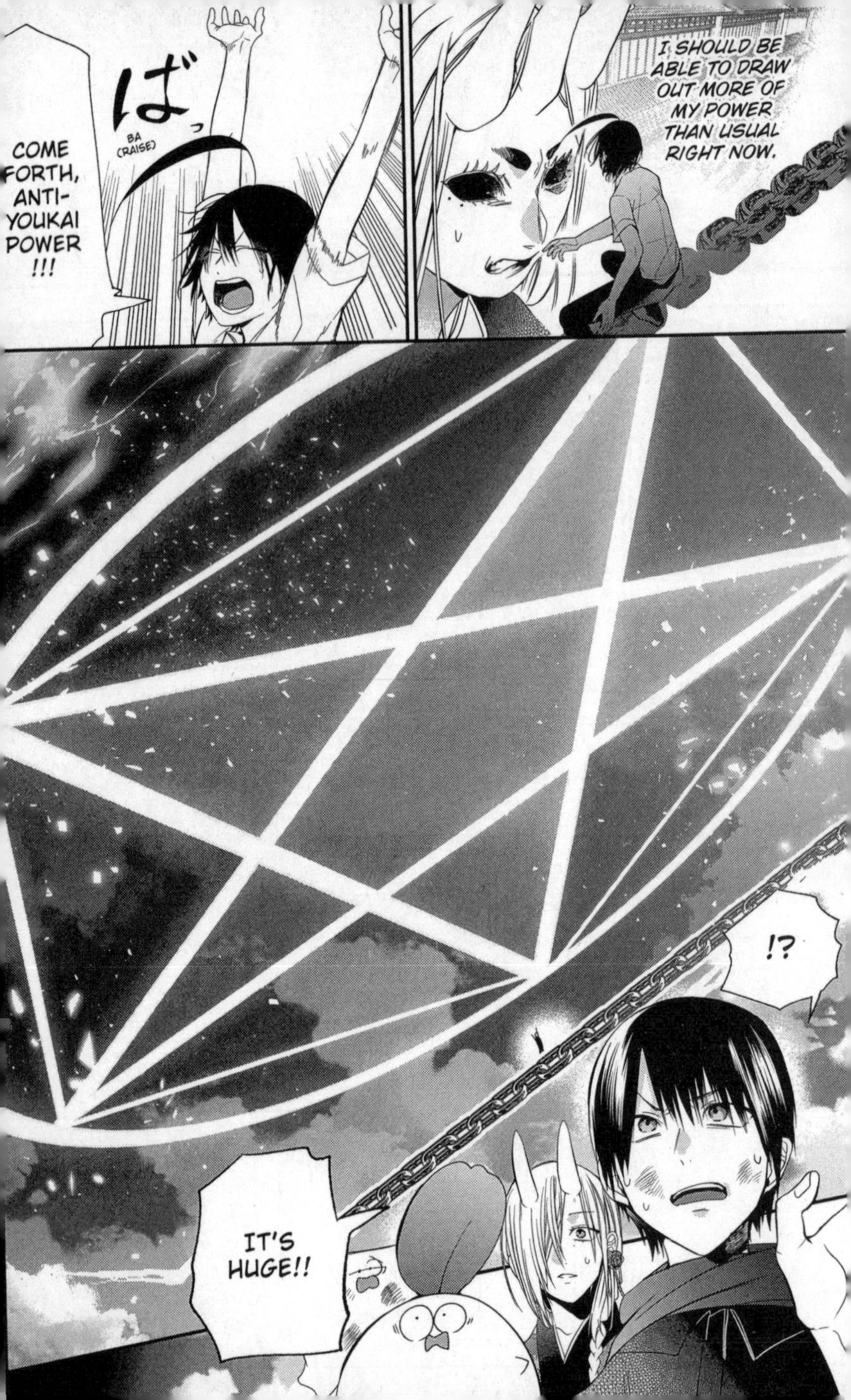
I SHOULD BE ABLE TO DRAW OUT MORE OF MY POWER THAN USUAL RIGHT NOW.
ばっ
BA (RAISE)
COME FORTH, ANTI-YOUKAI POWER!!!
!?
IT'S HUGE!!

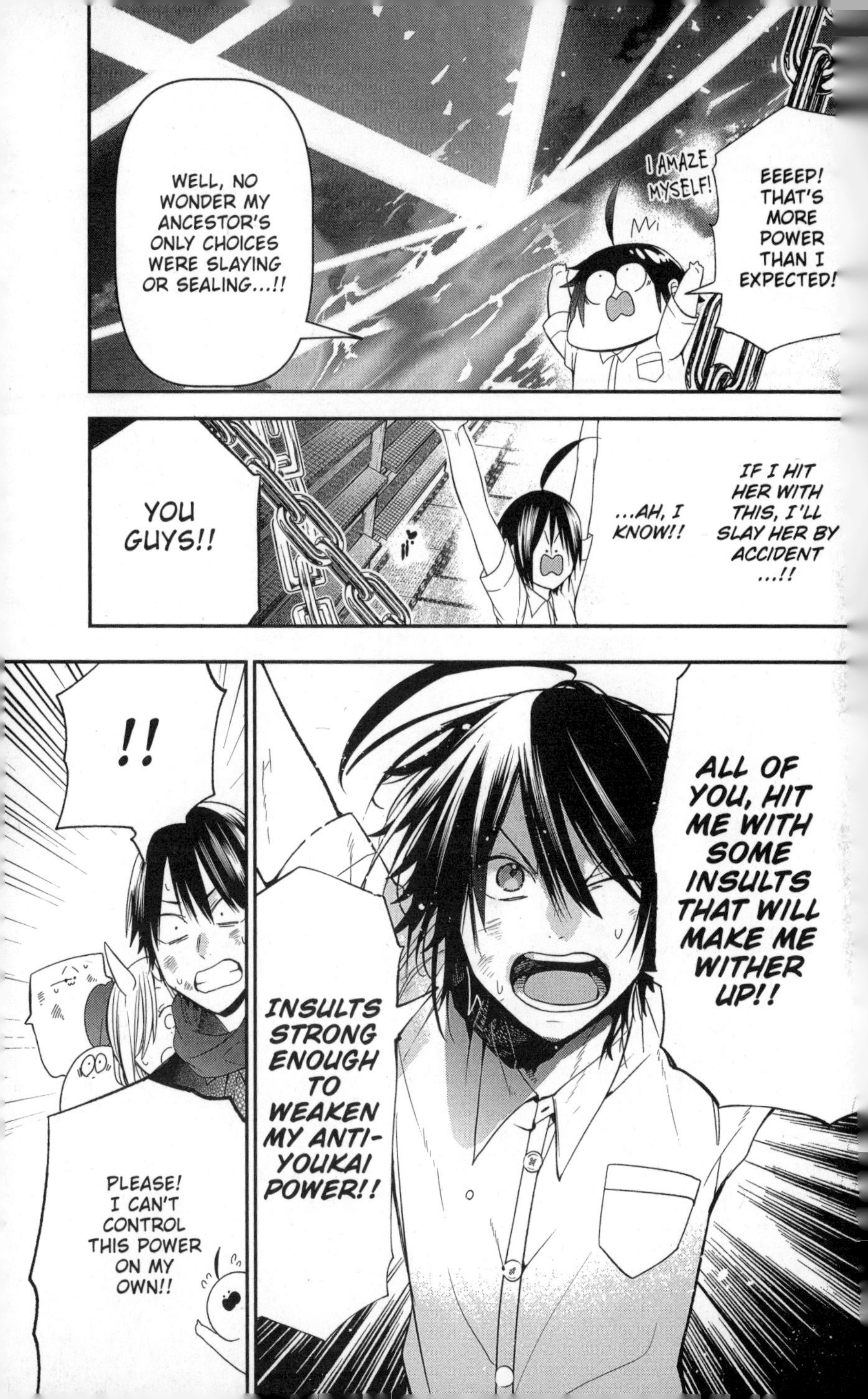
EEEEP! THAT'S MORE POWER THAN I EXPECTED!
I AMAZE MYSELF!
WELL, NO WONDER MY ANCESTOR'S ONLY CHOICES WERE SLAYING OR SEALING...!!
IF I HIT HER WITH THIS, I'LL SLAY HER BY ACCIDENT ...!!
...AH, I KNOW!!
YOU GUYS!!
ALL OF YOU, HIT ME WITH SOME INSULTS THAT WILL MAKE ME WITHER UP!!
INSULTS STRONG ENOUGH TO WEAKEN MY ANTI-YOUKAI POWER!!
PLEASE! I CAN'T CONTROL THIS POWER ON MY OWN!!
!!

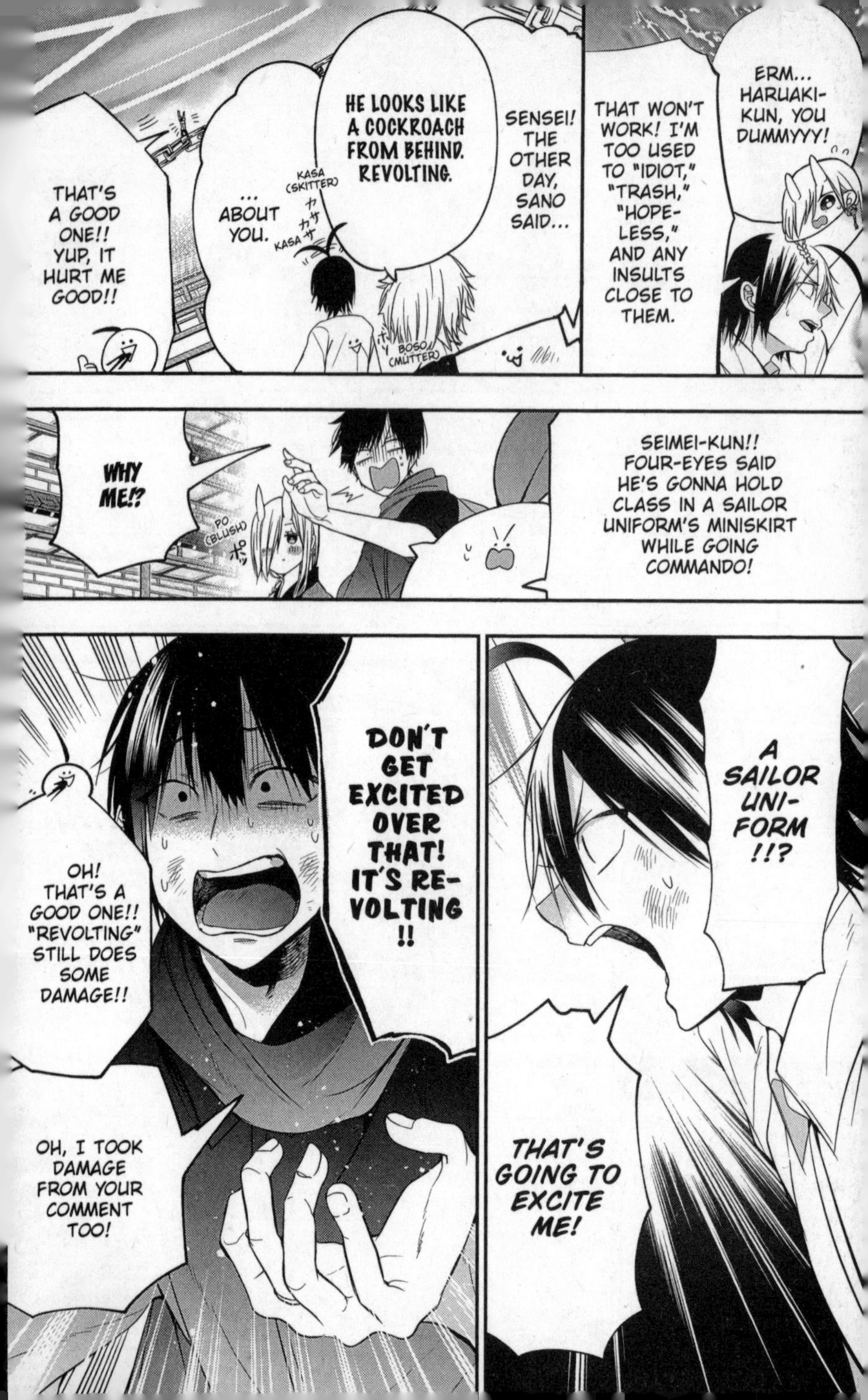
ERM... HARUAKI-KUN, YOU DUMMYYY!
THAT WON'T WORK! I'M TOO USED TO "IDIOT," "TRASH," "HOPE-LESS," AND ANY INSULTS CLOSE TO THEM.
SENSEI! THE OTHER DAY, SANO SAID...
HE LOOKS LIKE A COCKROACH FROM BEHIND. REVOLTING.
KASA (SKITTER) KASA
... ABOUT YOU.
BOSO (MUTTER)
THAT'S A GOOD ONE!! YUP, IT HURT ME GOOD!!
SEIMEI-KUN!! FOUR-EYES SAID HE'S GONNA HOLD CLASS IN A SAILOR UNIFORM'S MINISKIRT WHILE GOING COMMANDO!
PO (BLUSH)
WHY ME!?
A SAILOR UNI-FORM!!?
THAT'S GOING TO EXCITE ME!
DON'T GET EXCITED OVER THAT! IT'S RE-VOLTING!!
OH! THAT'S A GOOD ONE!! "REVOLTING" STILL DOES SOME DAMAGE!!
OH, I TOOK DAMAGE FROM YOUR COMMENT TOO!

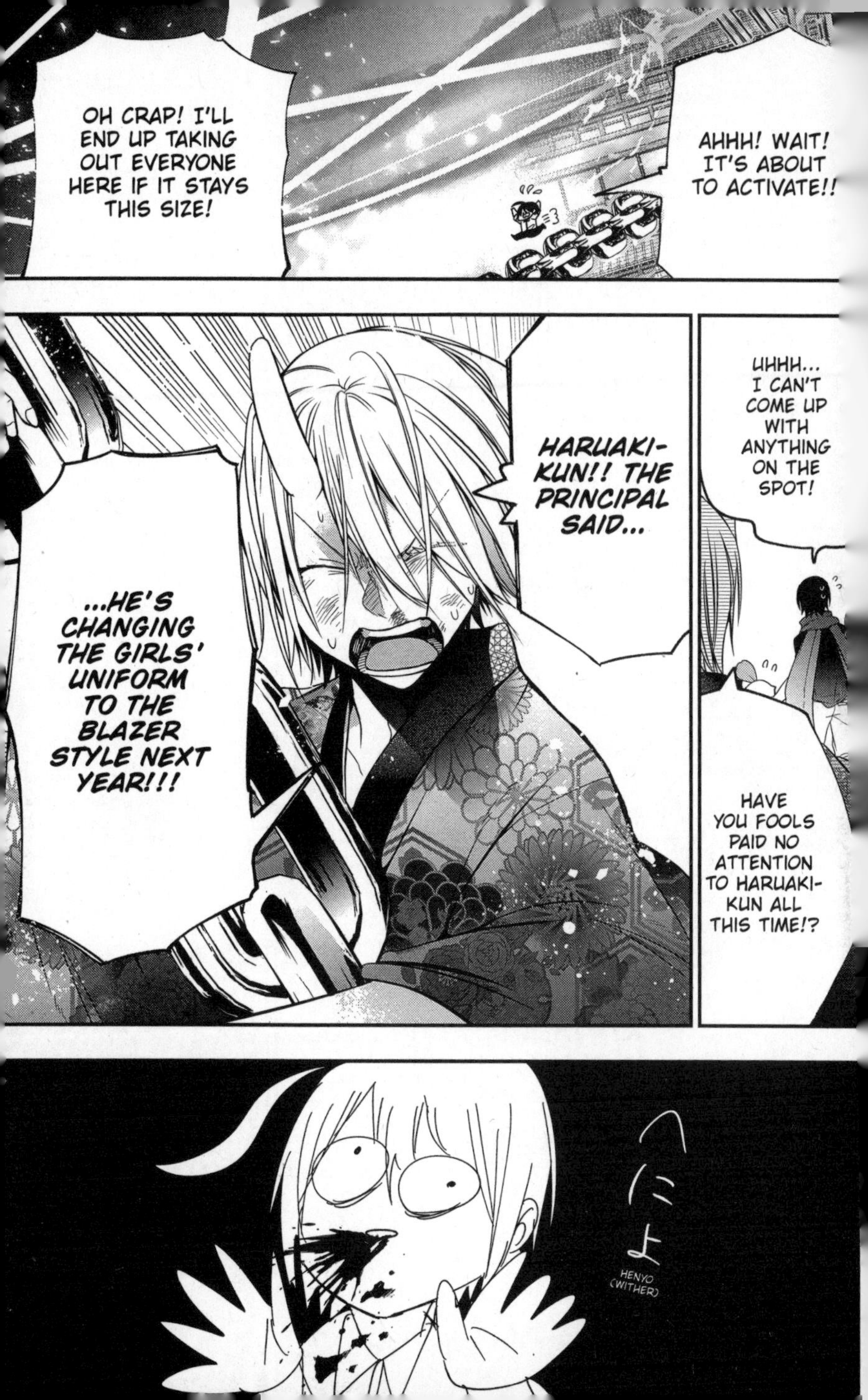
AHHH! WAIT! IT'S ABOUT TO ACTIVATE!!
OH CRAP! I'LL END UP TAKING OUT EVERYONE HERE IF IT STAYS THIS SIZE!
UHHH... I CAN'T COME UP WITH ANYTHING ON THE SPOT!
HAVE YOU FOOLS PAID NO ATTENTION TO HARUAKI-KUN ALL THIS TIME!?
HARUAKI-KUN!! THE PRINCIPAL SAID...
...HE'S CHANGING THE GIRLS' UNIFORM TO THE BLAZER STYLE NEXT YEAR!!!
HENYO (WITHER)

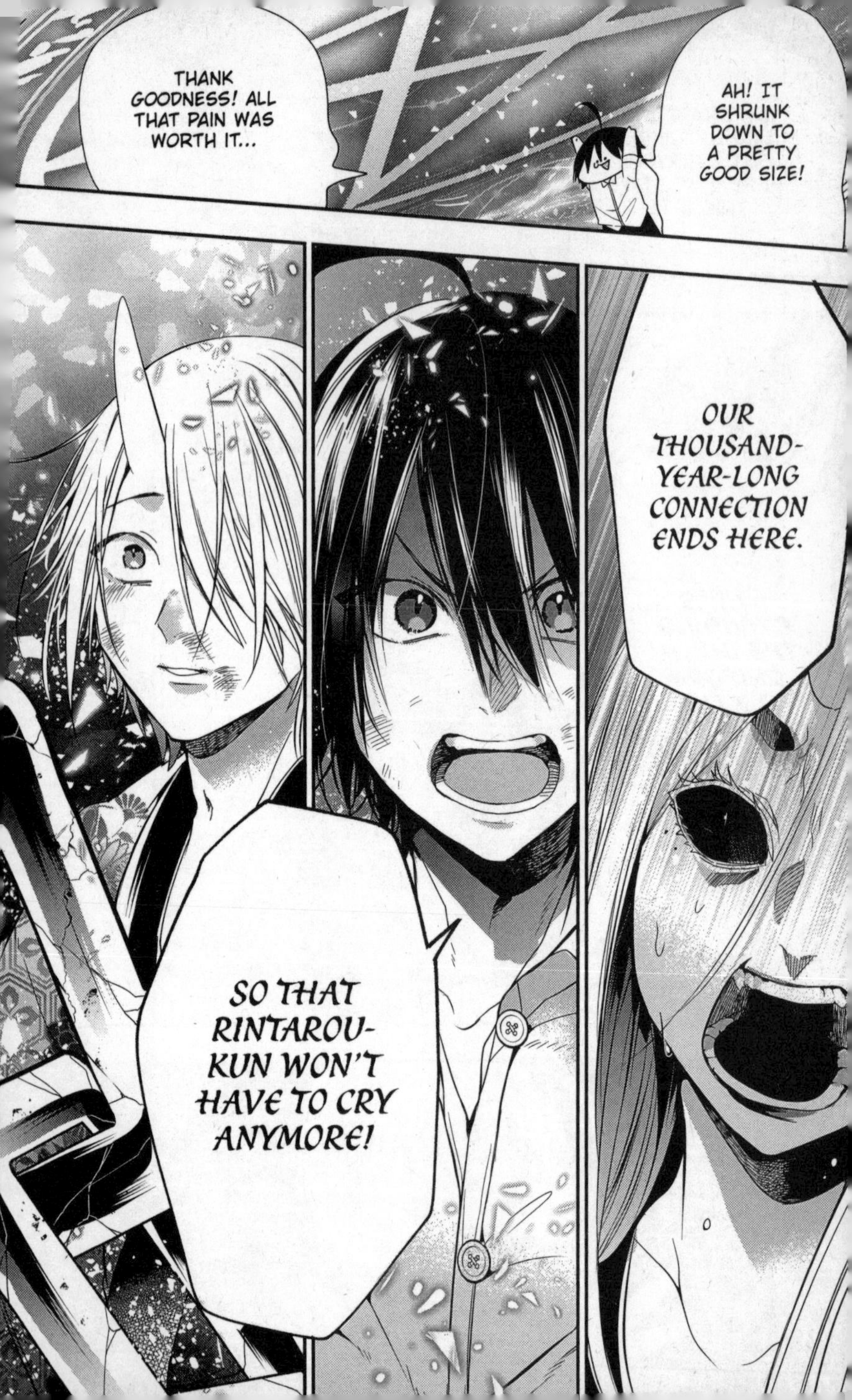
AH! IT SHRUNK DOWN TO A PRETTY GOOD SIZE!
THANK GOODNESS! ALL THAT PAIN WAS WORTH IT...
OUR THOUSAND-YEAR-LONG CONNECTION ENDS HERE.
SO THAT RINTAROU-KUN WON'T HAVE TO CRY ANYMORE!

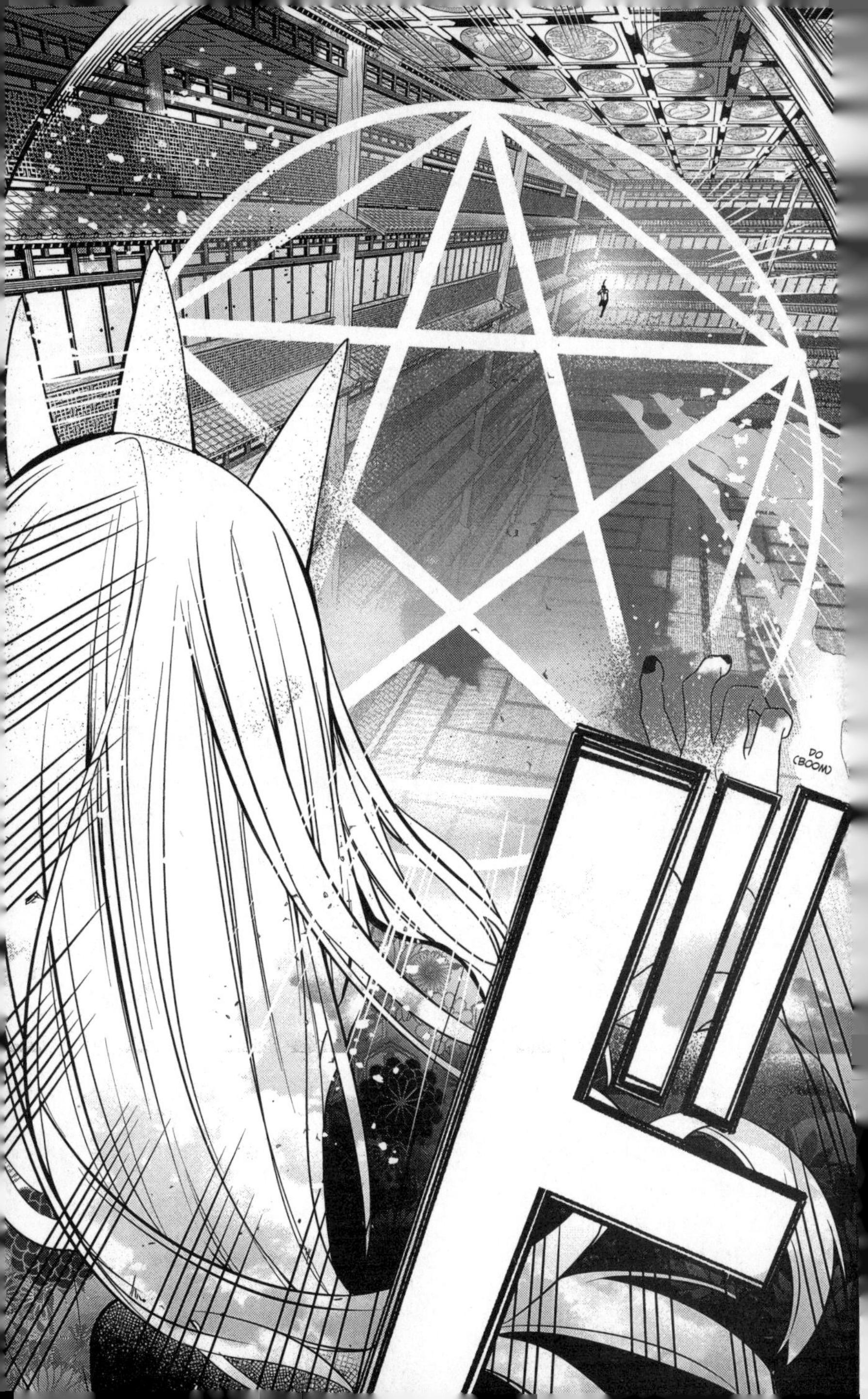
DO
(BOOM)

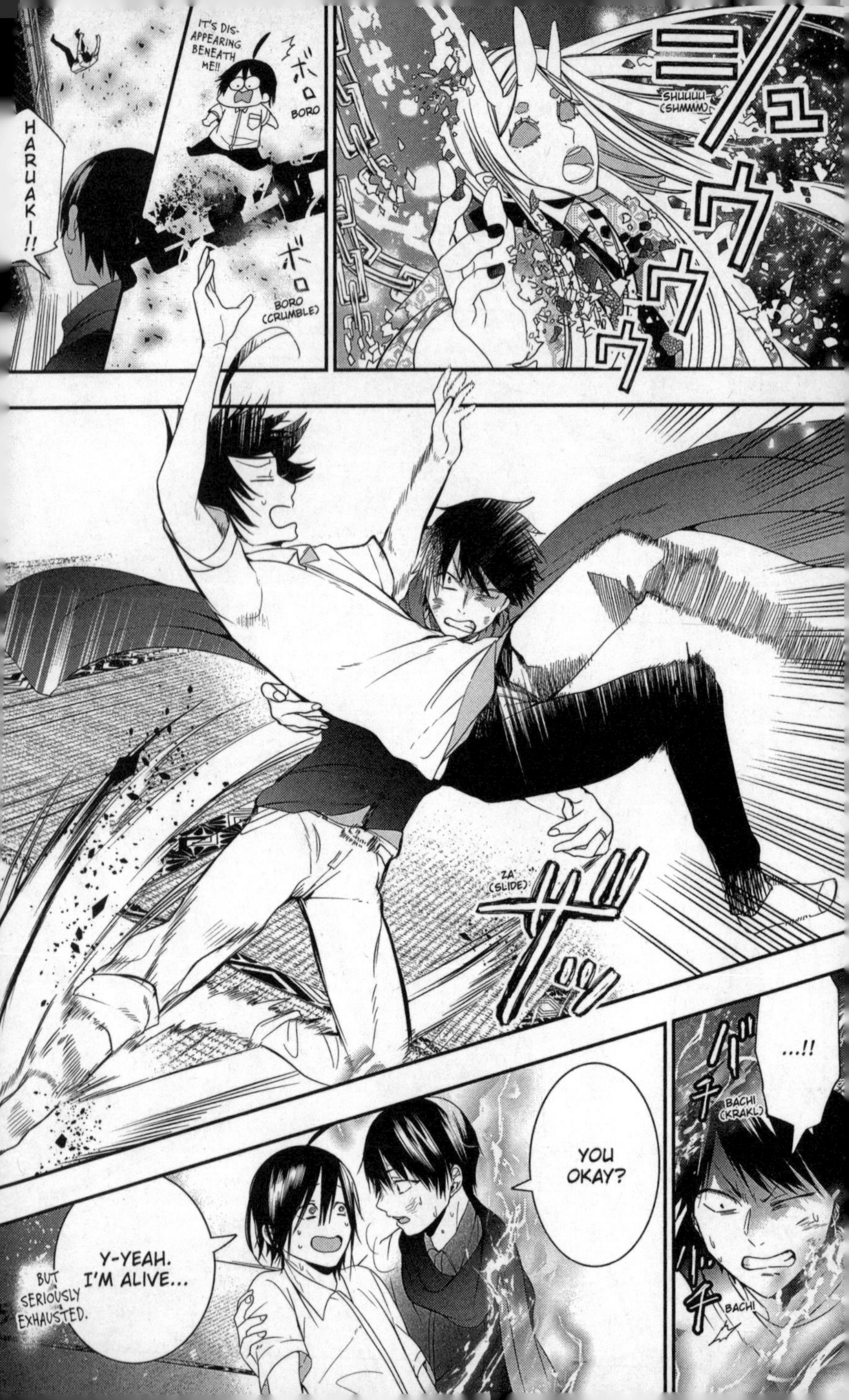
シュウウウ
SHUUUU (SHMMM)
IT'S DIS-APPEARING BENEATH ME!!
ボロ
BORO
ボロ
BORO (CRUMBLE)
HARUAKI!!
ザッ
ZA (SLIDE)
...!!
バチ
BACHI (KRAKL)
バチ
BACHI
YOU OKAY?
Y-YEAH. I'M ALIVE...
BUT SERIOUSLY EXHAUSTED.

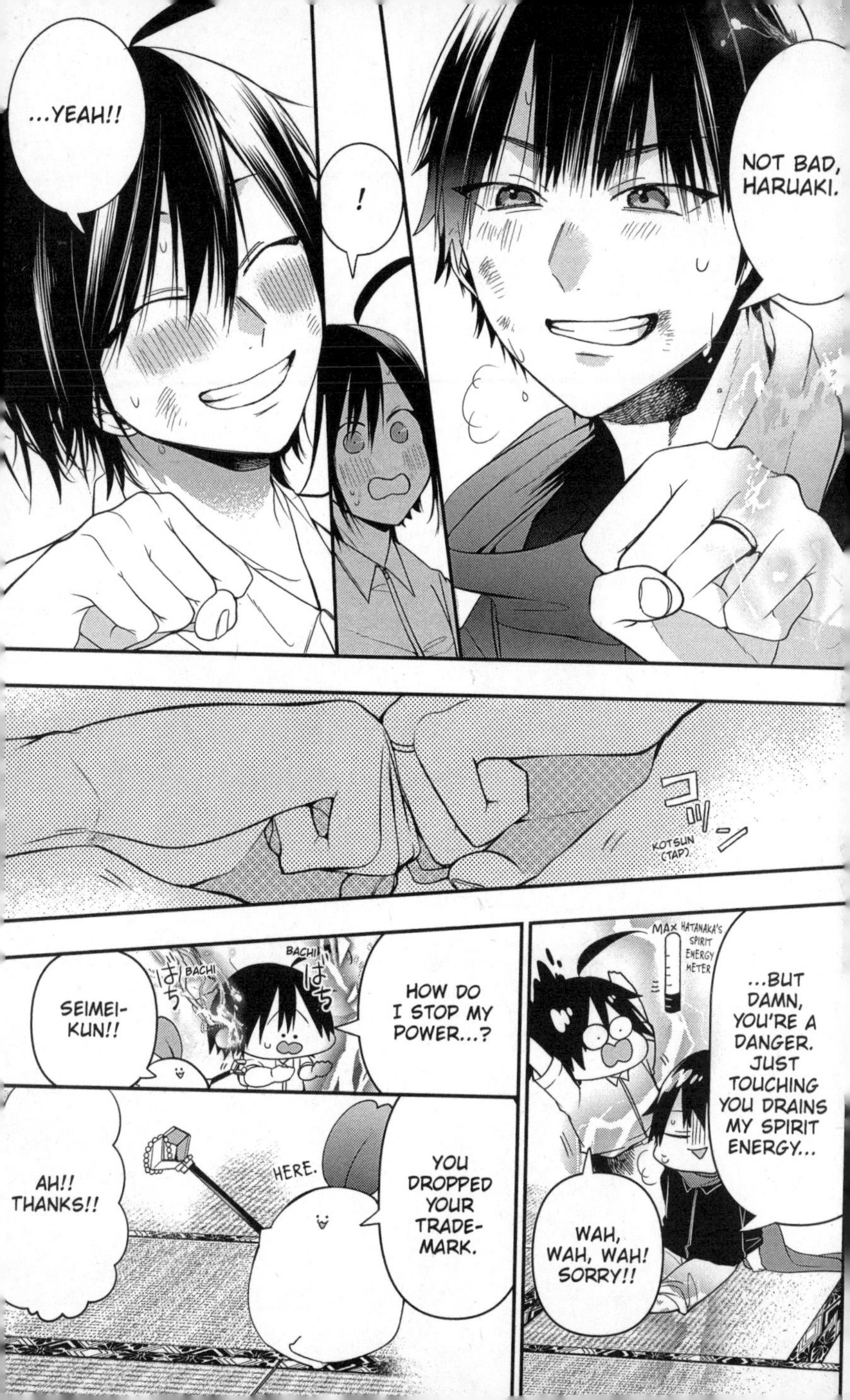
NOT BAD, HARUAKI.
!
...YEAH!!
KOTSUN (TAP)
MAX
HATANAKA'S SPIRIT ENERGY METER
...BUT DAMN, YOU'RE A DANGER. JUST TOUCHING YOU DRAINS MY SPIRIT ENERGY...
WAH, WAH, WAH! SORRY!!
HOW DO I STOP MY POWER...?
BACHI
BACHI
SEIMEI-KUN!!
YOU DROPPED YOUR TRADE-MARK.
HERE.
AH!! THANKS!!

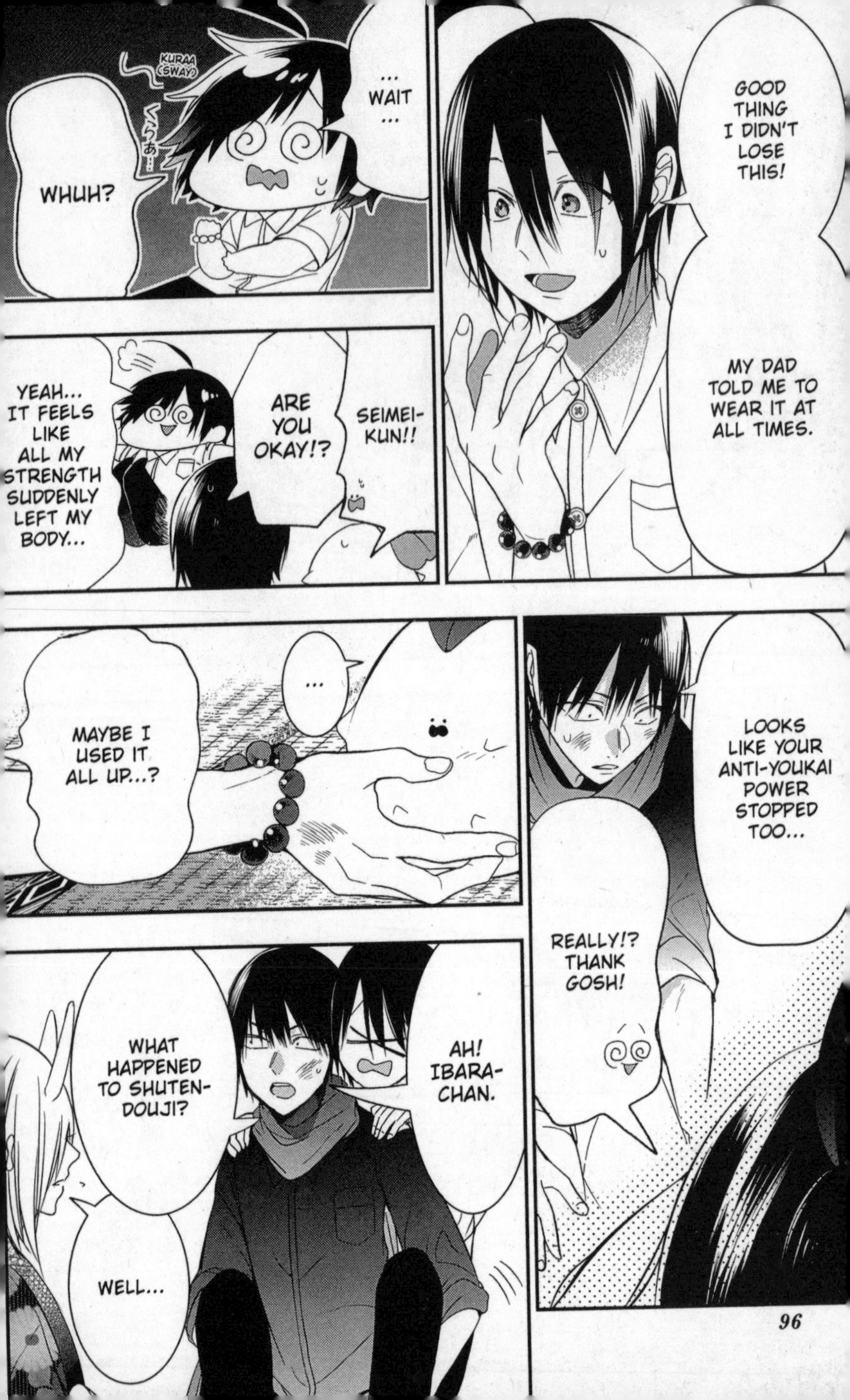
GOOD THING I DIDN'T LOSE THIS!
MY DAD TOLD ME TO WEAR IT AT ALL TIMES.
... WAIT ...
KURAA (SWAY)
くらぁ…
WHUH?
SEIMEI-KUN!!
ARE YOU OKAY!?
YEAH... IT FEELS LIKE ALL MY STRENGTH SUDDENLY LEFT MY BODY...
LOOKS LIKE YOUR ANTI-YOUKAI POWER STOPPED TOO...
REALLY!? THANK GOSH!
...
MAYBE I USED IT ALL UP...?
AH! IBARA-CHAN.
WHAT HAPPENED TO SHUTEN-DOUJI?
WELL...

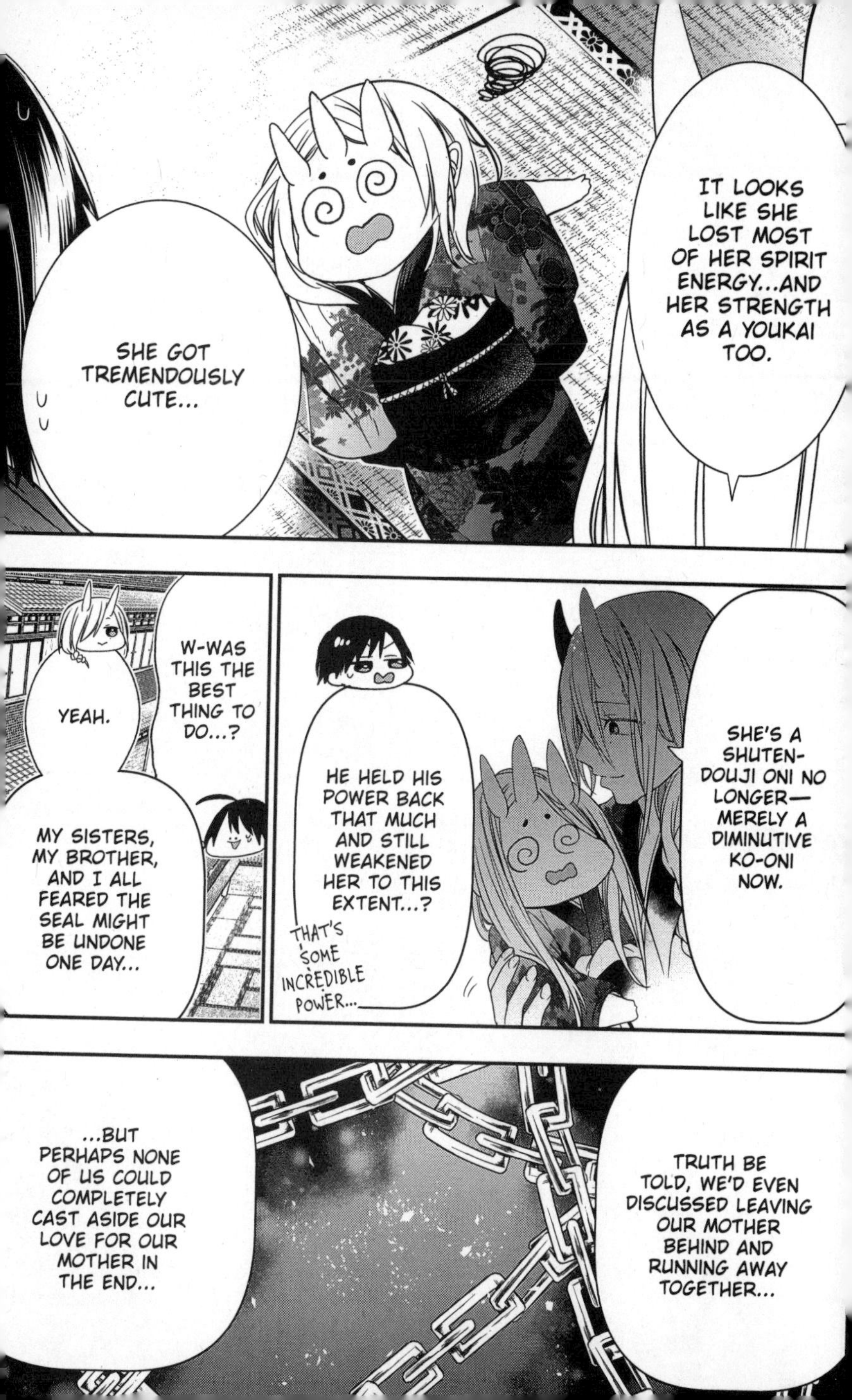
IT LOOKS LIKE SHE LOST MOST OF HER SPIRIT ENERGY...AND HER STRENGTH AS A YOUKAI TOO.
SHE GOT TREMENDOUSLY CUTE...
SHE'S A SHUTEN-DOUJI ONI NO LONGER—MERELY A DIMINUTIVE KO-ONI NOW.
HE HELD HIS POWER BACK THAT MUCH AND STILL WEAKENED HER TO THIS EXTENT...?
THAT'S SOME INCREDIBLE POWER...
W-WAS THIS THE BEST THING TO DO...?
YEAH.
MY SISTERS, MY BROTHER, AND I ALL FEARED THE SEAL MIGHT BE UNDONE ONE DAY...
TRUTH BE TOLD, WE'D EVEN DISCUSSED LEAVING OUR MOTHER BEHIND AND RUNNING AWAY TOGETHER...
...BUT PERHAPS NONE OF US COULD COMPLETELY CAST ASIDE OUR LOVE FOR OUR MOTHER IN THE END...

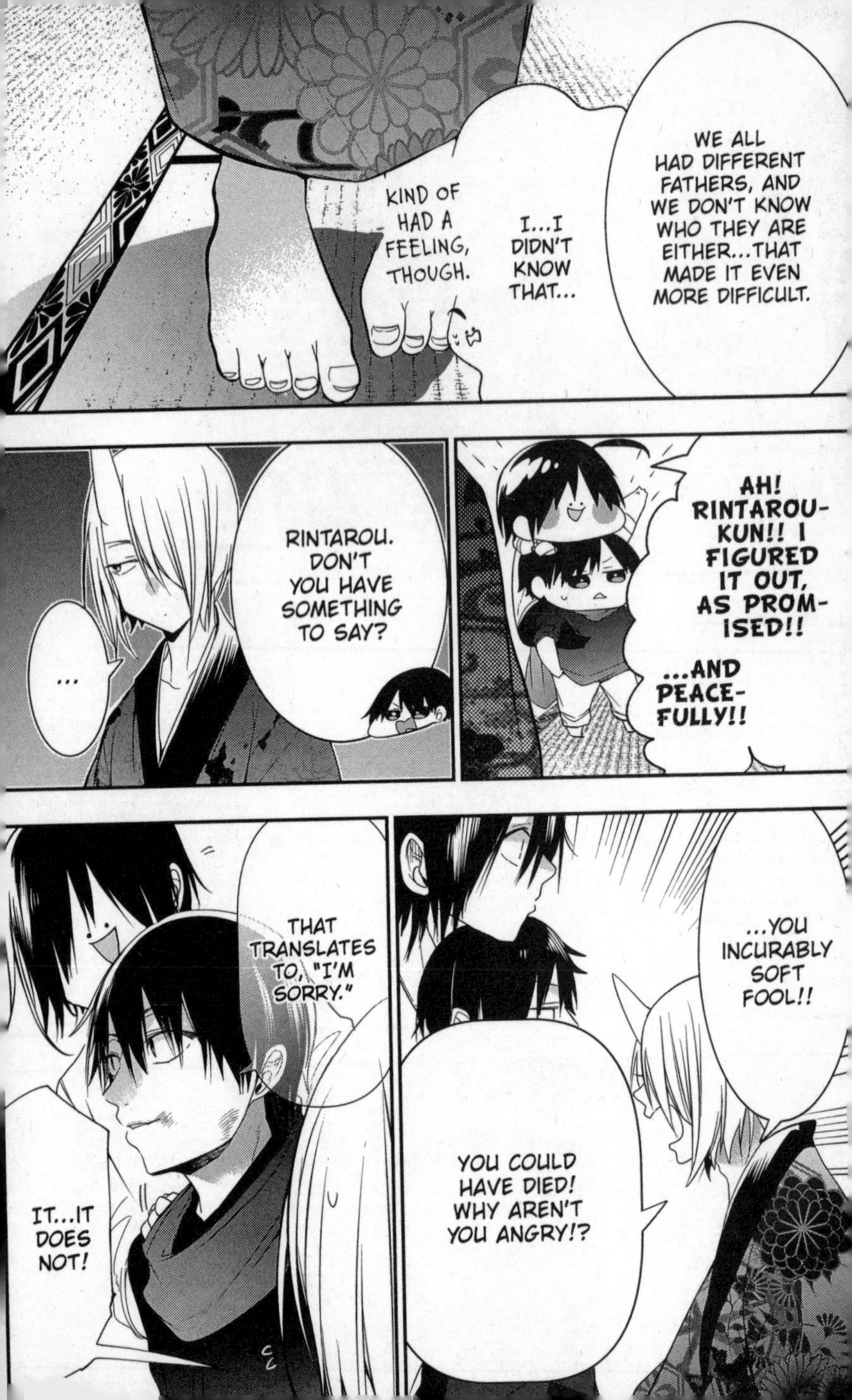
WE ALL HAD DIFFERENT FATHERS, AND WE DON'T KNOW WHO THEY ARE EITHER...THAT MADE IT EVEN MORE DIFFICULT.
I...I DIDN'T KNOW THAT...
KIND OF HAD A FEELING, THOUGH.
AH! RINTAROU-KUN!! I FIGURED IT OUT, AS PROMISED!!
...AND PEACEFULLY!!
RINTAROU. DON'T YOU HAVE SOMETHING TO SAY?
...
...YOU INCURABLY SOFT FOOL!!
YOU COULD HAVE DIED! WHY AREN'T YOU ANGRY!?
THAT TRANSLATES TO, "I'M SORRY."
IT...IT DOES NOT!

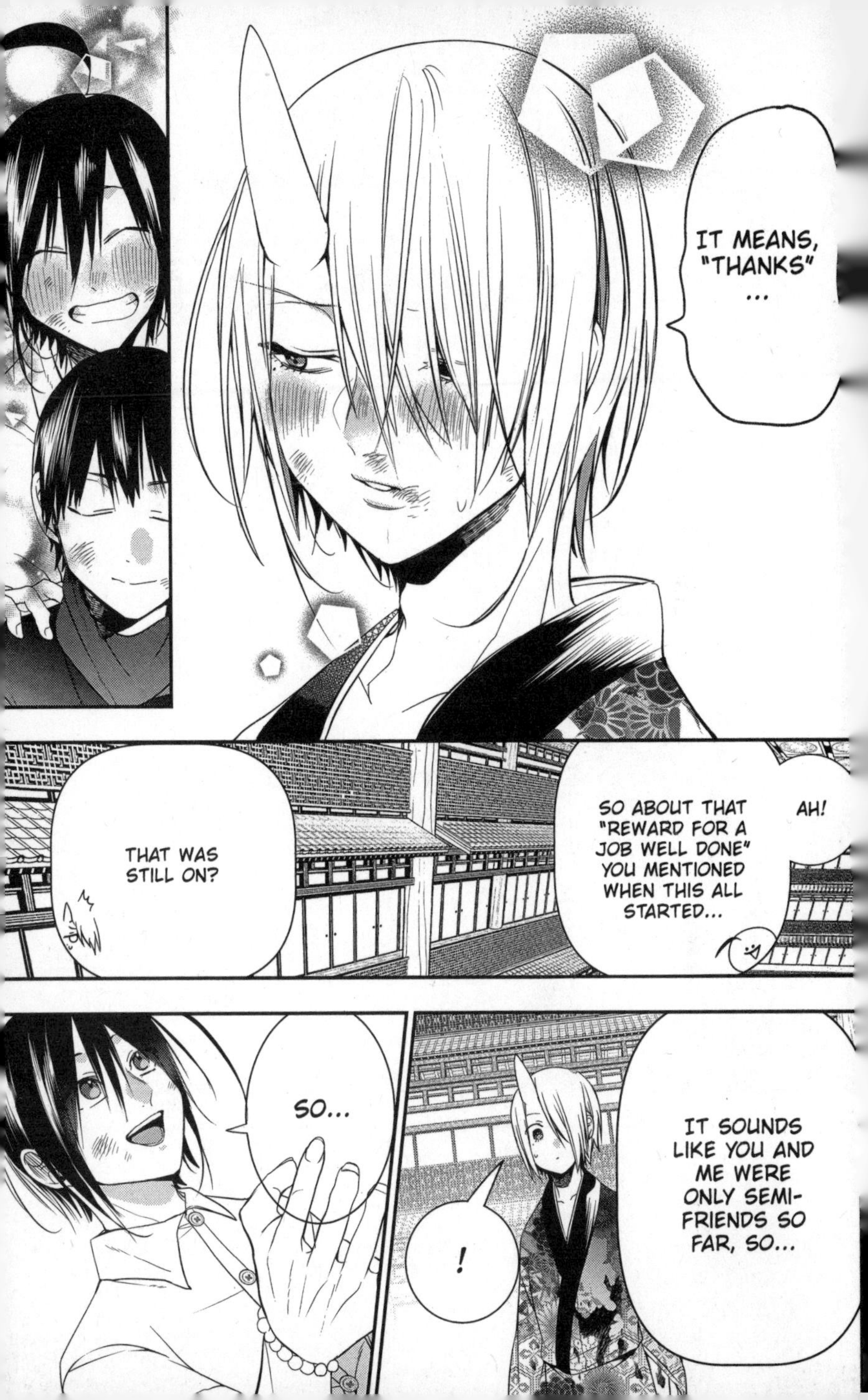
IT MEANS, "THANKS" ...
AH!
SO ABOUT THAT "REWARD FOR A JOB WELL DONE" YOU MENTIONED WHEN THIS ALL STARTED...
THAT WAS STILL ON?
IT SOUNDS LIKE YOU AND ME WERE ONLY SEMI-FRIENDS SO FAR, SO...
!
SO...

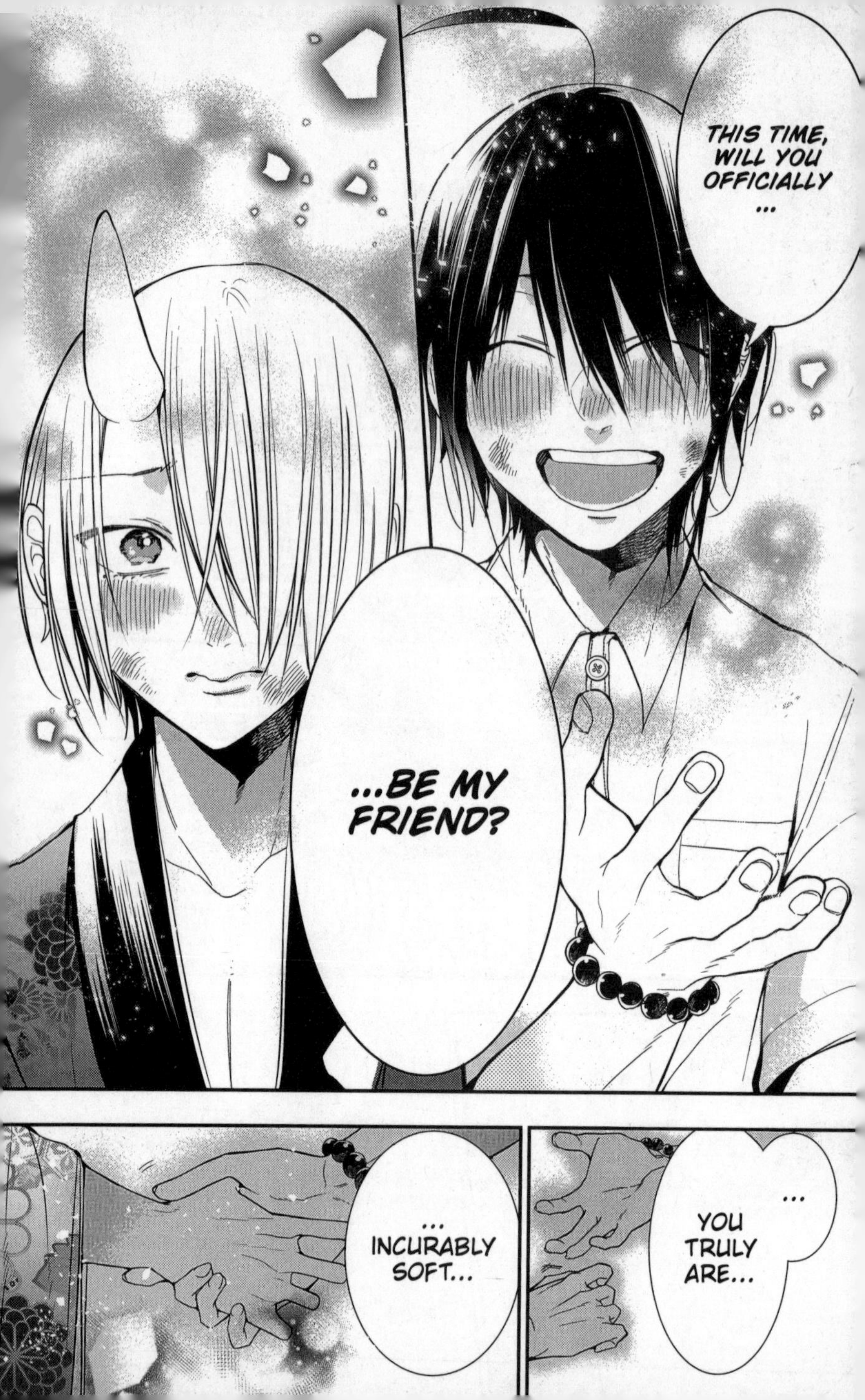
THIS TIME, WILL YOU OFFICIALLY ...
...BE MY FRIEND?
... YOU TRULY ARE...
... INCURABLY SOFT...

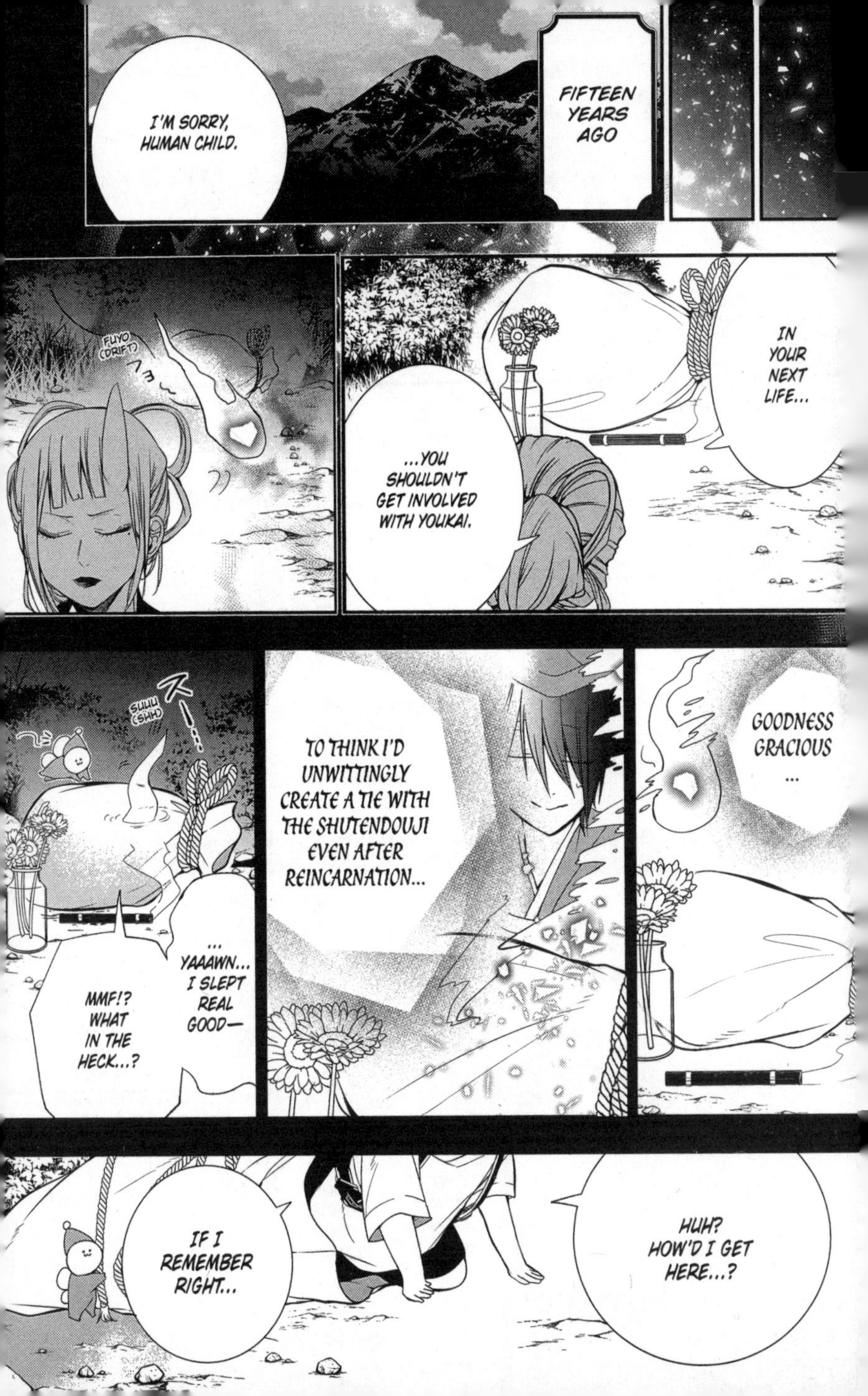
FIFTEEN YEARS AGO
I'M SORRY, HUMAN CHILD.
IN YOUR NEXT LIFE...
...YOU SHOULDN'T GET INVOLVED WITH YOUKAI.
FUYO (DRIFT)
GOODNESS GRACIOUS ...
TO THINK I'D UNWITTINGLY CREATE A TIE WITH THE SHUTENDOUJI EVEN AFTER REINCARNATION...
SUUU (SHH)
... YAAAWN... I SLEPT REAL GOOD—
MMF!? WHAT IN THE HECK...?
HUH? HOW'D I GET HERE...?
IF I REMEMBER RIGHT...

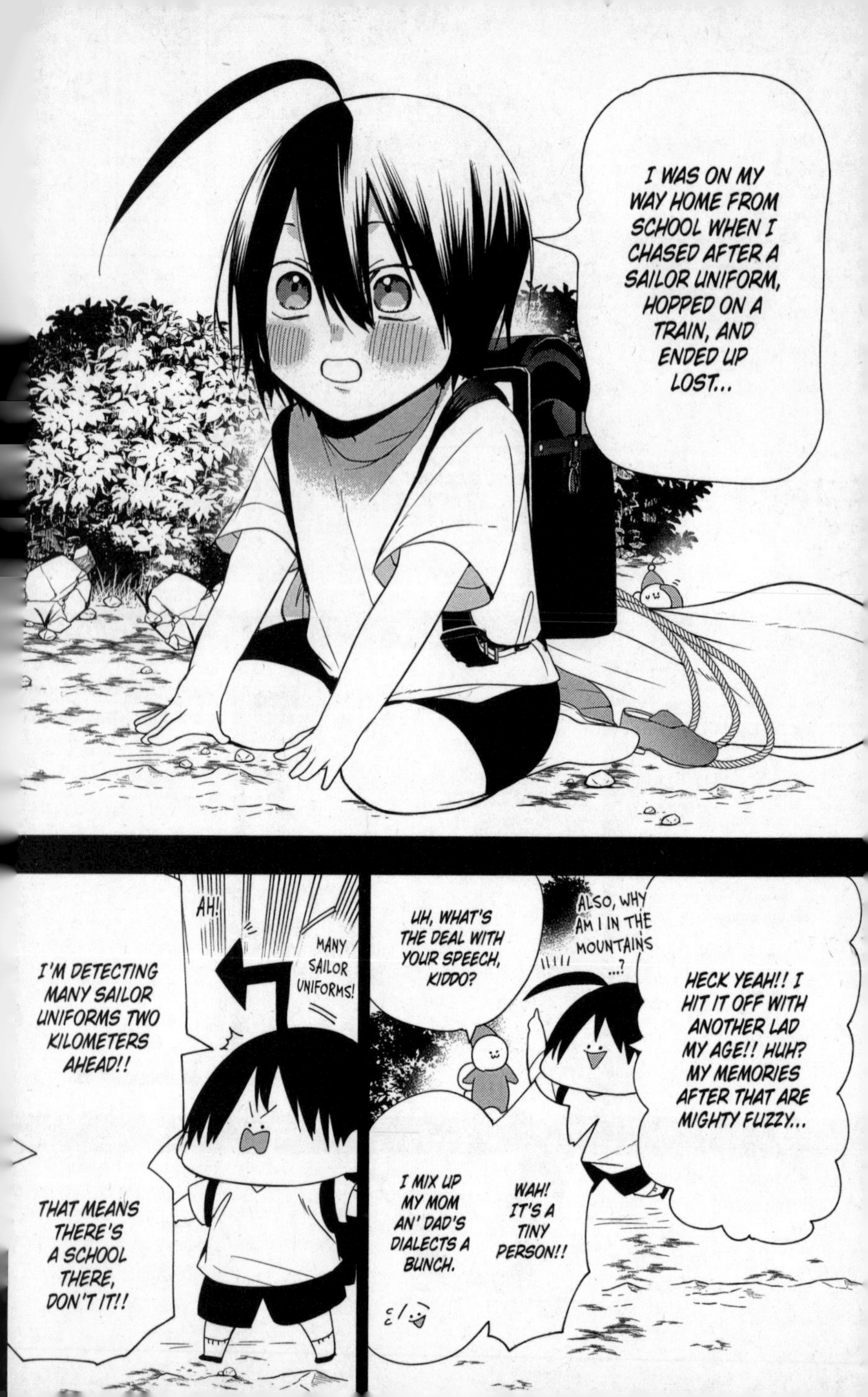
I WAS ON MY WAY HOME FROM SCHOOL WHEN I CHASED AFTER A SAILOR UNIFORM, HOPPED ON A TRAIN, AND ENDED UP LOST...
HECK YEAH!! I HIT IT OFF WITH ANOTHER LAD MY AGE!! HUH? MY MEMORIES AFTER THAT ARE MIGHTY FUZZY...
ALSO, WHY AM I IN THE MOUNTAINS ...?
UH, WHAT'S THE DEAL WITH YOUR SPEECH, KIDDO?
WAH! IT'S A TINY PERSON!!
I MIX UP MY MOM AN' DAD'S DIALECTS A BUNCH.
AH!
MANY SAILOR UNIFORMS!
I'M DETECTING MANY SAILOR UNIFORMS TWO KILOMETERS AHEAD!!
THAT MEANS THERE'S A SCHOOL THERE, DON'T IT!!

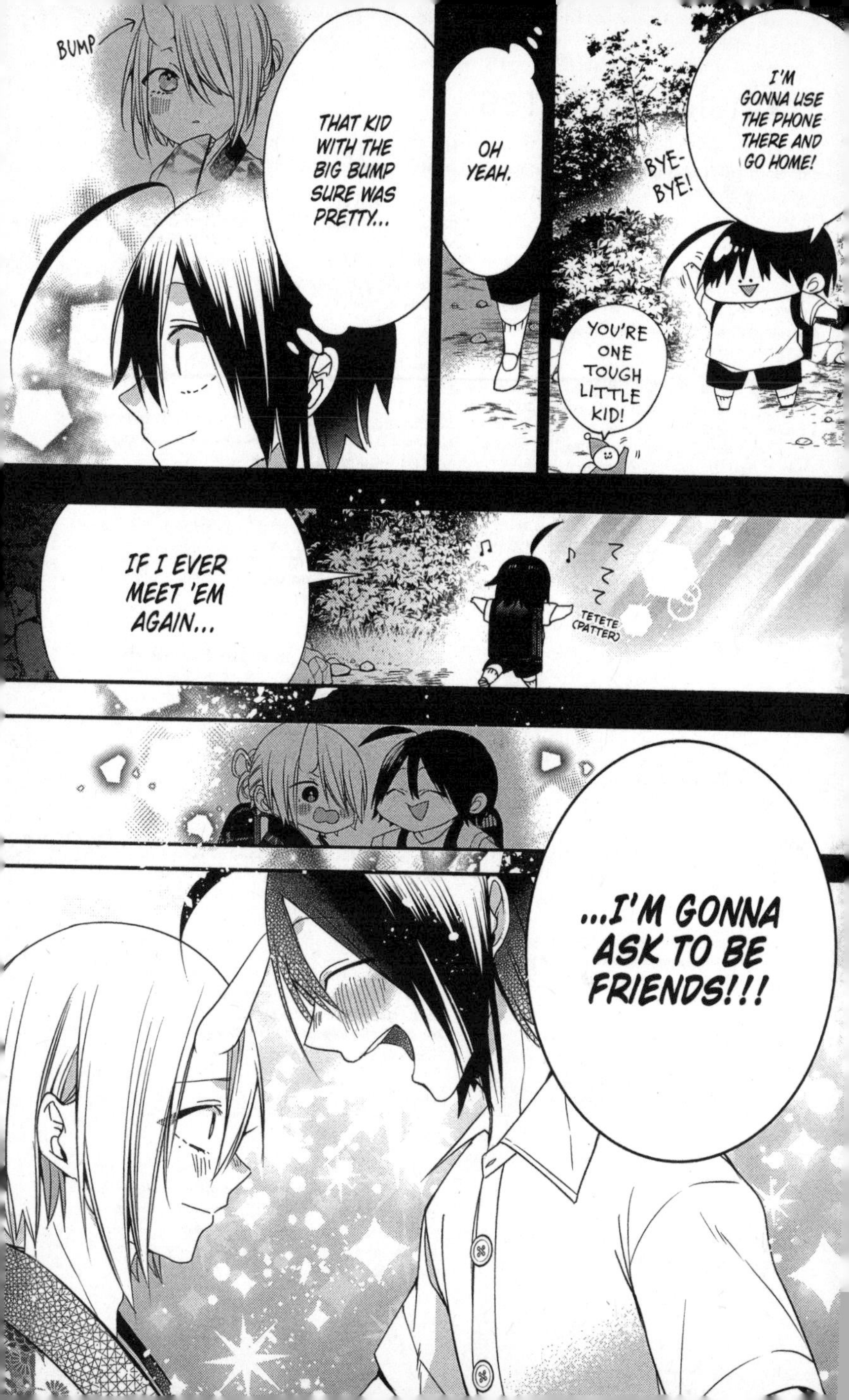
I'M GONNA USE THE PHONE THERE AND GO HOME!
BYE-BYE!
YOU'RE ONE TOUGH LITTLE KID!
OH YEAH.
THAT KID WITH THE BIG BUMP SURE WAS PRETTY...
BUMP
TETETE (PATTER)
IF I EVER MEET 'EM AGAIN...
...I'M GONNA ASK TO BE FRIENDS!!!

Translation Notes

PAGE 13
Umibouzu (literally "sea monks") appear in the sea, like vaguely humanoid, black, inky blobs, and smash into ships like waves.

PAGE 15
The **dorotabou** is a one-eyed youkai that rises out of the muddy waters of rice paddy fields. The legend of the dorotabou purportedly took place in the north, which is why the umibouzu knows that Hijita is from Tohoku — the northeast region of Japan's main island, Honshu.

Funayuurei (literally "ship ghost") are ghosts of people who've died in shipwrecks. They sink ships by using a ladle to fill them with water, hoping to add to their ranks. One way to foil them is to throw a ladle with no bottom into the sea. They may also attempt to make ships lose their way on stormy nights.

PAGE 23
Abe no Seimei (921 to 1005) is a historical figure and legend — a diviner for the imperial court said to have all kinds of supernatural powers.

The **shutendouji** (lit. little drunkard) was the commander of a gang of oni (ogres) that once terrorized Kyoto. Mount Ooe served as their hideout.

PAGE 27
The city of **Kyoto**, capital of Kyoto Prefecture, was a historic capital of Japan (from 794 to 1868) and is considered a cultural center of the country, so it might be a perfect location for a secret youkai city. Kyoto is also less than an hour away from Osaka (where Haruaki's family lives) by train, so Haruaki would have had easy access to the city.

PAGE 30
Ibarakidouji is an oni who was the shutendouji's most important underling.

PAGE 31
The confection **yatsuhashi** is one of Kyoto's famous local products and a common Kyoto souvenir. It's a gift you'd bring to friends and family on a return trip from Kyoto, not to people actually living in Kyoto...

PAGE 32
Nagoya, the largest city in central Japan, is located on the coast of central Honshu in the Chuubu region (the area just east of the Kansai region, where Kyoto and Osaka are).

PAGE 37
Onmyouji are specialists in magic and divination. Abe no Seimei is the most famous onmyouji.

PAGE 45
Kansai, where Kyoto and Osaka are, is located in the southern-central region of Japan's main island.

PAGE 68
The **ittan-momen** is a flying bolt of cloth.

PAGE 74
Golden Week is a week of holidays that starts on April 29.

PAGE 97
The **ko-oni** (literally "small oni/ogre") is just a mini oni (or sometimes an oni child).

PAGE 109
The **rokurokubi** is a youkai who can stretch its neck out very long.

The **kitsune** is a fox youkai. They may have up to nine tails and can shapeshift into human form. Some are tricksters, and some might use their magic for the good of humans.

Odawara is a **chouchin-kozou** ("paper lantern boy") youkai.

PAGE 110
The author **Akanameko's** name is a reference to the akaname youkai, the "filth-licker" who lives in dirty bathrooms and public baths licking up all the filth there.

PAGE 138
The name **teketeke** comes from the sound this youkai makes when it moves along on its arms, dragging its upper torso. According to urban legend, it's the vengeful spirit of someone (usually a young woman) who was cut in half when hit by a train.

PAGE 139
The **yakubyougami** is a god of pestilence.

PAGE 153
Urban legend **Sukima-san**, also known as sukima-onna or literally "gap woman," is a youkai who can fit into tiny gaps. She can even watch you in your own home from the tiny gap between your dresser and the wall...

PAGE 158
Yakou-san (sometimes pronounced yagyou-san; literally "mister night travel") is an oni who appears on certain days riding a headless horse. Those unfortunate enough to encounter him will be flung away or get kicked by the horse. Some say the horse itself is actually Yakou-san.

PAGE 162
Daidarabocchi: A youkai giant so big that it's said to have created mountains and lakes.

PAGE 168
In the Japanese version, Haruaki quotes the saying **teki ni shio wo okuru** — literally "send salt to your enemies," meaning to play fair or act with humanity even with an enemy. The saying originates from warlord Shingen Takeda supplying salt to enemy warlord Kenshin Uesugi.

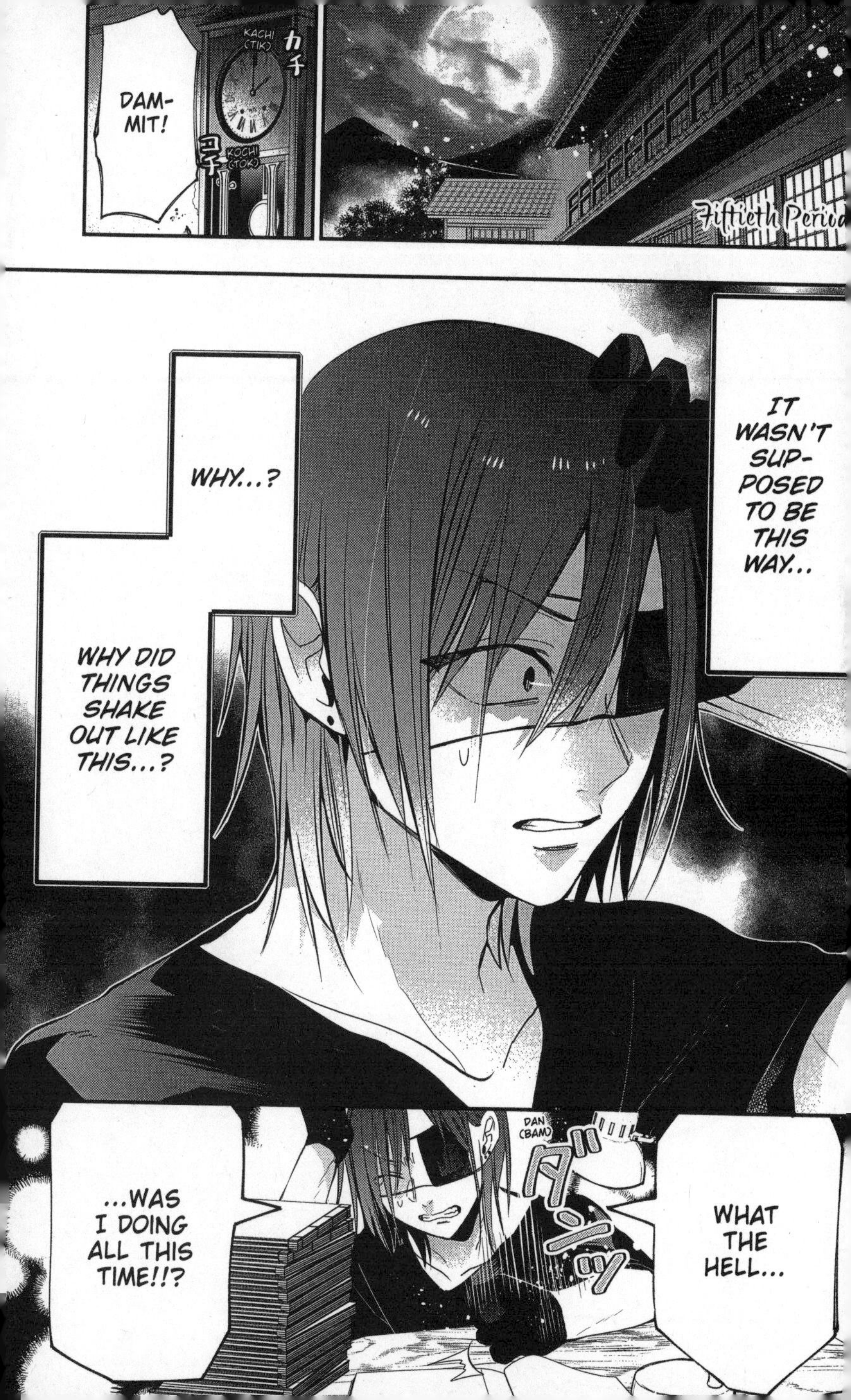
Fiftieth Period
カチ
KACHI (TIK)
コチ
KOCHI (TOK)
DAM-MIT!
IT WASN'T SUP-POSED TO BE THIS WAY...
WHY...?
WHY DID THINGS SHAKE OUT LIKE THIS...?
WHAT THE HELL...
DAN (BAM)
...WAS I DOING ALL THIS TIME!!?

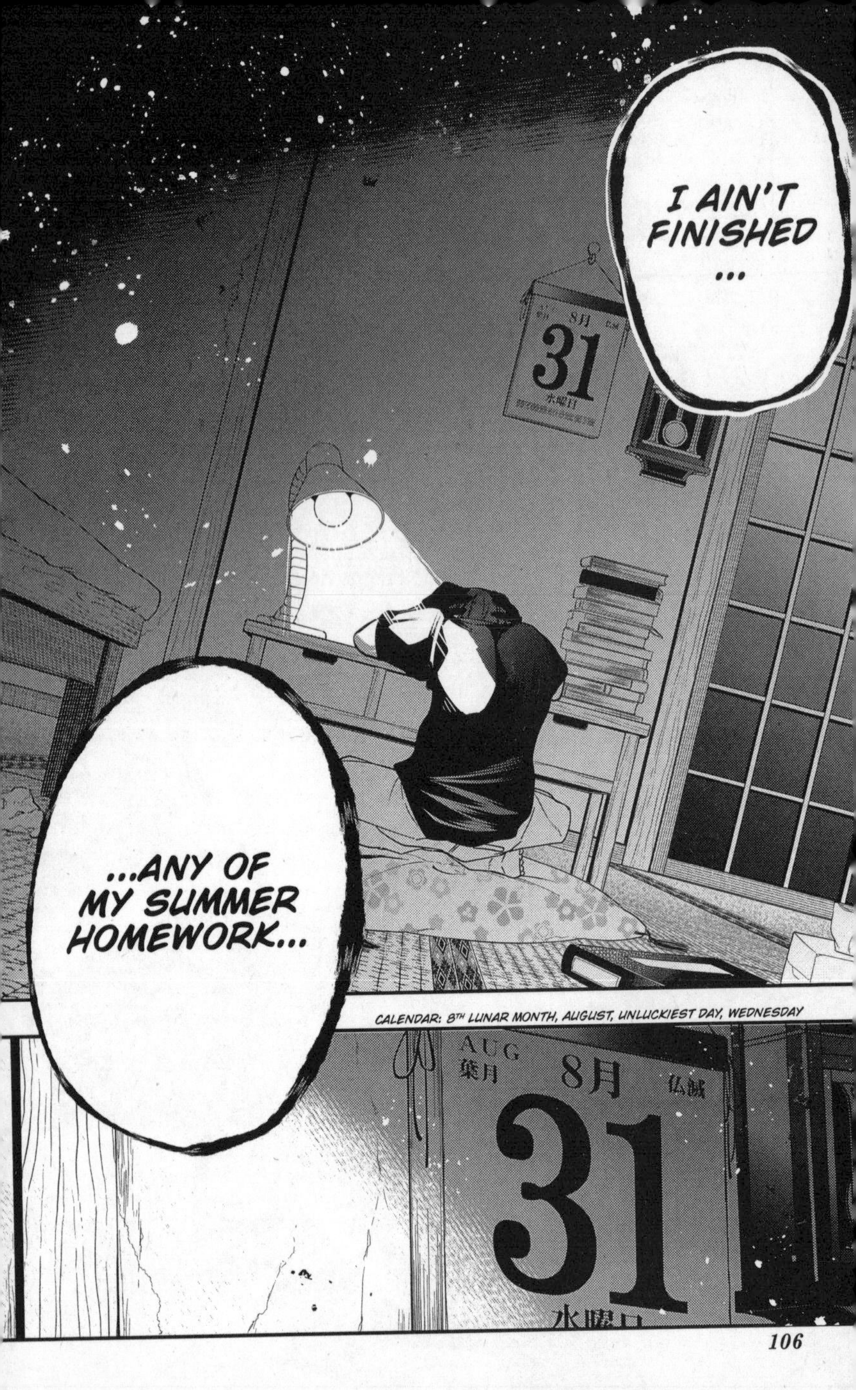
I AIN'T FINISHED ...
...ANY OF MY SUMMER HOMEWORK...
CALENDAR: 8TH LUNAR MONTH, AUGUST, UNLUCKIEST DAY, WEDNESDAY
AUG
8月
31

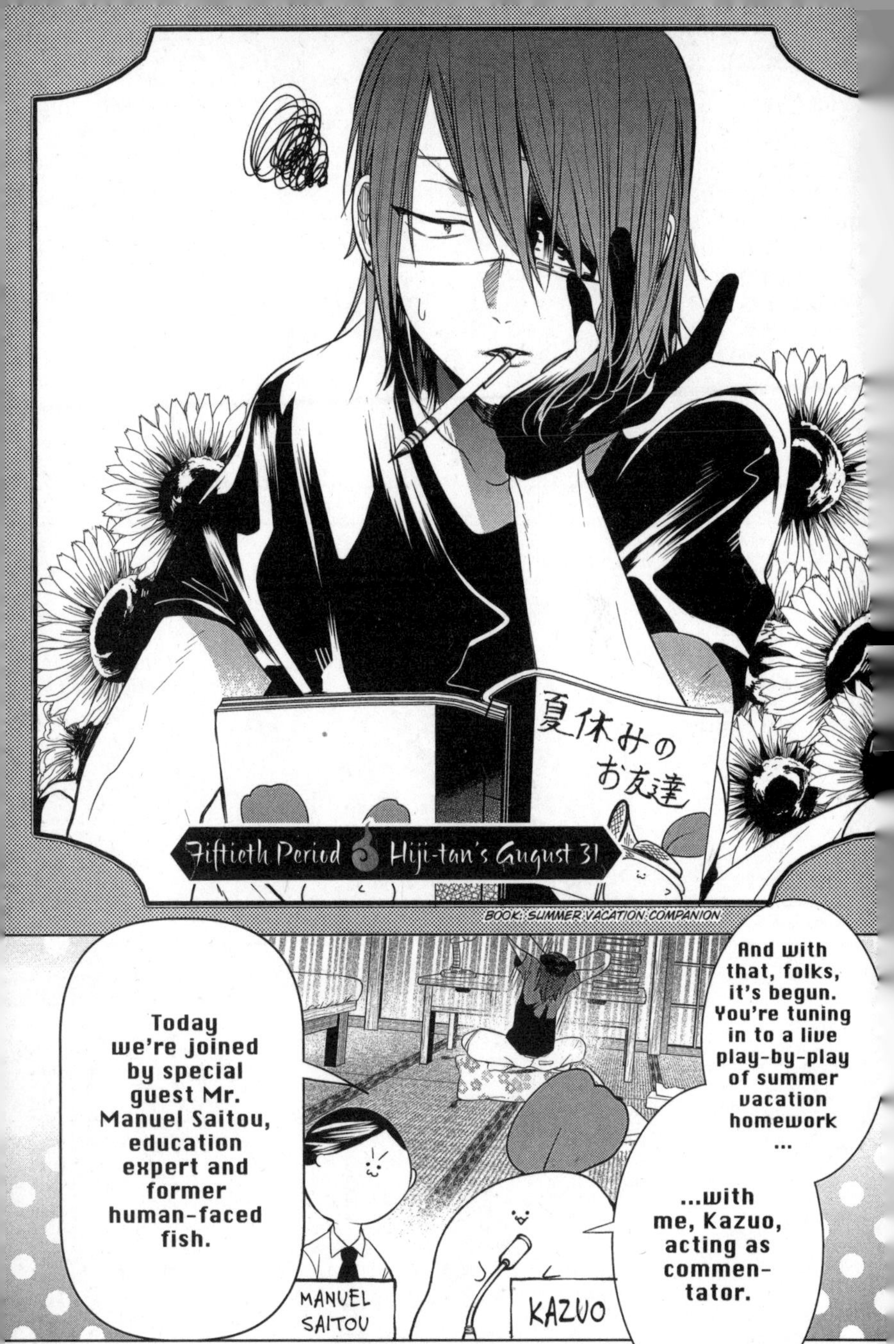
夏休みの
お友達
Fiftieth Period Hiji-tan's August 31
BOOK: SUMMER VACATION COMPANION
And with that, folks, it's begun. You're tuning in to a live play-by-play of summer vacation homework ...
...with me, Kazuo, acting as commentator.
Today we're joined by special guest Mr. Manuel Saitou, education expert and former human-faced fish.
MANUEL SAITOU
KAZUO

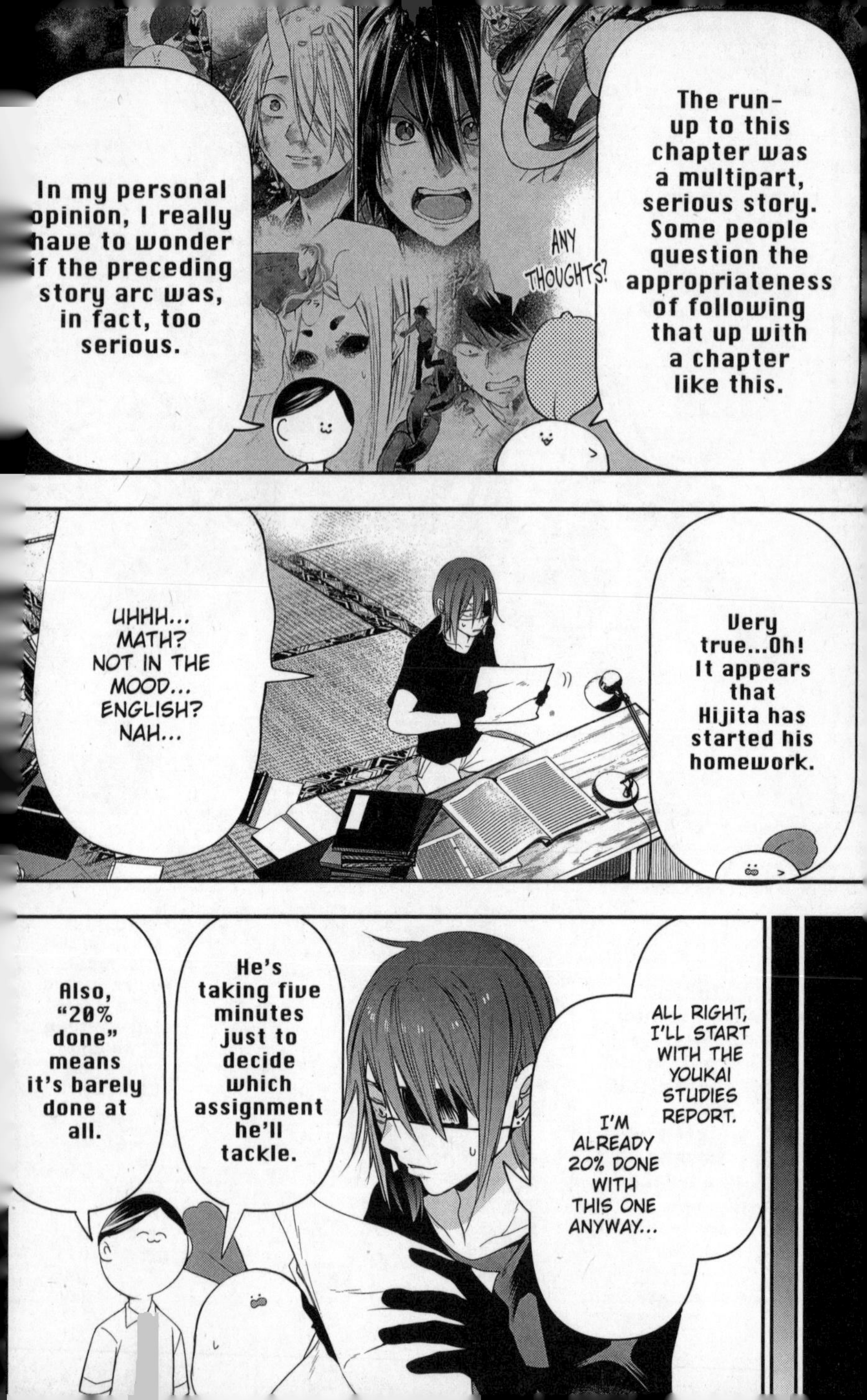
The run-up to this chapter was a multipart, serious story. Some people question the appropriateness of following that up with a chapter like this.
ANY THOUGHTS?
In my personal opinion, I really have to wonder if the preceding story arc was, in fact, too serious.
Very true...Oh! It appears that Hijita has started his homework.
UHHH... MATH? NOT IN THE MOOD... ENGLISH? NAH...
ALL RIGHT, I'LL START WITH THE YOUKAI STUDIES REPORT.
I'M ALREADY 20% DONE WITH THIS ONE ANYWAY...
He's taking five minutes just to decide which assignment he'll tackle.
Also, "20% done" means it's barely done at all.

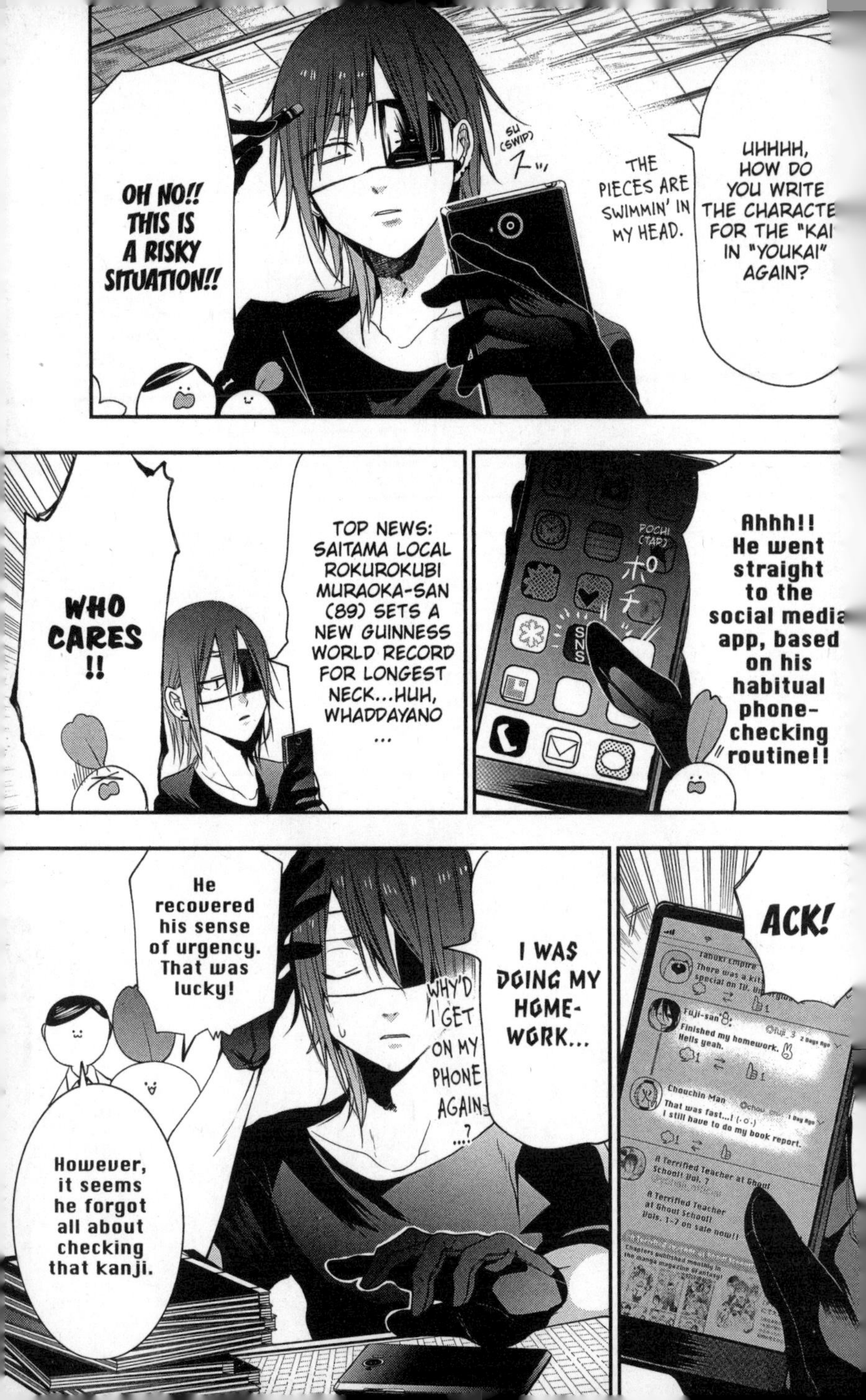

UHHHH, HOW DO YOU WRITE THE CHARACTE FOR THE "KAI IN "YOUKAI" AGAIN?
THE PIECES ARE SWIMMIN' IN MY HEAD.
SU (SWIP)
OH NO!! THIS IS A RISKY SITUATION!!
POCHI (TAP)
SNS
Ahhh!! He went straight to the social media app, based on his habitual phone-checking routine!!
TOP NEWS: SAITAMA LOCAL ROKUROKUBI MURAOKA-SAN (89) SETS A NEW GUINNESS WORLD RECORD FOR LONGEST NECK...HUH, WHADDAYANO ...
WHO CARES !!
ACK!
Tanuki Empire
Fuji-san @fuji_3 2 Days Ago
Finished my homework. Hells yeah.
Chouchin Man
That was fast...! (·o·) 1 Day Ago
I still have to do my book report.
A Terrified Teacher at Ghoul School! Vol. 7
A Terrified Teacher at Ghoul School! Vols. 1–7 on sale now!!
I WAS DOING MY HOME-WORK...
WHY'D I GET ON MY PHONE AGAIN-...?
He recovered his sense of urgency. That was lucky!
However, it seems he forgot all about checking that kanji.

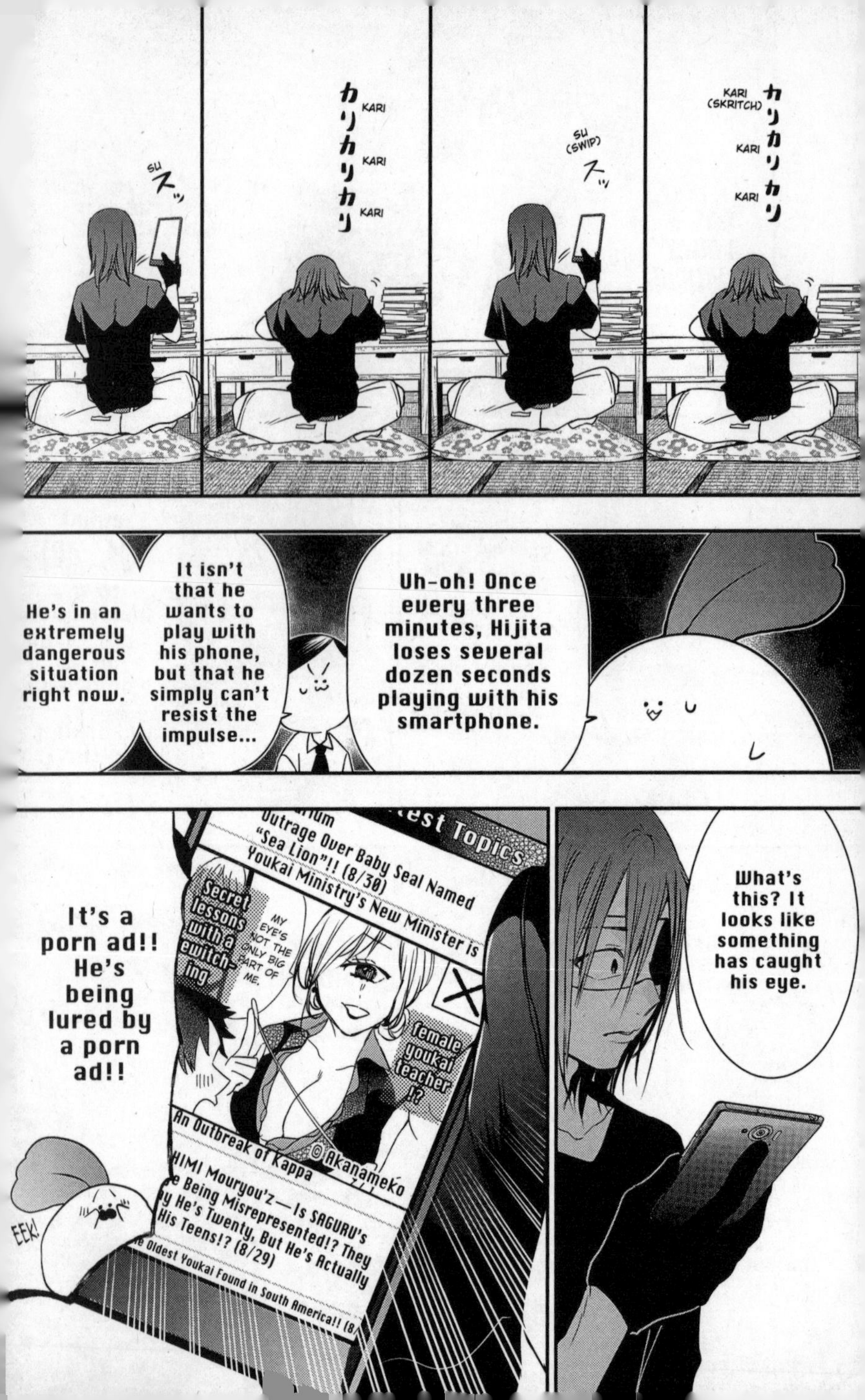

カリカリ
KARI (SKRITCH)
KARI
KARI
SU (SWIP)
スッ
カリカリカリ
KARI
KARI
KARI
SU
スッ
Uh-oh! Once every three minutes, Hijita loses several dozen seconds playing with his smartphone.
It isn't that he wants to play with his phone, but that he simply can't resist the impulse...
He's in an extremely dangerous situation right now.
What's this? It looks like something has caught his eye.
test Topics
arium
Outrage Over Baby Seal Named "Sea Lion"!! (8/30)
Youkai Ministry's New Minister is
Secret lessons with a ewitching female youkai teacher!?
MY EYE'S NOT THE ONLY BIG PART OF ME.
© Akanameko
An Outbreak of Kappa
HIMI Mouryou'z—Is SAGURU's
e Being Misrepresented!? They
y He's Twenty, But He's Actually
His Teens!? (8/29)
e Oldest Youkai Found in South America!! (8
It's a porn ad!! He's being lured by a porn ad!!
EEK!

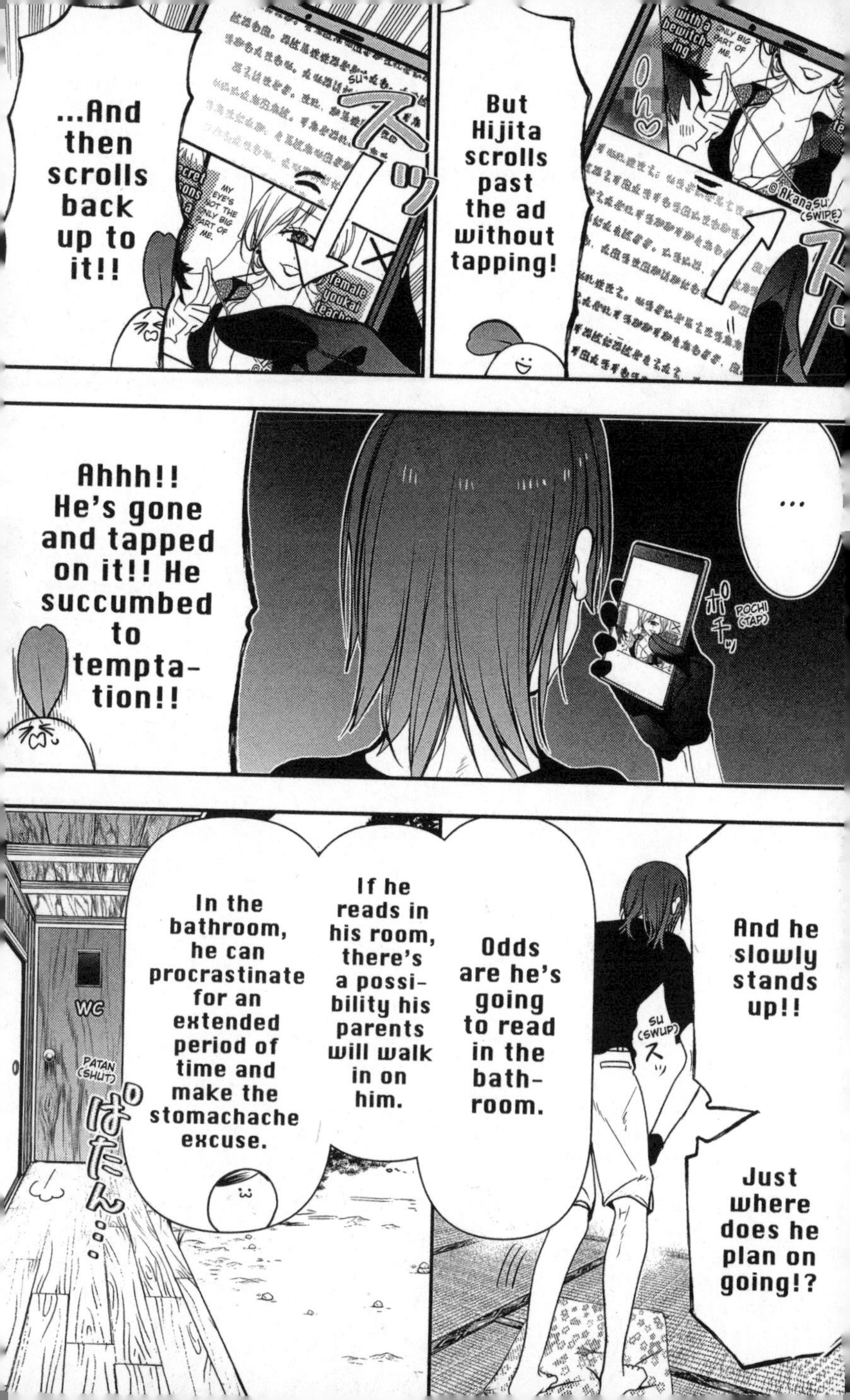

But Hijita scrolls past the ad without tapping!
with a bewitching
ONLY BIG PART OF ME.
© Akanasu
SU (SWIPE)
...And then scrolls back up to it!!
MY EYE'S NOT THE ONLY BIG PART OF ME.
female youkai teacher
...
POCHI (TAP)
Ahhh!! He's gone and tapped on it!! He succumbed to temptation!!
And he slowly stands up!!
SU (SWUP)
Just where does he plan on going!?
Odds are he's going to read in the bathroom.
If he reads in his room, there's a possibility his parents will walk in on him.
In the bathroom, he can procrastinate for an extended period of time and make the stomachache excuse.
WC
PATAN (SHUT)

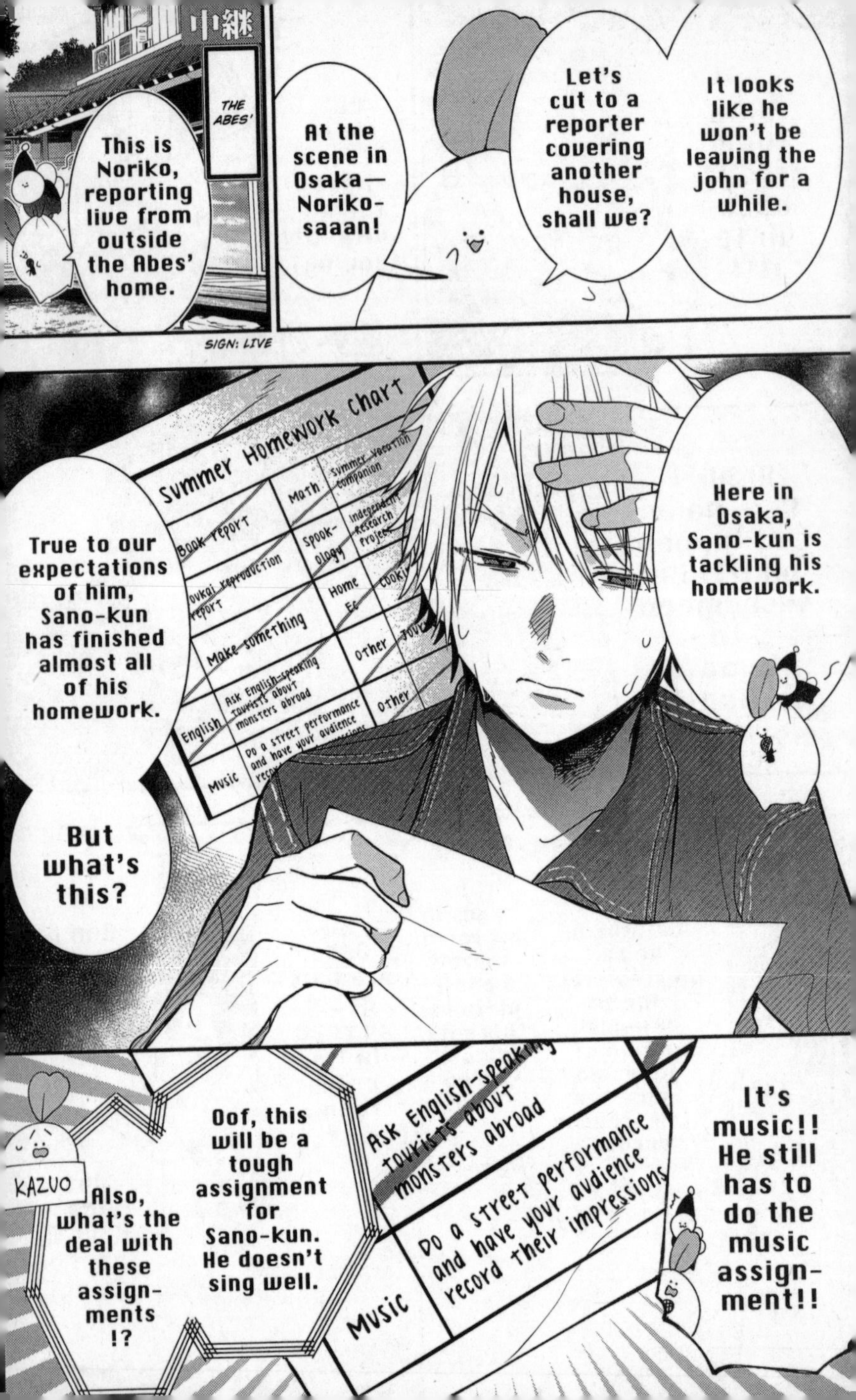
It looks like he won't be leaving the john for a while.
Let's cut to a reporter covering another house, shall we?
At the scene in Osaka—Noriko-saaan!
THE ABES'
This is Noriko, reporting live from outside the Abes' home.
SIGN: LIVE
Here in Osaka, Sano-kun is tackling his homework.
Summer Homework Chart
Book report
Math
Summer Vacation Companion
Spook-ology
Independent Research Project
Youkai reproduction report
Home Ec
Make something
Other
English
Ask English-speaking tourists about monsters abroad
Other
Music
True to our expectations of him, Sano-kun has finished almost all of his homework.
But what's this?
It's music!! He still has to do the music assignment!!
Ask English-speaking tourists about monsters abroad
Music
Do a street performance and have your audience record their impressions
Oof, this will be a tough assignment for Sano-kun. He doesn't sing well.
Also, what's the deal with these assignments!?
KAZUO

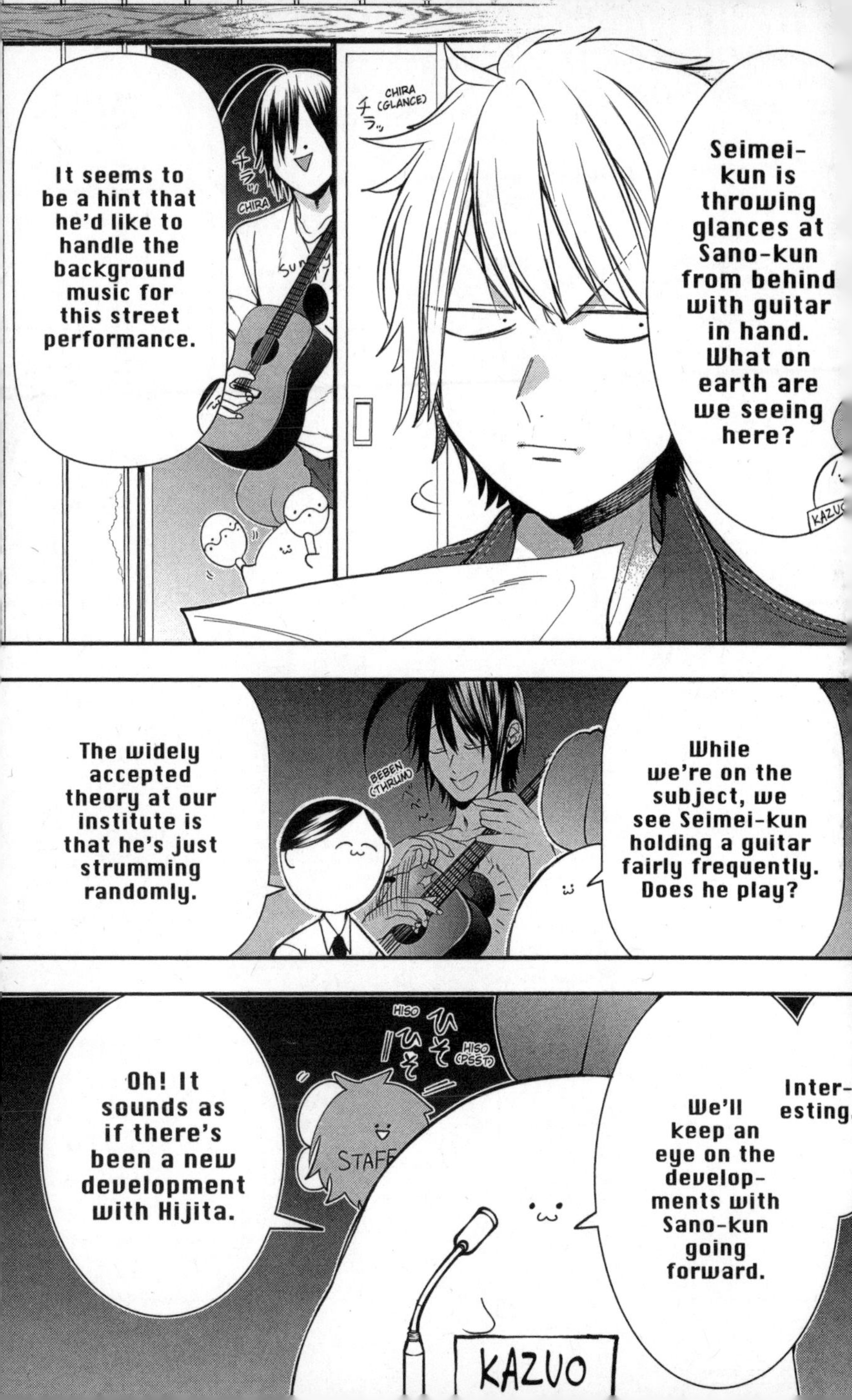
Seimei-kun is throwing glances at Sano-kun from behind with guitar in hand. What on earth are we seeing here?
チラッ
CHIRA (GLANCE)
It seems to be a hint that he'd like to handle the background music for this street performance.
チラッ
CHIRA
While we're on the subject, we see Seimei-kun holding a guitar fairly frequently. Does he play?
BEBEN (THRUM)
The widely accepted theory at our institute is that he's just strumming randomly.
Inter-esting.
We'll keep an eye on the develop-ments with Sano-kun going forward.
KAZUO
ひそひそ
HISO HISO (PSST)
Oh! It sounds as if there's been a new development with Hijita.

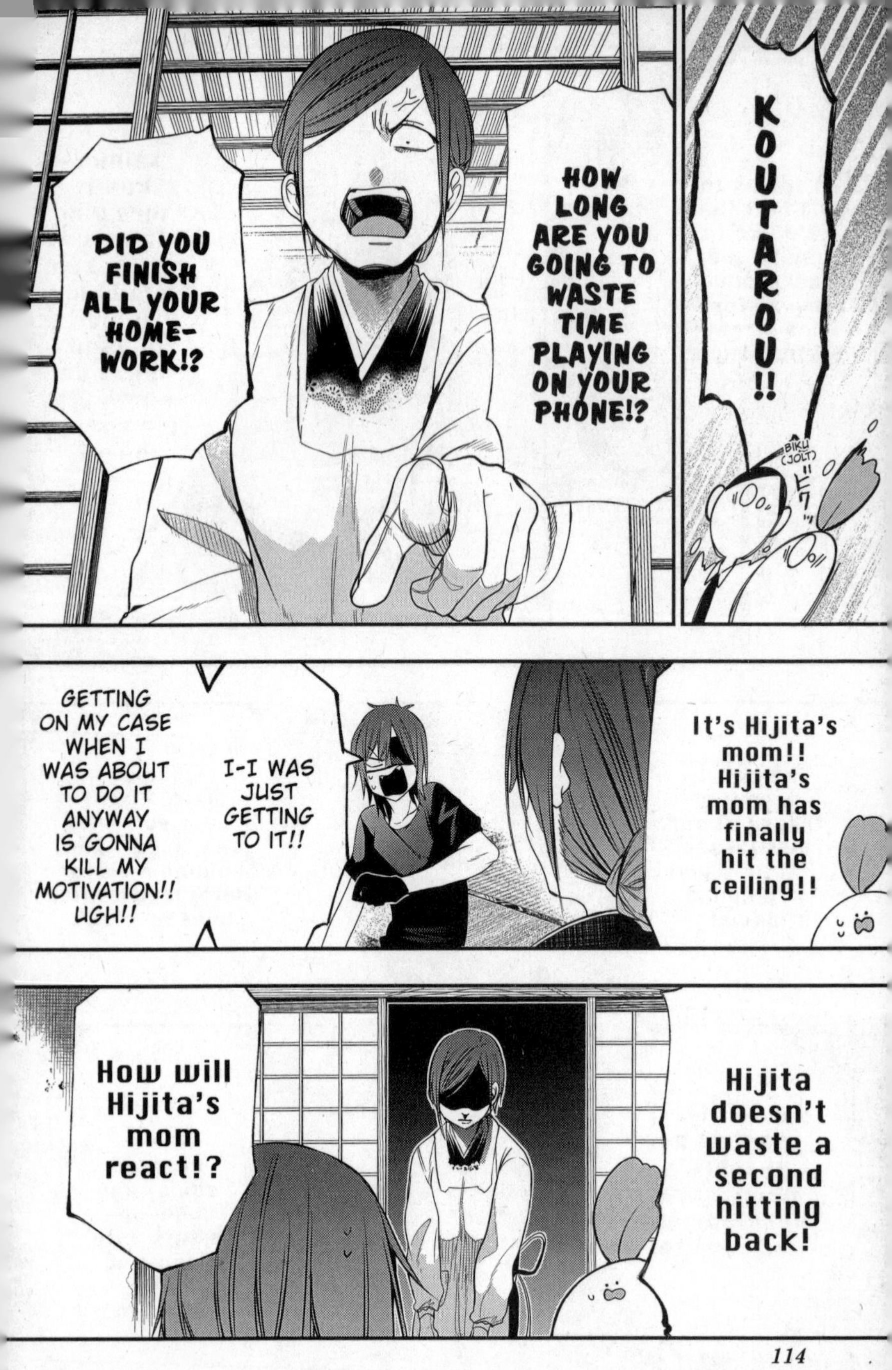
KOUTAROU!!
BIKU (JOLT)
HOW LONG ARE YOU GOING TO WASTE TIME PLAYING ON YOUR PHONE!?
DID YOU FINISH ALL YOUR HOME-WORK!?
It's Hijita's mom!! Hijita's mom has finally hit the ceiling!!
I-I WAS JUST GETTING TO IT!!
GETTING ON MY CASE WHEN I WAS ABOUT TO DO IT ANYWAY IS GONNA KILL MY MOTIVATION!! UGH!!
Hijita doesn't waste a second hitting back!
How will Hijita's mom react!?

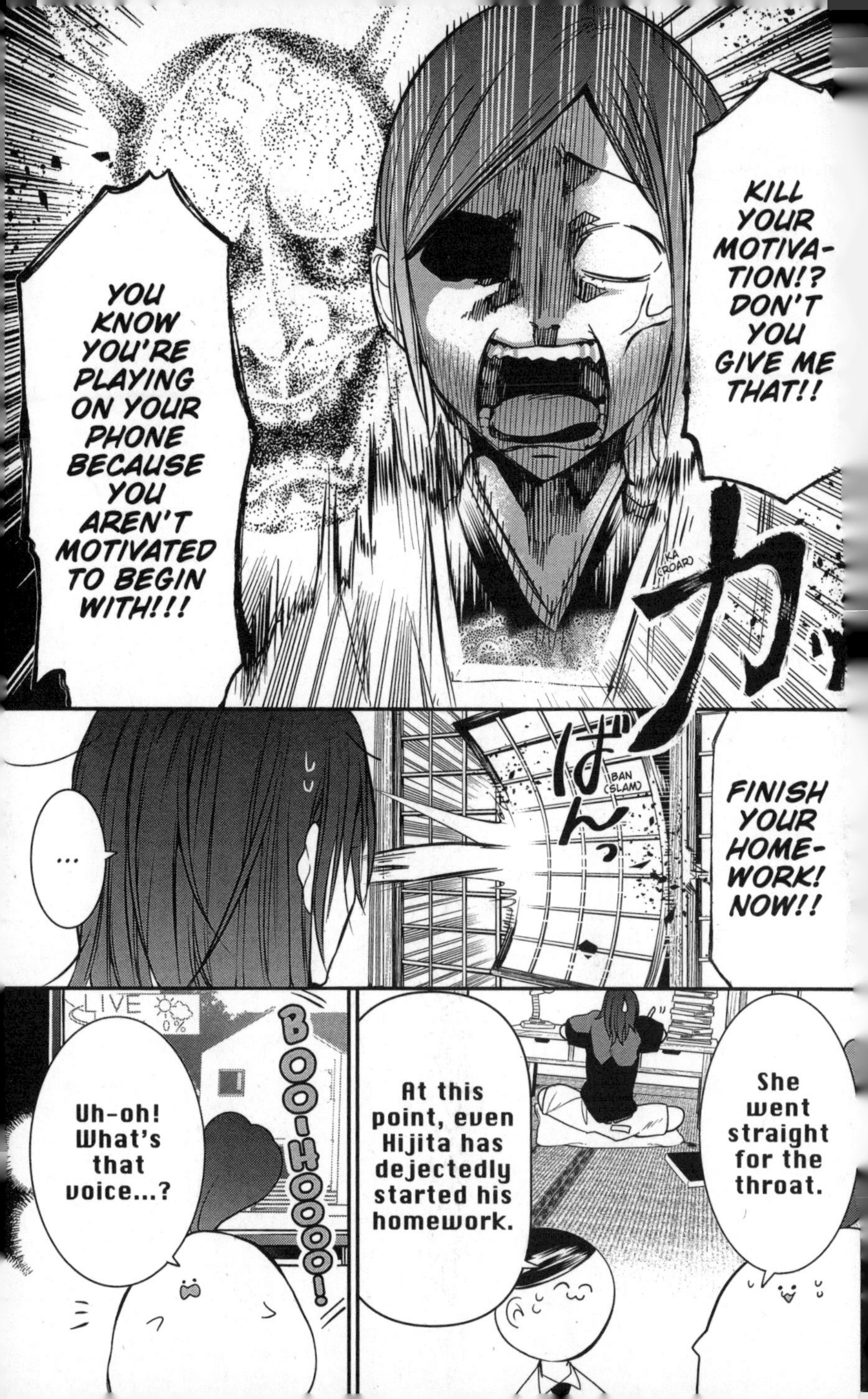
KILL YOUR MOTIVA-TION!? DON'T YOU GIVE ME THAT!!
YOU KNOW YOU'RE PLAYING ON YOUR PHONE BECAUSE YOU AREN'T MOTIVATED TO BEGIN WITH!!!
カッ
KA (ROAR)
FINISH YOUR HOME-WORK! NOW!!
ばんっ
BAN (SLAM)
...
She went straight for the throat.
At this point, even Hijita has dejectedly started his homework.
BOO-HOOOOO!
LIVE
0%
Uh-oh! What's that voice...?

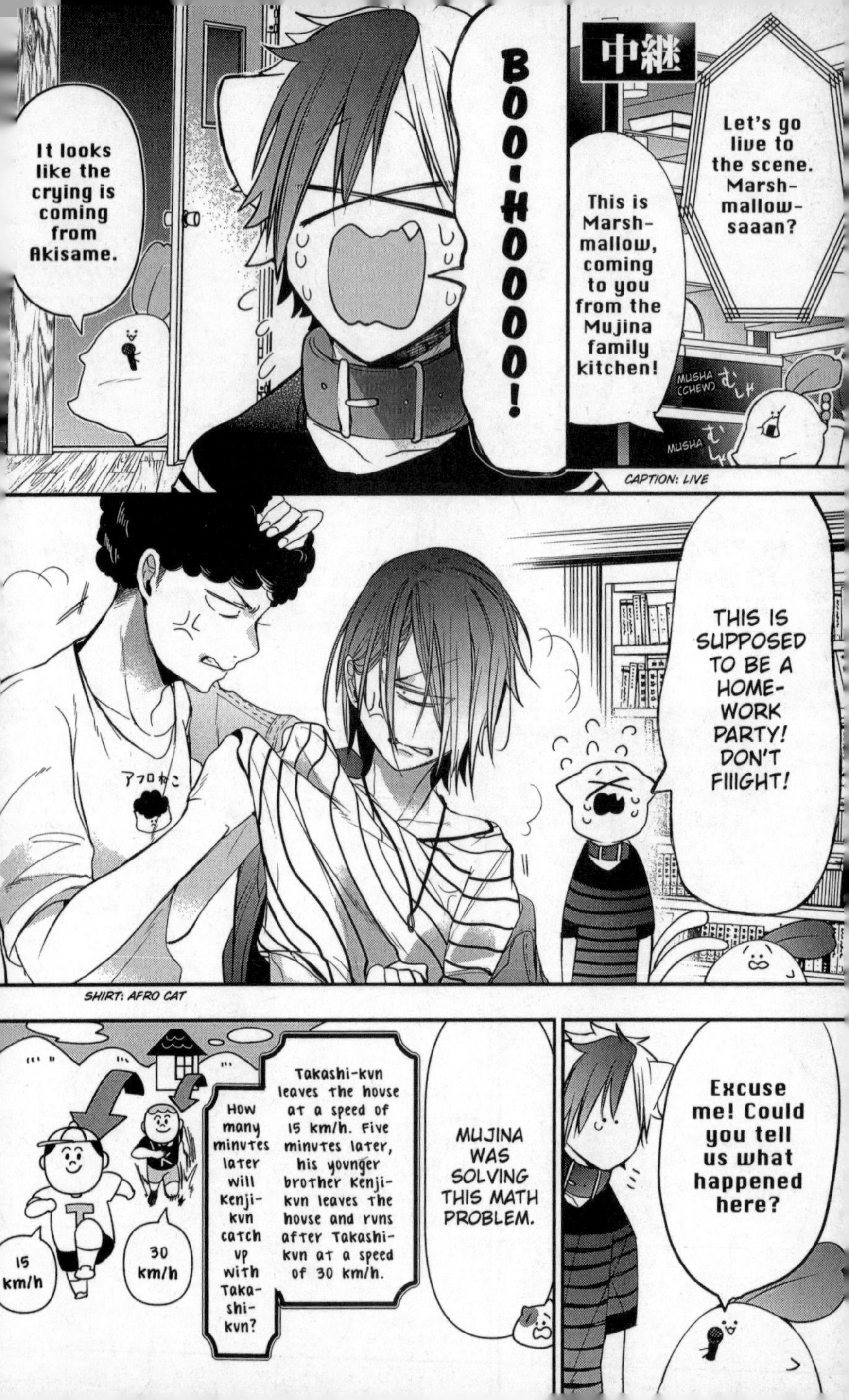
中継
Let's go live to the scene. Marsh-mallow-saaan?
This is Marsh-mallow, coming to you from the Mujina family kitchen!
MUSHA (CHEW) むしゃ
MUSHA むしゃ
CAPTION: LIVE
BOO-HOOOOOO!
It looks like the crying is coming from Akisame.
THIS IS SUPPOSED TO BE A HOME-WORK PARTY! DON'T FIIIGHT!
アフロねこ
SHIRT: AFRO CAT
Excuse me! Could you tell us what happened here?
MUJINA WAS SOLVING THIS MATH PROBLEM.
Takashi-kun leaves the house at a speed of 15 km/h. Five minutes later, his younger brother Kenji-kun leaves the house and runs after Takashi-kun at a speed of 30 km/h.
How many minutes later will Kenji-kun catch up with Takashi-kun?
30 km/h
15 km/h

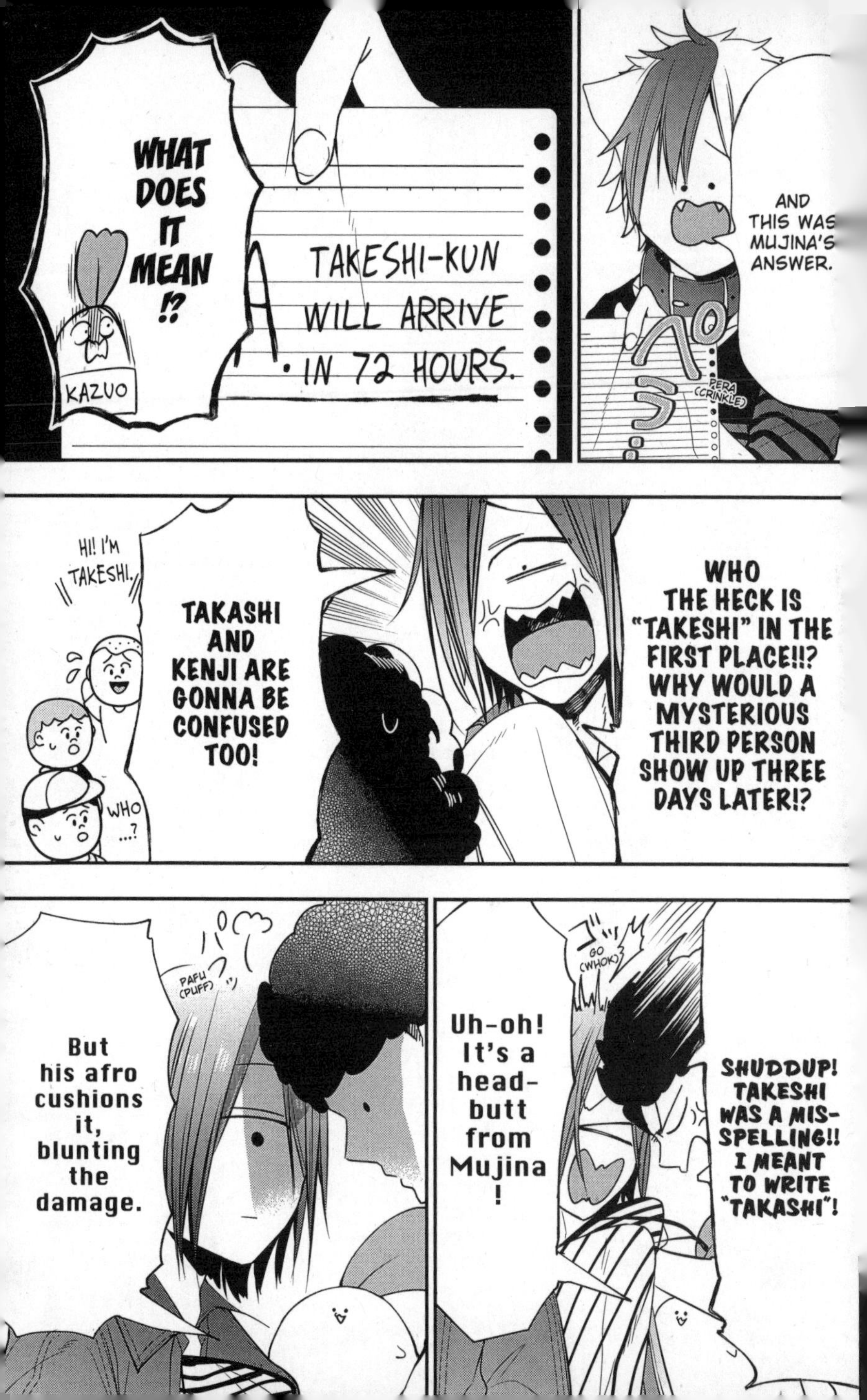

AND THIS WAS MUJINA'S ANSWER.
PERA (CRINKLE)
A
TAKESHI-KUN WILL ARRIVE IN 72 HOURS.
WHAT DOES IT MEAN!?
KAZUO
WHO THE HECK IS "TAKESHI" IN THE FIRST PLACE!!? WHY WOULD A MYSTERIOUS THIRD PERSON SHOW UP THREE DAYS LATER!?
TAKASHI AND KENJI ARE GONNA BE CONFUSED TOO!
HI! I'M TAKESHI.
WHO ...?
GO (WHOK)
SHUDDUP! TAKESHI WAS A MIS-SPELLING!! I MEANT TO WRITE "TAKASHI"!
Uh-oh! It's a head-butt from Mujina!
PAFU (PUFF)
But his afro cushions it, blunting the damage.

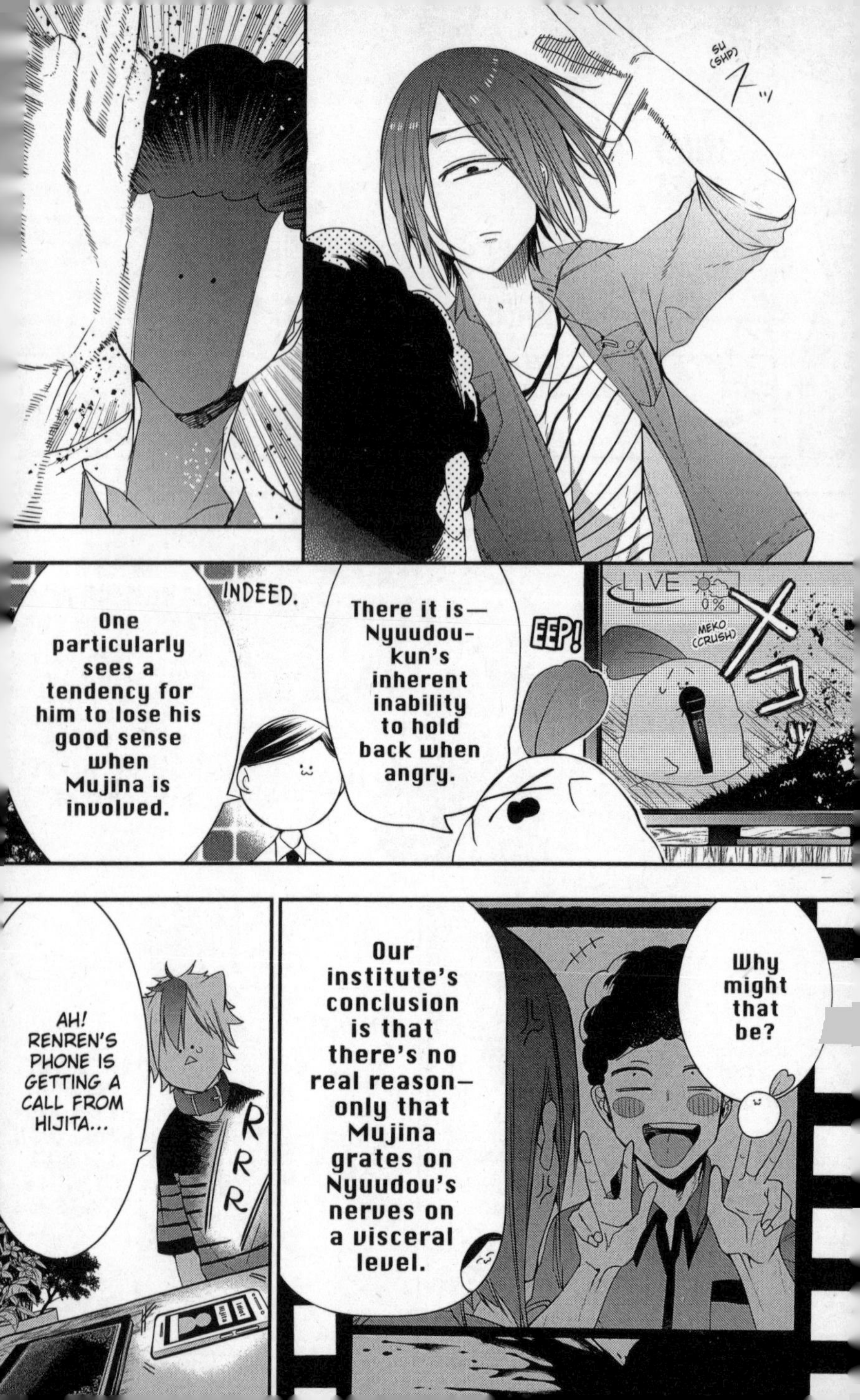
SU (SHP)
LIVE
0%
MEKO (CRUSH)
EEP!
There it is—Nyuudou-kun's inherent inability to hold back when angry.
INDEED.
One particularly sees a tendency for him to lose his good sense when Mujina is involved.
Why might that be?
Our institute's conclusion is that there's no real reason—only that Mujina grates on Nyuudou's nerves on a visceral level.
AH! RENREN'S PHONE IS GETTING A CALL FROM HIJITA...
RRR

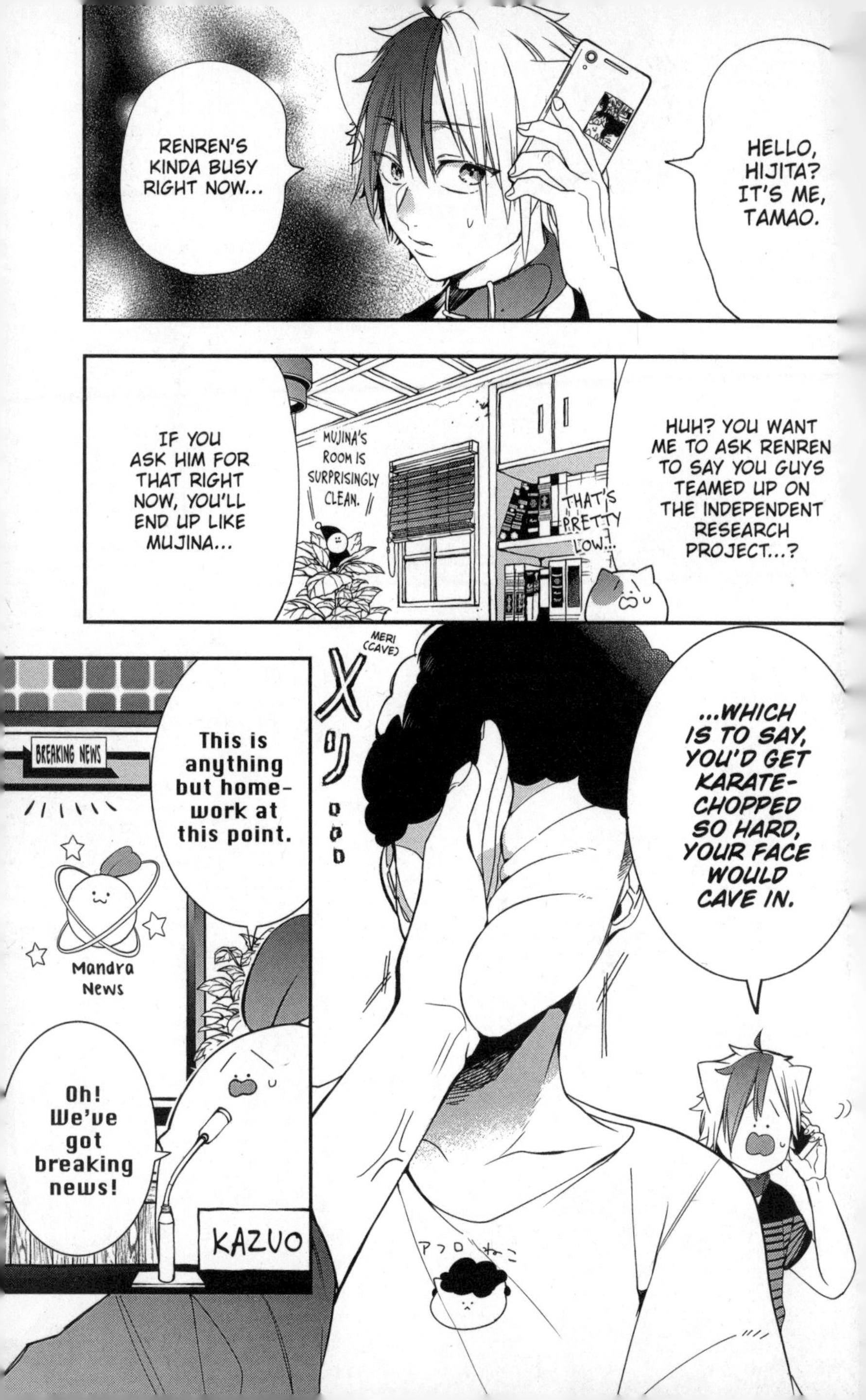
HELLO, HIJITA? IT'S ME, TAMAO.
RENREN'S KINDA BUSY RIGHT NOW...
HUH? YOU WANT ME TO ASK RENREN TO SAY YOU GUYS TEAMED UP ON THE INDEPENDENT RESEARCH PROJECT...?
THAT'S PRETTY LOW...
MUJINA'S ROOM IS SURPRISINGLY CLEAN.
IF YOU ASK HIM FOR THAT RIGHT NOW, YOU'LL END UP LIKE MUJINA...
...WHICH IS TO SAY, YOU'D GET KARATE-CHOPPED SO HARD, YOUR FACE WOULD CAVE IN.
MERI (CAVE)
メリ
アフロねこ
This is anything but home-work at this point.
BREAKING NEWS
Mandra News
Oh! We've got breaking news!
KAZUO

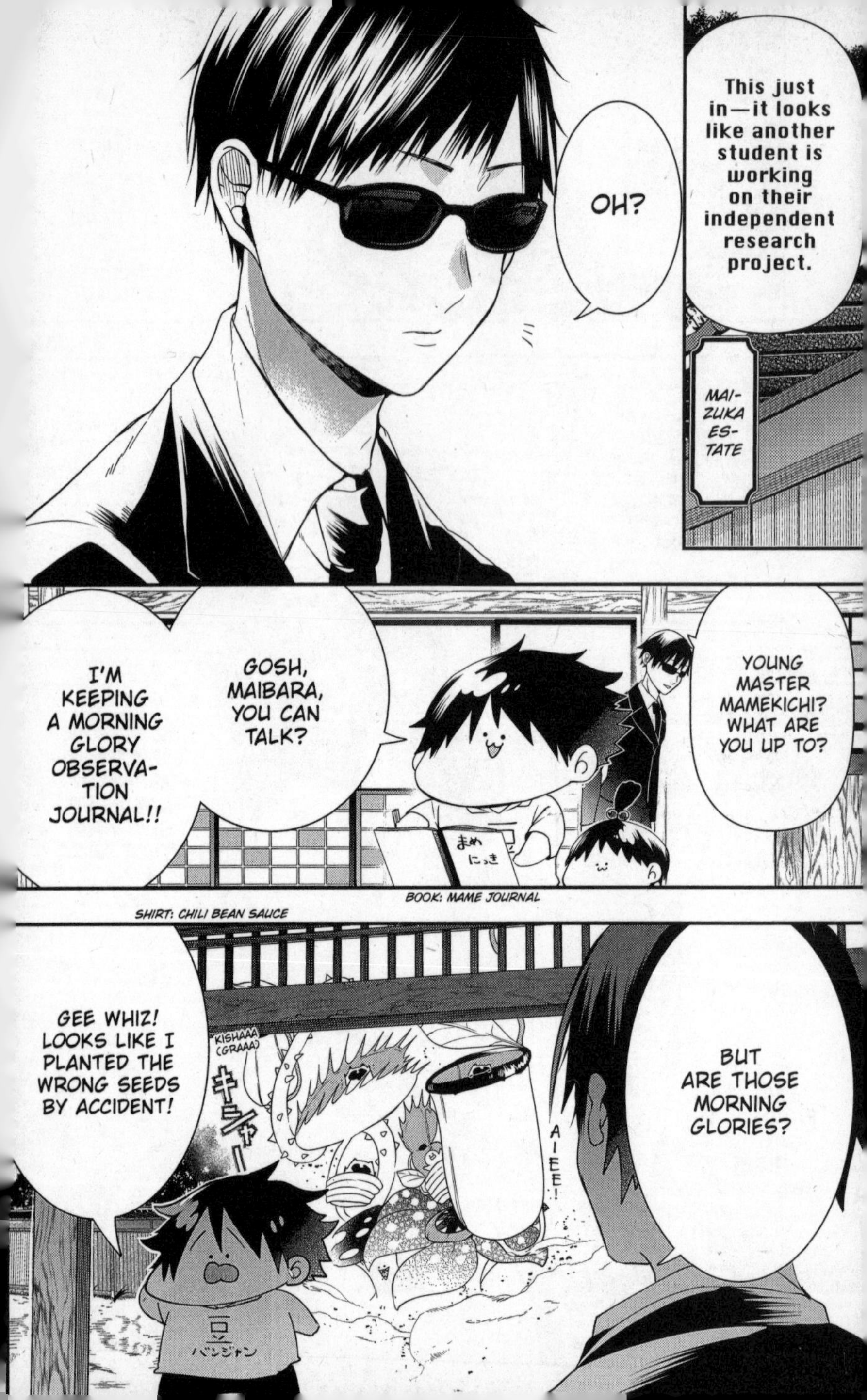
This just in—it looks like another student is working on their independent research project.
MAIZUKA ESTATE
OH?
YOUNG MASTER MAMEKICHI? WHAT ARE YOU UP TO?
GOSH, MAIBARA, YOU CAN TALK?
I'M KEEPING A MORNING GLORY OBSERVATION JOURNAL!!
まめ にっき
BOOK: MAME JOURNAL
SHIRT: CHILI BEAN SAUCE
BUT ARE THOSE MORNING GLORIES?
AIEEE!
KISHAAA (GRAAA)
キシャー
GEE WHIZ! LOOKS LIKE I PLANTED THE WRONG SEEDS BY ACCIDENT!
豆 バンジャン

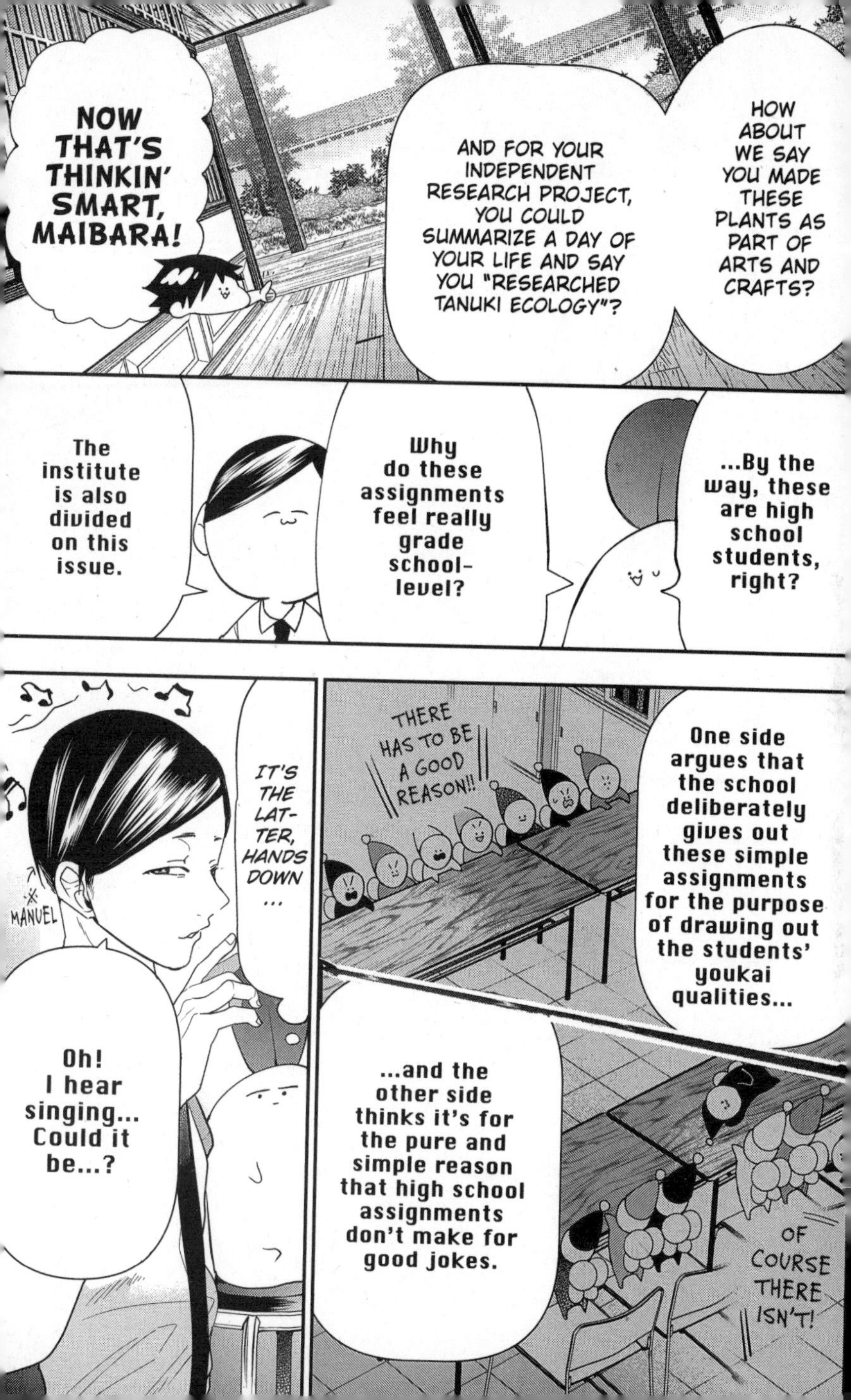
HOW ABOUT WE SAY YOU MADE THESE PLANTS AS PART OF ARTS AND CRAFTS?
AND FOR YOUR INDEPENDENT RESEARCH PROJECT, YOU COULD SUMMARIZE A DAY OF YOUR LIFE AND SAY YOU "RESEARCHED TANUKI ECOLOGY"?
NOW THAT'S THINKIN' SMART, MAIBARA!
...By the way, these are high school students, right?
Why do these assignments feel really grade school-level?
The institute is also divided on this issue.
One side argues that the school deliberately gives out these simple assignments for the purpose of drawing out the students' youkai qualities...
THERE HAS TO BE A GOOD REASON!!
...and the other side thinks it's for the pure and simple reason that high school assignments don't make for good jokes.
OF COURSE THERE ISN'T!
IT'S THE LAT-TER, HANDS DOWN...
※MANUEL
Oh! I hear singing... Could it be...?

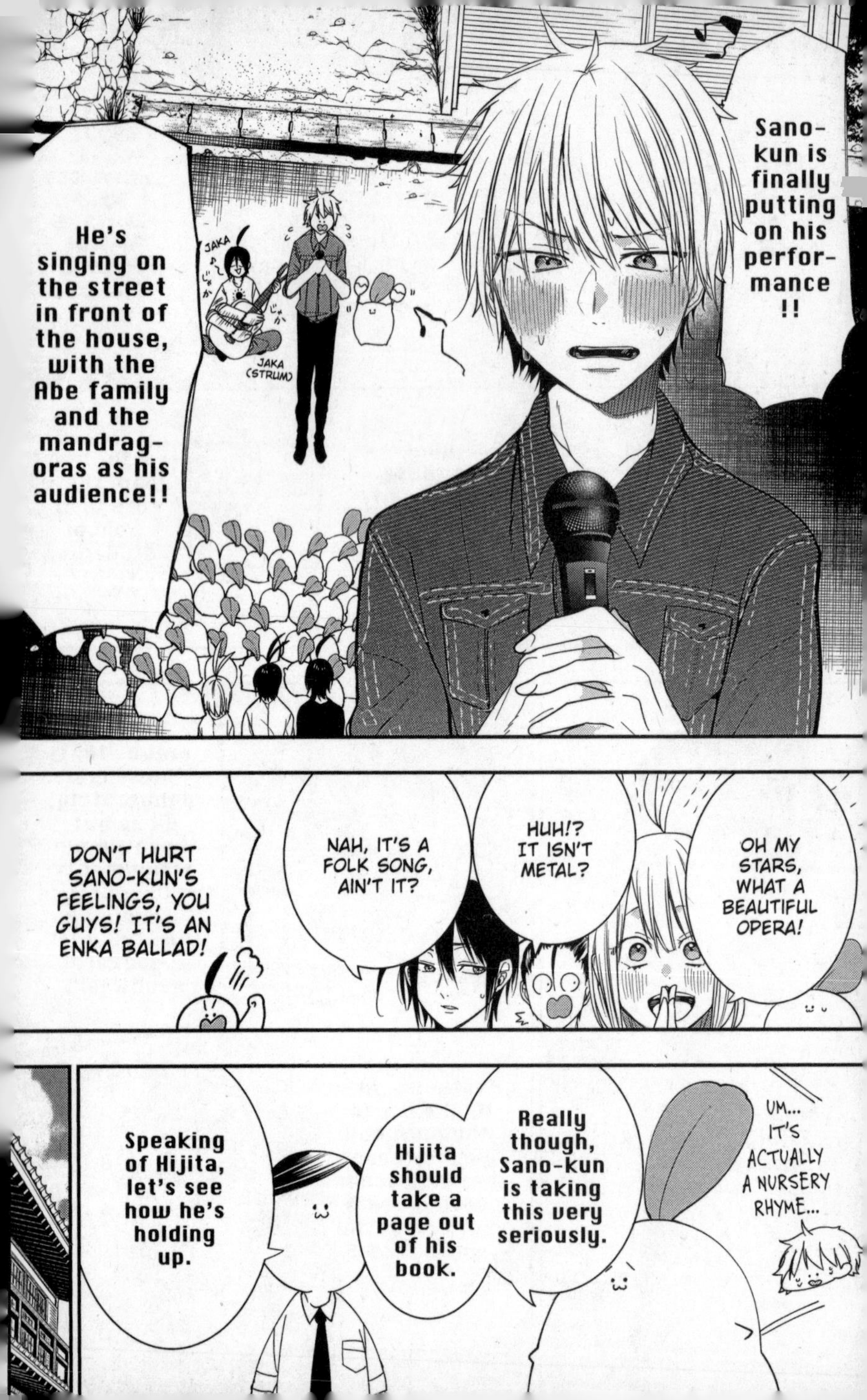
Sano-kun is finally putting on his performance!!
He's singing on the street in front of the house, with the Abe family and the mandragoras as his audience!!
JAKA
JAKA (STRUM)
OH MY STARS, WHAT A BEAUTIFUL OPERA!
HUH!? IT ISN'T METAL?
NAH, IT'S A FOLK SONG, AIN'T IT?
DON'T HURT SANO-KUN'S FEELINGS, YOU GUYS! IT'S AN ENKA BALLAD!
UM... IT'S ACTUALLY A NURSERY RHYME...
Really though, Sano-kun is taking this very seriously.
Hijita should take a page out of his book.
Speaking of Hijita, let's see how he's holding up.

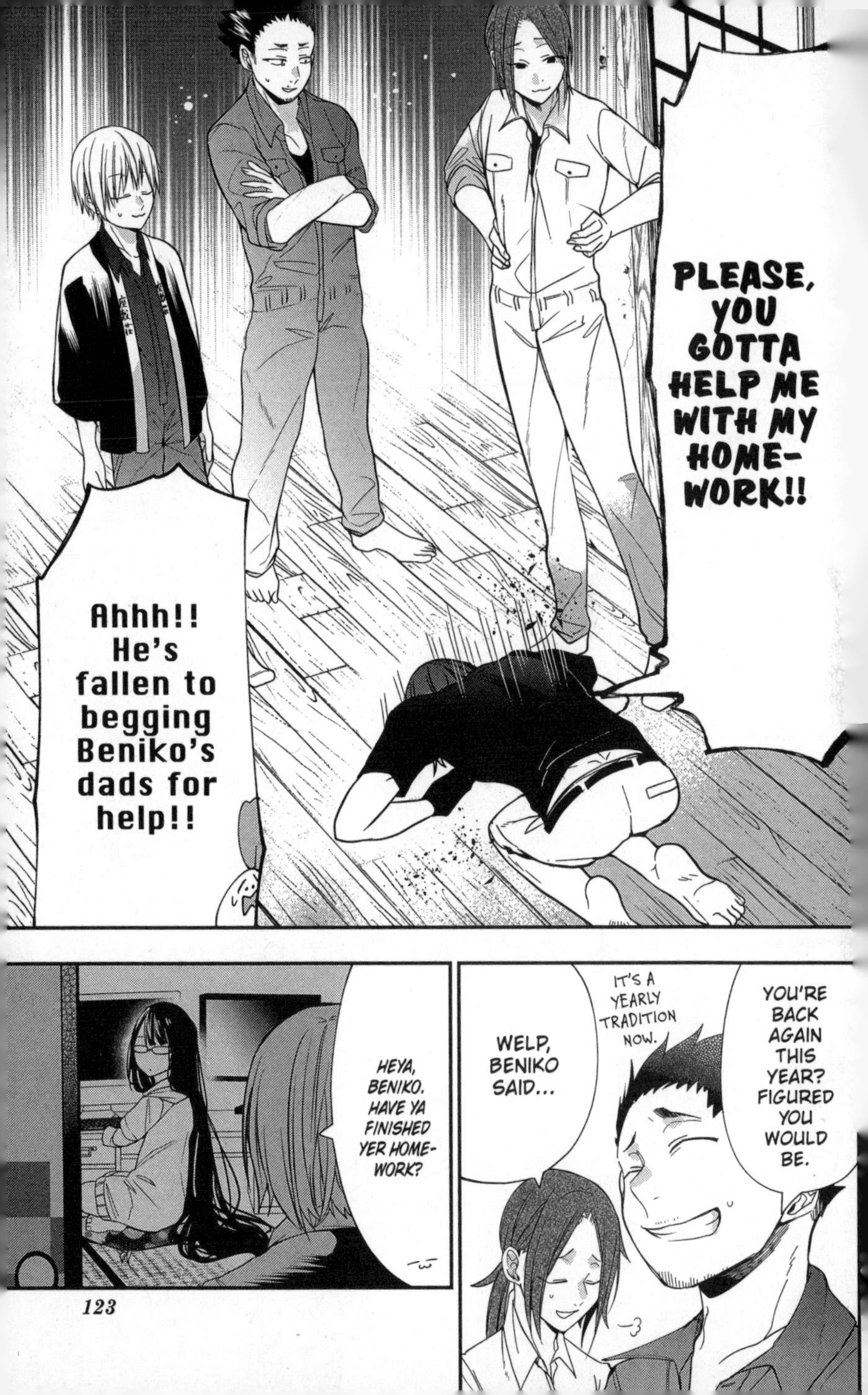
PLEASE, YOU GOTTA HELP ME WITH MY HOME-WORK!!
Ahhh!! He's fallen to begging Beniko's dads for help!!
YOU'RE BACK AGAIN THIS YEAR? FIGURED YOU WOULD BE.
IT'S A YEARLY TRADITION NOW.
WELP, BENIKO SAID...
HEYA, BENIKO. HAVE YA FINISHED YER HOME-WORK?

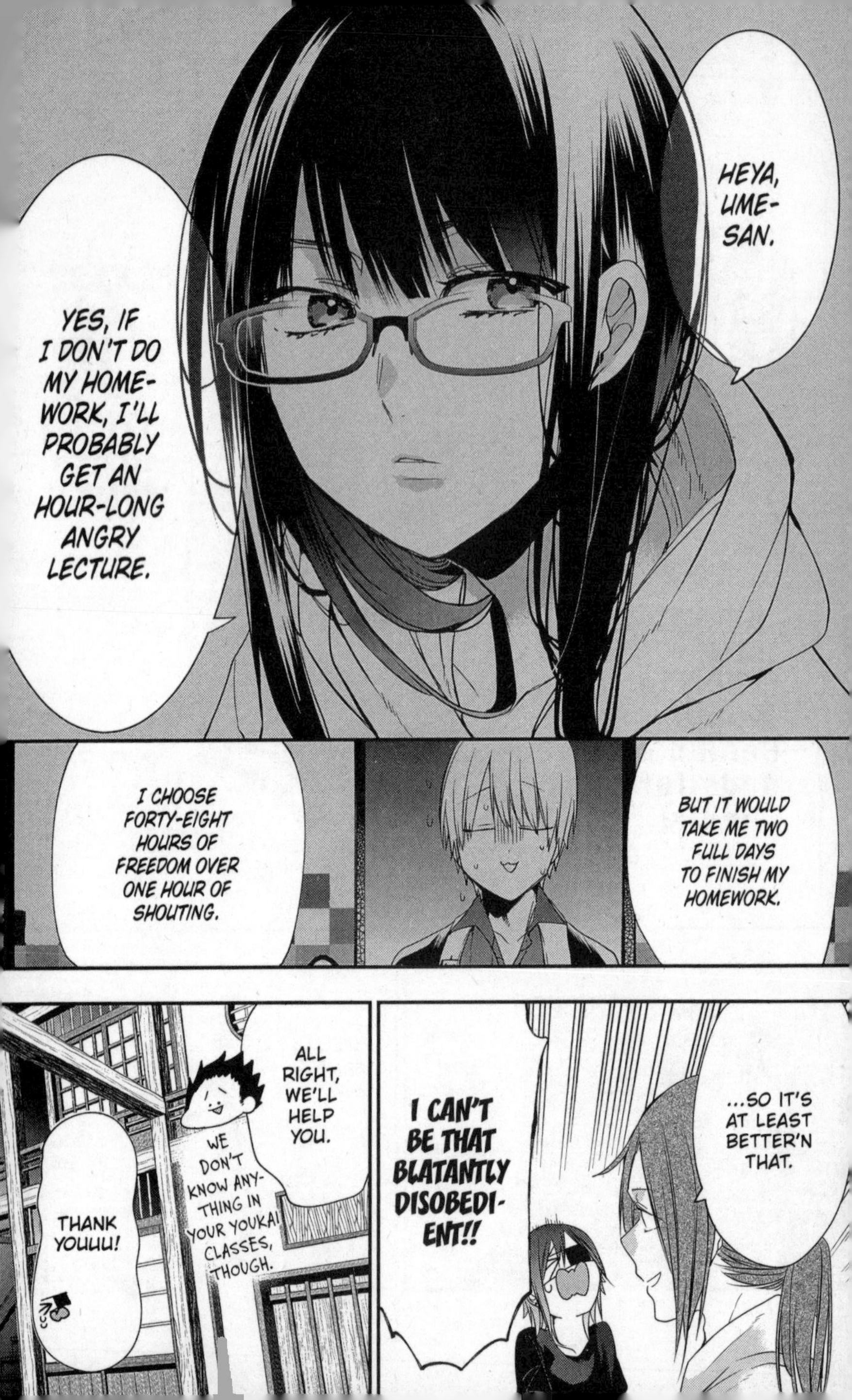
HEYA, UME-SAN.
YES, IF I DON'T DO MY HOME-WORK, I'LL PROBABLY GET AN HOUR-LONG ANGRY LECTURE.
BUT IT WOULD TAKE ME TWO FULL DAYS TO FINISH MY HOMEWORK.
I CHOOSE FORTY-EIGHT HOURS OF FREEDOM OVER ONE HOUR OF SHOUTING.
...SO IT'S AT LEAST BETTER'N THAT.
I CAN'T BE THAT BLATANTLY DISOBEDI-ENT!!
ALL RIGHT, WE'LL HELP YOU.
WE DON'T KNOW ANY-THING IN YOUR YOUKAI CLASSES, THOUGH.
THANK YOUUU!

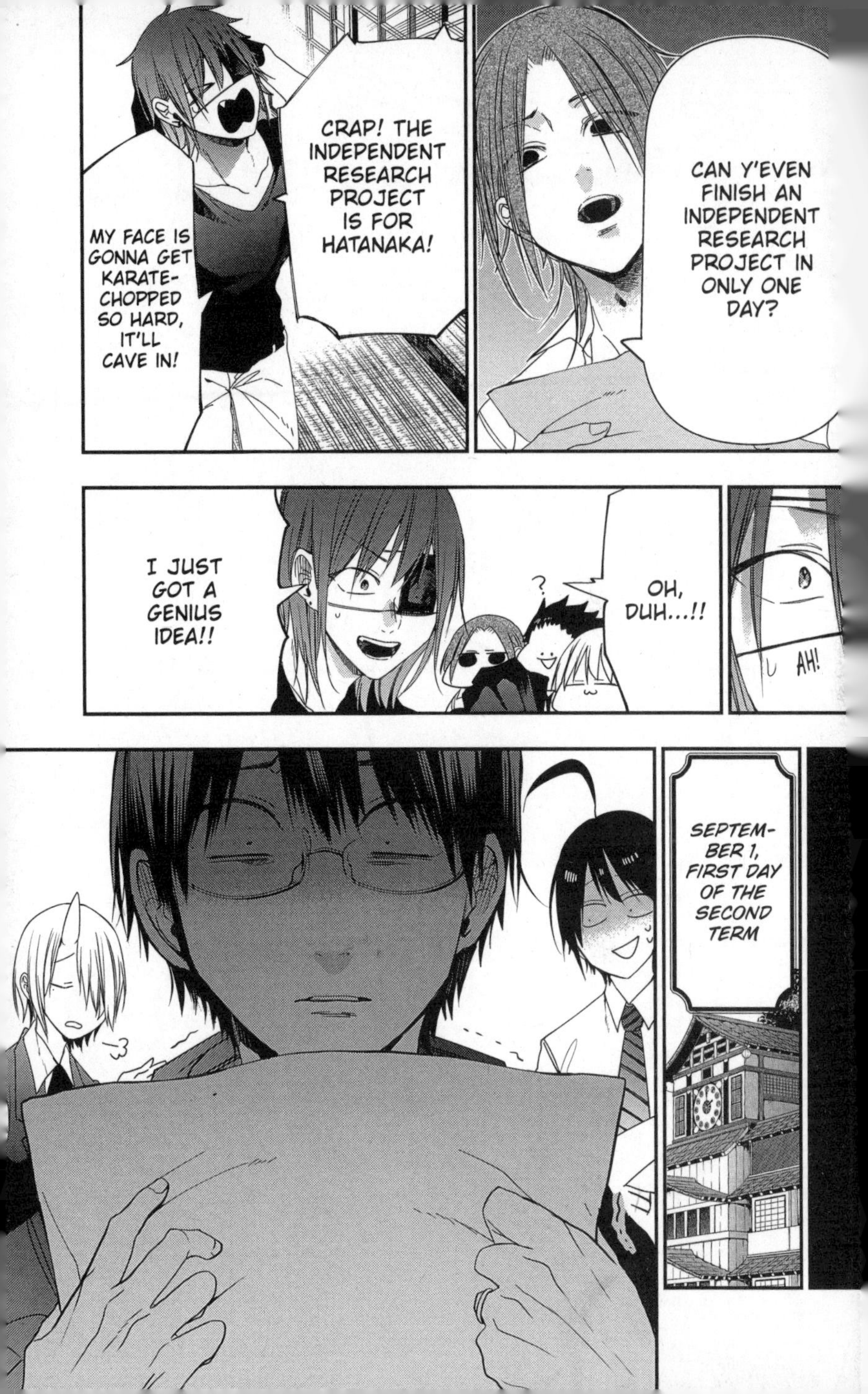
CAN Y'EVEN FINISH AN INDEPENDENT RESEARCH PROJECT IN ONLY ONE DAY?
CRAP! THE INDEPENDENT RESEARCH PROJECT IS FOR HATANAKA!
MY FACE IS GONNA GET KARATE-CHOPPED SO HARD, IT'LL CAVE IN!
AH!
OH, DUH...!!
?
I JUST GOT A GENIUS IDEA!!
SEPTEMBER 1, FIRST DAY OF THE SECOND TERM

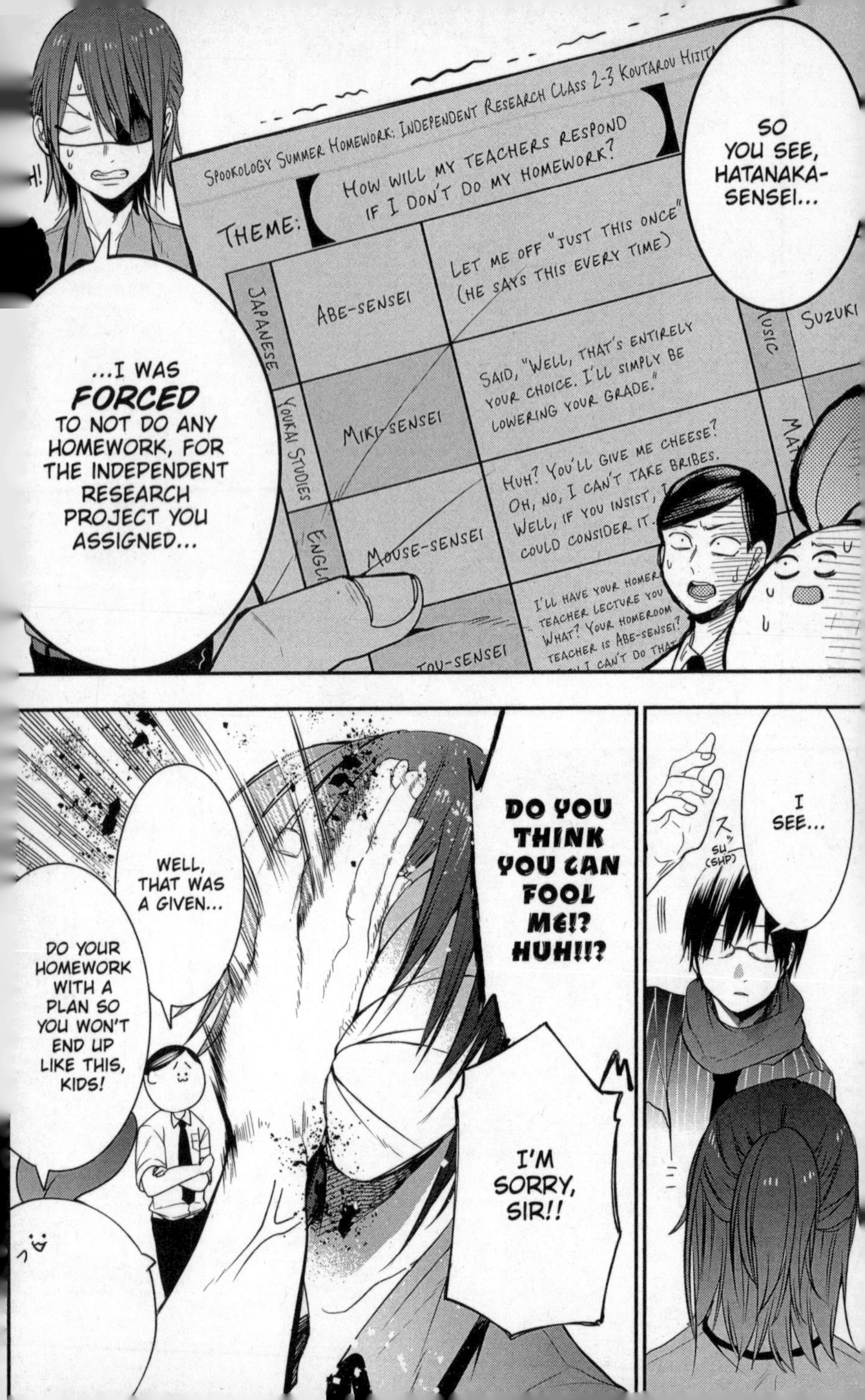
SO YOU SEE, HATANAKA-SENSEI...
SPOOKOLOGY SUMMER HOMEWORK: INDEPENDENT RESEARCH CLASS 2-3 KOUTAROU
THEME: HOW WILL MY TEACHERS RESPOND IF I DON'T DO MY HOMEWORK?
JAPANESE
ABE-SENSEI
LET ME OFF "JUST THIS ONCE" (HE SAYS THIS EVERY TIME)
YOUKAI STUDIES
MIKI-SENSEI
SAID, "WELL, THAT'S ENTIRELY YOUR CHOICE. I'LL SIMPLY BE LOWERING YOUR GRADE."
MOUSE-SENSEI
HUH? YOU'LL GIVE ME CHEESE? OH, NO, I CAN'T TAKE BRIBES.
SUZUKI
...I WAS FORCED TO NOT DO ANY HOMEWORK, FOR THE INDEPENDENT RESEARCH PROJECT YOU ASSIGNED...
I SEE...
SU (SHP)
DO YOU THINK YOU CAN FOOL ME!? HUH!!?
I'M SORRY, SIR!!
WELL, THAT WAS A GIVEN...
DO YOUR HOMEWORK WITH A PLAN SO YOU WON'T END UP LIKE THIS, KIDS!

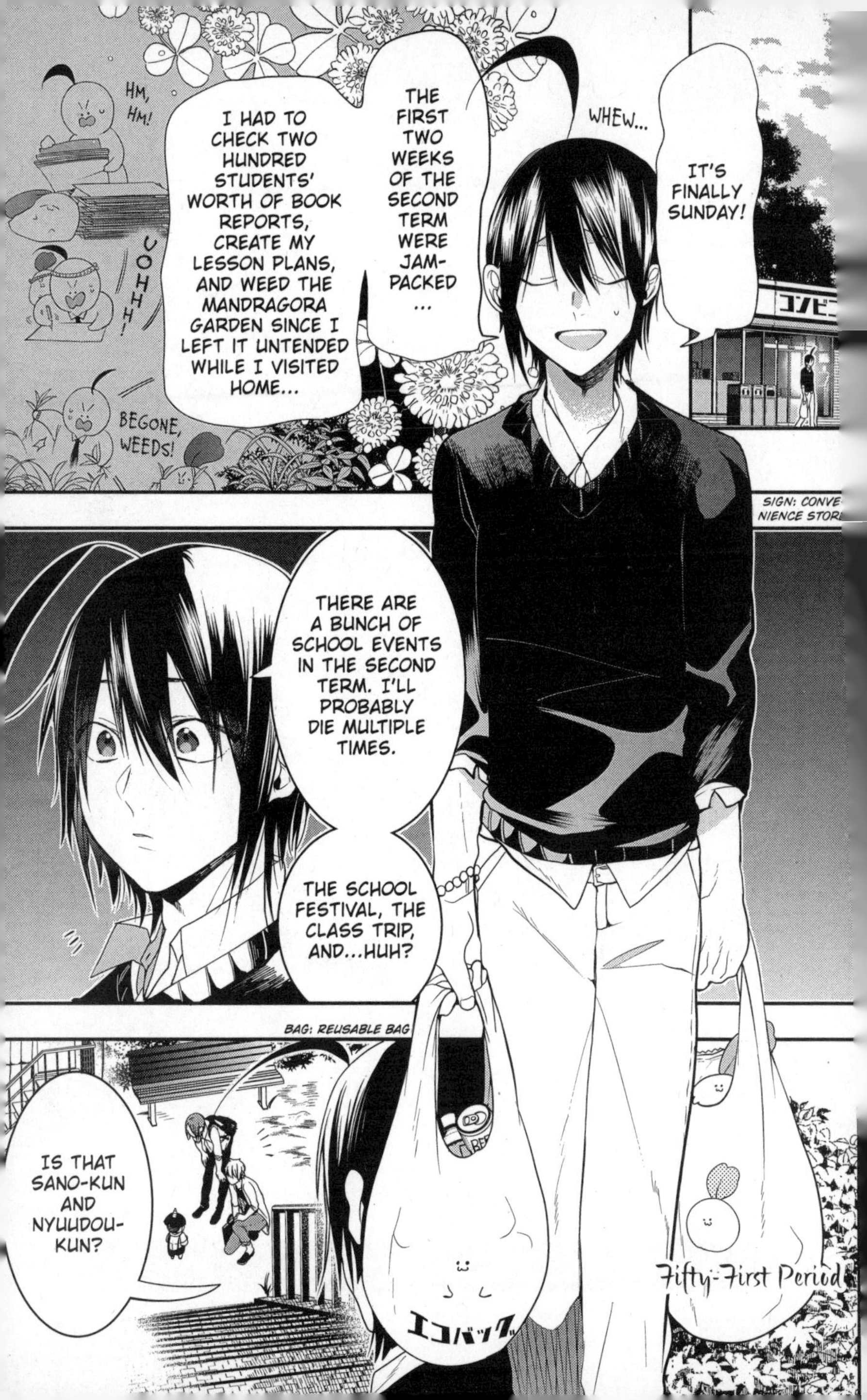

WHEW...
IT'S FINALLY SUNDAY!
SIGN: CONVE-NIENCE STORE
THE FIRST TWO WEEKS OF THE SECOND TERM WERE JAM-PACKED...
I HAD TO CHECK TWO HUNDRED STUDENTS' WORTH OF BOOK REPORTS, CREATE MY LESSON PLANS, AND WEED THE MANDRAGORA GARDEN SINCE I LEFT IT UNTENDED WHILE I VISITED HOME...
HM, HM!
UOHHH!
BEGONE, WEEDS!
THERE ARE A BUNCH OF SCHOOL EVENTS IN THE SECOND TERM. I'LL PROBABLY DIE MULTIPLE TIMES.
THE SCHOOL FESTIVAL, THE CLASS TRIP, AND...HUH?
BAG: REUSABLE BAG
エコバッグ
Fifty-First Period
IS THAT SANO-KUN AND NYUUDOU-KUN?

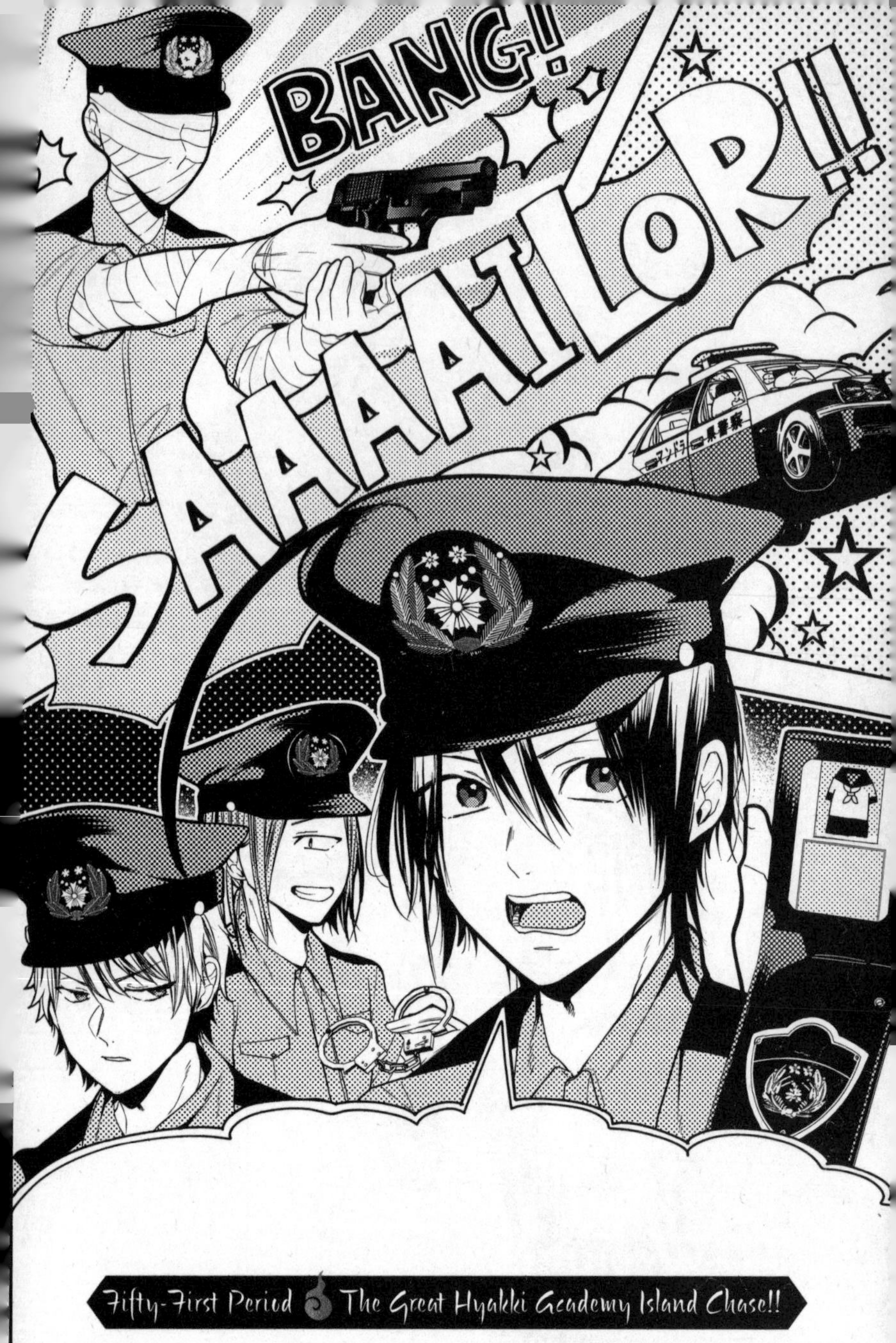
BANG!
SAAAILOR!!

Fifty-First Period The Great Hyakki Academy Island Chase!!

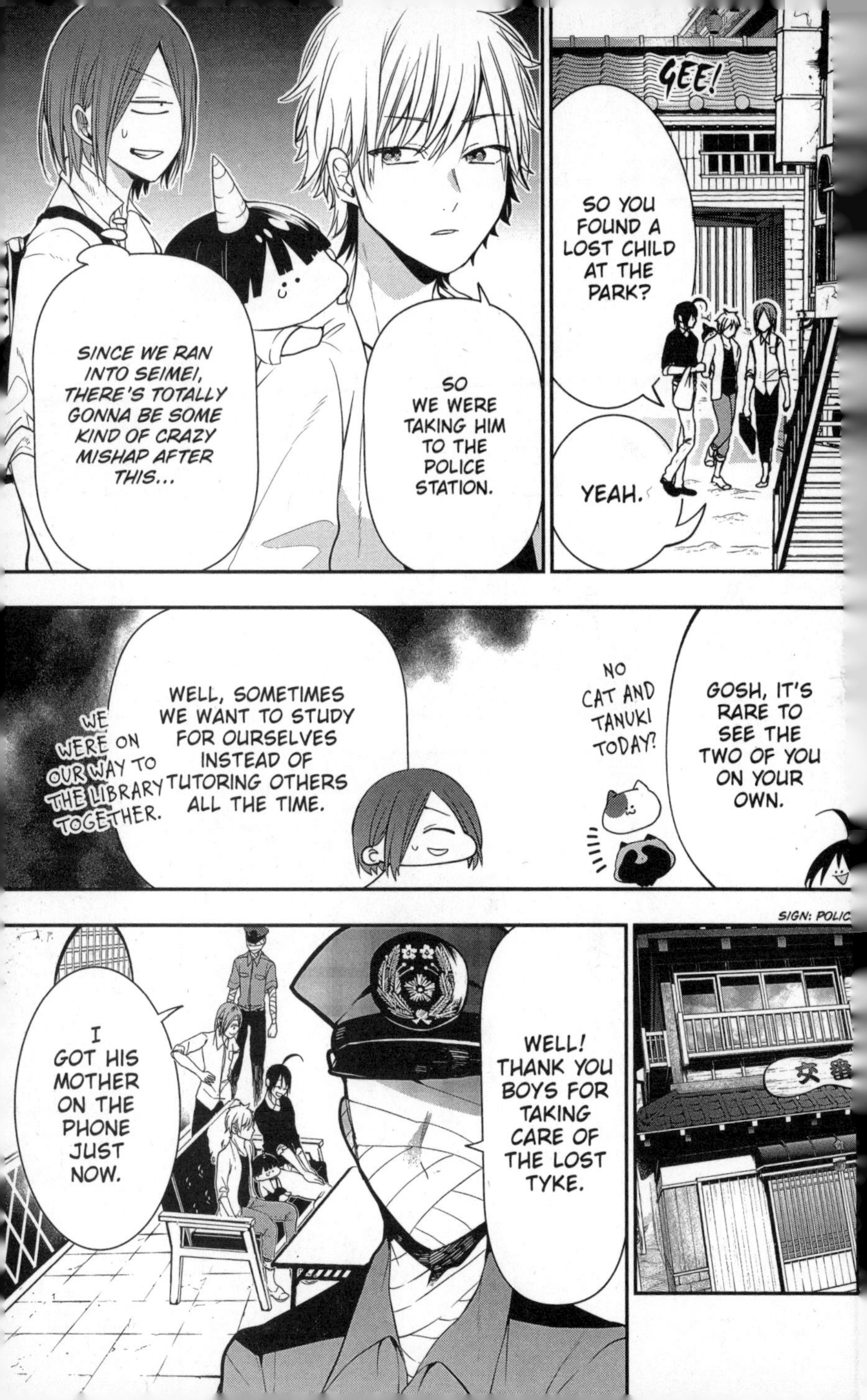
GEE!
SO YOU FOUND A LOST CHILD AT THE PARK?
YEAH.
SO WE WERE TAKING HIM TO THE POLICE STATION.
SINCE WE RAN INTO SEIMEI, THERE'S TOTALLY GONNA BE SOME KIND OF CRAZY MISHAP AFTER THIS...
GOSH, IT'S RARE TO SEE THE TWO OF YOU ON YOUR OWN.
NO CAT AND TANUKI TODAY?
WELL, SOMETIMES WE WANT TO STUDY FOR OURSELVES INSTEAD OF TUTORING OTHERS ALL THE TIME.
WE WERE ON OUR WAY TO THE LIBRARY TOGETHER.
SIGN: POLIC
交番
WELL! THANK YOU BOYS FOR TAKING CARE OF THE LOST TYKE.
I GOT HIS MOTHER ON THE PHONE JUST NOW.

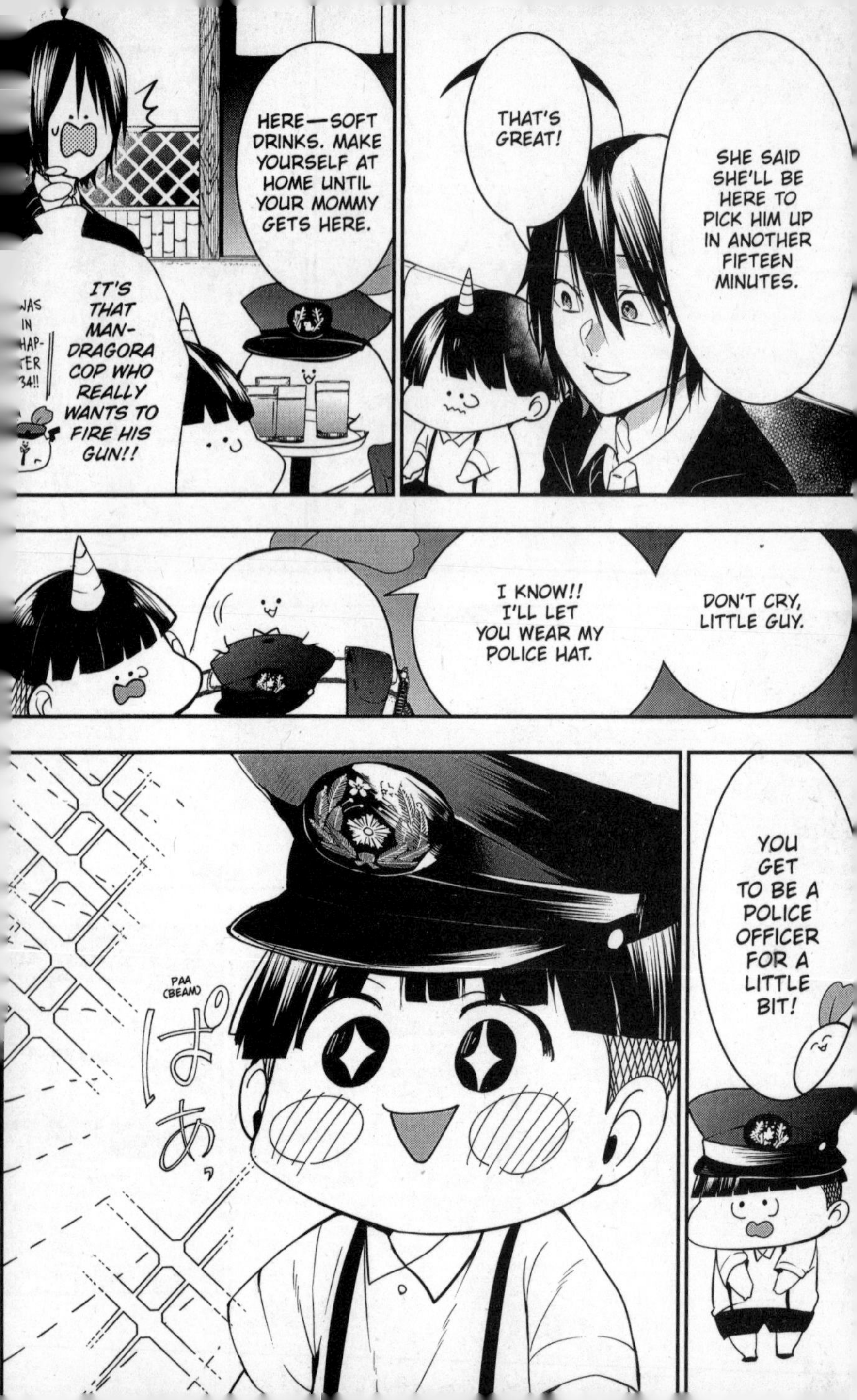
SHE SAID SHE'LL BE HERE TO PICK HIM UP IN ANOTHER FIFTEEN MINUTES.
THAT'S GREAT!
HERE—SOFT DRINKS. MAKE YOURSELF AT HOME UNTIL YOUR MOMMY GETS HERE.
IT'S THAT MAN-DRAGORA COP WHO REALLY WANTS TO FIRE HIS GUN!!
WAS IN HAP-TER 34!!
DON'T CRY, LITTLE GUY.
I KNOW!! I'LL LET YOU WEAR MY POLICE HAT.
YOU GET TO BE A POLICE OFFICER FOR A LITTLE BIT!
PAA (BEAM)
ぱあっ

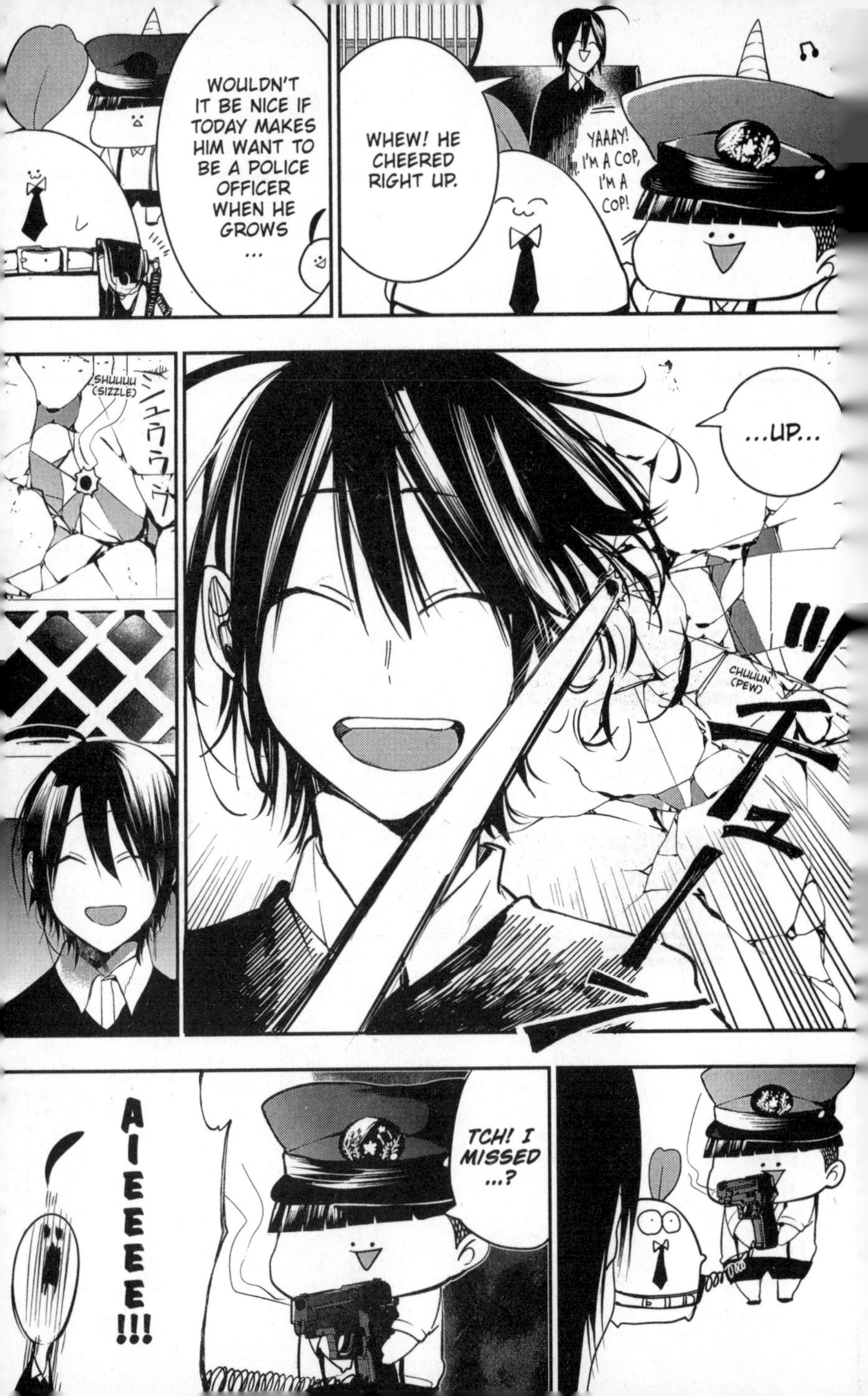
YAAAY! I'M A COP, I'M A COP!
WHEW! HE CHEERED RIGHT UP.
WOULDN'T IT BE NICE IF TODAY MAKES HIM WANT TO BE A POLICE OFFICER WHEN HE GROWS ...
...UP...
CHUUUN (PEW)
SHUUUU (SIZZLE)
シュウウウ
TCH! I MISSED ...?
AIEEEEE!!!

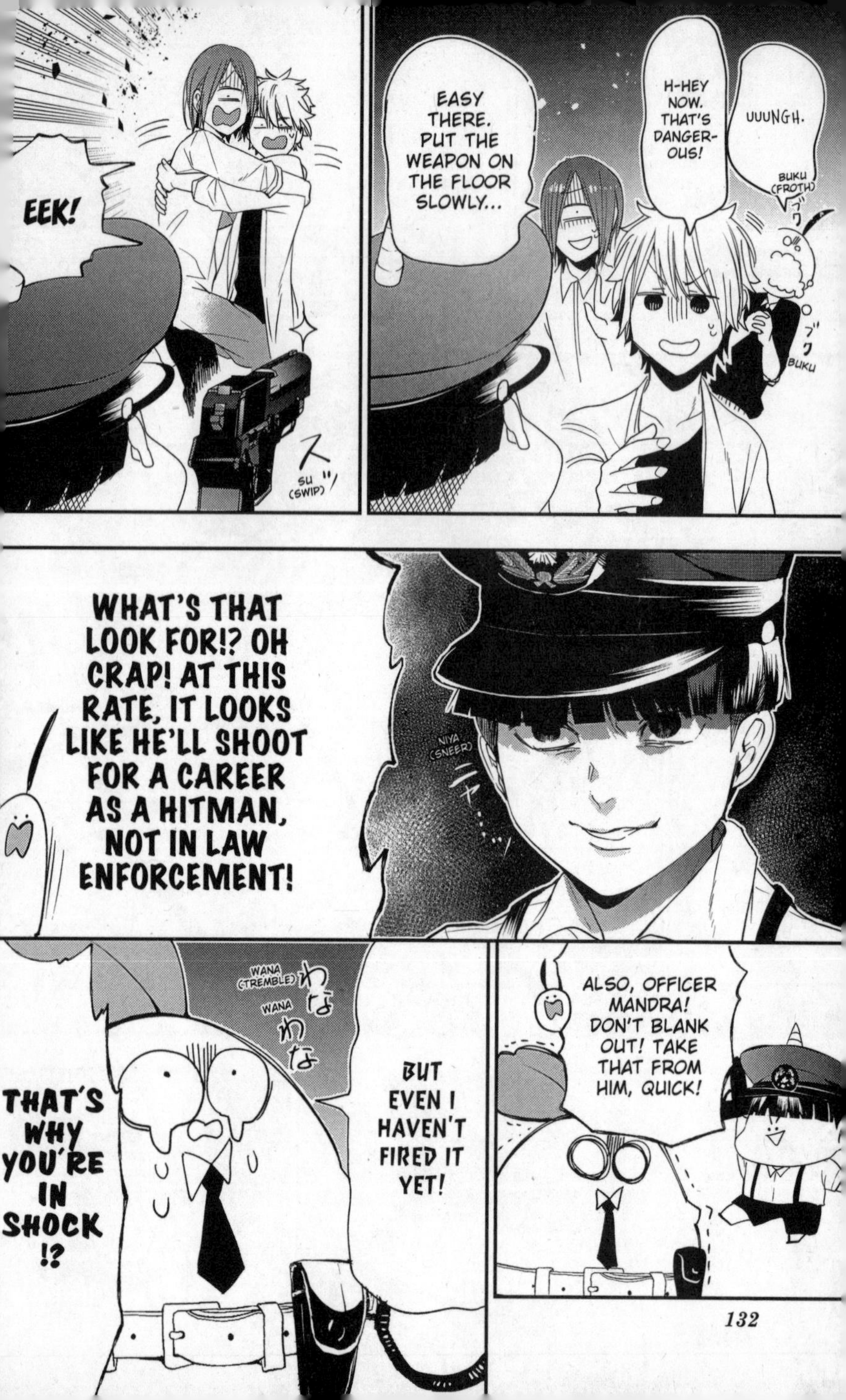
UUUNGH.
BUKU (FROTH)
H-HEY NOW. THAT'S DANGER-OUS!
EASY THERE. PUT THE WEAPON ON THE FLOOR SLOWLY...
BUKU
EEK!
SU (SWIP)
NIYA (SNEER)
WHAT'S THAT LOOK FOR!? OH CRAP! AT THIS RATE, IT LOOKS LIKE HE'LL SHOOT FOR A CAREER AS A HITMAN, NOT IN LAW ENFORCEMENT!
ALSO, OFFICER MANDRA! DON'T BLANK OUT! TAKE THAT FROM HIM, QUICK!
WANA (TREMBLE)
WANA
BUT EVEN I HAVEN'T FIRED IT YET!
THAT'S WHY YOU'RE IN SHOCK!?

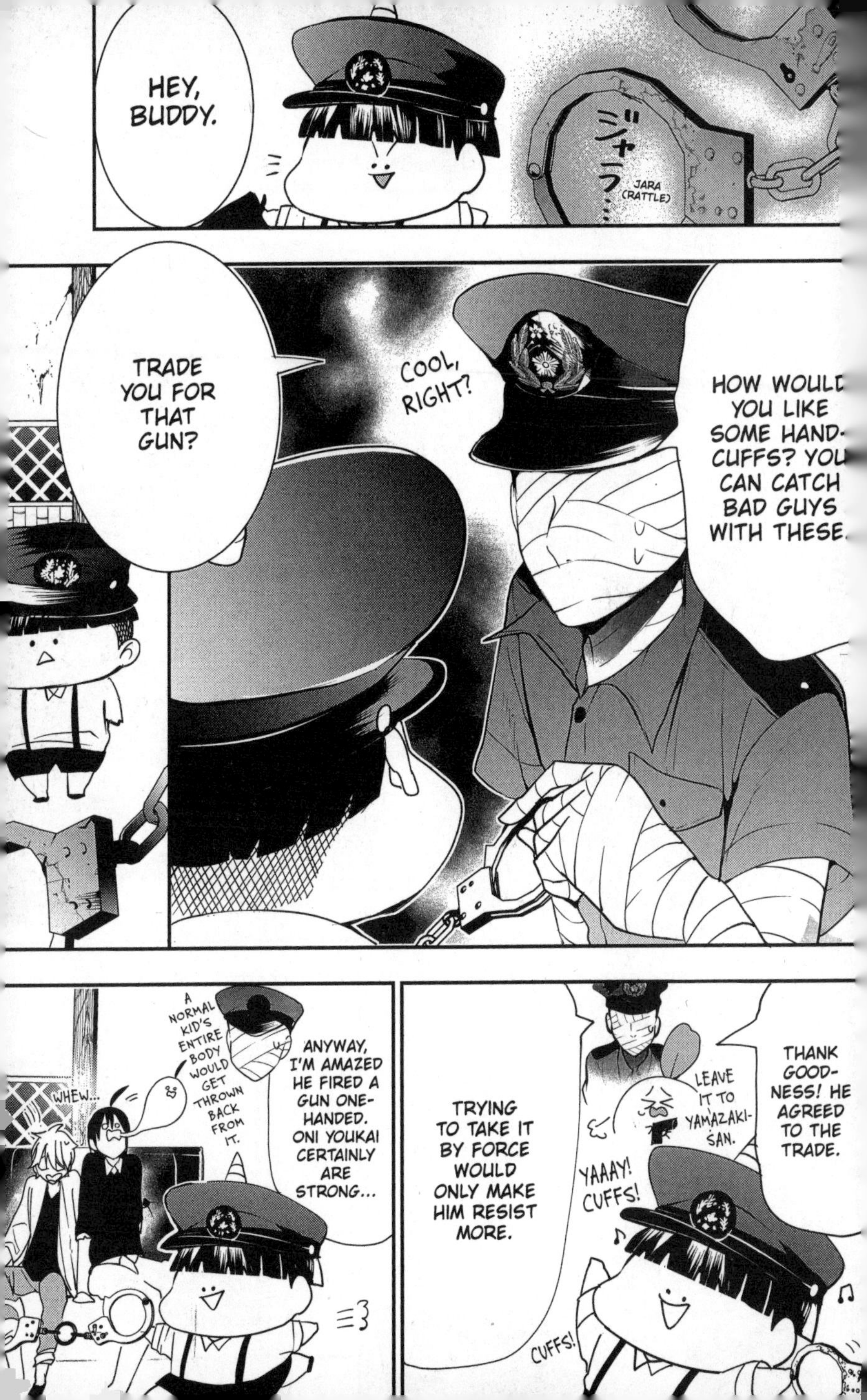
ジャラ…
JARA (RATTLE)
HEY, BUDDY.
HOW WOULD YOU LIKE SOME HAND-CUFFS? YOU CAN CATCH BAD GUYS WITH THESE.
COOL, RIGHT?
TRADE YOU FOR THAT GUN?
THANK GOODNESS! HE AGREED TO THE TRADE.
LEAVE IT TO YAMAZAKI-SAN.
YAAAY! CUFFS!
TRYING TO TAKE IT BY FORCE WOULD ONLY MAKE HIM RESIST MORE.
CUFFS!
ANYWAY, I'M AMAZED HE FIRED A GUN ONE-HANDED. ONI YOUKAI CERTAINLY ARE STRONG...
A NORMAL KID'S ENTIRE BODY WOULD GET THROWN BACK FROM IT.
WHEW...

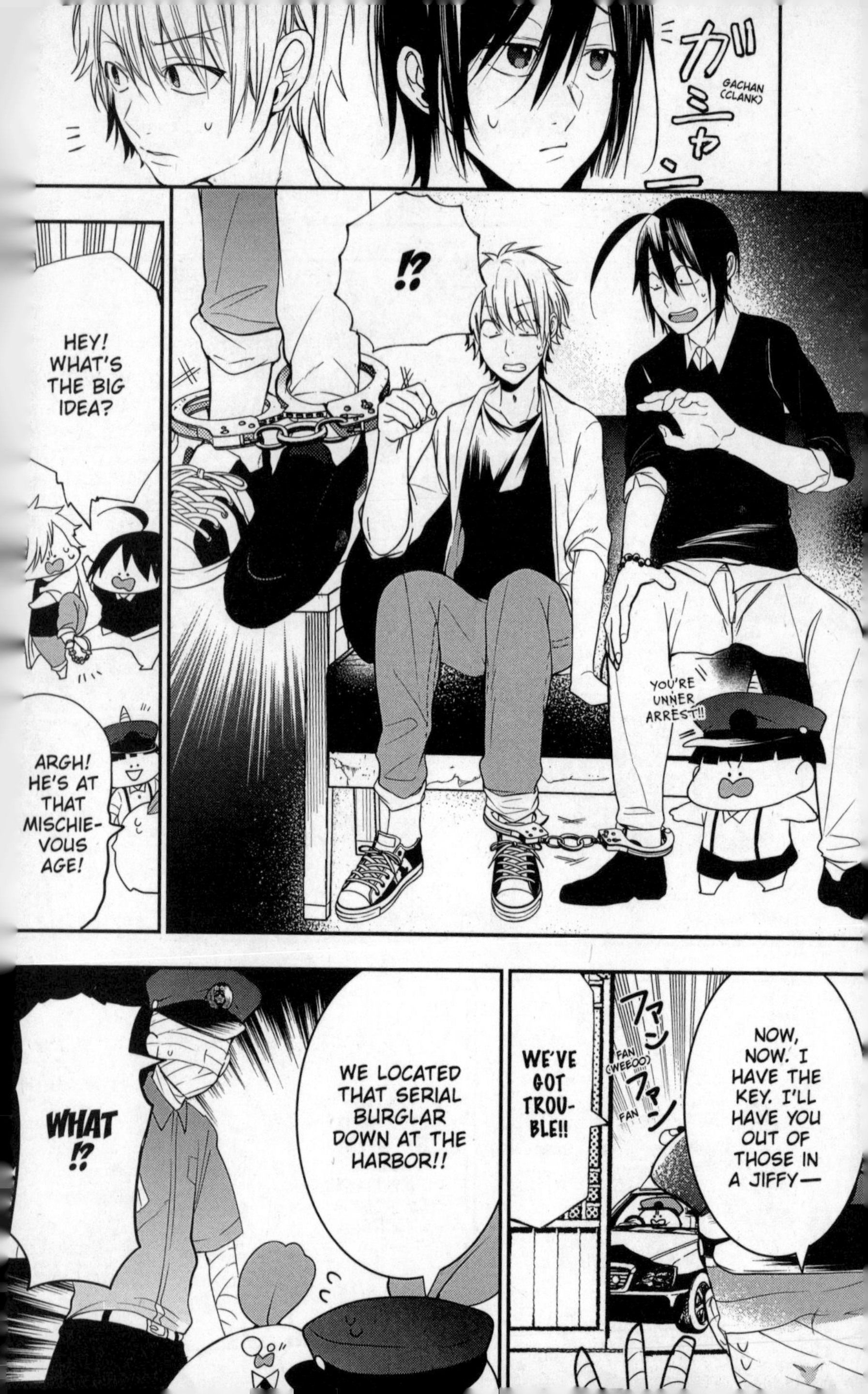

ガチャン
GACHAN (CLANK)
!?
YOU'RE UNNER ARREST!!
HEY! WHAT'S THE BIG IDEA?
ARGH! HE'S AT THAT MISCHIEVOUS AGE!
NOW, NOW. I HAVE THE KEY. I'LL HAVE YOU OUT OF THOSE IN A JIFFY—
ファン
FAN (WEEOO)
ファン
FAN
WE'VE GOT TROUBLE!!
WE LOCATED THAT SERIAL BURGLAR DOWN AT THE HARBOR!!
WHAT!?

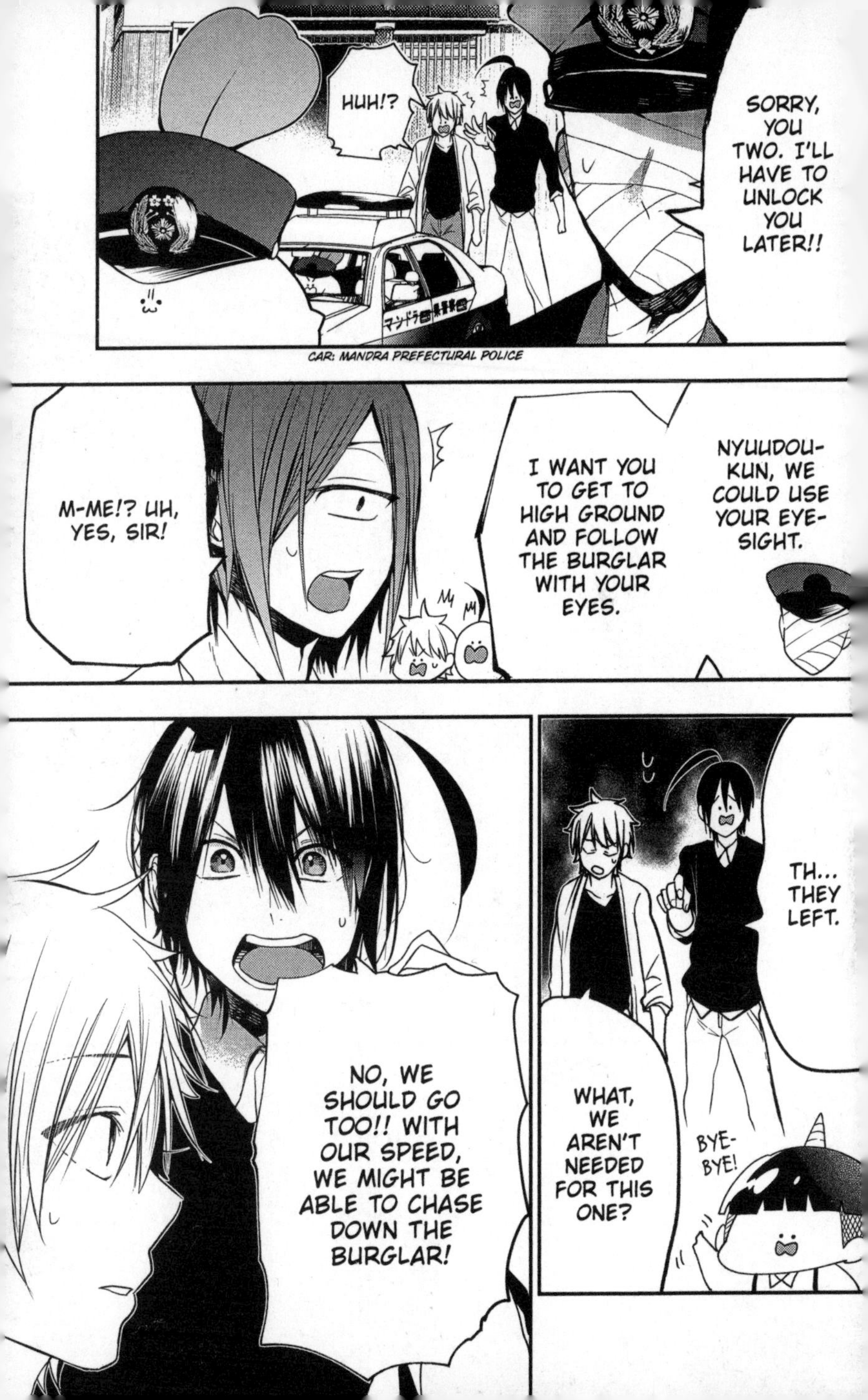
SORRY, YOU TWO. I'LL HAVE TO UNLOCK YOU LATER!!
HUH!?
CAR: MANDRA PREFECTURAL POLICE
NYUUDOU-KUN, WE COULD USE YOUR EYE-SIGHT.
I WANT YOU TO GET TO HIGH GROUND AND FOLLOW THE BURGLAR WITH YOUR EYES.
M-ME!? UH, YES, SIR!
TH... THEY LEFT.
BYE-BYE!
WHAT, WE AREN'T NEEDED FOR THIS ONE?
NO, WE SHOULD GO TOO!! WITH OUR SPEED, WE MIGHT BE ABLE TO CHASE DOWN THE BURGLAR!

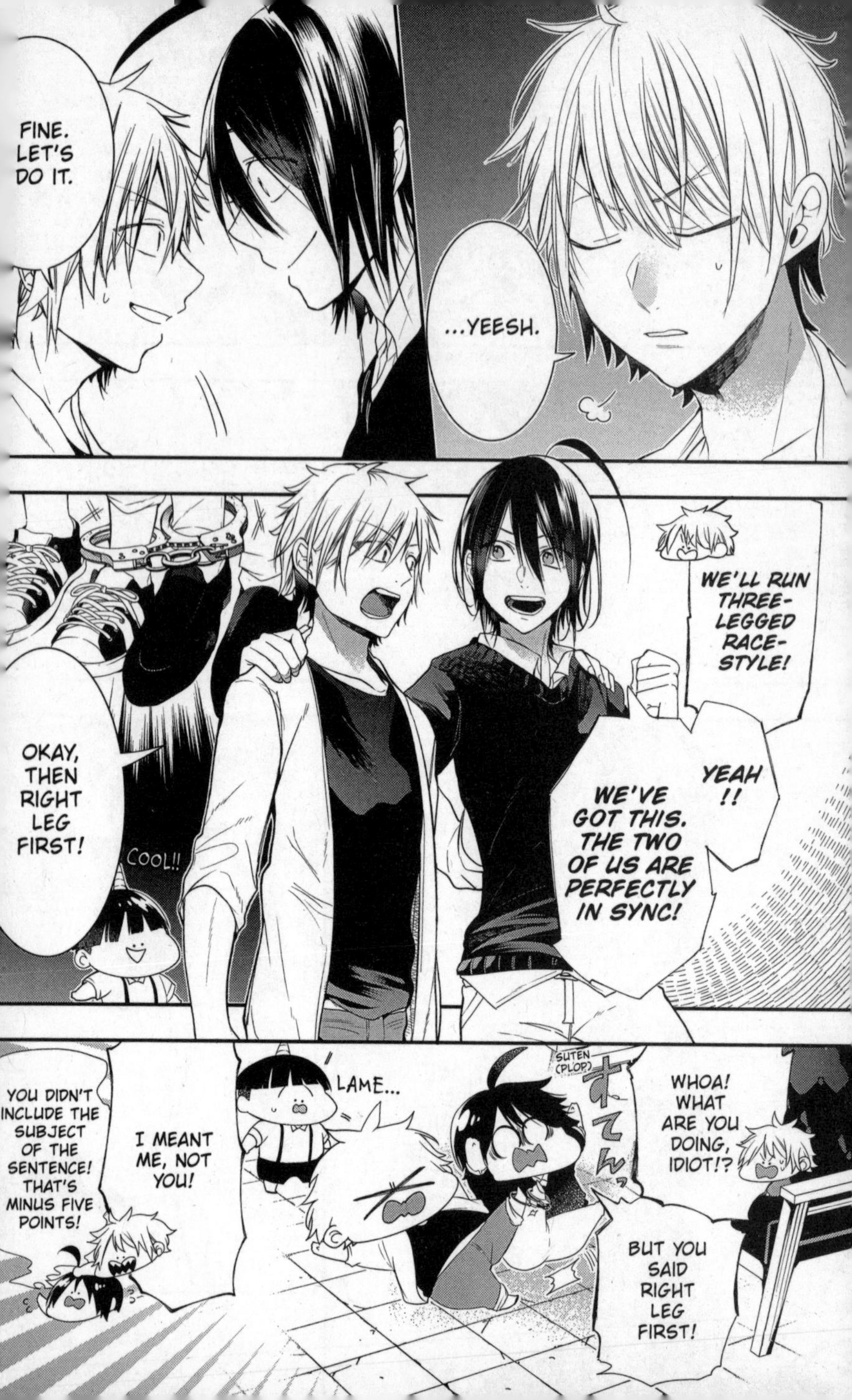
...YEESH.
FINE. LET'S DO IT.
WE'LL RUN THREE-LEGGED RACE-STYLE!
YEAH!!
WE'VE GOT THIS. THE TWO OF US ARE PERFECTLY IN SYNC!
OKAY, THEN RIGHT LEG FIRST!
COOL!!
SUTEN (PLOP)
WHOA! WHAT ARE YOU DOING, IDIOT!?
BUT YOU SAID RIGHT LEG FIRST!
LAME...
I MEANT ME, NOT YOU!
YOU DIDN'T INCLUDE THE SUBJECT OF THE SENTENCE! THAT'S MINUS FIVE POINTS!

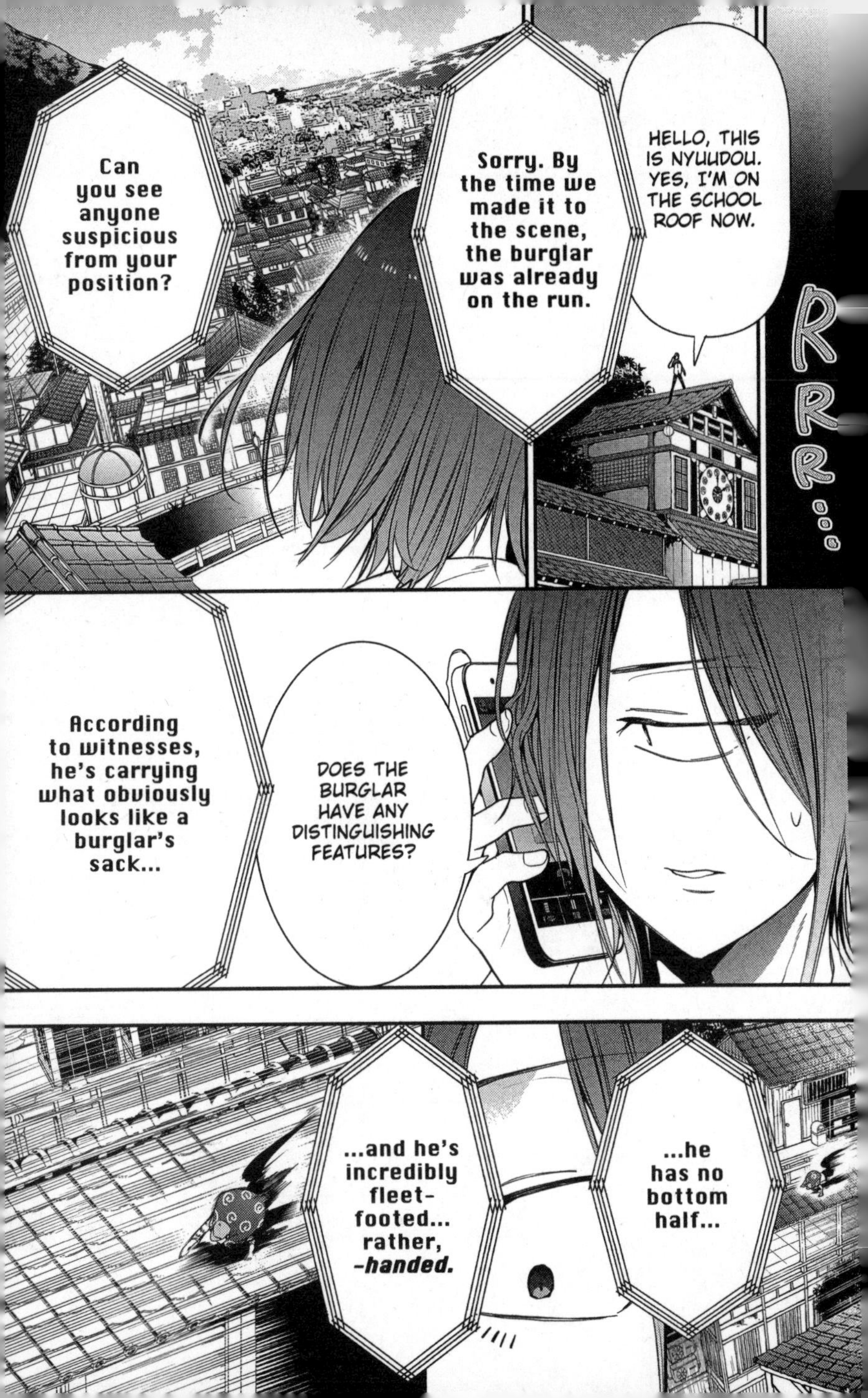
RRR...
HELLO, THIS IS NYUUDOU. YES, I'M ON THE SCHOOL ROOF NOW.
Sorry. By the time we made it to the scene, the burglar was already on the run.
Can you see anyone suspicious from your position?
DOES THE BURGLAR HAVE ANY DISTINGUISHING FEATURES?
According to witnesses, he's carrying what obviously looks like a burglar's sack...
...he has no bottom half...
...and he's incredibly fleet-footed... rather, -handed.

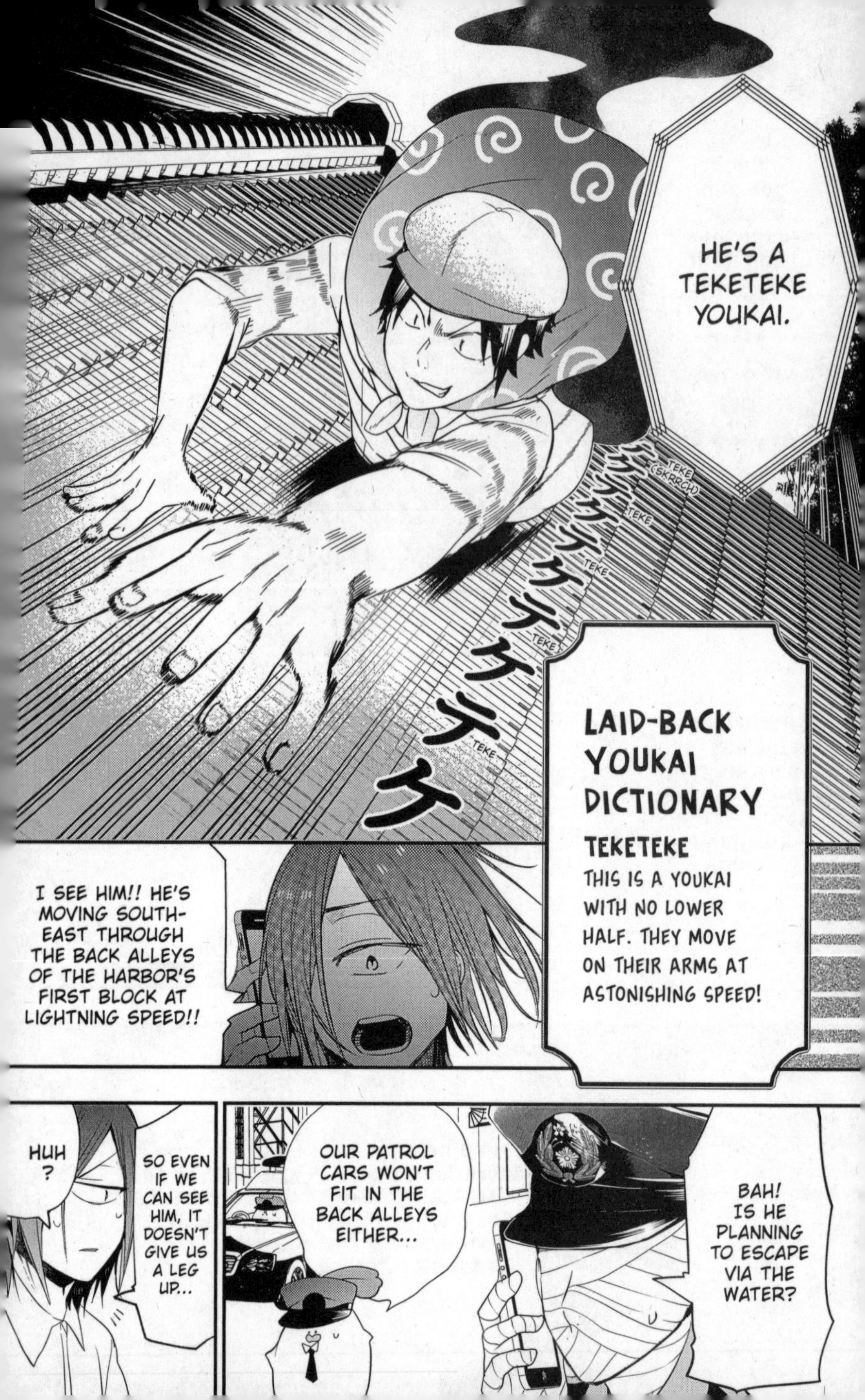
HE'S A TEKETEKE YOUKAI.
TEKE (SKRRCH)
TEKE
TEKE
TEKE
TEKE
LAID-BACK YOUKAI DICTIONARY
TEKETEKE
THIS IS A YOUKAI WITH NO LOWER HALF. THEY MOVE ON THEIR ARMS AT ASTONISHING SPEED!
I SEE HIM!! HE'S MOVING SOUTH-EAST THROUGH THE BACK ALLEYS OF THE HARBOR'S FIRST BLOCK AT LIGHTNING SPEED!!
BAH! IS HE PLANNING TO ESCAPE VIA THE WATER?
OUR PATROL CARS WON'T FIT IN THE BACK ALLEYS EITHER...
SO EVEN IF WE CAN SEE HIM, IT DOESN'T GIVE US A LEG UP...
HUH?

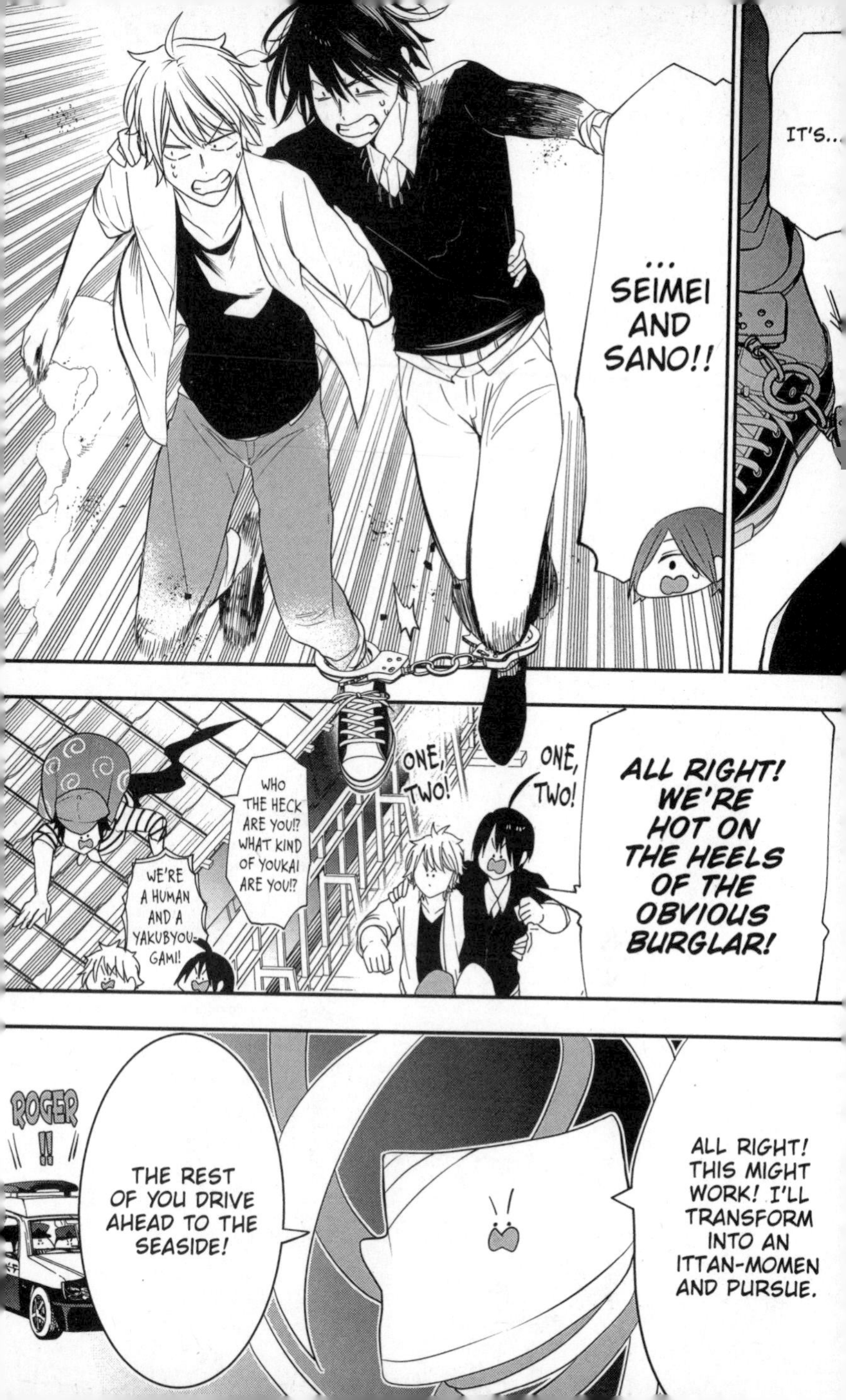
IT'S...
...SEIMEI AND SANO!!
ALL RIGHT! WE'RE HOT ON THE HEELS OF THE OBVIOUS BURGLAR!
ONE, TWO!
ONE, TWO!
WHO THE HECK ARE YOU!? WHAT KIND OF YOUKAI ARE YOU!?
WE'RE A HUMAN AND A YAKUBYOU-GAMI!
ALL RIGHT! THIS MIGHT WORK! I'LL TRANSFORM INTO AN ITTAN-MOMEN AND PURSUE.
THE REST OF YOU DRIVE AHEAD TO THE SEASIDE!
ROGER!!

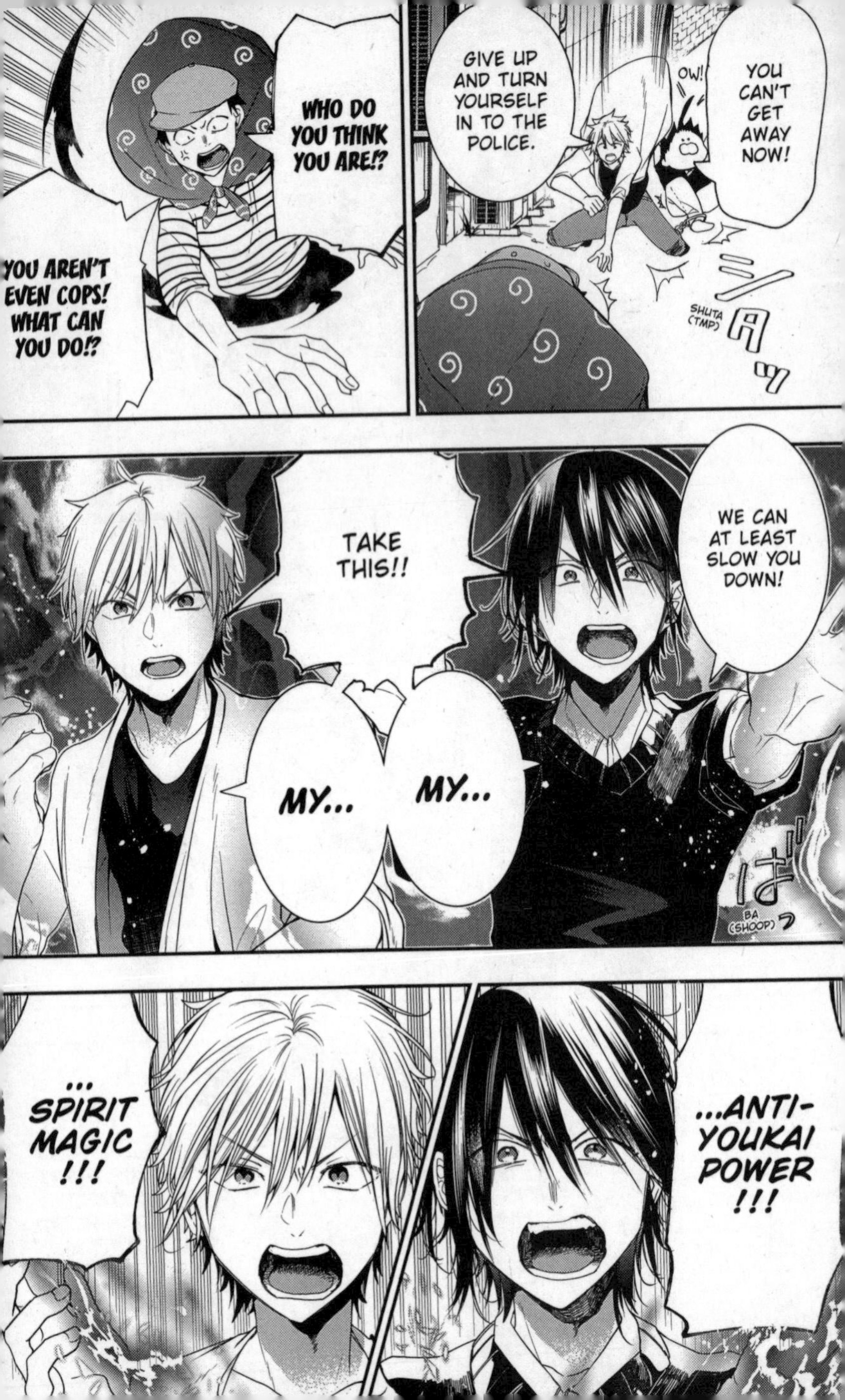
YOU CAN'T GET AWAY NOW!
OW!
GIVE UP AND TURN YOURSELF IN TO THE POLICE.
SHUTA (TMP)
WHO DO YOU THINK YOU ARE!?
YOU AREN'T EVEN COPS! WHAT CAN YOU DO!?
WE CAN AT LEAST SLOW YOU DOWN!
TAKE THIS!!
BA (SHOOP)
MY...
MY...
...ANTI-YOUKAI POWER!!!
...SPIRIT MAGIC!!!

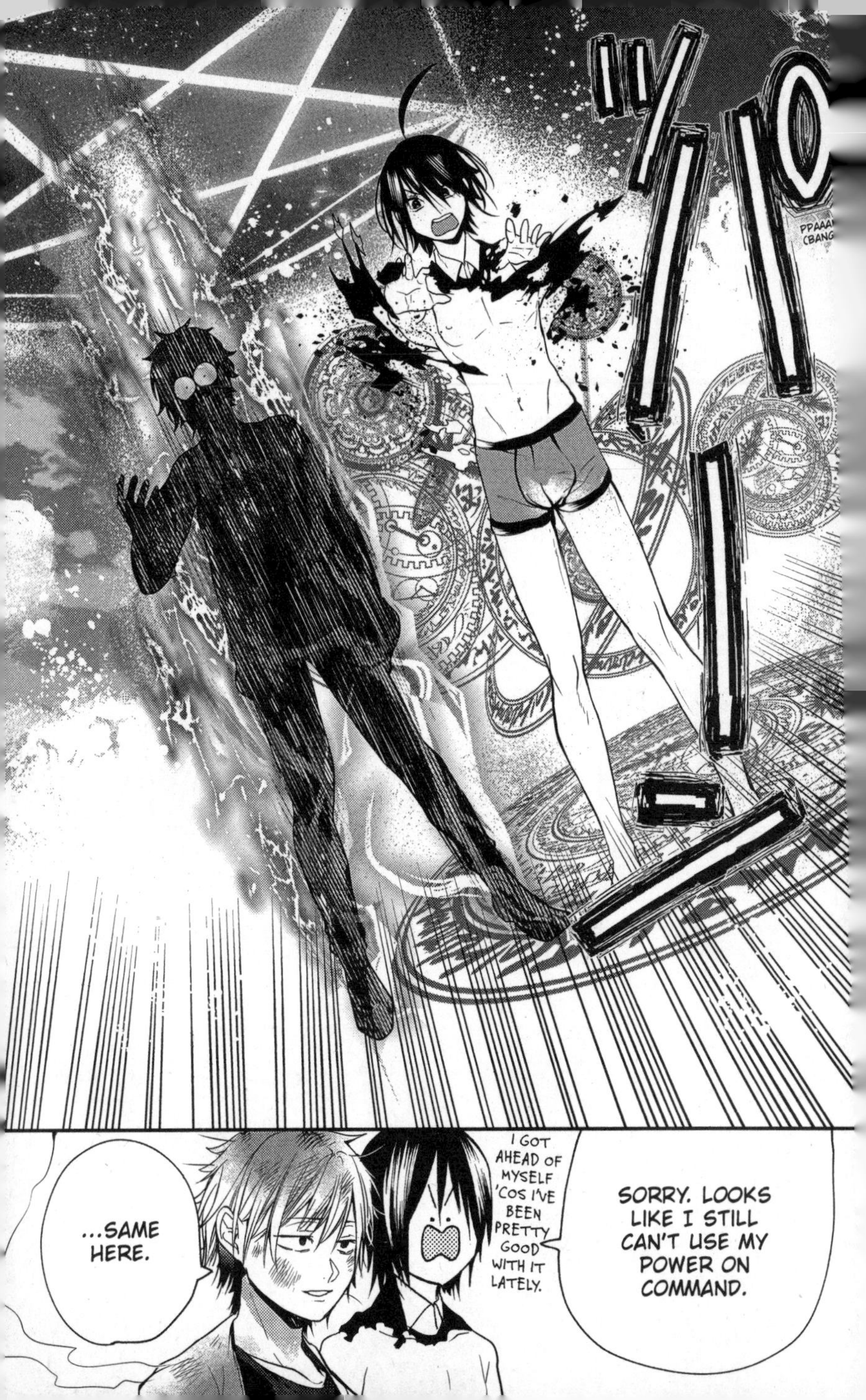
PPAAA
(BANG
SORRY. LOOKS LIKE I STILL CAN'T USE MY POWER ON COMMAND.
I GOT AHEAD OF MYSELF 'COS I'VE BEEN PRETTY GOOD WITH IT LATELY.
...SAME HERE.

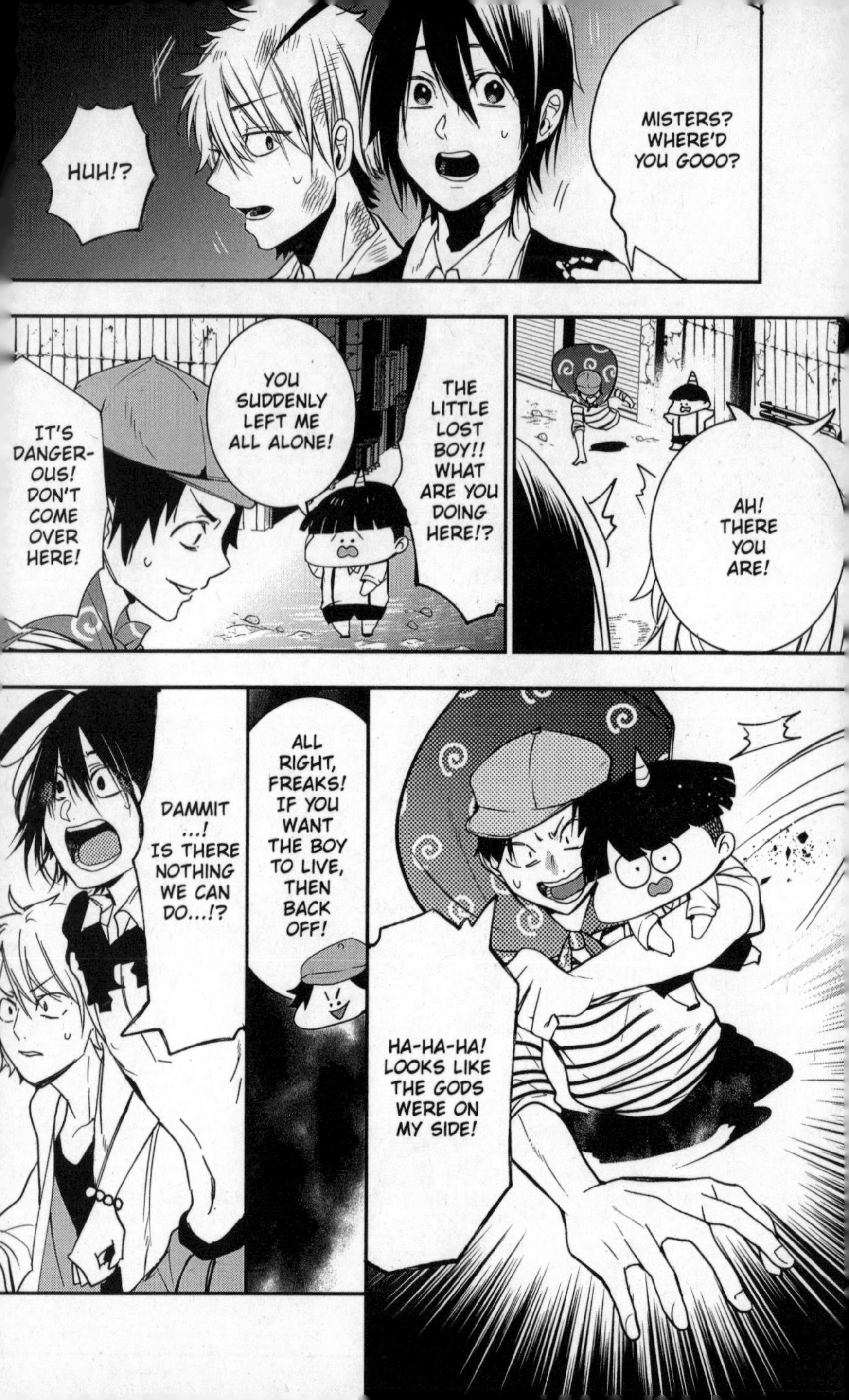
MISTERS? WHERE'D YOU GOOO?
HUH!?
AH! THERE YOU ARE!
THE LITTLE LOST BOY!! WHAT ARE YOU DOING HERE!?
YOU SUDDENLY LEFT ME ALL ALONE!
IT'S DANGER-OUS! DON'T COME OVER HERE!
HA-HA-HA! LOOKS LIKE THE GODS WERE ON MY SIDE!
ALL RIGHT, FREAKS! IF YOU WANT THE BOY TO LIVE, THEN BACK OFF!
DAMMIT...! IS THERE NOTHING WE CAN DO...!?

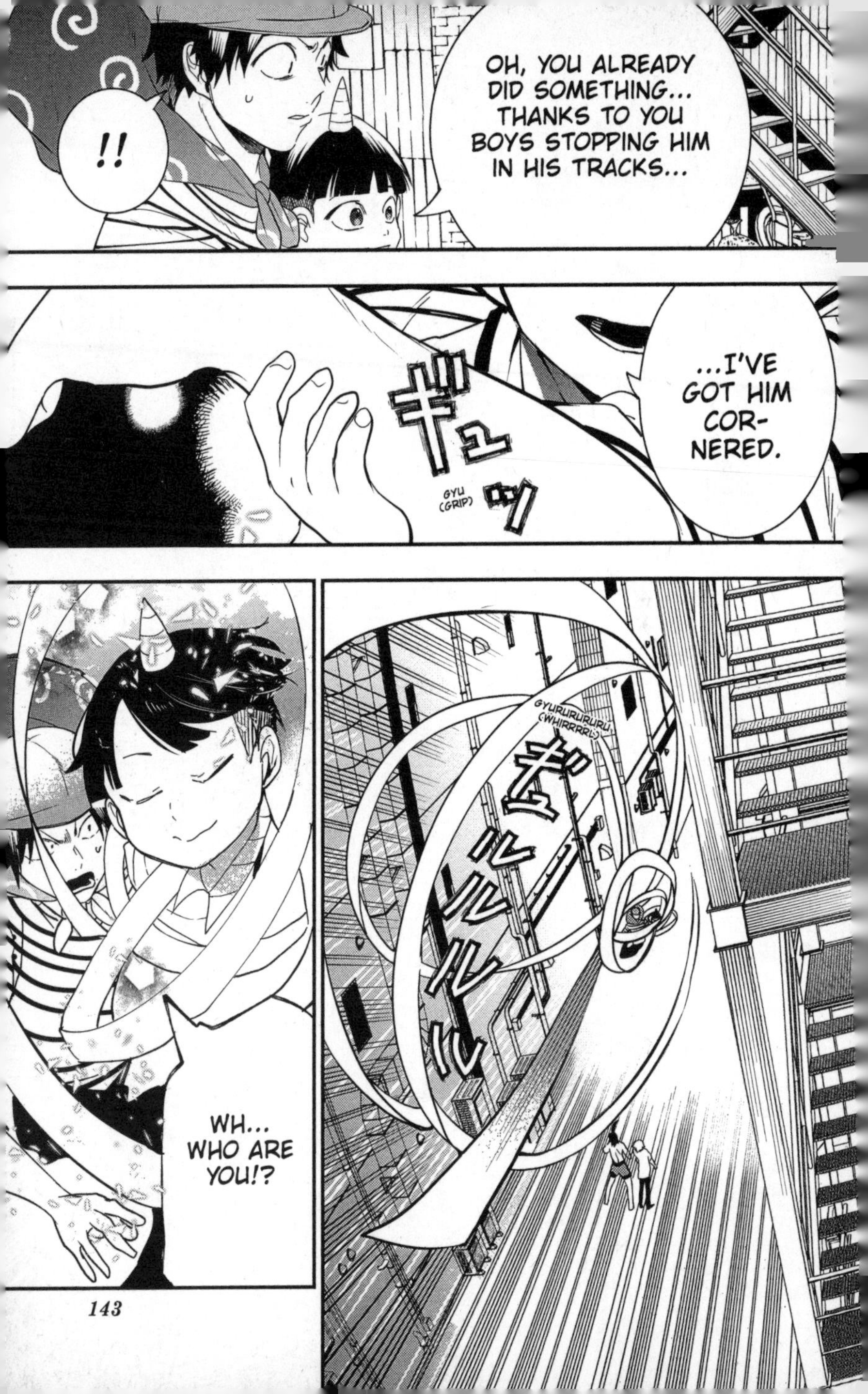

OH, YOU ALREADY DID SOMETHING... THANKS TO YOU BOYS STOPPING HIM IN HIS TRACKS...
!!
...I'VE GOT HIM COR-NERED.
GYU (GRIP)
GYURURURURU (WHIRRRRL)
WH... WHO ARE YOU!?

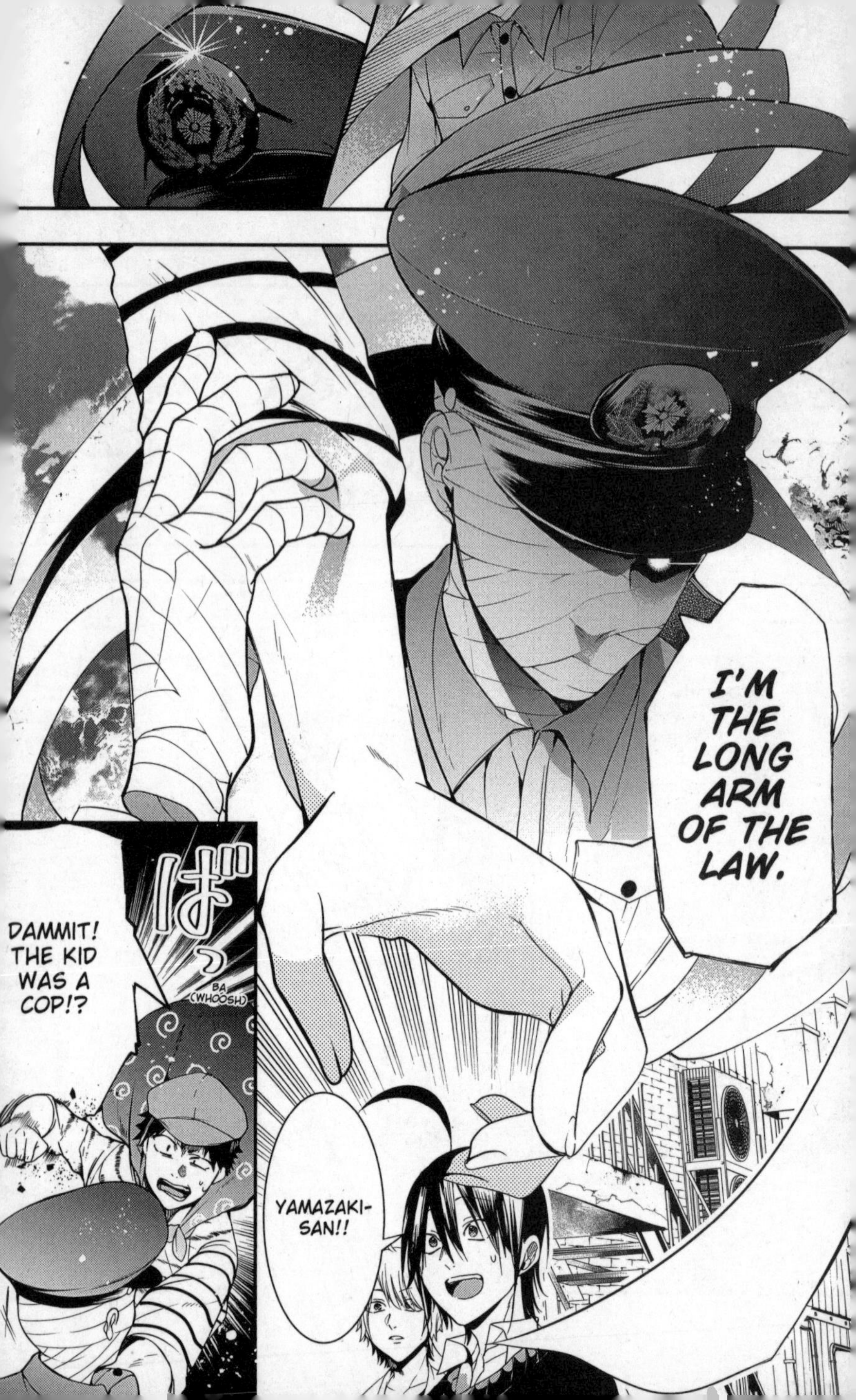

I'M THE LONG ARM OF THE LAW.
ばっ
BA (WHOOSH)
YAMAZAKI-SAN!!
DAMMIT! THE KID WAS A COP!?

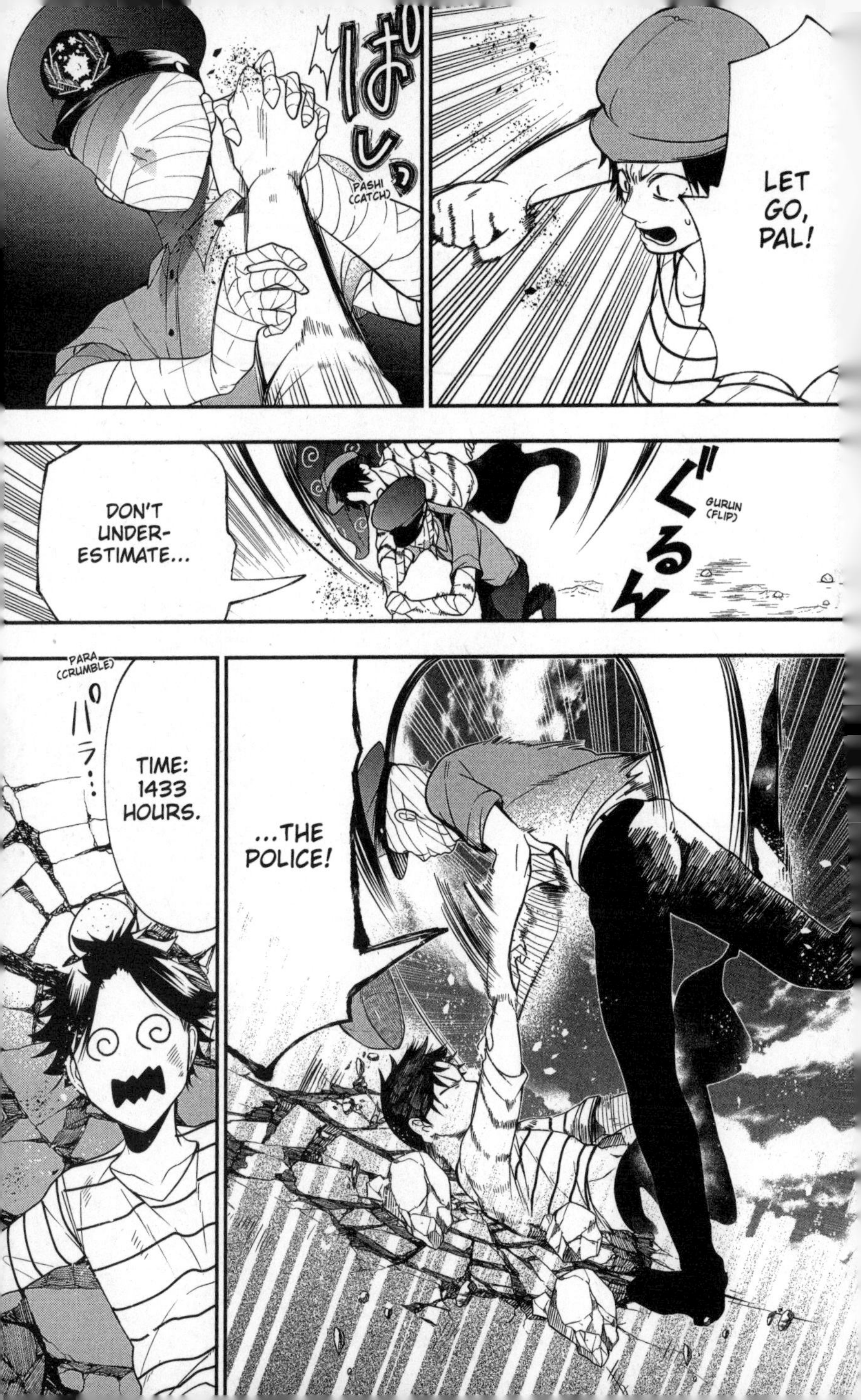
LET GO, PAL!
ぱしっ
PASHI (CATCH)
ぐるん
GURUN (FLIP)
DON'T UNDER-ESTIMATE...
...THE POLICE!
パラ…
PARA (CRUMBLE)
TIME: 1433 HOURS.

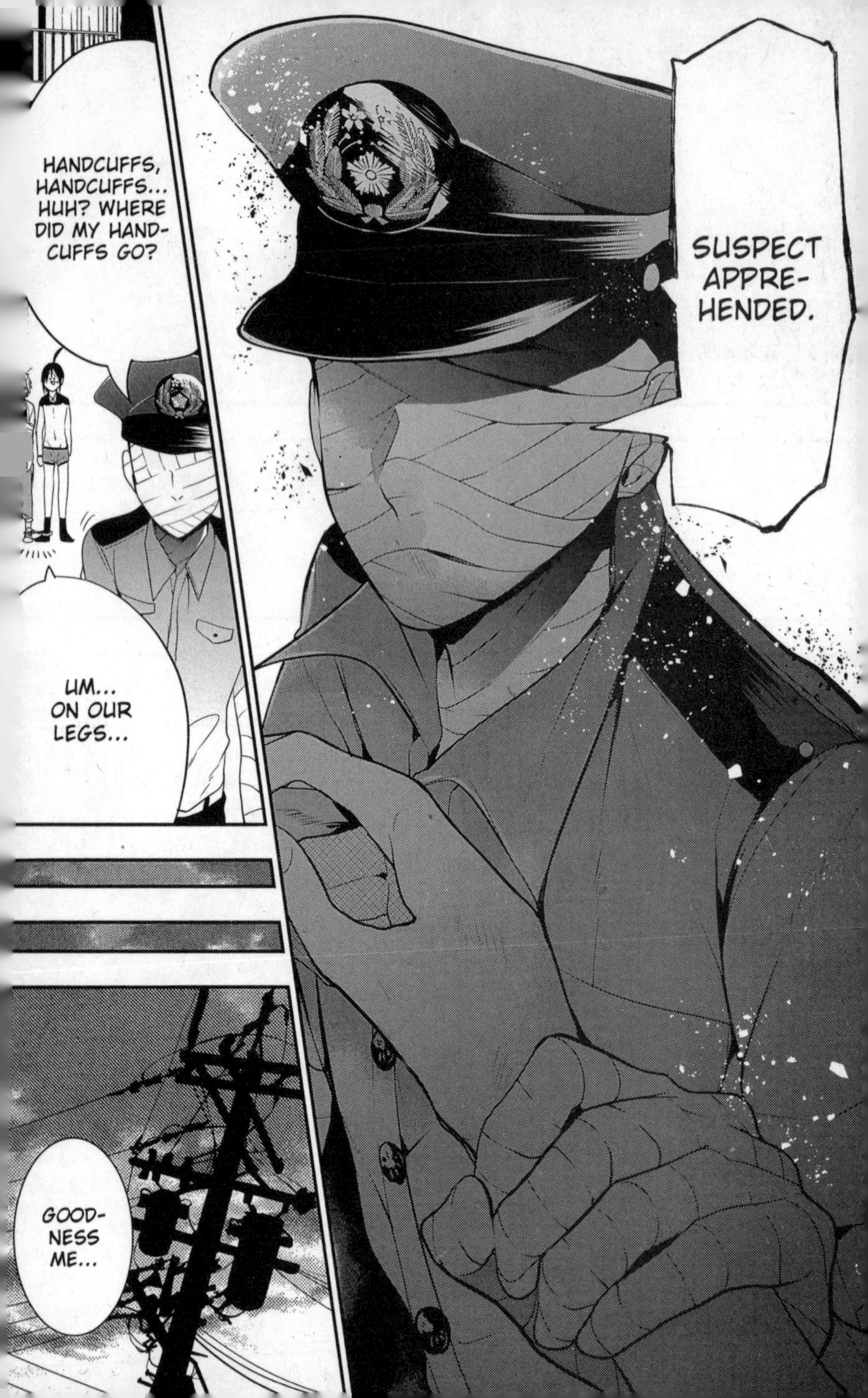
SUSPECT APPREHENDED.
HANDCUFFS, HANDCUFFS... HUH? WHERE DID MY HAND-CUFFS GO?
UM... ON OUR LEGS...
GOOD-NESS ME...

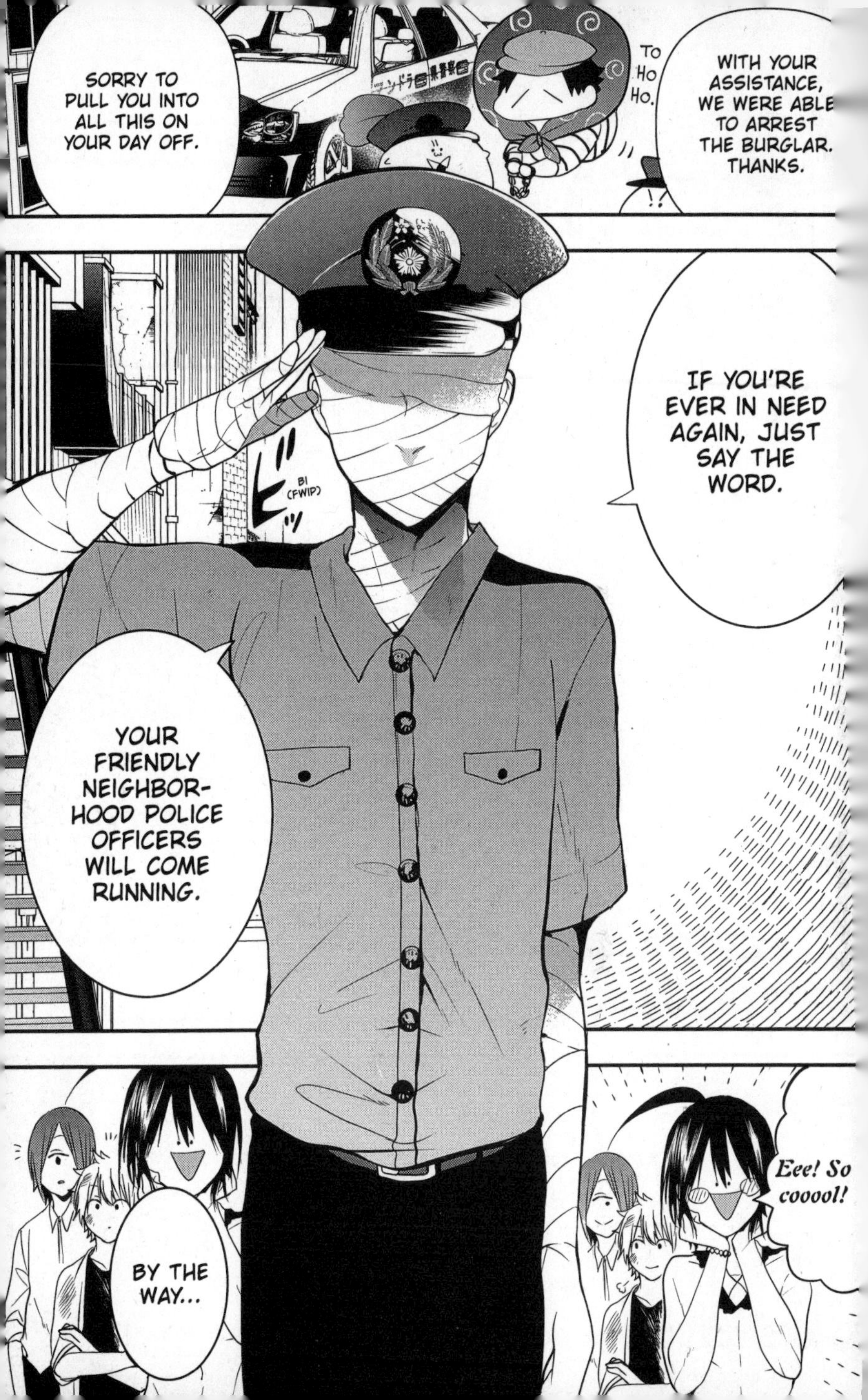

WITH YOUR ASSISTANCE, WE WERE ABLE TO ARREST THE BURGLAR. THANKS.
TO HO HO.
SORRY TO PULL YOU INTO ALL THIS ON YOUR DAY OFF.
IF YOU'RE EVER IN NEED AGAIN, JUST SAY THE WORD.
BI (FWIP)
YOUR FRIENDLY NEIGHBOR-HOOD POLICE OFFICERS WILL COME RUNNING.
Eee! So cooool!
BY THE WAY...

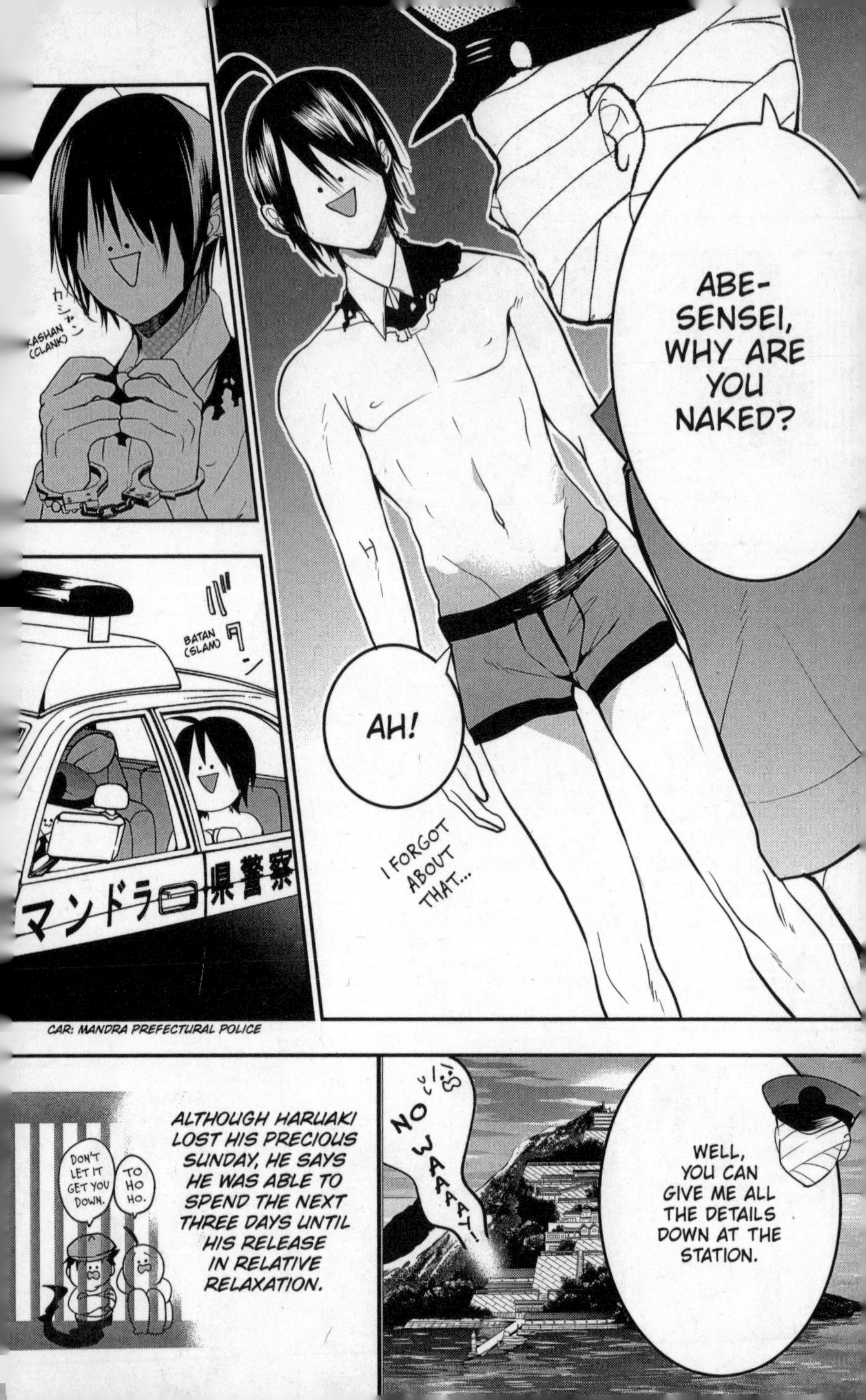

ABE-SENSEI, WHY ARE YOU NAKED?
AH!
I FORGOT ABOUT THAT...
カシャン
KASHAN (CLANK)
バタン
BATAN (SLAM)
マンドラ県警察
CAR: MANDRA PREFECTURAL POLICE
WELL, YOU CAN GIVE ME ALL THE DETAILS DOWN AT THE STATION.
NOWAAAAT!
ALTHOUGH HARUAKI LOST HIS PRECIOUS SUNDAY, HE SAYS HE WAS ABLE TO SPEND THE NEXT THREE DAYS UNTIL HIS RELEASE IN RELATIVE RELAXATION.
DON'T LET IT GET YOU DOWN.
TO HO HO.

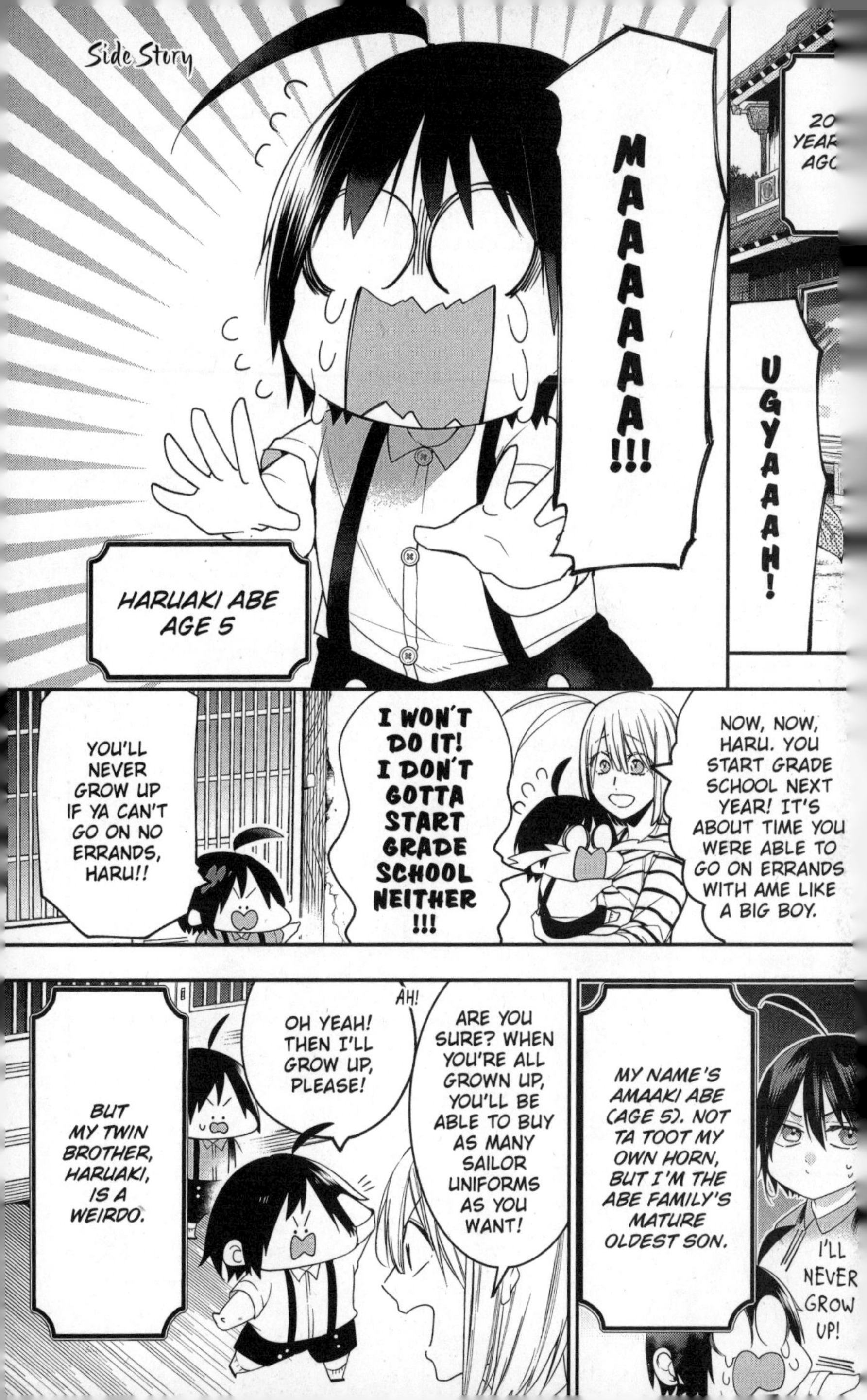
20 YEAR AGO
UGYAAAAH!
Side Story
MAAAAAAAA!!!
HARUAKI ABE AGE 5
NOW, NOW, HARU. YOU START GRADE SCHOOL NEXT YEAR! IT'S ABOUT TIME YOU WERE ABLE TO GO ON ERRANDS WITH AME LIKE A BIG BOY.
I WON'T DO IT! I DON'T GOTTA START GRADE SCHOOL NEITHER!!!
YOU'LL NEVER GROW UP IF YA CAN'T GO ON NO ERRANDS, HARU!!
MY NAME'S AMAAKI ABE (AGE 5). NOT TA TOOT MY OWN HORN, BUT I'M THE ABE FAMILY'S MATURE OLDEST SON.
I'LL NEVER GROW UP!
AH!
ARE YOU SURE? WHEN YOU'RE ALL GROWN UP, YOU'LL BE ABLE TO BUY AS MANY SAILOR UNIFORMS AS YOU WANT!
OH YEAH! THEN I'LL GROW UP, PLEASE!
BUT MY TWIN BROTHER, HARUAKI, IS A WEIRDO.

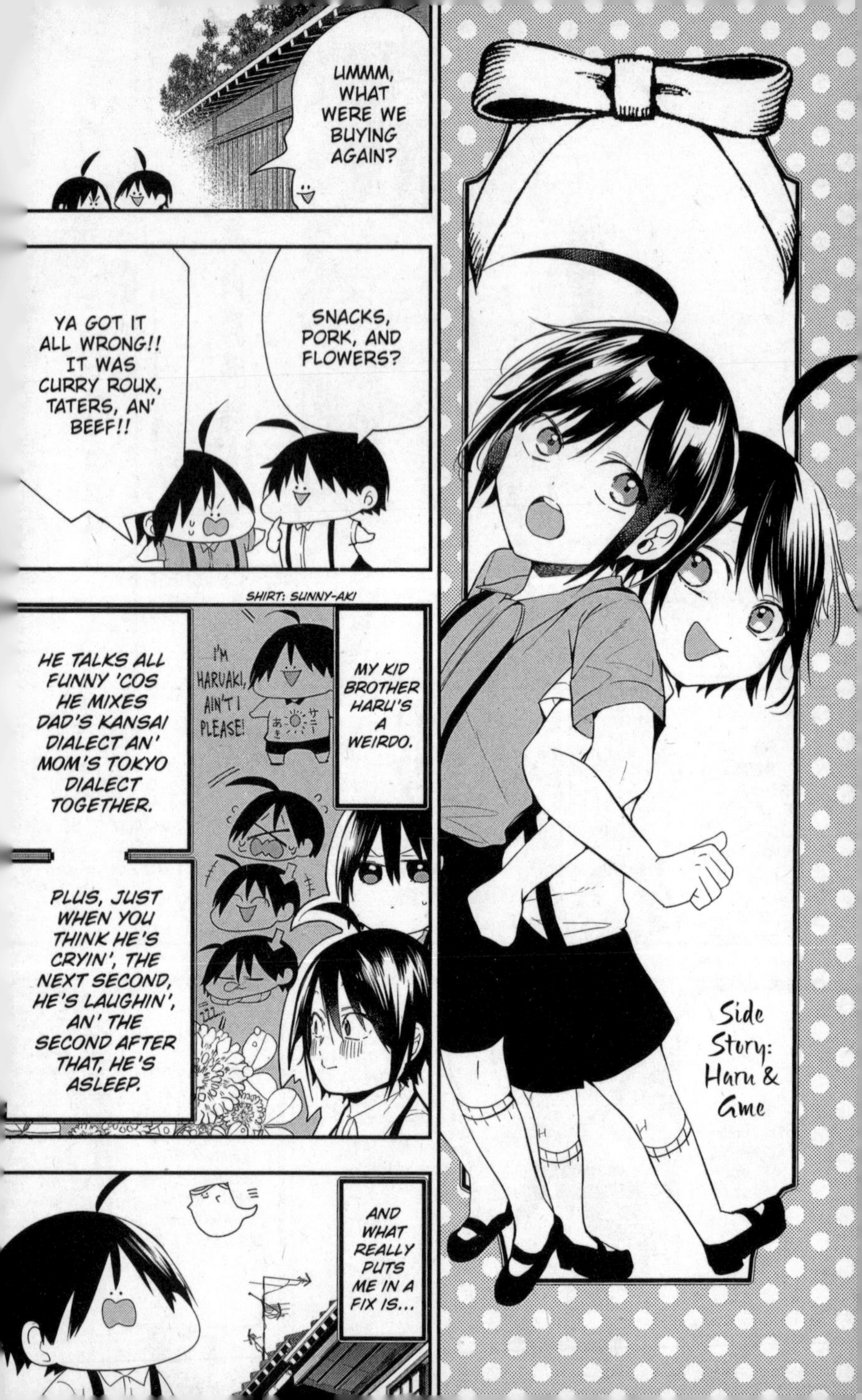
Side Story: Haru & Ame
UMMM, WHAT WERE WE BUYING AGAIN?
SNACKS, PORK, AND FLOWERS?
YA GOT IT ALL WRONG!! IT WAS CURRY ROUX, TATERS, AN' BEEF!!
SHIRT: SUNNY-AKI
MY KID BROTHER HARU'S A WEIRDO.
I'M HARUAKI, AIN'T I PLEASE!
HE TALKS ALL FUNNY 'COS HE MIXES DAD'S KANSAI DIALECT AN' MOM'S TOKYO DIALECT TOGETHER.
PLUS, JUST WHEN YOU THINK HE'S CRYIN', THE NEXT SECOND, HE'S LAUGHIN', AN' THE SECOND AFTER THAT, HE'S ASLEEP.
AND WHAT REALLY PUTS ME IN A FIX IS...

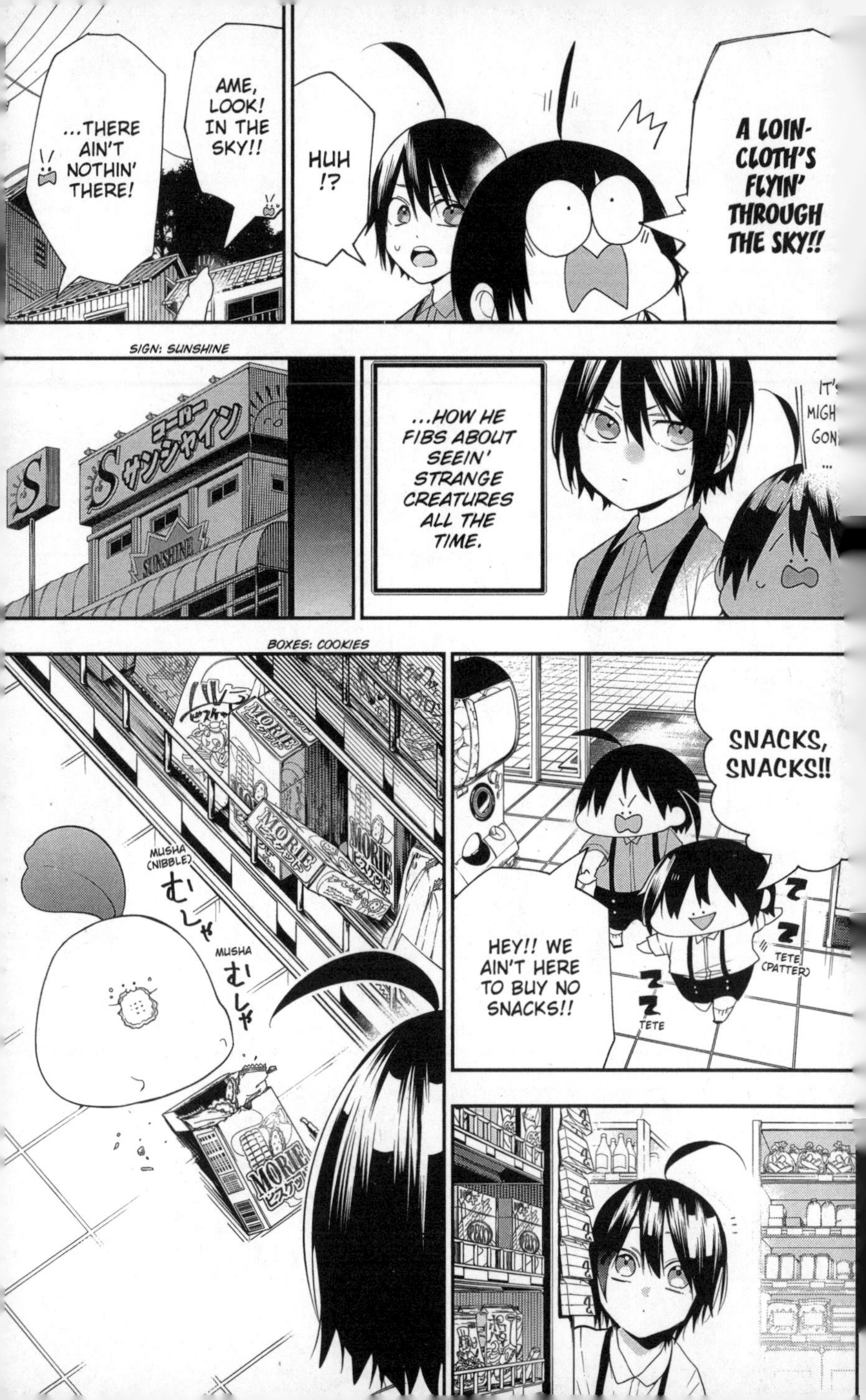
A LOIN-CLOTH'S FLYIN' THROUGH THE SKY!!
HUH !?
AME, LOOK! IN THE SKY!!
...THERE AIN'T NOTHIN' THERE!
SIGN: SUNSHINE
IT'S MIGH GON ...
...HOW HE FIBS ABOUT SEEIN' STRANGE CREATURES ALL THE TIME.
ヨーカー
サンシャイン
SUNSHINE
BOXES: COOKIES
SNACKS, SNACKS!!
HEY!! WE AIN'T HERE TO BUY NO SNACKS!!
TETE (PATTER)
TETE
MORIE
ビスケット
MUSHA (NIBBLE)
むしゃ
MUSHA
むしゃ

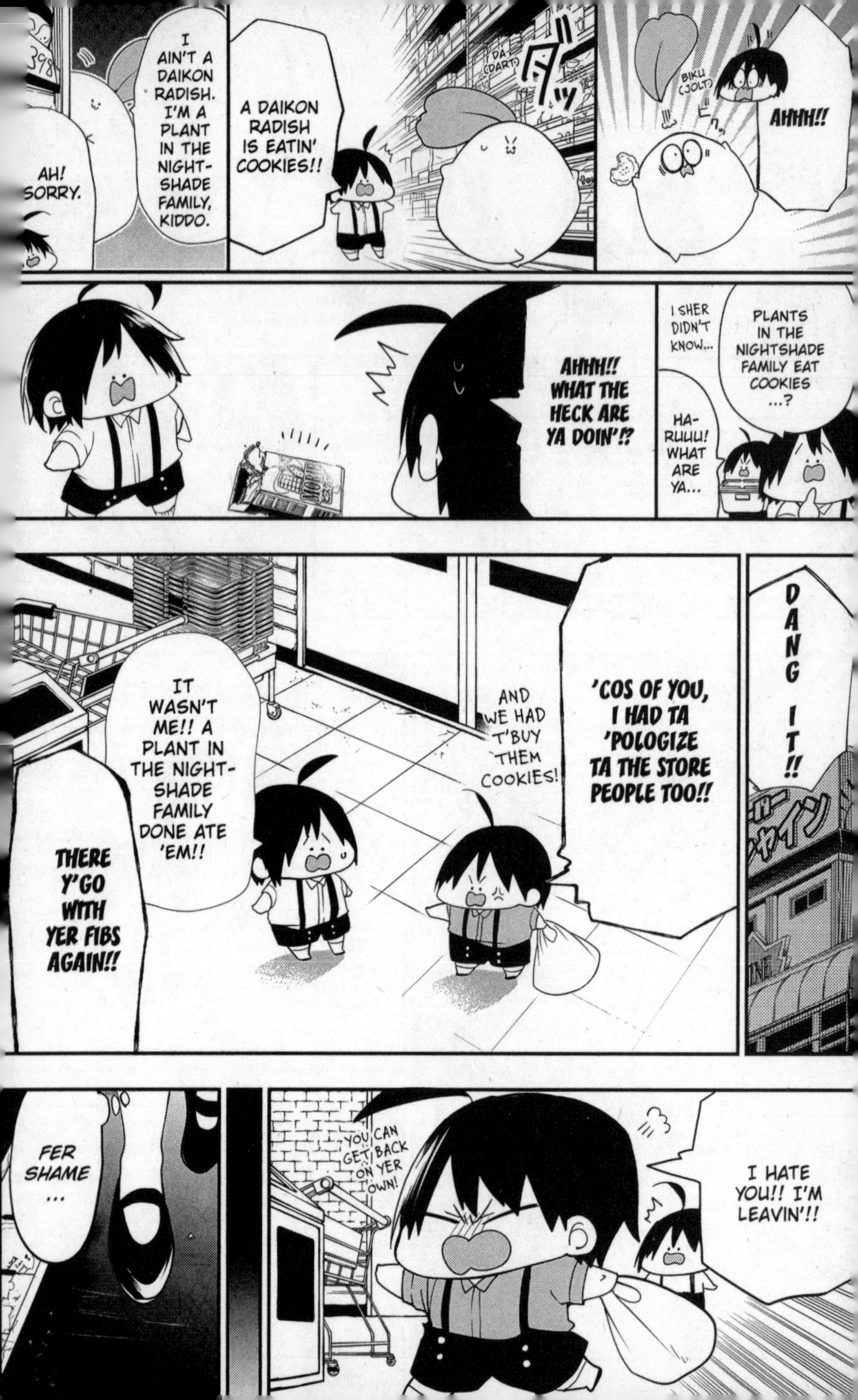
AHHH!!
BIKU (JOLT)
DA (DART)
A DAIKON RADISH IS EATIN' COOKIES!!
I AIN'T A DAIKON RADISH. I'M A PLANT IN THE NIGHTSHADE FAMILY, KIDDO.
AH! SORRY.
PLANTS IN THE NIGHTSHADE FAMILY EAT COOKIES ...?
I SHER DIDN'T KNOW...
HA-RUUU! WHAT ARE YA...
AHHH!! WHAT THE HECK ARE YA DOIN'!?
DANG IT!!
'COS OF YOU, I HAD TA 'POLOGIZE TA THE STORE PEOPLE TOO!!
AND WE HAD T'BUY THEM COOKIES!
IT WASN'T ME!! A PLANT IN THE NIGHTSHADE FAMILY DONE ATE 'EM!!
THERE Y'GO WITH YER FIBS AGAIN!!
I HATE YOU!! I'M LEAVIN'!!
YOU CAN GET BACK ON YER OWN!
FER SHAME ...

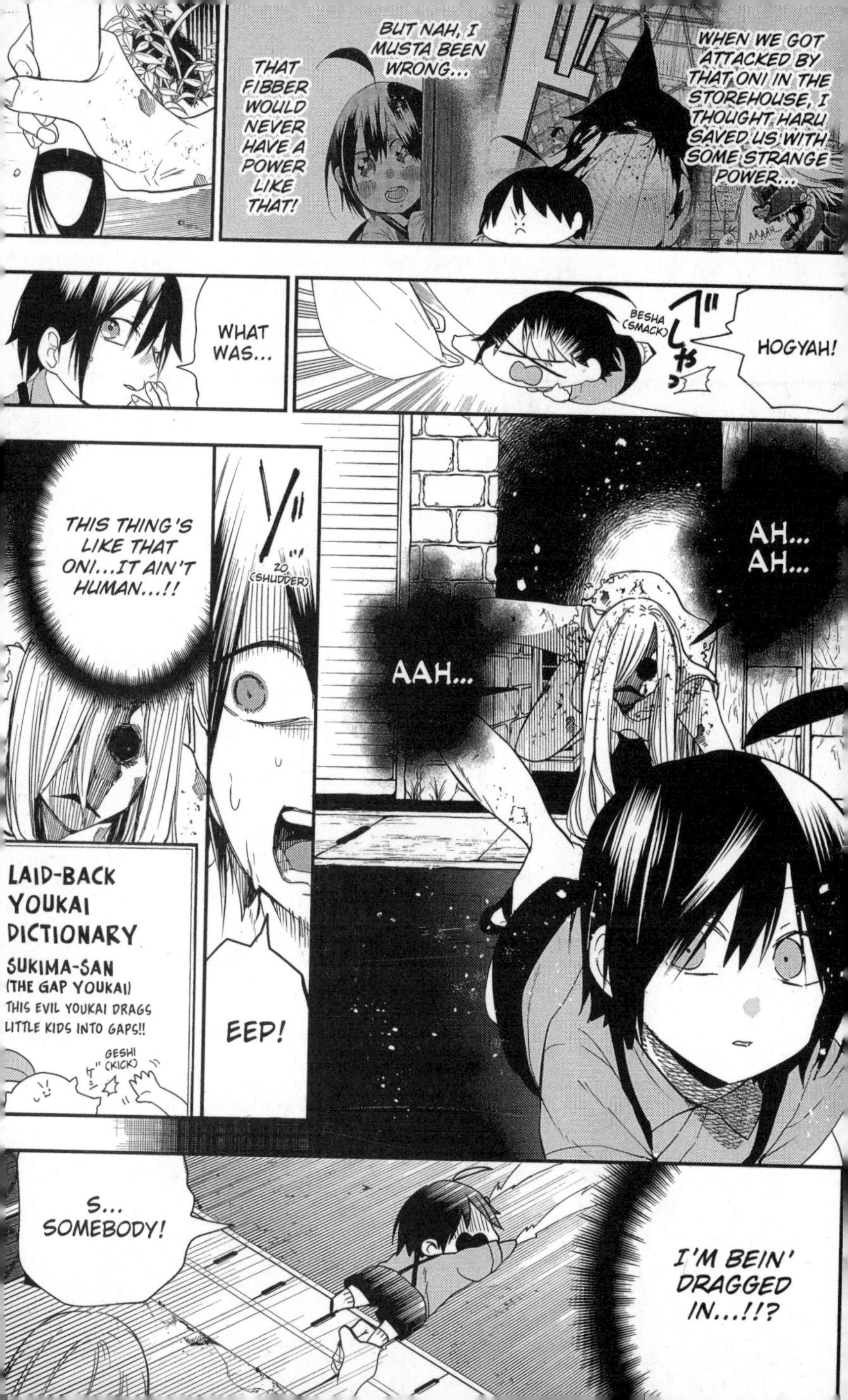
WHEN WE GOT ATTACKED BY THAT ONI IN THE STOREHOUSE, I THOUGHT HARU SAVED US WITH SOME STRANGE POWER...
BUT NAH, I MUSTA BEEN WRONG...
THAT FIBBER WOULD NEVER HAVE A POWER LIKE THAT!
HOGYAH!
BESHA (SMACK)
WHAT WAS...
AH... AH...
AAH...
ZO (SHUDDER)
THIS THING'S LIKE THAT ONI...IT AIN'T HUMAN...!!
EEP!
LAID-BACK YOUKAI DICTIONARY
SUKIMA-SAN (THE GAP YOUKAI)
THIS EVIL YOUKAI DRAGS LITTLE KIDS INTO GAPS!!
GESHI (KICK)
I'M BEIN' DRAGGED IN...!!?
S... SOMEBODY!

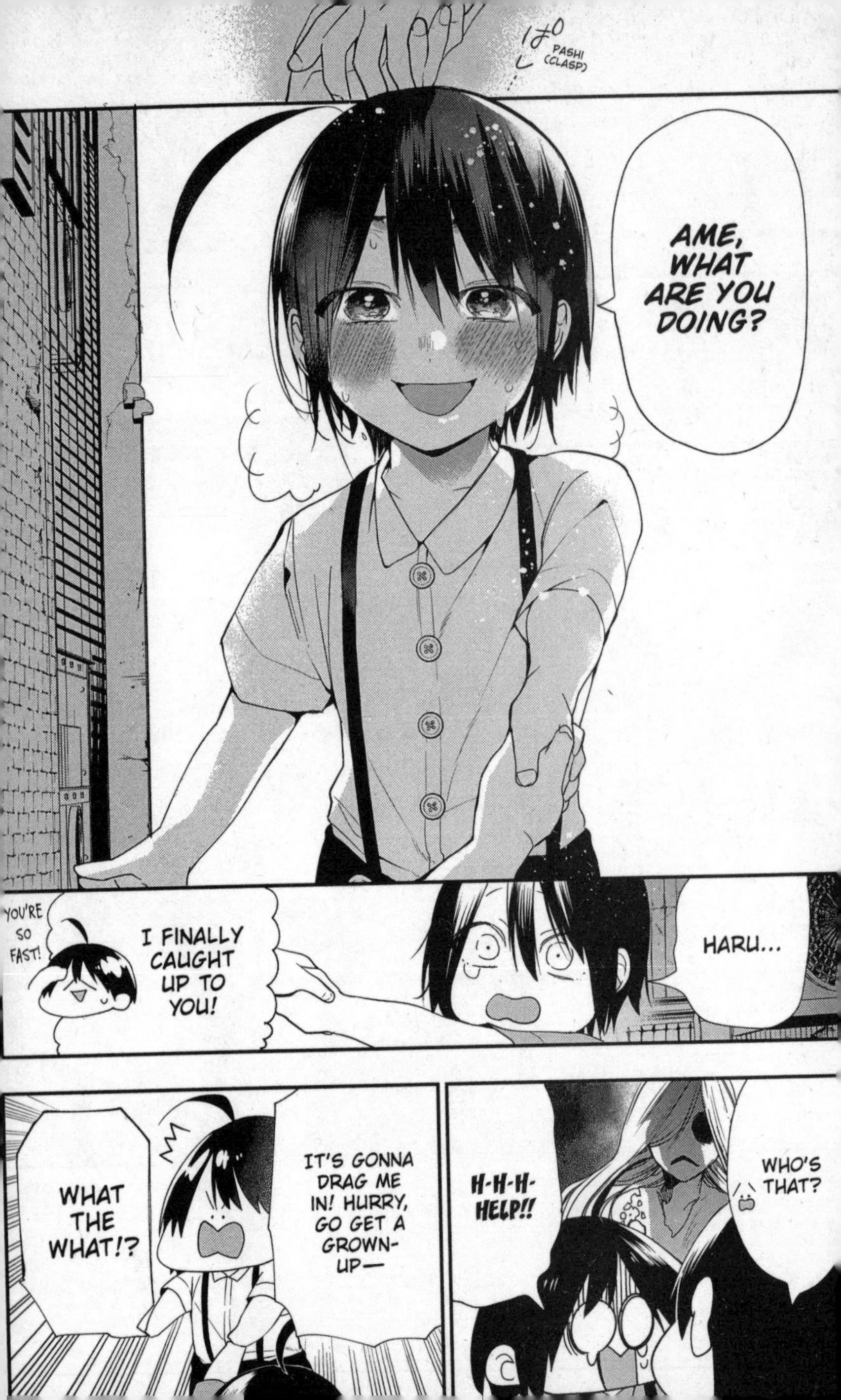
ぱし
PASHI (CLASP)
AME, WHAT ARE YOU DOING?
HARU...
I FINALLY CAUGHT UP TO YOU!
YOU'RE SO FAST!
WHO'S THAT?
H-H-H-HELP!!
IT'S GONNA DRAG ME IN! HURRY, GO GET A GROWN-UP—
WHAT THE WHAT!?

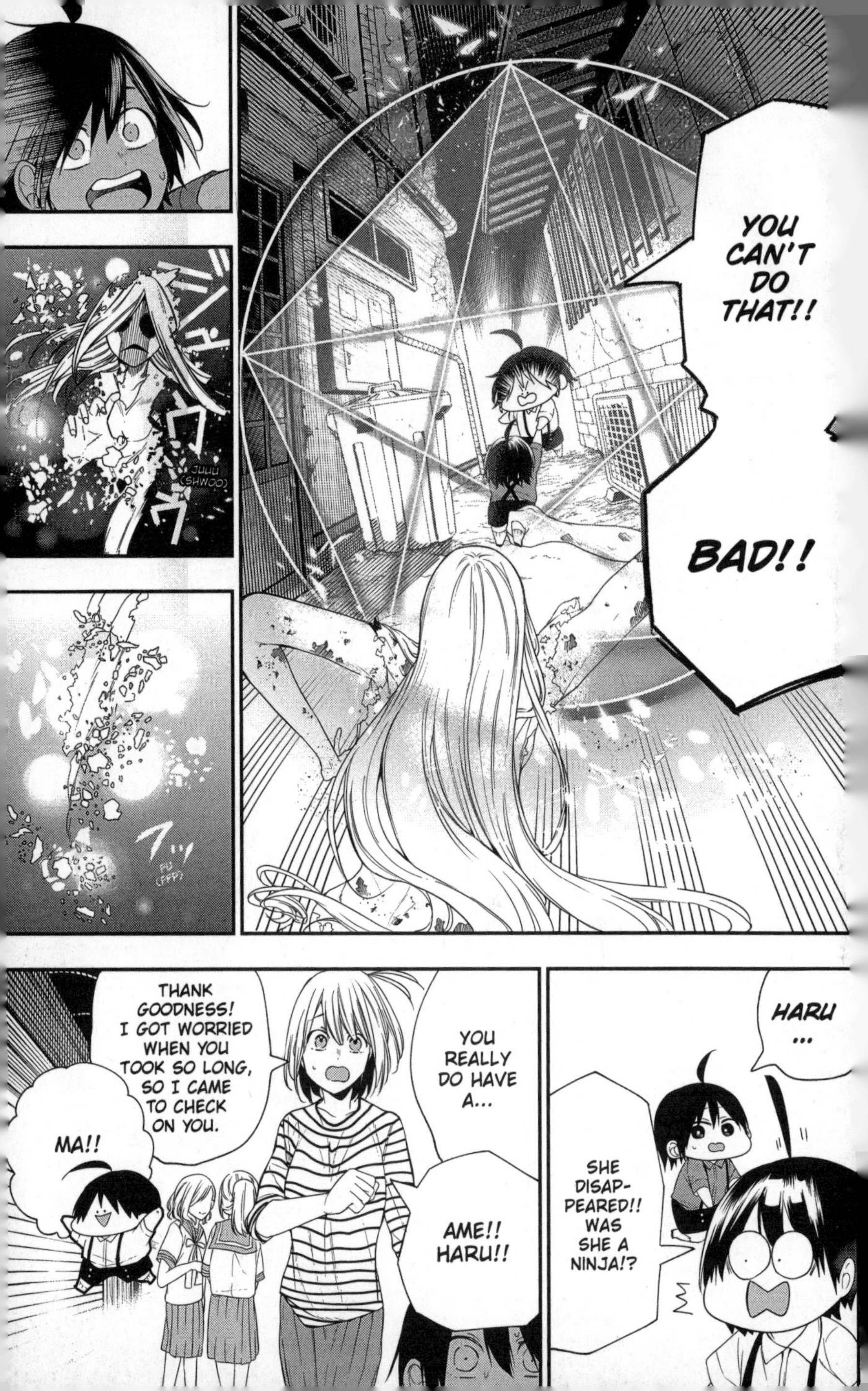
YOU CAN'T DO THAT!!
BAD!!
JUUU (SHWOO)
FU (FFP)
HARU ...
SHE DISAP-PEARED!! WAS SHE A NINJA!?
YOU REALLY DO HAVE A...
THANK GOODNESS! I GOT WORRIED WHEN YOU TOOK SO LONG, SO I CAME TO CHECK ON YOU.
AME!! HARU!!
MA!!

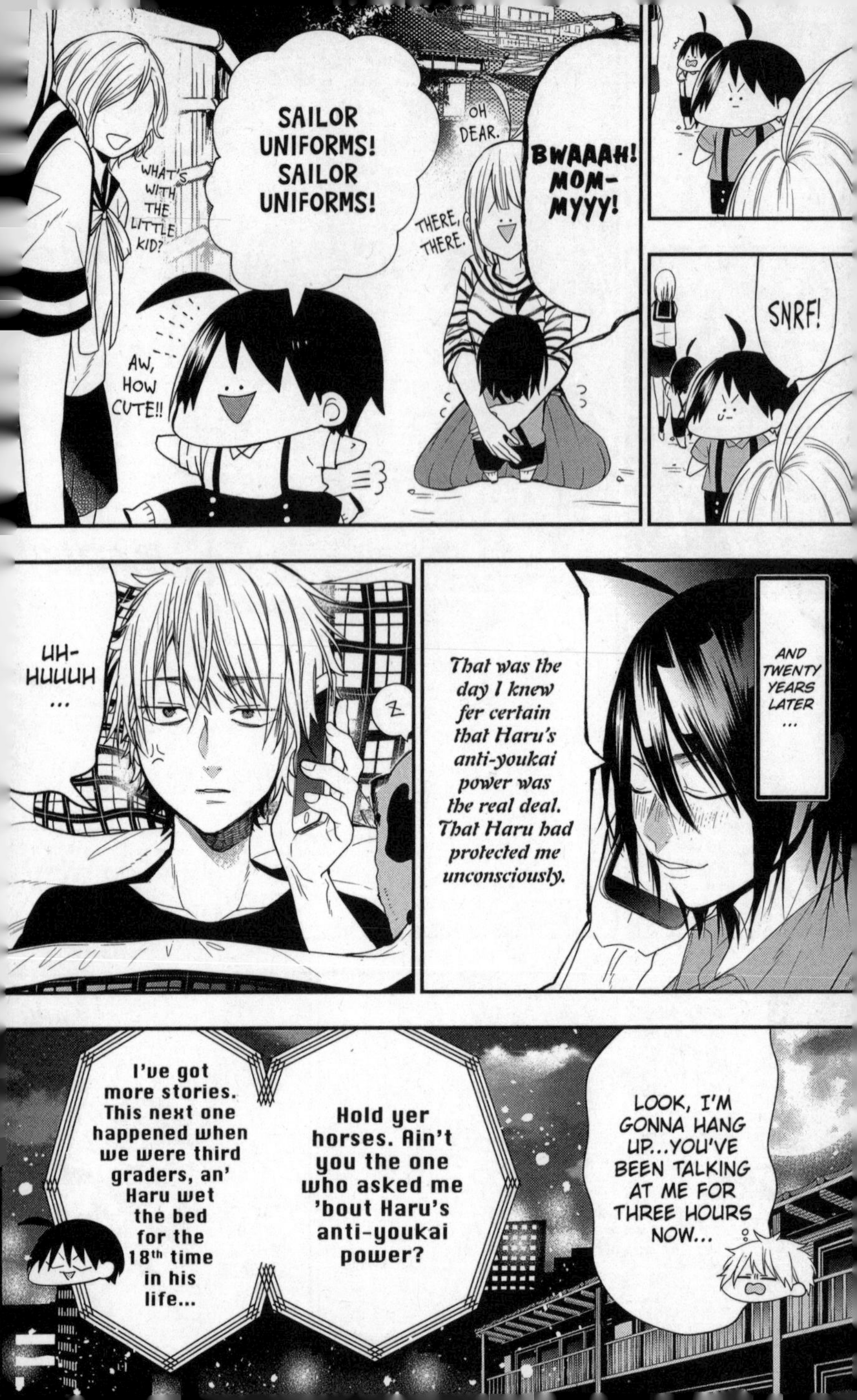
SNRF!
BWAAAH! MOM-MYYY!
OH DEAR.
THERE, THERE.
SAILOR UNIFORMS! SAILOR UNIFORMS!
WHAT'S WITH THE LITTLE KID?
AW, HOW CUTE!!
AND TWENTY YEARS LATER...
That was the day I knew for certain that Haru's anti-youkai power was the real deal. That Haru had protected me unconsciously.
UH-HUUUH...
Z
LOOK, I'M GONNA HANG UP...YOU'VE BEEN TALKING AT ME FOR THREE HOURS NOW...
Hold yer horses. Ain't you the one who asked me 'bout Haru's anti-youkai power?
I've got more stories. This next one happened when we were third graders, an' Haru wet the bed for the 18th time in his life...

Fifty-Second Period

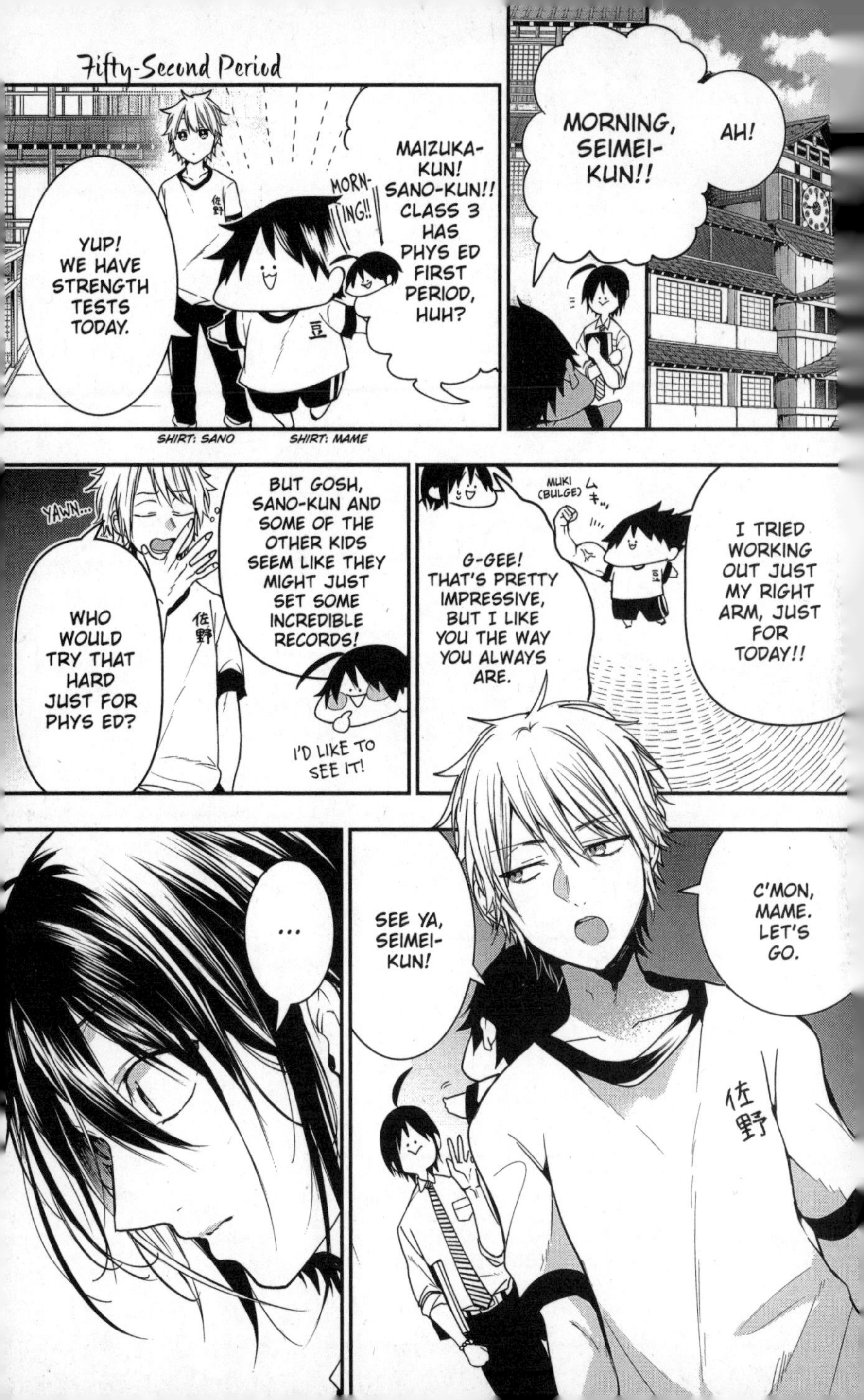
AH!
MORNING, SEIMEI-KUN!!
MAIZUKA-KUN! SANO-KUN!! CLASS 3 HAS PHYS ED FIRST PERIOD, HUH?
MORN-ING!!
YUP! WE HAVE STRENGTH TESTS TODAY.
SHIRT: SANO
SHIRT: MAME
I TRIED WORKING OUT JUST MY RIGHT ARM, JUST FOR TODAY!!
MUKI (BULGE)
G-GEE! THAT'S PRETTY IMPRESSIVE, BUT I LIKE YOU THE WAY YOU ALWAYS ARE.
BUT GOSH, SANO-KUN AND SOME OF THE OTHER KIDS SEEM LIKE THEY MIGHT JUST SET SOME INCREDIBLE RECORDS!
I'D LIKE TO SEE IT!
YAWN...
WHO WOULD TRY THAT HARD JUST FOR PHYS ED?
C'MON, MAME. LET'S GO.
SEE YA, SEIMEI-KUN!
...

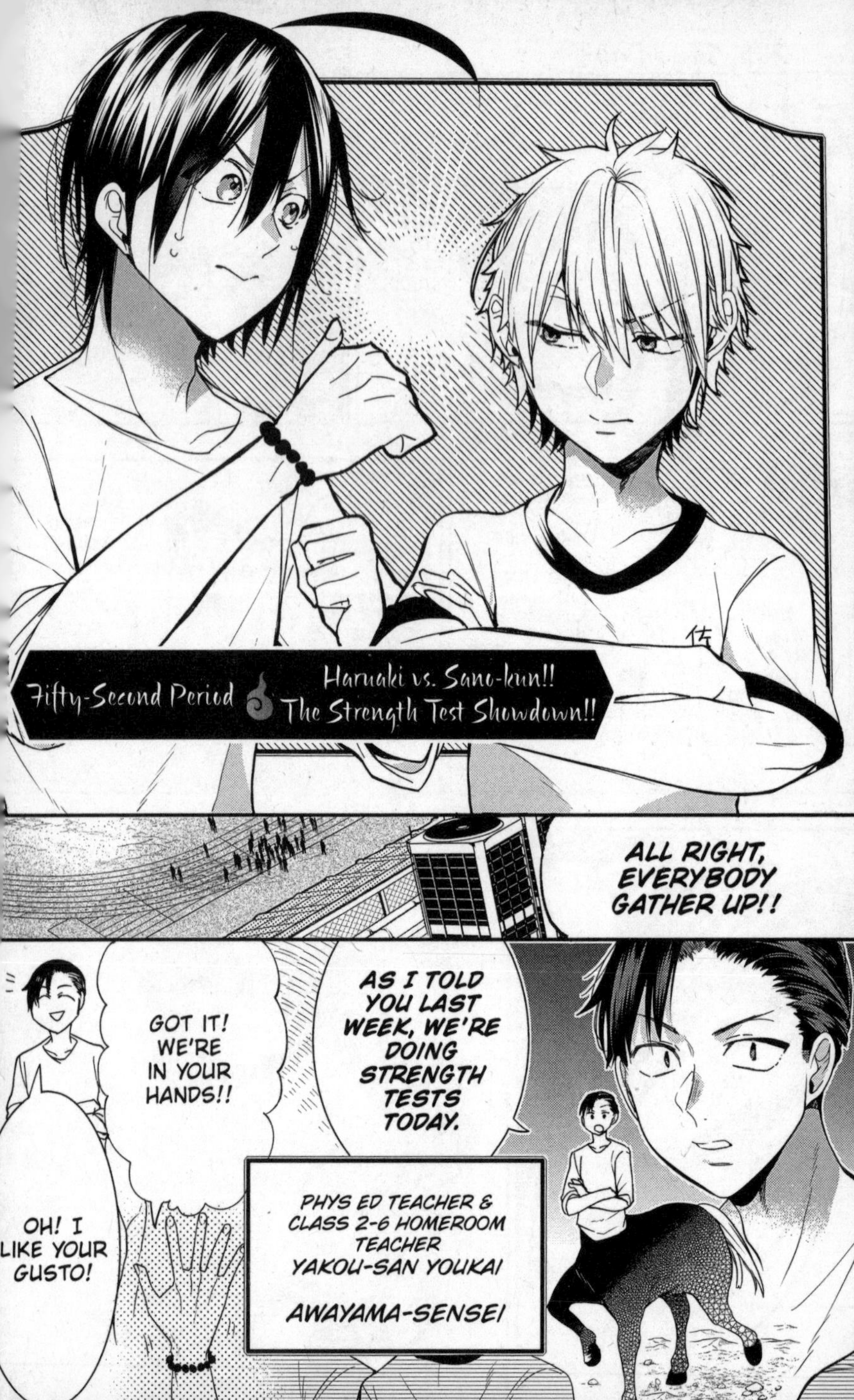
Fifty-Second Period
Haruaki vs. Sano-kun!! The Strength Test Showdown!!
佐
ALL RIGHT, EVERYBODY GATHER UP!!
AS I TOLD YOU LAST WEEK, WE'RE DOING STRENGTH TESTS TODAY.
PHYS ED TEACHER & CLASS 2-6 HOMEROOM TEACHER YAKOU-SAN YOUKAI
AWAYAMA-SENSEI
GOT IT! WE'RE IN YOUR HANDS!!
OH! I LIKE YOUR GUSTO!

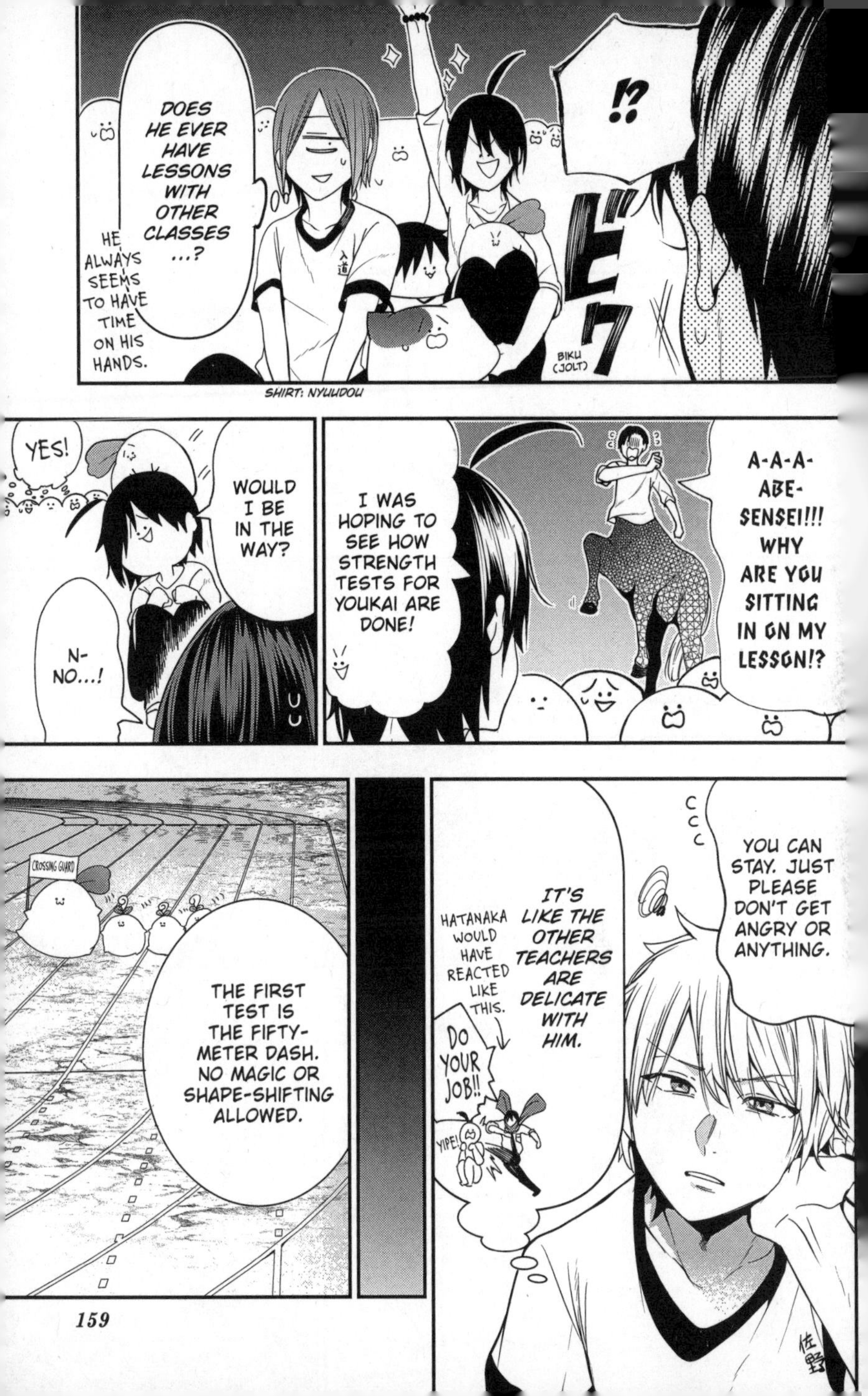
!?
ビク
BIKU (JOLT)
DOES HE EVER HAVE LESSONS WITH OTHER CLASSES...?
HE ALWAYS SEEMS TO HAVE TIME ON HIS HANDS.
SHIRT: NYUUDOU
A-A-A-ABE-SENSEI!!! WHY ARE YOU SITTING IN ON MY LESSON!?
I WAS HOPING TO SEE HOW STRENGTH TESTS FOR YOUKAI ARE DONE!
WOULD I BE IN THE WAY?
YES!
N-NO...!
YOU CAN STAY. JUST PLEASE DON'T GET ANGRY OR ANYTHING.
IT'S LIKE THE OTHER TEACHERS ARE DELICATE WITH HIM.
HATANAKA WOULD HAVE REACTED LIKE THIS.
DO YOUR JOB!!
YIPE!
CROSSING GUARD
THE FIRST TEST IS THE FIFTY-METER DASH. NO MAGIC OR SHAPE-SHIFTING ALLOWED.

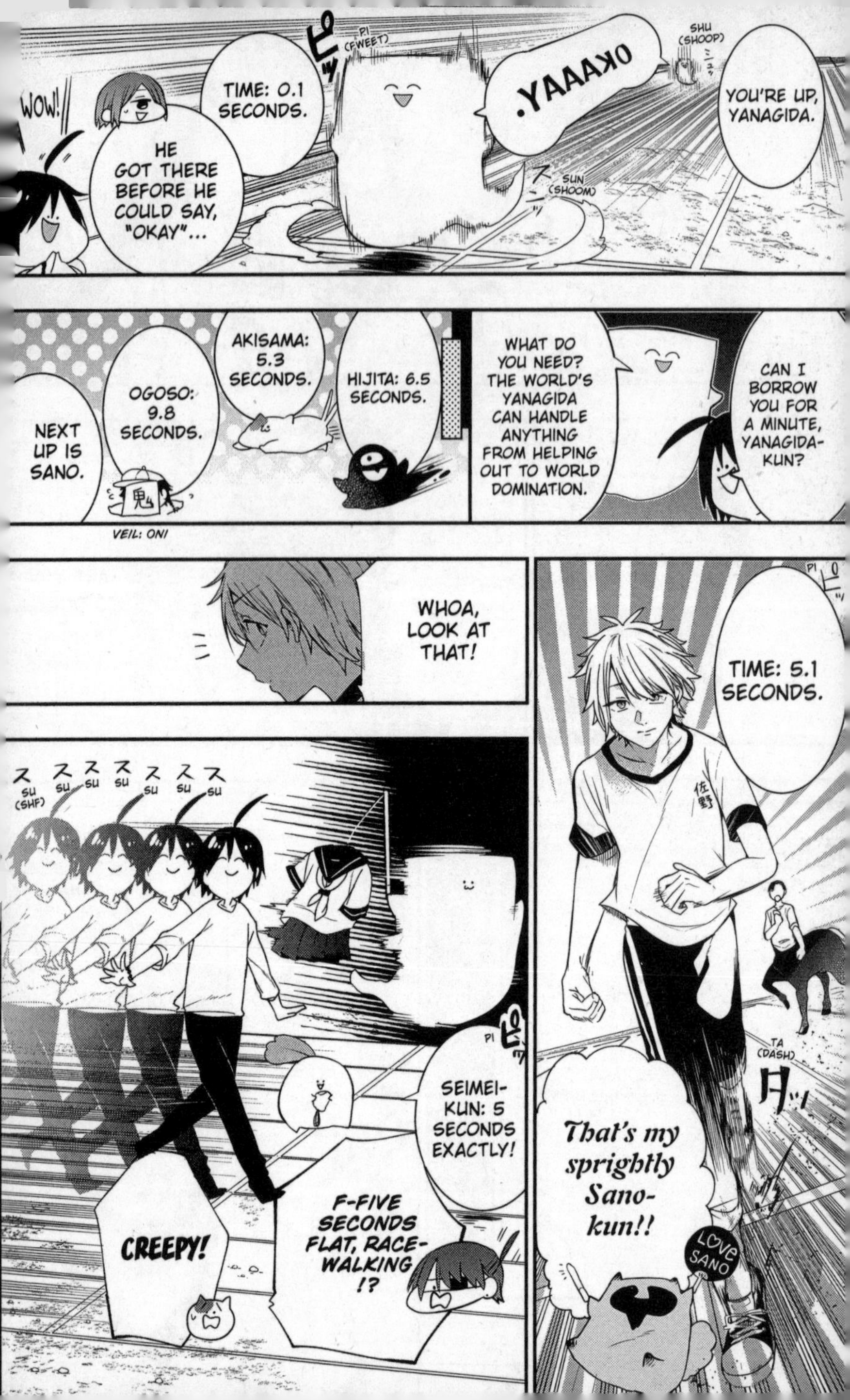
SHU (SHOOP)
YOU'RE UP, YANAGIDA.
OKAAAY.
PI (FWEET)
SUN (SHOOM)
TIME: 0.1 SECONDS.
HE GOT THERE BEFORE HE COULD SAY, "OKAY"...
WOW!
CAN I BORROW YOU FOR A MINUTE, YANAGIDA-KUN?
WHAT DO YOU NEED? THE WORLD'S YANAGIDA CAN HANDLE ANYTHING FROM HELPING OUT TO WORLD DOMINATION.
HIJITA: 6.5 SECONDS.
AKISAMA: 5.3 SECONDS.
OGOSO: 9.8 SECONDS.
NEXT UP IS SANO.
鬼
VEIL: ONI
PI
TIME: 5.1 SECONDS.
佐野
TA (DASH)
That's my sprightly Sano-kun!!
LOVE SANO
WHOA, LOOK AT THAT!
PI
SEIMEI-KUN: 5 SECONDS EXACTLY!
F-FIVE SECONDS FLAT, RACE-WALKING!?
CREEPY!
SU (SHF) SU SU SU SU SU SU

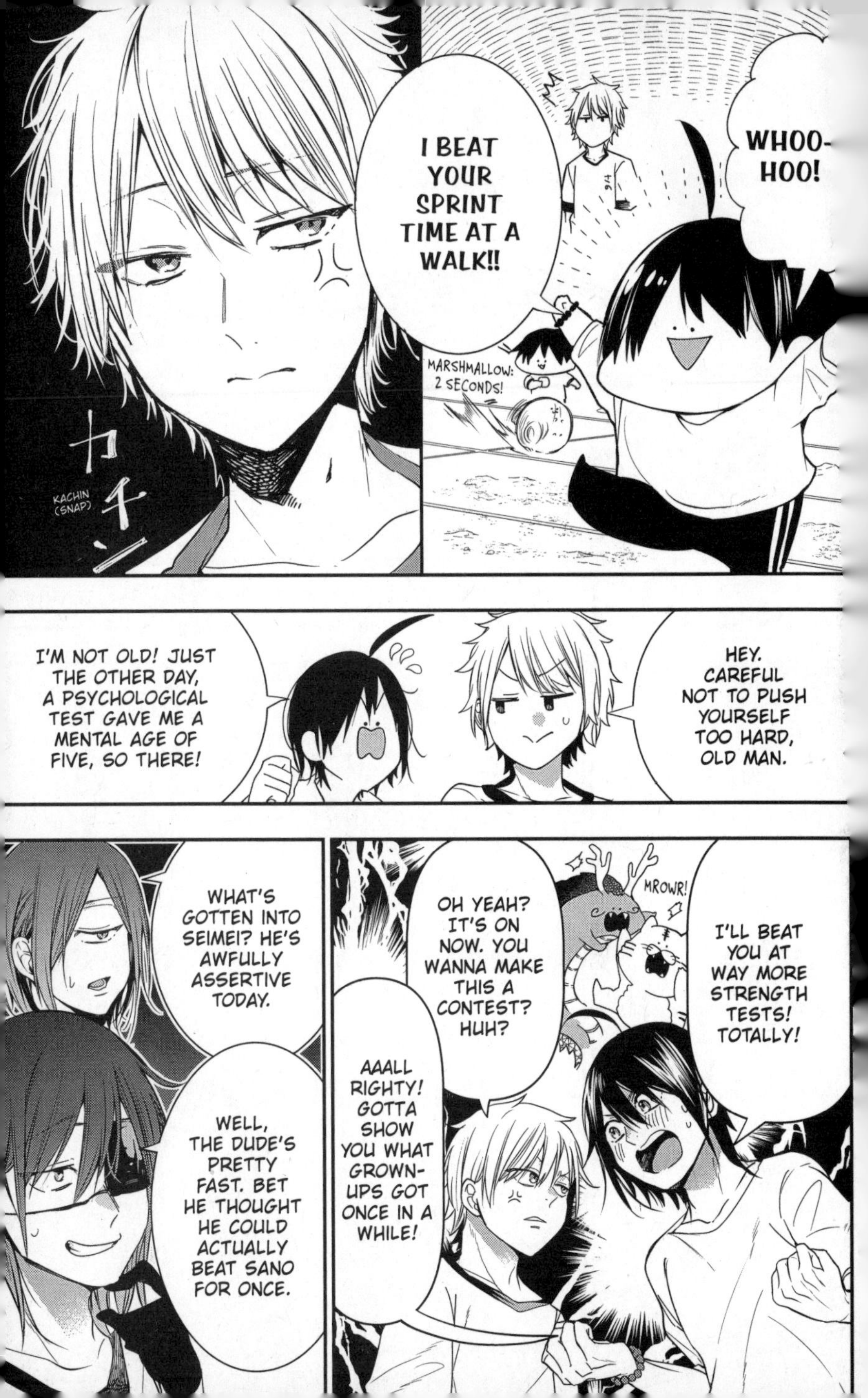
WHOO-HOO!
I BEAT YOUR SPRINT TIME AT A WALK!!
MARSHMALLOW: 2 SECONDS!
KACHIN (SNAP)
HEY. CAREFUL NOT TO PUSH YOURSELF TOO HARD, OLD MAN.
I'M NOT OLD! JUST THE OTHER DAY, A PSYCHOLOGICAL TEST GAVE ME A MENTAL AGE OF FIVE, SO THERE!
I'LL BEAT YOU AT WAY MORE STRENGTH TESTS! TOTALLY!
MROWR!
OH YEAH? IT'S ON NOW. YOU WANNA MAKE THIS A CONTEST? HUH?
AAALL RIGHTY! GOTTA SHOW YOU WHAT GROWN-UPS GOT ONCE IN A WHILE!
WHAT'S GOTTEN INTO SEIMEI? HE'S AWFULLY ASSERTIVE TODAY.
WELL, THE DUDE'S PRETTY FAST. BET HE THOUGHT HE COULD ACTUALLY BEAT SANO FOR ONCE.

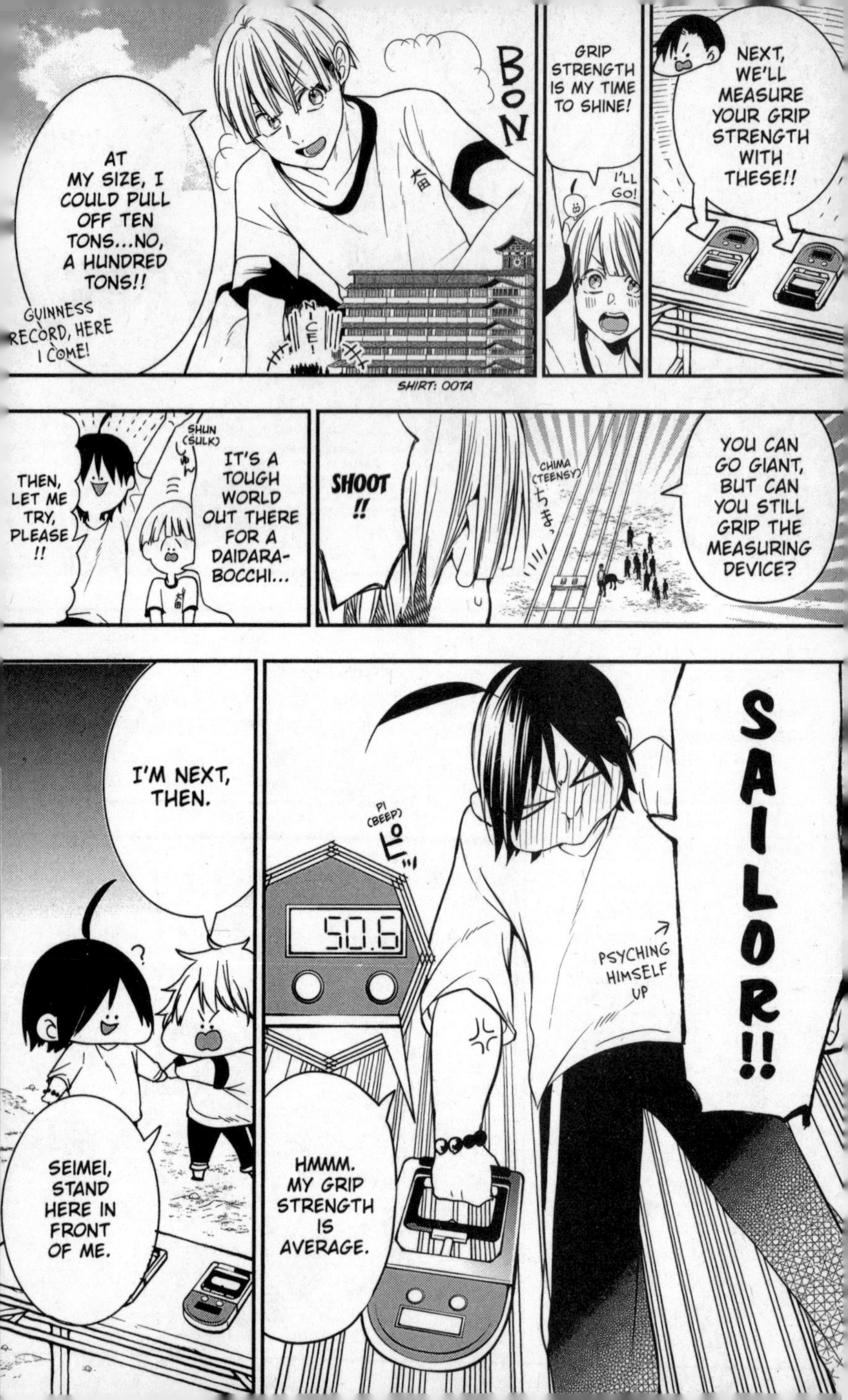
NEXT, WE'LL MEASURE YOUR GRIP STRENGTH WITH THESE!!
GRIP STRENGTH IS MY TIME TO SHINE!
I'LL GO!
BON
AT MY SIZE, I COULD PULL OFF TEN TONS...NO, A HUNDRED TONS!!
GUINNESS RECORD, HERE I COME!
NICE!
SHIRT: OOTA
YOU CAN GO GIANT, BUT CAN YOU STILL GRIP THE MEASURING DEVICE?
CHIMA (TEENSY)
SHOOT!!
IT'S A TOUGH WORLD OUT THERE FOR A DAIDARA-BOCCHI...
SHUN (SULK)
THEN, LET ME TRY, PLEASE!!
SAILOR!!
PSYCHING HIMSELF UP
PI (BEEP)
50.6
HMMM. MY GRIP STRENGTH IS AVERAGE.
I'M NEXT, THEN.
SEIMEI, STAND HERE IN FRONT OF ME.

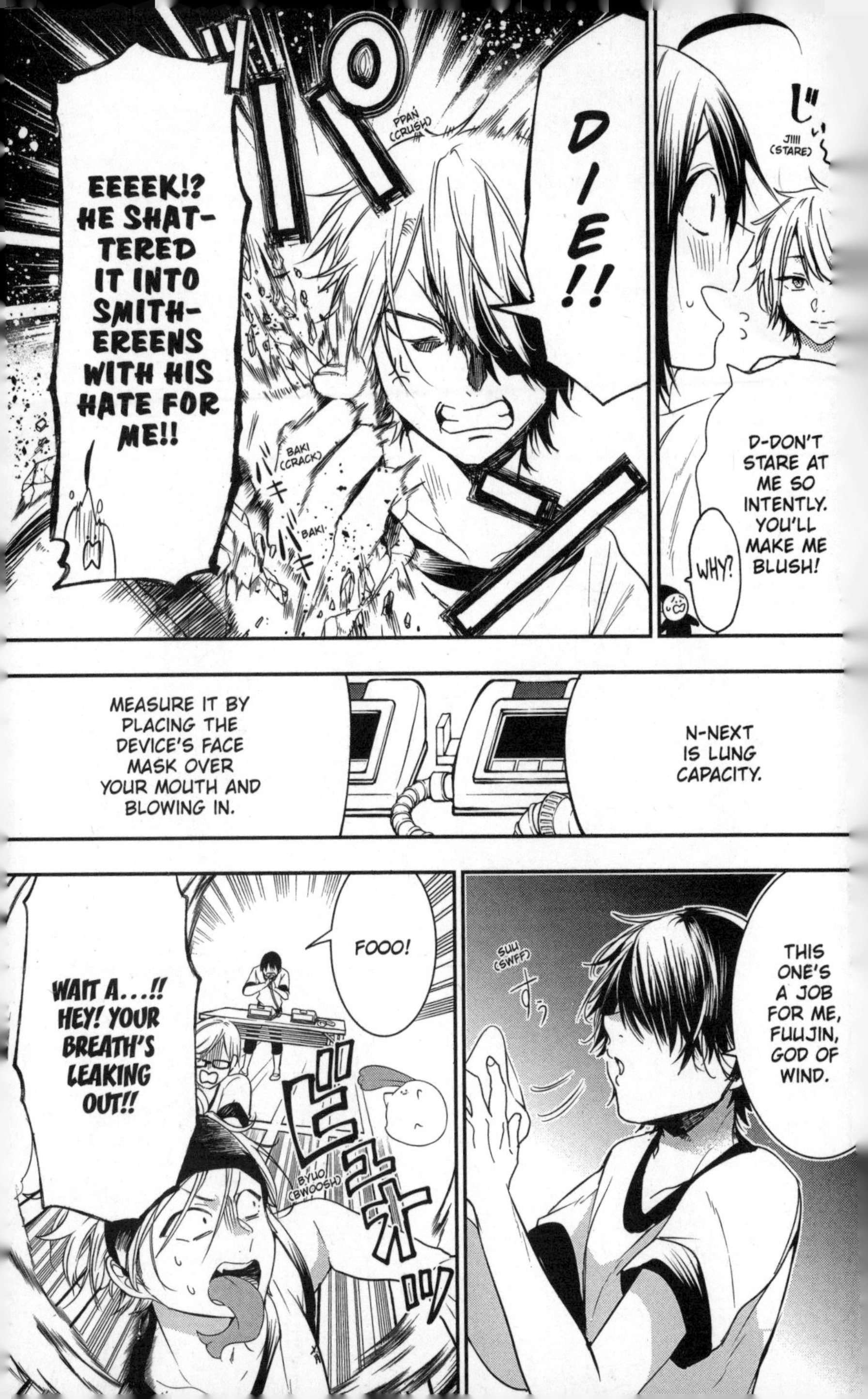
JIII (STARE)
D-DON'T STARE AT ME SO INTENTLY. YOU'LL MAKE ME BLUSH!
WHY?
PPAN (CRUSH)
DIE!!
EEEEK!? HE SHAT-TERED IT INTO SMITH-EREENS WITH HIS HATE FOR ME!!
BAKI (CRACK)
BAKI
N-NEXT IS LUNG CAPACITY.
MEASURE IT BY PLACING THE DEVICE'S FACE MASK OVER YOUR MOUTH AND BLOWING IN.
SUU (SWFF)
THIS ONE'S A JOB FOR ME, FUUJIN, GOD OF WIND.
FOOO!
WAIT A...!! HEY! YOUR BREATH'S LEAKING OUT!!
BYUO (BWOOSH)

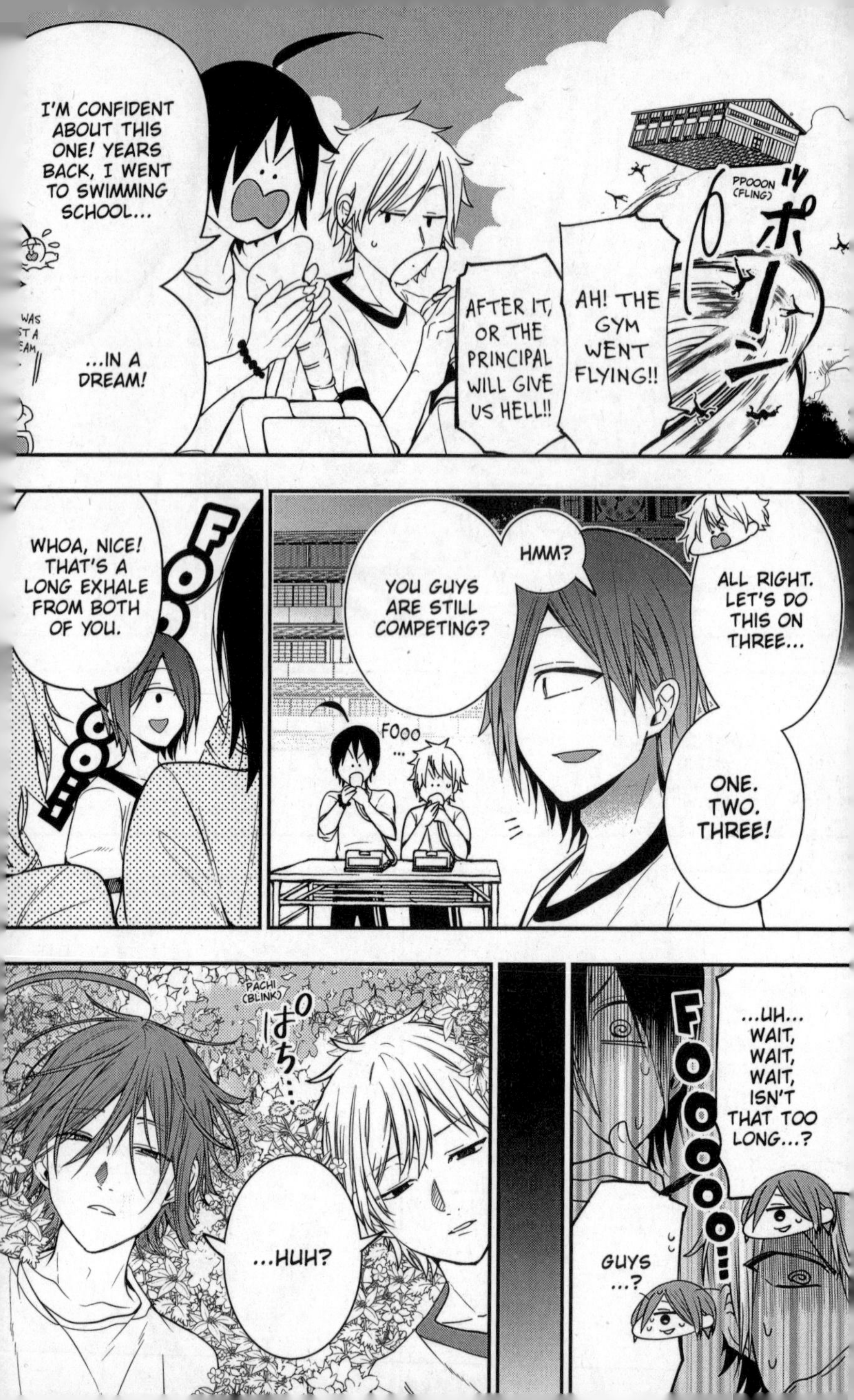
PPOOON (FLING)
AH! THE GYM WENT FLYING!!
AFTER IT, OR THE PRINCIPAL WILL GIVE US HELL!!
I'M CONFIDENT ABOUT THIS ONE! YEARS BACK, I WENT TO SWIMMING SCHOOL...
...IN A DREAM!
ALL RIGHT. LET'S DO THIS ON THREE...
HMM?
YOU GUYS ARE STILL COMPETING?
ONE. TWO. THREE!
FOOO...
FOOO...
WHOA, NICE! THAT'S A LONG EXHALE FROM BOTH OF YOU.
...UH... WAIT, WAIT, WAIT, ISN'T THAT TOO LONG...?
FOOOOO...
GUYS ...?
PACHI (BLINK)
...HUH?

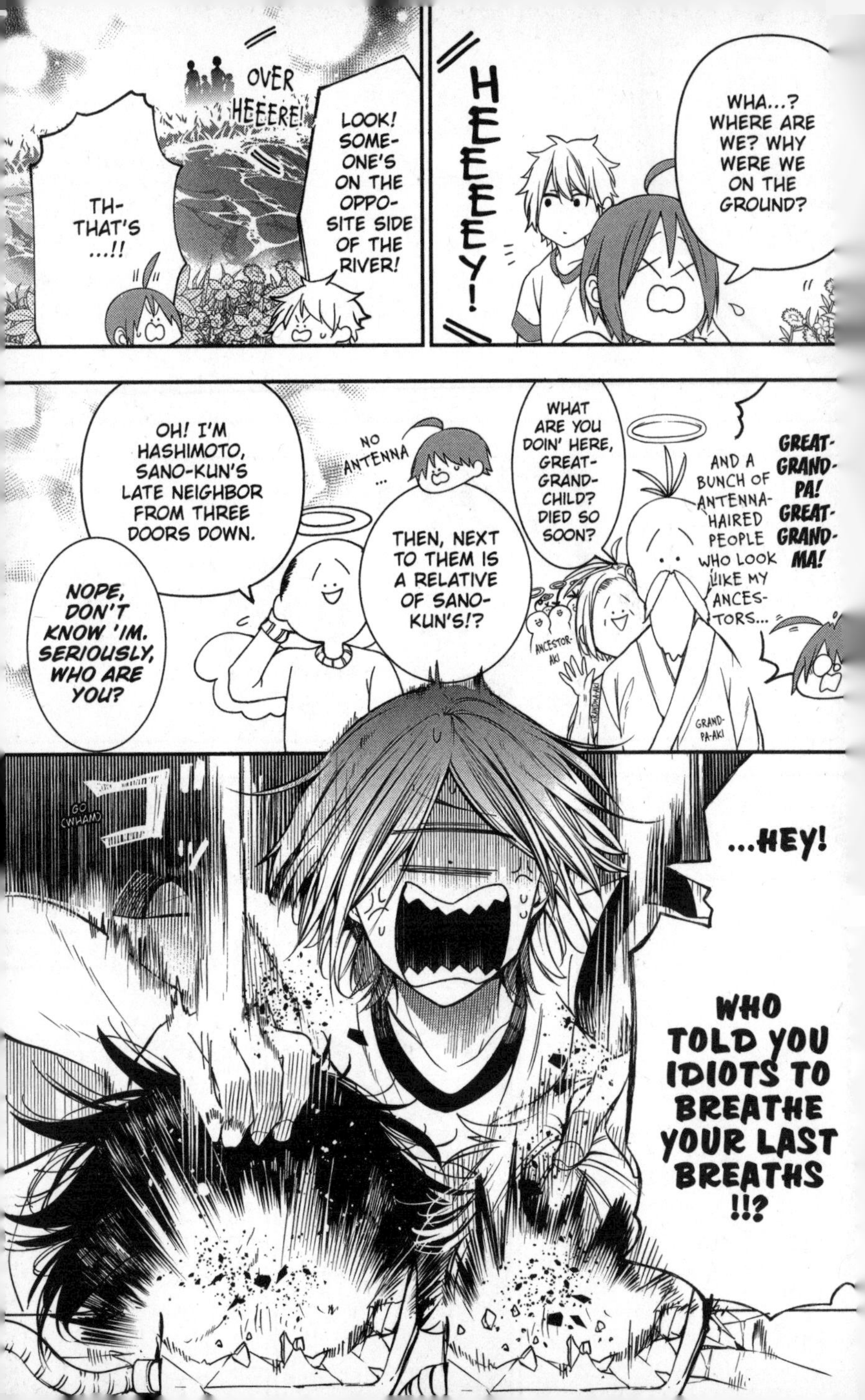
WHA...? WHERE ARE WE? WHY WERE WE ON THE GROUND?
HEEEEEY!
LOOK! SOME-ONE'S ON THE OPPO-SITE SIDE OF THE RIVER!
OVER HEEERE!
TH-THAT'S ...!!
GREAT-GRANDPA! GREAT-GRANDMA!
AND A BUNCH OF ANTENNA-HAIRED PEOPLE WHO LOOK LIKE MY ANCES-TORS...
WHAT ARE YOU DOIN' HERE, GREAT-GRAND-CHILD? DIED SO SOON?
GRAND-PA-AKI
GRANDMA-AKI
ANCESTOR-AKI
THEN, NEXT TO THEM IS A RELATIVE OF SANO-KUN'S!?
NO ANTENNA ...
OH! I'M HASHIMOTO, SANO-KUN'S LATE NEIGHBOR FROM THREE DOORS DOWN.
NOPE, DON'T KNOW 'IM. SERIOUSLY, WHO ARE YOU?
...HEY!
WHO TOLD YOU IDIOTS TO BREATHE YOUR LAST BREATHS!!?
GO (WHAM)

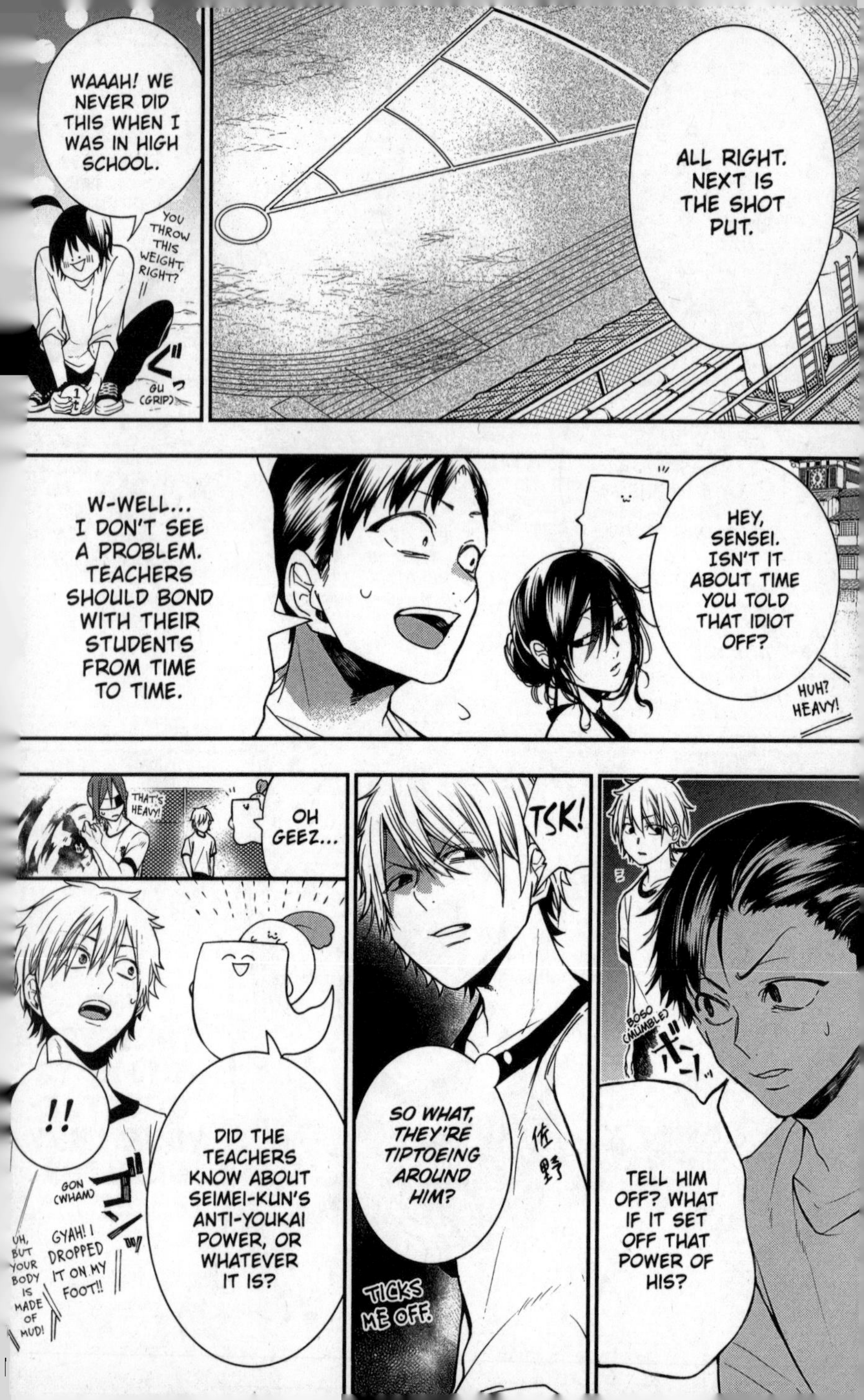
ALL RIGHT. NEXT IS THE SHOT PUT.
WAAAH! WE NEVER DID THIS WHEN I WAS IN HIGH SCHOOL.
YOU THROW THIS WEIGHT, RIGHT?
GU (GRIP)
HEY, SENSEI. ISN'T IT ABOUT TIME YOU TOLD THAT IDIOT OFF?
HUH? HEAVY!
W-WELL... I DON'T SEE A PROBLEM. TEACHERS SHOULD BOND WITH THEIR STUDENTS FROM TIME TO TIME.
BOSO (MUMBLE)
TELL HIM OFF? WHAT IF IT SET OFF THAT POWER OF HIS?
TSK!
SO WHAT, THEY'RE TIPTOEING AROUND HIM?
TICKS ME OFF.
THAT'S HEAVY!
OH GEEZ...
DID THE TEACHERS KNOW ABOUT SEIMEI-KUN'S ANTI-YOUKAI POWER, OR WHATEVER IT IS?
!!
GON (WHAM)
GYAH! I DROPPED IT ON MY FOOT!!
UH, BUT YOUR BODY IS MADE OF MUD!

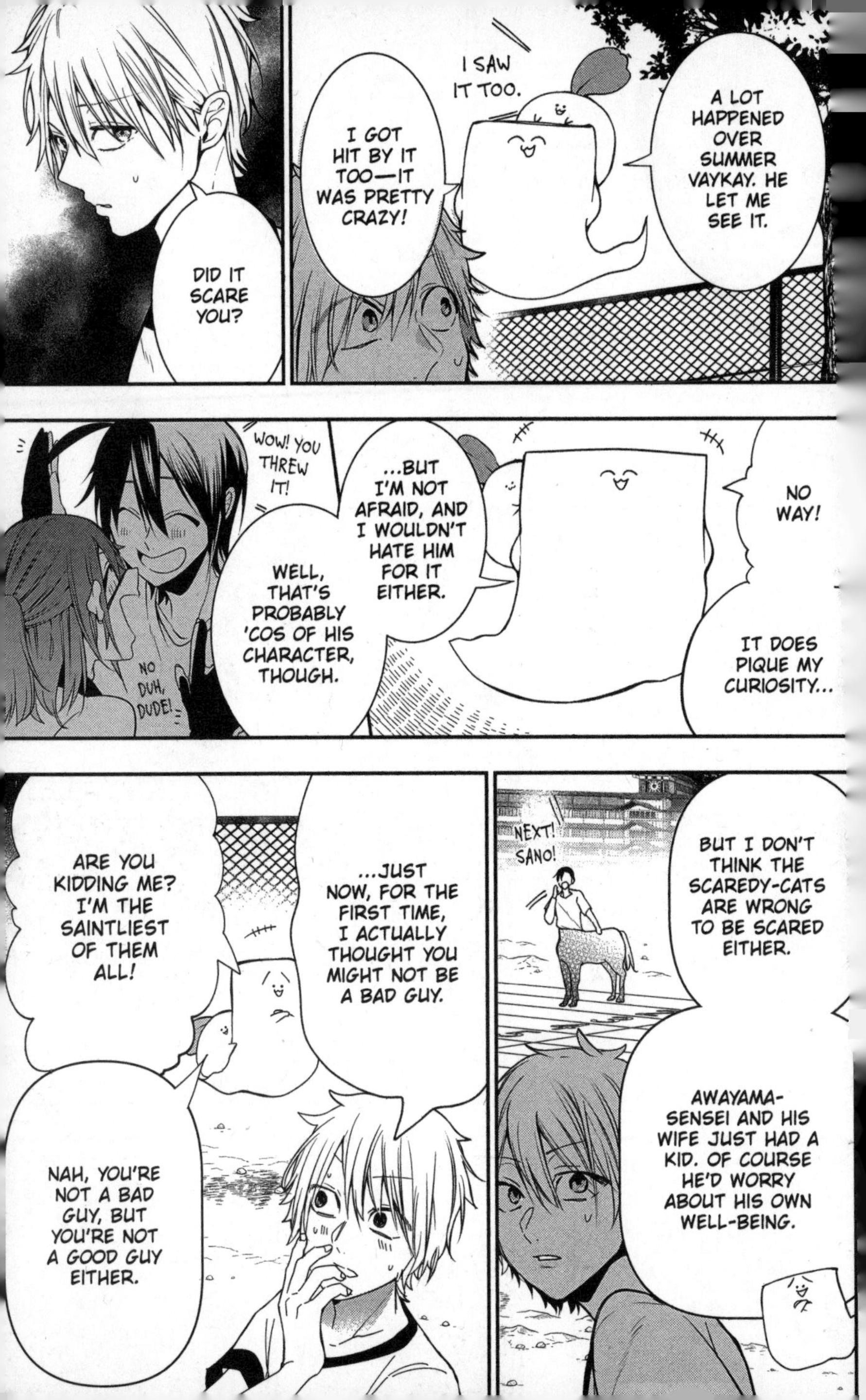
A LOT HAPPENED OVER SUMMER VAYKAY. HE LET ME SEE IT.
I SAW IT TOO.
I GOT HIT BY IT TOO—IT WAS PRETTY CRAZY!
DID IT SCARE YOU?
NO WAY!
IT DOES PIQUE MY CURIOSITY...
...BUT I'M NOT AFRAID, AND I WOULDN'T HATE HIM FOR IT EITHER.
WOW! YOU THREW IT!
WELL, THAT'S PROBABLY 'COS OF HIS CHARACTER, THOUGH.
NO DUH, DUDE!
BUT I DON'T THINK THE SCAREDY-CATS ARE WRONG TO BE SCARED EITHER.
NEXT! SANO!
AWAYAMA-SENSEI AND HIS WIFE JUST HAD A KID. OF COURSE HE'D WORRY ABOUT HIS OWN WELL-BEING.
...JUST NOW, FOR THE FIRST TIME, I ACTUALLY THOUGHT YOU MIGHT NOT BE A BAD GUY.
ARE YOU KIDDING ME? I'M THE SAINTLIEST OF THEM ALL!
NAH, YOU'RE NOT A BAD GUY, BUT YOU'RE NOT A GOOD GUY EITHER.

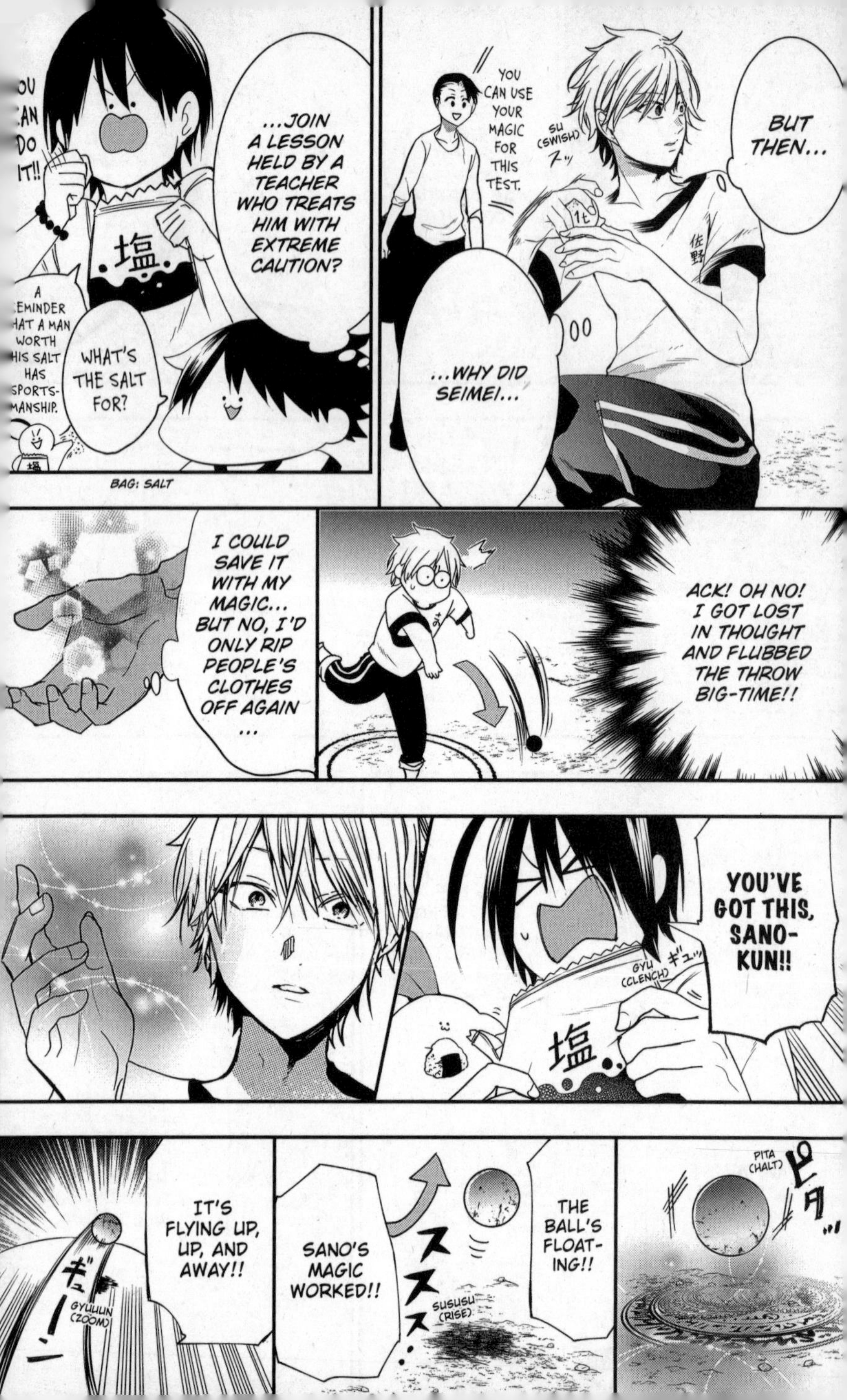
BUT THEN...
SU (SWISH)
YOU CAN USE YOUR MAGIC FOR THIS TEST.
...WHY DID SEIMEI...
...JOIN A LESSON HELD BY A TEACHER WHO TREATS HIM WITH EXTREME CAUTION?
OU AN DO IT!!
WHAT'S THE SALT FOR?
EMINDER HAT A MAN WORTH HIS SALT HAS SPORTS-MANSHIP.
BAG: SALT
ACK! OH NO! I GOT LOST IN THOUGHT AND FLUBBED THE THROW BIG-TIME!!
I COULD SAVE IT WITH MY MAGIC... BUT NO, I'D ONLY RIP PEOPLE'S CLOTHES OFF AGAIN...
YOU'VE GOT THIS, SANO-KUN!!
GYU (CLENCH)
PITA (HALT)
THE BALL'S FLOAT-ING!!
SANO'S MAGIC WORKED!!
SUSUSU (RISE)
IT'S FLYING UP, UP, AND AWAY!!
GYUUUN (ZOOM)

THERE'S ONLY ONE TEST LEFT...? CRAP, I'M LOSING...!

WELL, PERSONALLY SPEAKING, I WOULD SAY THIS MAGIC WAS A FLUB.

MEKO (SMASH)

1t

KAKUN (DROP)

	Haruaki-kun	Sano-kun
Grip strength	X	O
50m	O	X
Lung capacity	—	—
Shot put	X	O
Side-stepping	O	X
Abs	O	X

REALLY? WE CAN?

AH... I KNOW. ABE-SENSEI AND SANO, WHY DON'T YOU GO FIRST?

YEAH.

I'LL MAKE THESE TWO FINISH FAST...

ALL RIGHT, FINALLY, I'LL TIME YOU IN THE 1,500-METER DASH.

TWO LAPS OF THIS TRACK IS 1,500 METERS EXACTLY.

GET SET...

ON YOUR MARKS...

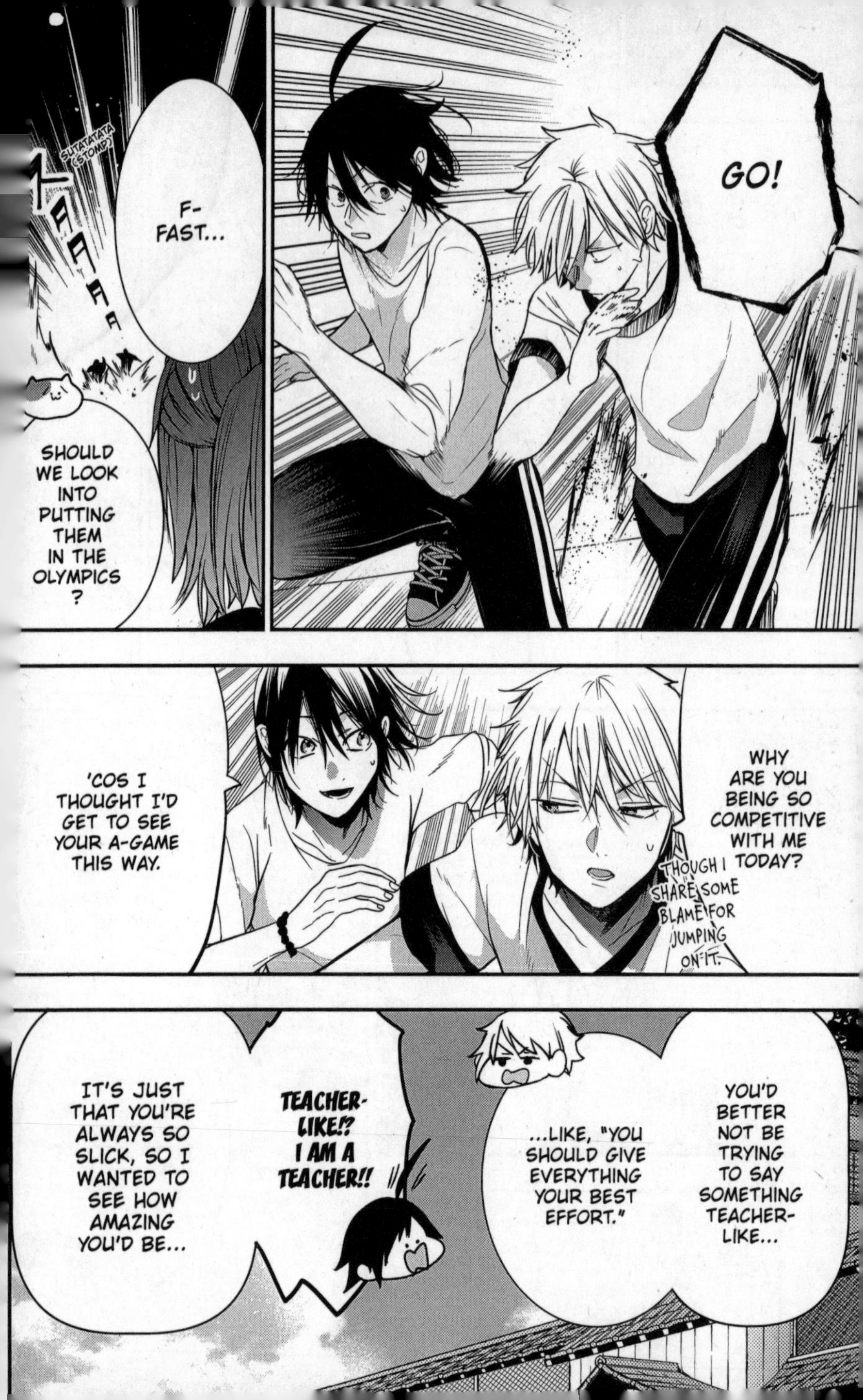
GO!
SUTATATATA (STOMP)
F- FAST...
SHOULD WE LOOK INTO PUTTING THEM IN THE OLYMPICS?
WHY ARE YOU BEING SO COMPETITIVE WITH ME TODAY?
THOUGH I SHARE SOME BLAME FOR JUMPING ON IT.
'COS I THOUGHT I'D GET TO SEE YOUR A-GAME THIS WAY.
YOU'D BETTER NOT BE TRYING TO SAY SOMETHING TEACHER-LIKE...
...LIKE, "YOU SHOULD GIVE EVERYTHING YOUR BEST EFFORT."
TEACHER-LIKE!? I AM A TEACHER!!
IT'S JUST THAT YOU'RE ALWAYS SO SLICK, SO I WANTED TO SEE HOW AMAZING YOU'D BE...

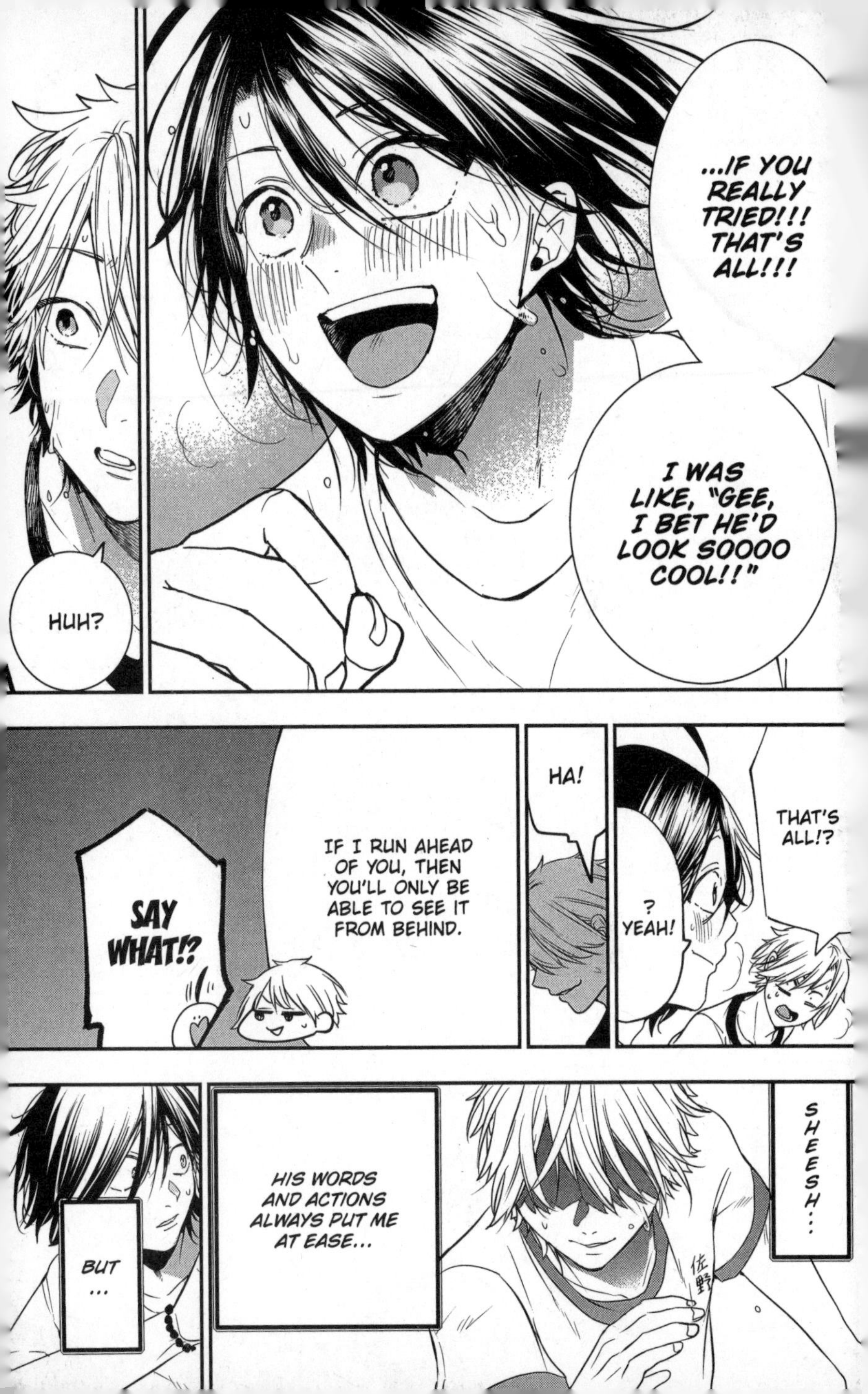
...IF YOU REALLY TRIED!!! THAT'S ALL!!!
I WAS LIKE, "GEE, I BET HE'D LOOK SOOOO COOL!!"
HUH?
THAT'S ALL!?
? YEAH!
HA!
IF I RUN AHEAD OF YOU, THEN YOU'LL ONLY BE ABLE TO SEE IT FROM BEHIND.
SAY WHAT!?
SHEESH...
佐野
HIS WORDS AND ACTIONS ALWAYS PUT ME AT EASE...
BUT...

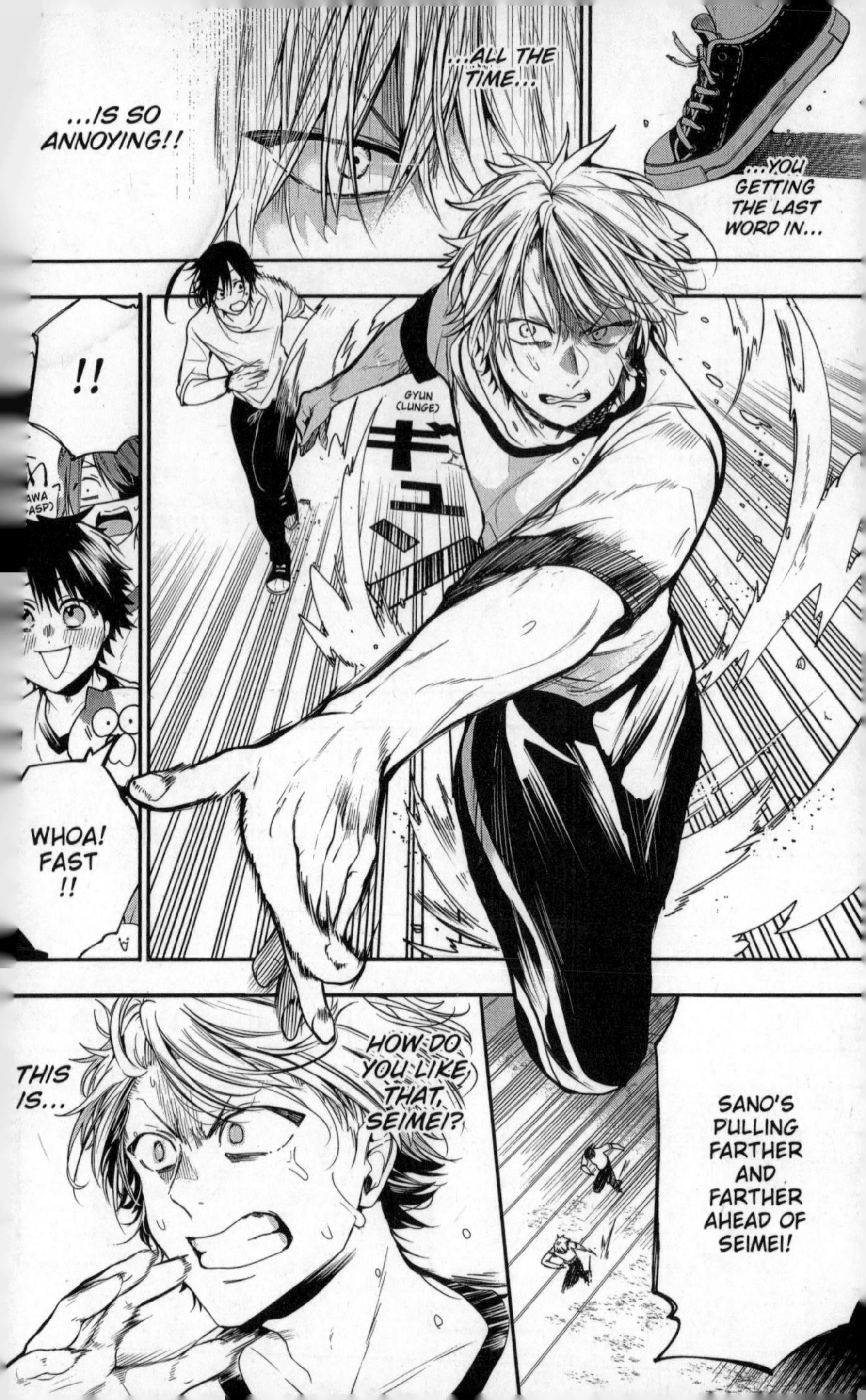
...YOU GETTING THE LAST WORD IN...
...ALL THE TIME...
...IS SO ANNOYING!!
GYUN (LUNGE)
!!
WHOA! FAST !!
SANO'S PULLING FARTHER AND FARTHER AHEAD OF SEIMEI!
HOW DO YOU LIKE THAT, SEIMEI?
THIS IS...

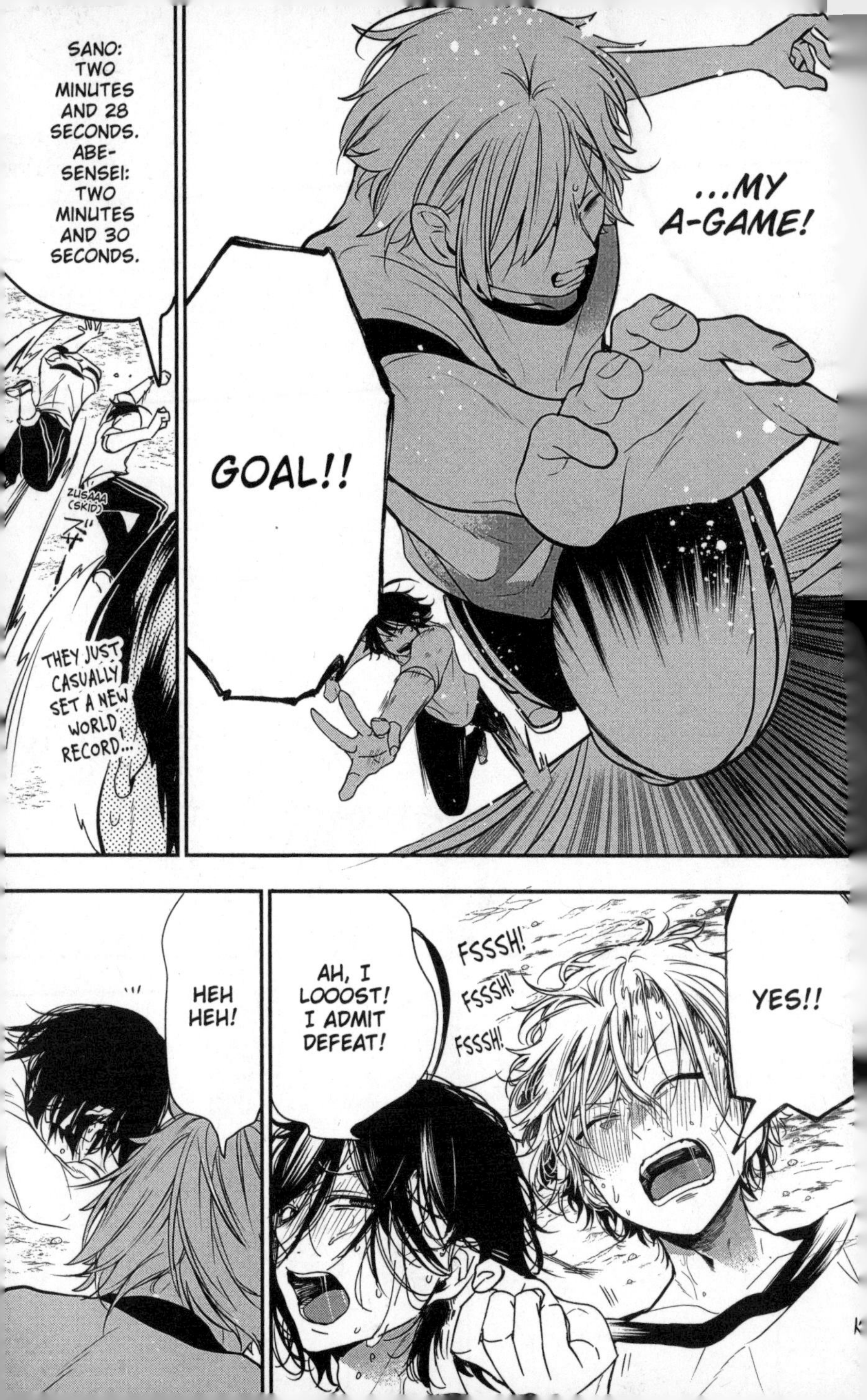
...MY A-GAME!
GOAL!!
SANO: TWO MINUTES AND 28 SECONDS. ABE-SENSEI: TWO MINUTES AND 30 SECONDS.
ZUSAAA (SKID)
THEY JUST CASUALLY SET A NEW WORLD RECORD...
YES!!
FSSSH!
FSSSH!
FSSSH!
AH, I LOOOST! I ADMIT DEFEAT!
HEH HEH!

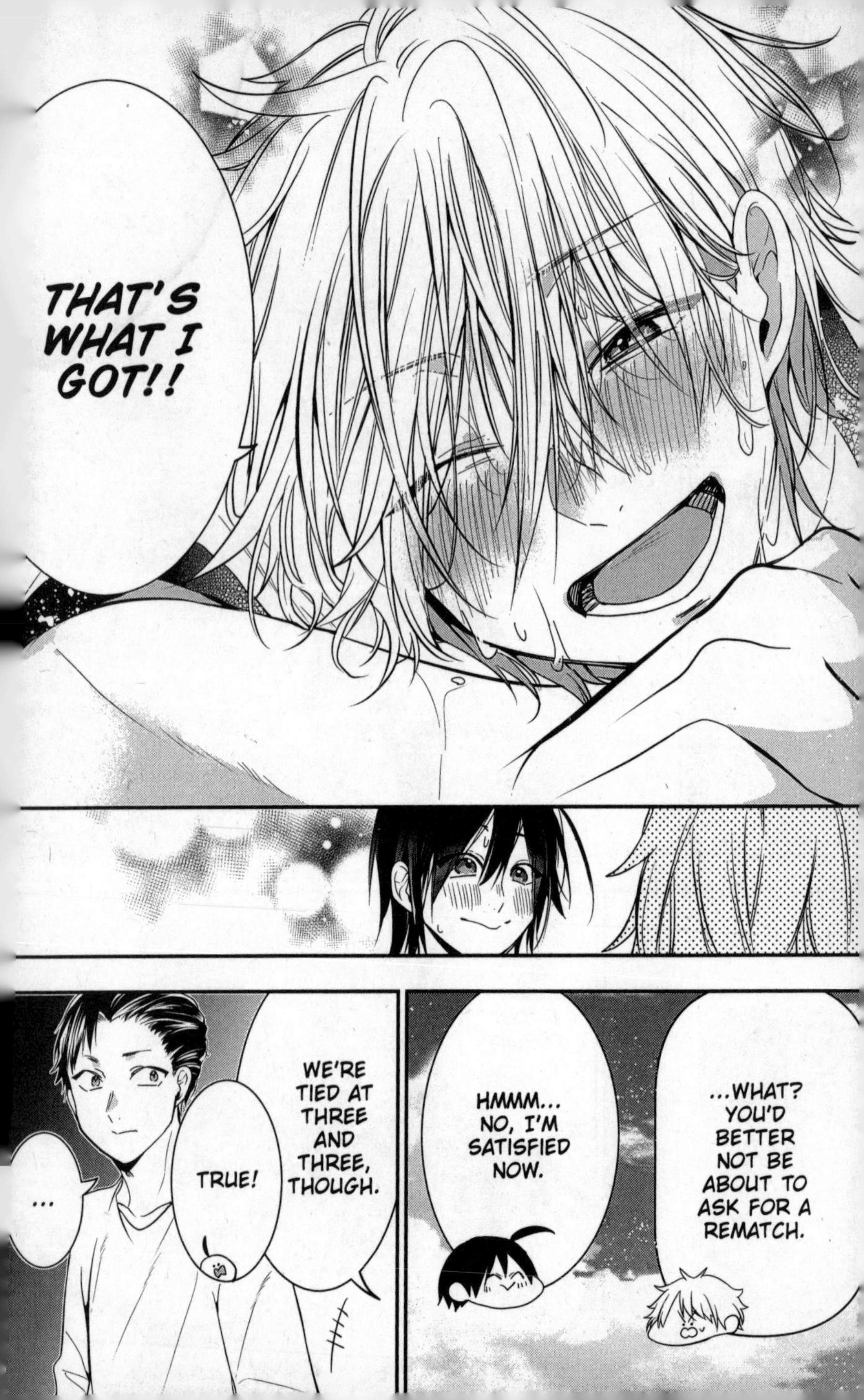
THAT'S WHAT I GOT!!
...WHAT? YOU'D BETTER NOT BE ABOUT TO ASK FOR A REMATCH.
HMMM... NO, I'M SATISFIED NOW.
WE'RE TIED AT THREE AND THREE, THOUGH.
TRUE!
...

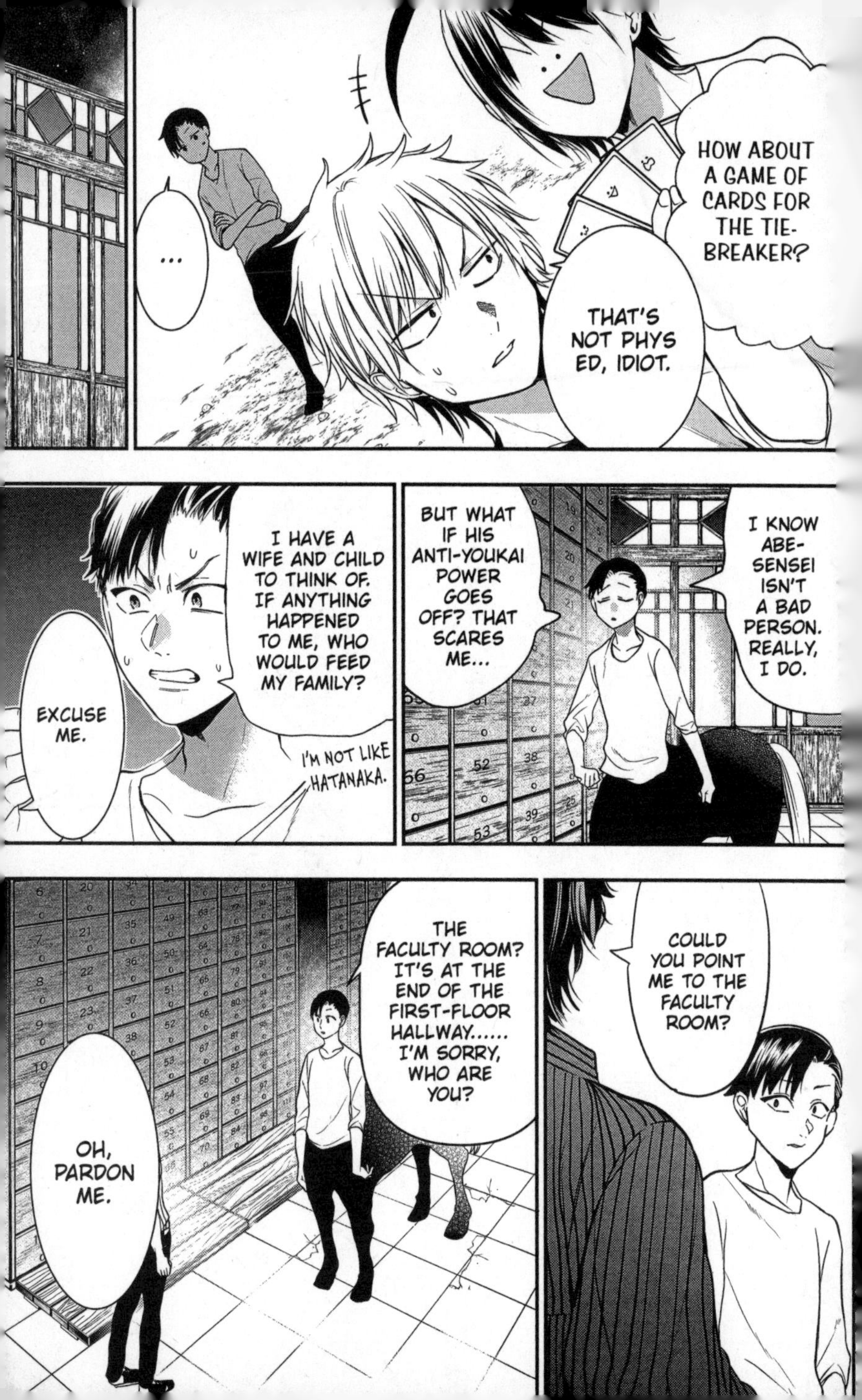
HOW ABOUT A GAME OF CARDS FOR THE TIE-BREAKER?
THAT'S NOT PHYS ED, IDIOT.
...
I KNOW ABE-SENSEI ISN'T A BAD PERSON. REALLY, I DO.
BUT WHAT IF HIS ANTI-YOUKAI POWER GOES OFF? THAT SCARES ME...
I HAVE A WIFE AND CHILD TO THINK OF. IF ANYTHING HAPPENED TO ME, WHO WOULD FEED MY FAMILY?
I'M NOT LIKE HATANAKA.
EXCUSE ME.
COULD YOU POINT ME TO THE FACULTY ROOM?
THE FACULTY ROOM? IT'S AT THE END OF THE FIRST-FLOOR HALLWAY...... I'M SORRY, WHO ARE YOU?
OH, PARDON ME.

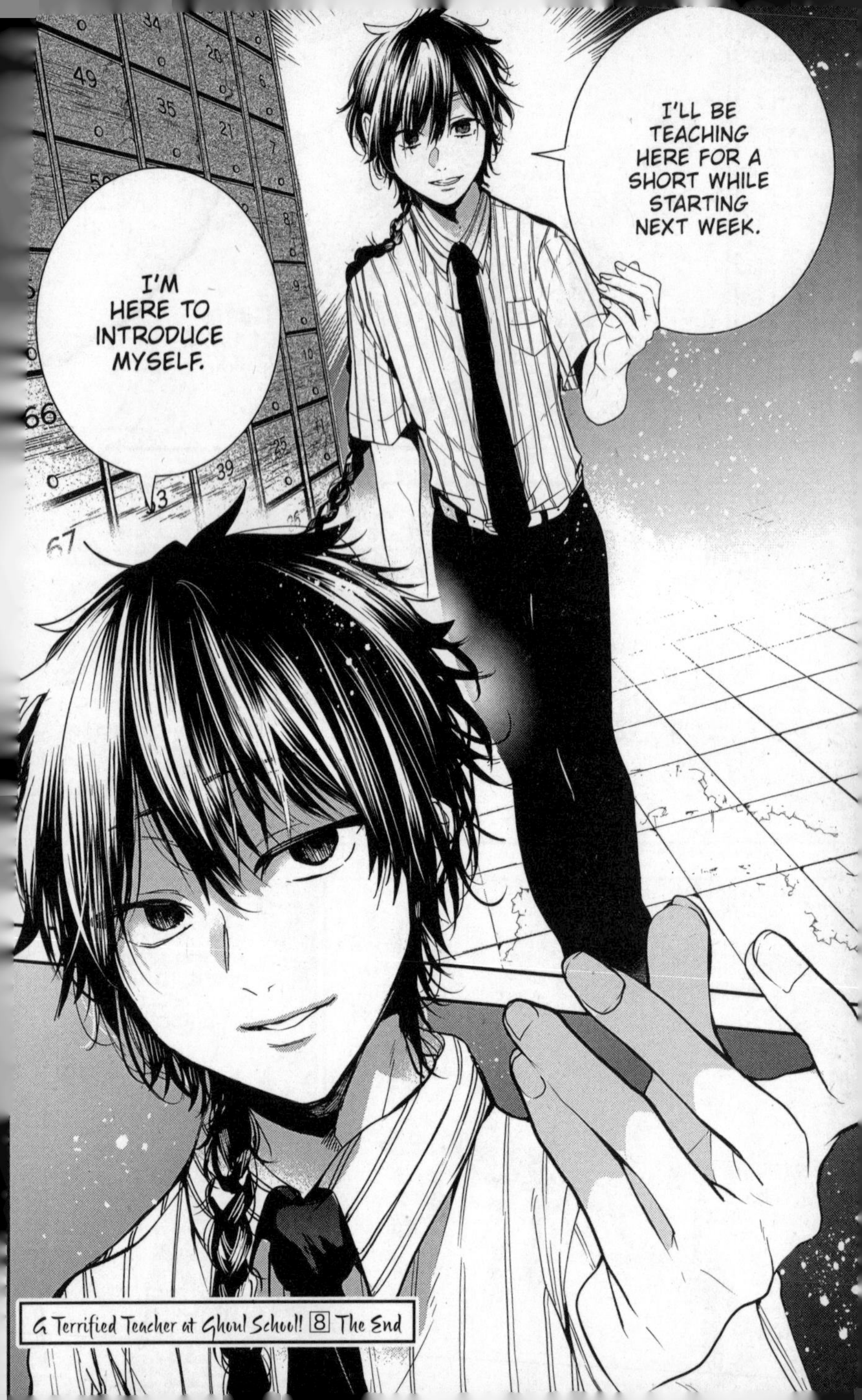
I'LL BE TEACHING HERE FOR A SHORT WHILE STARTING NEXT WEEK.
I'M HERE TO INTRODUCE MYSELF.
A Terrified Teacher at Ghoul School! 8 The End

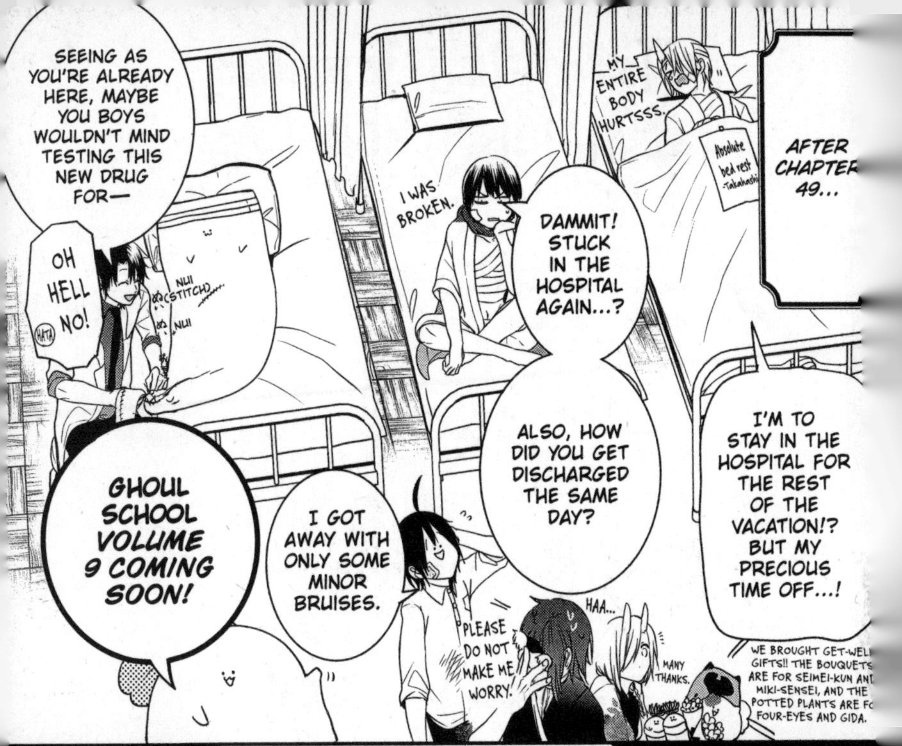
AFTER CHAPTER 49...
MY ENTIRE BODY HURTSSS.
Absolute bed rest -Takahashi
I'M TO STAY IN THE HOSPITAL FOR THE REST OF THE VACATION!? BUT MY PRECIOUS TIME OFF...!
DAMMIT! STUCK IN THE HOSPITAL AGAIN...?
I WAS BROKEN.
ALSO, HOW DID YOU GET DISCHARGED THE SAME DAY?
SEEING AS YOU'RE ALREADY HERE, MAYBE YOU BOYS WOULDN'T MIND TESTING THIS NEW DRUG FOR—
OH HELL NO!
HATA
NUI (STITCH)
NUI
WE BROUGHT GET-WELL GIFTS!! THE BOUQUETS ARE FOR SEIMEI-KUN AND MIKI-SENSEI, AND THE POTTED PLANTS ARE FOR FOUR-EYES AND GIDA.
MANY THANKS.
HAA...
PLEASE DO NOT MAKE ME WORRY.
I GOT AWAY WITH ONLY SOME MINOR BRUISES.
GHOUL SCHOOL VOLUME 9 COMING SOON!

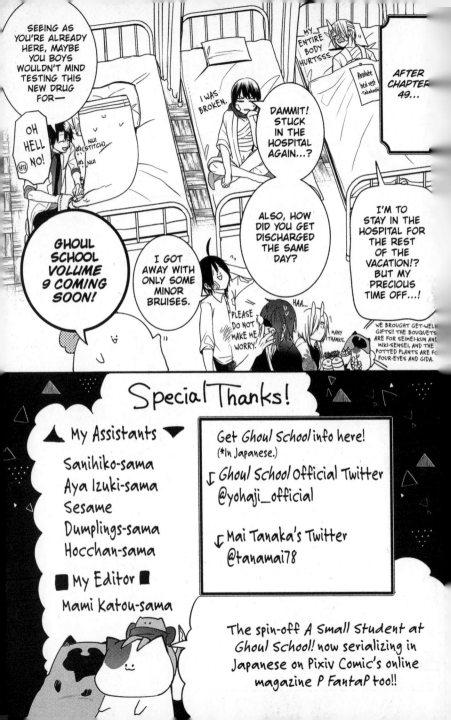

Special Thanks!

My Assistants

Sanihiko-sama
Aya Izuki-sama
Sesame
Dumplings-sama
Hocchan-sama

My Editor

Mami Katou-sama

Get *Ghoul School* info here!
(*In Japanese.)

Ghoul School Official Twitter
@yohaji_official

Mai Tanaka's Twitter
@tanamai78

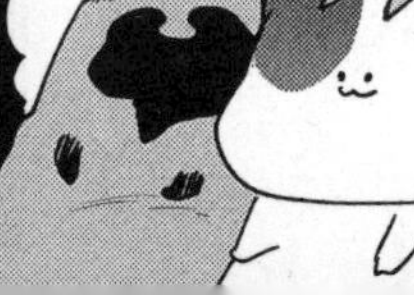

The spin-off *A Small Student at Ghoul School!* now serializing in Japanese on Pixiv Comic's online magazine *P FantaP* too!!

A Terrified Teacher at Ghoul School! Vol. 8

Mai Tanaka

🔥 **Translation: AMANDA HALEY**

🔥 **Lettering: LYS BLAKESLEE, RACHEL J. PIERCE**

YOKAI GAKKO NO SENSEI HAJIMEMASHITA! Vol. 8 © 2019 Mai Tanaka/ SQUARE ENIX CO., LTD. First published in Japan in 2019 by SQUARE ENIX CO., LTD. English translation rights arranged with SQUARE ENIX CO., LTD. and Yen Press, LLC through Tuttle-Mori Agency, Inc., Tokyo.

English translation © 2019 by SQUARE ENIX CO., LTD.

Yen Press
150 West 30th Street, 19th Floor
New York, NY 10001

Visit us at yenpress.com
facebook.com/yenpress
twitter.com/yenpress
yenpress.tumblr.com
instagram.com/yenpress

First Yen Press Edition:
December 2019

Yen Press is an imprint of Yen Press, LLC.
The Yen Press name and logo are trademarks of Yen Press, LLC.

The publisher is not responsible for websites (or their content) that are not owned by the publisher.

Library of Congress Control Number: 2017954141

ISBNs: 978-1-9753-8736-5 (paperback)
978-1-9753-8737-2 (ebook)

10 9 8 7 6 5 4 3 2 1

BVG

Printed in the United States of America